"Fast-paced...An exciting Border romance with plenty of action...A terrific historical gender war."

—Midwest Book Review

BORDER LASS

"5 Stars! A thrilling tale, rife with villains and notorious plots...Scott demonstrates again her expertise in the realm of medieval Scotland."

—FallenAngelReviews.com

"4½ Stars! TOP PICK! Readers will be thrilled...a tautly written, deeply emotional love story steeped in the rich history of the Borders."

—RT Book Reviews

"Scott excels in creating memorable characters."

—FreshFiction.com

BORDER WEDDING

"5 Stars! Scott has possibly written the best historical in ages!"

—FallenAngelReviews.com

"4½ Stars! TOP PICK! Not only do her characters leap off the pages, the historical events do too. This is more than entertainment and romance; this is historical romance as it was meant to be."

—RT Book Reviews

"Wonderful...full of adventure and history."
—*Midwest Book Review*

KING OF STORMS

"4 Stars! An exhilarating novel...with a lively love story."
—*RT Book Reviews*

"A terrific tale...Rich in history and romance, fans will enjoy the search for the Templar treasure and the Stone of Scone."
—*Midwest Book Review*

"Enchanting...a thrilling adventure...a *must* read... *King of Storms* is a page-turner. A sensual, action-packed romance sure to satisfy every heart."
—**FreshFiction.com**

KNIGHT'S TREASURE

"Filled with tension, deceptions, and newly awakened passions. Scott gets better and better."
—**NovelTalk.com**

HIGHLAND PRINCESS

"Delightful historical...Grips the audience from the onset and never [lets] go."
—*Affaire de Coeur*

"A fabulous medieval Scottish romance."
—*Midwest Book Review*

Other Books by Amanda Scott

AMANDA SCOTT

Highland Master

FOREVER

NEW YORK   BOSTON

This book is a work of fiction. Names, characters, places, and incidents are the product of the author's imagination or are used fictitiously. Any resemblance to actual events, locales, or persons, living or dead, is coincidental.

Copyright © 2011 by Lynne Scott-Drennan
Excerpt from *Highland Hero* copyright © 2011 Lynne Scott-Drennan

Forever
Hachette Book Group
237 Park Avenue
New York, NY 10017
Visit our website at www.HachetteBookGroup.com

Forever is an imprint of Grand Central Publishing. The Forever name and logo is a trademark of Hachette Book Group, Inc.

The publisher is not responsible for websites (or their content) that are not owned by the publisher.

Printed in the United States of America

First Printing: February 2011

10 9 8 7 6 5 4 3 2 1

For Paige Lori
when she is old enough to read it
and for the true Highland wildcat

Scottish Highlands 1400

····· Highland Line

Author's Note

For readers who appreciate a quick guide to the meanings and/or pronunciation of certain words used in this story:

Aodán = AY den (ay as in hay)

Ay-de-mi = AY de me (also ay as in hay, an expletive)

Boreas = the North Wind (Greek mythology)

Finlagh = FIN lay

Forbye = besides or however

Garron = a small, sure-footed Highland horse or pony, alternative to foot travel

Himself = the way by which clan members, especially those who are not of the nobility, refer to a clan or confederation chief—in this instance, the Mackintosh

Lug(s) = ear(s)

Moigh = Moy (now the word is spelled so)

Rothesay = ROSS-ee

Rothiemurchus = Roth-ee MUR kus

Tadhg = TAY

"The Mackintosh" refers to the chief of Clan Mackintosh, who is also the head or Captain of Clan Chattan. The title "captain" is unique to Clan Chattan.

Tocher = a bride's dowry

Prologue ───────────────

Perth, Scotland, September 1396

Abrupt silence filled the air when the young dark-haired warrior's opponent fell. The lad looked swiftly for the next one but saw no one nearby still standing.

Then, hearing moans and weaker cries of the wounded and dying, the warrior realized that his sense of silence was no more than that the screeching of the pipes that always accompanied combat had abruptly ceased when his own fight had.

Not only had the pipes of battle fallen silent, but so also had the noble audience that watched from tiered seats overlooking the field. They had cheered at the beginning, for he had heard them before all his senses had focused on his first opponent.

The broad, usually green meadowlike expanse of the North Inch of Perth had altered gruesomely now to a field of bodies and gore.

Man after man had he slain in that trial by combat between Camerons and Clan Chattan, two of the most powerful Highland clan federations. Each, by order of the King of Scots, had produced thirty champions to fight.

The royal intent was to end decades of feuding over land and other bones of contention.

The young warrior extended his gaze to sweep the rest of the field for any remaining opponent. He saw only three men standing and one kneeling, all some distance away from where he stood near the wide, fast-moving river Tay.

St. John's town of Perth and nearby Scone Abbey having served as royal and sacred places for centuries, Perth's North Inch had long been a site for trial by combat. The field was fenced off from the town just southeast of it on the river, and the river provided as effective a barrier as the fences did, if not more so.

The town overlooked the Tay estuary at the first place narrow enough to bridge. If a man should fall in, the swift and powerful river would sweep him into the Firth of Tay and thence to the sea or, more likely, drown him long before then.

Therefore, the day's combatants had tried to keep clear of the precipitous riverbank. But when other ground grew slippery with gore and cluttered with the fallen, the area near the water remained as the only option.

None of the four who were still visibly alive looked as if he cared a whit about the young warrior. The lad remained wary but was grateful to rest, knowing that if he had to fight one or all of them, the likelihood was that he would die.

The others wore clothing similar to his—saffron-colored, knee-length tunics and wide leather sword belts. Each also wore a leather targe strapped to one arm to parry sword strokes. And each one wore his long hair in a single plait, as most Highland warriors did, to keep flying strands out of his face as he fought.

Although he could not discern their clan badges from where he stood, the lad knew they were all members of Clan Chattan, the enemy.

"Fin."

His sharp ears heard the voice, weak though it was, and he turned quickly.

Amidst the nearby bodies, he saw a slight but insistent movement and hurried toward it. Dropping to a knee beside the man who had made it and fighting back a rush of fear and icy despair, he exclaimed, "Father!"

"I'm spent," Teàrlach MacGillony muttered, clearly exerting himself more than a man in his condition should. "But I must—"

"Don't talk!" Fin said urgently.

"I must. Ye be all we ha' left from this dreadful day, lad. So 'tis your sacred duty tae stay alive. How many o' the villains be still upstanding?"

"I can see four," Fin said. "One is kneeling—retching, I think." With a catch in his voice, he added, "Except for me, all of our men have fallen."

"Then them ye see be just taking a breath," his father said. "Ye'll ha' to stand against them unless his grace, the King, stops the slaughter. But his brother, Albany, does sit by his side. The King is weak, but Albany is not. He is evil, is what *he* is. 'Twas his idea, all this, but his grace does ha' the power to stop it."

Fin looked again toward the tiers. Not only did the King and the Duke of Albany sit there but also members of the royal court, the clergy, and many of Perth's townspeople. Banners waved, and vendors doubtless still sold the ale, whisky, buns, and sweets that at the beginning of the day had made the event seem like a fair.

"Albany is speaking to his grace now," Fin said.

"Aye, nae doots telling him that there must be a true victor, so that the feuding betwixt the Camerons and Clan Chattan will stop. But hear me, lad. Our people did count on me as their war leader today, and I failed them. Ye must not."

"You accounted for several of these dead, sir," Fin said.

"I did, aye, but your sword sped more to their Maker than mine did. And, if ye truly be the last man o' ours standing, ye ha' a duty that ye must see to."

"What is it?"

"Vengeance," his father said, gasping. "Swear that ye'll seek it against their war leader and...and others. Ye ken fine...after such slaughter...the right o' vengeance be sacred. 'Tis a holy bequest that ye...as sole survivor, must accept." Gasping more harshly for each breath, he added, "Swear it...to me."

"I do swear it, sir, aye," Fin said hastily. To his father, clearly dying, he could give no other reply.

"Bless ye, my..."

Teàrlach MacGillony gasped no more.

Tears sprang to Fin's eyes, but a cry from the audience startled him from his grief. Glancing toward the tiers, he saw Albany waving for combat to continue.

The pipes kept silent. The King sat with his head bowed, making no sign, but people would see naught amiss in that. The King was weak, and Albany, as Governor of the Realm in his grace's stead, had long been the one who made such decisions.

Looking toward the men of Clan Chattan, Fin saw that three of them faced the tiers. The fourth, a tall and lanky chap, spoke to the others. Then, his sword at the ready, he turned toward Fin. The others followed but stopped well back of him.

As the man approached, he kept his head down and watched where he walked, doubtless to avoid treading on the fallen.

Fin hefted his sword, drew a deep breath, and set himself.

When the other man looked up at last, his gaze caught Fin's and held it.

Fin stared, then found voice enough to say, "Hawk?"

The other stopped six feet away. With a movement of his head so slight that Fin wondered if he had imagined it, he indicated the river nearby to his right.

The men behind him were talking to each other, cheerful now, confident of the outcome. They were far enough away that they could not have heard Fin speak, nor would they hear him if he spoke again.

"What are you trying to say?" he asked.

"Go," Hawk said, although his lips barely moved. "I cannot fight you. Someone from your side must live to tell your version of what happened here today."

"They'll flay you!"

"Nay, Lion. I'll be a hero. But think on that later. Now go, and go quickly before Albany sends his own men to dispatch the lot of us."

Hawk being one of the few men Fin trusted without question, he whirled, thrust his sword into the sling on his back, and dove in, wondering at himself and realizing only as the water swallowed him that he must look like a coward. By then, the river was bearing him swiftly past the town and onward, inexorably, to the sea.

The weight and cumbrous nature of the sword strapped to his back threatened to sink him, but he did not fight it. The farther the current took him before he surfaced, the safer he would be, and if he died on the way, so be it.

Then another, horrifying, thought struck. He'd sworn *two* oaths that day.

The first had been to accept the results of the combat and do no harm to any man on the opposing side. Every man there, as one voice, had sworn to that oath.

But then his war leader—his own dying father—had demanded a second oath, of vengeance, an oath that Fin could not keep without breaking his first one. Such a dilemma threatened his honor and that of his clan. But *all* oaths were sacred.

Might one oath be *more* sacred? Had his father known what he had asked?

He began kicking toward the surface, angling southward, knowing of only one place where he might find an answer. He could get there more easily from the shore opposite Perth...if he could get there at all.

Chapter 1 _____

The Highlands, early June 1401

The odd gurgling punctuated with harsher sounds that composed the Scottish jay's birdsong gave no hint of what lay far below its perch, on the forest floor.

The fair-haired young woman silently wending her way through the forest toward the jay's tall pine tree sensed nothing amiss. Nor, apparently, did the large wolf dog moving through the thick growth of pines, birch, and aspen a few feet to her right like a graceful, tarnished-silver ghost.

Most of the winter's snow had melted, and the day was a temperate one.

The breeze hushing through the canopy overhead and the still damp forest floor beneath eighteen-year-old Lady Catriona Mackintosh's bare feet made keeping silent easier than it would be after warmer temperatures dried the ground and foliage.

When a fat furry brown vole scurried out of her path and two squirrels chased each other up a nearby tree, she smiled, feeling a stab of pride in her ability to move so silently that her presence did not disturb the forest creatures.

She listened for sounds of the fast-flowing burn ahead. But before she heard any, the breeze dropped and the dog halted, stiffening to alertness as it raised its long snout. Then, trembling, it turned its head and looked at her.

Raising her right hand toward it, palm outward, Catriona stopped, too, and tried to sense what it sensed.

The dog watched her. She could tell that the scent it had caught on the air was not that of a wolf or a deer. Its expression was uncharacteristically wary. And its trembling likewise indicated wariness rather than the quivering, bowstring-taut excitement that it displayed when catching the scent of a favored prey.

The dog turned away again and bared its teeth but made no sound. She had trained it well and felt another rush of pride at this proof of her skill.

Moving forward, easing her toes gently under the mixture of rotting leaves and pine needles that carpeted the forest floor, as she had before, she glanced at the dog again. It would stop her if it sensed danger lurking ahead.

Instead, as she moved, the dog moved faster, making its own path between trees and through shrubbery to range silently before her.

She was accustomed to its protective instincts. Once, she had nearly walked into a wolf that had drifted from its pack and had gone so still at her approach that she failed to sense its presence. The wolf dog had leaped between them, stopping her and snarling at the wolf, startling it so that it made a strident bolt for safety. She had no doubt that the dog would kill any number of wolves to protect her.

That it glided steadily ahead but continued to glance back told her that although it did not like what it smelled, it was not afraid.

She felt no fear either, because she carried her dirk, and her brothers had taught her to use it. Moreover, she trusted her own instincts nearly as much as the dog's. She was sure that no predator, human or otherwise, lay in wait ahead of her.

The jay still sang. The squirrels chattered.

Birds usually fell silent at a predator's approach. And when squirrels shrieked warnings of danger, they did so in loud, staccato bursts as the harbinger raced ahead of the threat. But the two squirrels had grown noisier, as if they were trying to outshriek the jay.

As that whimsical thought struck, Catriona glanced up to see if she could spy the squirrels or the bird. Instead, she saw a huge black raven swooping toward the tall pine and heard the larger bird's deep croak as it sent the jay squawking into flight. The raven's arrival shot a chill up her spine. Ravens sought out carrion, dead things. This one perched in the tree and stared fixedly downward as it continued its croaking call to inform others of its kind that it had discovered a potential feast.

The dog increased its pace as if it, too, recognized the raven's call.

Catriona hurried after it and soon heard water rushing ahead. Following the dog into a clearing, she could see the turbulent burn running through it. The huge raven, on its branch overhead, raucously protested her presence. Others circled above, great black shadows against the overcast sky, cawing hopefully.

The dog growled, and at last she saw what had drawn the ravens.

A man wearing rawhide boots, a saffron-colored tunic with a large red and green mantle over it—the sort that

Highlanders called a plaid—lay facedown on the damp ground, unconscious or dead, his legs stretched toward the tumbling burn. Strapped slantwise across his back was a great sword in its sling, and a significant amount of blood had pooled by his head.

The dog had scented the blood.

So had the ravens.

⁓

Sir Finlagh Cameron awoke slowly. His first awareness was that his head ached unbearably. His second was of a warm breeze in his right ear and a huffing sound. He seemed to be facedown, his left cheek resting on an herbal-scented pillow.

What, he wondered, had happened to him?

Just as it finally dawned on him that he was lying on dampish ground atop leafy plants of some sort, a long wet tongue laved his right cheek and ear.

Opening his eyes, he beheld two…no, four silvery gray legs, much too close.

Tensing, but straining to keep still as the animal licked him again, well aware that wolves littered all Highland forests, he shifted his gaze beyond the four legs to see if there were any more. He did see two more legs, but either his vision was defective or his mind was playing tricks on him.

The two legs were bare, shapely, and tanned.

He shut his eyes and opened them again. The legs looked the same.

Slowly and carefully, he tried to lift his head to see more of both creatures, only to wince at the jolt of pain that shot through his head as he did. But, framed by the arch of the beast's legs and body, he glimpsed bare feet and ankles, clearly human, then bare calves, decidedly feminine.

By straining, he could also see bare knees and bare...

A snapping sound diverted him, and the animal beside him backed off. It was larger than he had expected and taller. But it was no wolf. On the contrary...

"Wolf dog or staghound," he muttered.

"So you are not dead after all."

The soft feminine voice carried a note of drollery and floated to him on the breeze, only he no longer felt a breeze. Doubtless, the dog's breath had been what he'd felt in his ear earlier. Coming to this conclusion reassured him that he hadn't lost his wits, whatever else had happened to him.

"Can you not talk to me?"

It was the same voice but nearer, although he had not sensed her approach in any way. But then, until the warm breath huffed into his ear, he had not sensed the dog either. He realized, too, that she had spoken the Gaelic. He had scarcely noticed, despite having spoken it little himself for several years.

Recalling the shapely legs and bare feet, he realized with some confusion that his eyes had somehow shut themselves. He opened them to the disappointing revelation that her bareness ended midthigh. A raggedy blue kirtle, kilted up the way a man would kilt up his plaid, covered most of the rest of her.

"I can talk," he said and felt again that odd sense of accomplishment. "I'm not so sure that I can move. My head feels as if someone tried to split it in two."

"You've shed blood on the leaves round your head, so you are injured," she said. Her voice was still soft, calm, and carrying that light note, as if she felt no fear of him or of anything else in the woods. "I can get your sword out of its sling if you will trust me to do it. And I can get the sling and belt off you, too. But you will have to lift yourself a bit for that. Then, mayhap you can turn over."

"Aye, sure," he said. If she had wanted to kill him, she'd have done it. And she was too small to wield his heavy sword as a weapon.

She managed without much difficulty to drag the sword from the sling on his back. But when he raised himself so she could reach the strap's buckle under him, he had to grit his teeth against the pain and dizziness that surged through his head.

Still, he decided by the time she unbuckled the stout strap and deftly slipped it free of his body that little was wrong with him other than an aching head.

"Now, if you can turn over," she said, "I will look and see how bad it is."

Exerting himself, he rolled over and looked up to see a pretty face with a smudge on one rosy cheek, and a long mass of unconfined, wild-looking, tawny hair.

Despite the look of concern on her face, her eyes twinkled.

Fin could not tell their exact color in the shadow of so many trees and with an overcast sky above, but they seemed to be light brown, rather than blue.

"Are you a sprite, or some other woodland creature?" he murmured, finding the effort to talk greater now. His eyelids drooped.

She chuckled low in her throat, a delightful sound and a stimulating one.

His eyes opened again, and he saw that she had dropped

to one knee to bend over him. As he took in the two soft-looking, well-tanned mounds of flesh that peeped over the low-cut bodice so close to him, his head seemed instantly clearer.

Her lips were moving, and he realized that she was speaking. Having missed the first bit, he listened intently to catch the rest, hoping thereby to reply sensibly.

"...would laugh to hear anyone mistake me for a sprite," she said, adding firmly, "Now, lie still, sir, if you please. You must know that I was leery of getting too near until I could be sure that you would not harm me."

"Never fear, lass. I would not."

"I can see that, but Boreas, my companion here, dislikes letting any stranger near me. Had you moved suddenly or thrashed about as some do when they regain conscious-ness after an injury, he might have mistaken you for a threat."

Having noted how quickly the wolf dog had stepped back after the snapping sound he'd heard—surely a snap of her slim fingers—he doubted that it would attack against her will. But he did not say so. His eyelids drifted shut again.

"Are you still awake?" No amusement now, only concern.

"Aye, sure, but fading," he murmured. "What is your name, lass?"

"Catriona. What's yours?"

He thought about it briefly, then said, "Fin...they call me Fin of the Battles."

"What happened to you, Fin of the Battles?" Her voice sounded more distant, as if she were floating away again.

"I wish I knew," he said, trying to concentrate. "I was

walking through the forest, listening to a damned impertinent jay that squawked and muttered at me for trespassing. The next thing I knew, your escort was huffing in my ear."

He drew a long breath and, without opening his eyes, tried moving his arms more than had been necessary to shift himself. Pain shot through his head again, and he felt more pain from some sort of scrape on his left arm. But both arms seemed obedient to his will. His toes and feet likewise obeyed him.

A hand touched his right shoulder, startling him. She had come up on his other side, and again he'd not heard her move. He was definitely *not* himself yet.

"Be still now," she said, kneeling gracefully beside him. As she bent nearer, he noted the bare softness of her breasts again before a cold, wet cloth touched his forehead and moved soothingly over it to cover his eyes.

He knew then that she must have gone to the burn that he could hear splashing nearby. He tried to decide if he remembered seeing that burn.

"That feels good," he murmured.

"It won't in a minute. You have a gash on the left side of your forehead with leaves, dirt, and hair stuck in it. You will have a fine scar to brag about."

"I don't brag."

"All men brag," she said, the note of humor strong again. "Most women do, too, come to that. But men brag like bairns, often and with great exaggeration."

"I don't." It seemed important that she should know that.

"Very well, you don't. You are unique amongst men. Now, hold still. Recall that Boreas will object to any sudden movement."

He braced himself. He was not afraid of the dog, but he hated pain. And he had already borne more than his share of it.

⁓

Catriona saw him stiffen and easily deduced the reason. All men, in her experience, disliked pain. Certainly, her father and two brothers did, although they were all fine, brave warriors. The excellent specimen of manhood before her looked as if he could hold his own against any one of them.

When he'd turned over, it had taken all of her willpower not to exclaim at his blood-streaked face. She reminded herself that head wounds always bled freely, and noted thankfully that all the blood seemed to come from the gash in his forehead.

In cleaning his face before she put the cloth over his eyes, she had decided that, besides being well formed, he was handsome in a rugged way. His deep-set eyes were especially fine, their light gray irises surprising in a darkly tanned face. His thick, black lashes were less surprising. For a reason known only to God, men always seemed to grow darker, thicker lashes than women did.

"Have you enemies hereabouts?" she asked as she gently plucked hair and forest detritus from his wound.

Instead of answering directly, he said, "I have not passed this way before. Are your people unfriendly to strangers?"

Having ripped two pieces from her red flannel under-skirt to soak in the burn, she'd used one to cover his eyes, hoping it would soothe him and keep him from staring at her as she cleansed his wound. The latter hope was not for his sake but for hers. Aware that she would be hurting him, she knew she would do a better job if she need not keep seeing the pain in his eyes each time she touched his wound.

Now, however, she plucked the cloth from his eyes, waited until he opened them and focused on her, and then raised her eyebrows and said, "*My* people?"

To her surprise, he smiled, just slightly. But it was enough to tell her that he had a nice smile and that her tone had tickled his sense of humor.

"Do you dare to laugh at me?" she demanded.

"Nay, lass, I would not laugh at such a kind benefactress. I am still wondering if your people are human or otherwise. Sithee, although you disclaim being a wood sprite, I *have* heard tales of wee folk in this area."

"I am human," she said. "Lie still now. Your wound is trying to clot, but I must rinse these cloths, and if you move too much, you'll start leaking again."

"Tell me first who your people are," he said as she stood. His voice was stronger, and his words came as a command from a man accustomed to obedience.

Catriona eyed him speculatively. "Do you not know *where* you are?"

"I am in Clan Chattan territory, in Strathspey, I think. But Clan Chattan boasts vast lands and numerous clans within it—six, I think, at last count."

"All controlled by one man," she said.

"The Mackintosh is chief of the whole confederation, aye," he said, almost nodding. She saw him remember her warning about that and catch himself.

Satisfied, she said, "That's right, although we call him our captain, to show that he is more powerful than other clan chiefs in our confederation." Moving swiftly back to the burn, she knelt and rinsed the bloody cloth in the churning, icy water. Then she dipped the other one, wrung them both out, and returned to him.

As she approached, she saw Boreas go into some bushes a short way beyond the man's head, sniffing the air. The dog pushed its snout into low, dense shrubbery, plucked an arrow from it, and trotted back to her with it in its mouth.

Taking the arrow, Catriona said, "I think Boreas has found the cause of your injury, sir. If so, I can tell you that this arrow came from no Clan Chattan bow."

"Nor any Lochaber one," he muttered.

"Are you from Lochaber then?"

Cursing himself for the slip, Fin said, "I grew up on the west side of the Great Glen. But have spent little time there of late. Do you ken aught else of this arrow?"

"Nay, but I do wish that Ivor were here," she said.

"Ivor?" He raised his left eyebrow, winced, and said ruefully, "I shall have to remember for a time *not* to express my feelings with facial movements."

Chuckling, deciding she liked the melodic sound of his voice, she said, "Ivor is the younger of my two brothers. He is also the finest archer in Scotland, so he knows the fletching of most Highland clans and taught me what little I know. But he, my father, and my brother James are in the Borders with the Lord of the North."

"What makes you think this Ivor is the finest archer in the land?" he asked. "Scotland boasts many fine archers. I'm deft with a bow and arrow myself."

"No doubt you are. I shoot well, too, come to that. But Ivor is the best."

"I know a chap who can beat anything that your Ivor might do," he said.

"No such person exists," she said çonfidently as she slipped the arrow under the linked girdle that kilted up her skirts. Then, kneeling again, she added, "Now, let me finish cleaning your wound. The only thing that I might bandage it with is a strip of my underskirt. But I fear that the flannel would chafe it and make it bleed more."

"I don't need a bandage," he said. "I heal quickly."

"See, you do brag, like any man. How much farther must you go?"

"A day's walk, mayhap two."

"Then you should come home with me and rest overnight. That gash *will* open again, because it does need bandaging and may even require a stitch or two."

His grimace revealed strong reluctance, either to stitches or to her invitation.

Before he could speak, she said, "Don't be so daft as to refuse. Someone wickedly attacked you, and that arrow knocked you headfirst against yon tree. You hit hard enough to make you bounce back and fall as you were when I found you."

"Sakes, lass, if you saw all that, did you not also see who shot me?"

"I saw none of that," she replied.

Looking narrowly at her, Fin said, "If you saw none of it, you cannot possibly know how I fell. Sakes, I don't know that much myself."

"Nevertheless, that or something like that *is* what happened," she insisted. "This arrow that Boreas found made the gash in your forehead because the blood on it is still sticky. You have a lump rising here by your ear"—he winced when she touched it—"and I see bark in your hair and down the collar of your shirt. Also, the sleeve of your jack is torn, and I see more bits of bark on your arm. The event depicts itself, sir. Moreover," she added, pointing, "he shot from across the burn."

He had to admit, if only to himself, that if she was right about the rest, she was right about the direction of the shot.

Deciding that he had lain long enough on the damp ground, he sat up and then had to hold himself steady and concentrate hard to fight off a new wave of dizziness. He tried to do so without letting her see how weak he felt.

Meeting her twinkling gaze, he grimaced, suspecting that her powers of observation were keener than his ability just then to conceal his feelings.

"That dizziness will pass if you give it time," she said, confirming his suspicion. "But you would be foolish *not* to come with me, because one can easily see that you are in no fit state to continue on your own."

The dog moved up beside her, eyeing him thoughtfully. Just looking at it reminded Fin that Highland forests sheltered many a wolf pack. The beasts would soon catch scent of his blood if he did aught to start the wound bleeding again.

"Would your kinsmen so easily welcome a stranger?" he asked.

"My lady mother welcomes all who come in peace," she said. "In my father's absence, I warrant she will be fain to have a strong man at hand, even overnight."

He realized then that she was of noble birth and that he

ought to have known it despite her untidiness. Commoners rarely owned wolf dogs or spoke as she did.

"How far is your home from here?" he asked.

"'Tis in the glen just over yon hill," she said, pointing toward the granite ridge above them to the northeast. "We'll go through the cut above those trees."

"Then I will gratefully accept your invitation."

Smiling in a way that made his body stir unexpectedly in response, she picked up his sword and sling and stood back to let him get to his feet.

When he stood and reached for the sword, she said, "I can carry it."

"Nay, then, I do not relinquish my weapon to anyone, woman or man."

He saw a flash of annoyance, but she handed him the belt. He strapped it into place and took the sword from her, feeling its weight more than usual as he reached back and slipped it into its sling. But he did so, he thought, without noticeable difficulty. She did not *seem* to notice, but he felt new tension between them.

The hill was steep, and it proved harder than he had expected to follow her up through the forest to the ridge. The waves of dizziness persisted, and halfway up, he began to feel weary, almost leaden. To be sure, he had traveled far that day.

But such profound weariness was abnormal for him.

When they reached the scree-filled cut below the sharp crest, the going grew easier. Still, the loose rocks underfoot and a number of huge boulders in their path required vigilance to avoid a misstep.

Fin stopped gratefully when the lass did but assured himself that naught was amiss with him but his recurrent dizziness and the strange lassitude. The sweeping prospect of the towering, still snowy Cairngorms beyond was spectacular.

"There," she said, pointing. "We need only row across the loch."

He looked down to see a curving, mile-long, deep-green loch that looked like a shard from a lass's looking glass, reflecting the wild beauty of heavily forested slopes and a few steep granite ones that surrounded it like the steep sides of a basin.

Following her gesture southeast to a much nearer point, his gaze fell on an island fortress some hundred yards from where the shore curved around the base of the steep hillside just below them. At the sight of that fortress, he felt a sense of unexpected disorientation and disbelief.

Maintaining an even tone of voice with effort, he said, "Is that not Castle Moigh, the very seat of the Mackintosh?"

"Nay," she said. "That is Loch an Eilein and my father's castle of Rothiemurchus. But you are not the first to mistake it for Moigh. See you, we Mackintoshes like islands. They provide more security than other sites do."

"So you must be kin to the Mackintosh."

"He is my grandfather," she said proudly.

"Then you can tell me exactly how far Loch Moigh lies from here."

"Aye, sure, but why do you want to know?"

"Sithee, I have come into Clan Chattan territory a-purpose to talk with the Mackintosh, to deliver a message to him."

Her eyes twinkled again. "Have you, in troth?" When he nodded, she added, "Then it is good that you did come with me, sir, because at present the Mackintosh and my lady grandmother are staying with my mother and me at Rothiemurchus."

"Our meeting today was fortunate then, was it not?"

"It was, aye," she agreed, turning away. "We'll go down now."

He recalled then her belief that, in her father's absence, her mother would welcome a "strong man" at Rothiemurchus.

"I trust that your grandfather is in good health and..." He hesitated, having seen enough of her to know that the words on his tongue might offend her.

She looked back, and he saw that the twinkle in her eyes had deepened. "If you were about to suggest that my grandfather is ill or has lost his wits—"

"I did not say that."

"But you nearly did say it, or something like it. Do you deny that?"

"Nay, but I did hear that he was too elderly to wield a sword with his once-legendary skill. And since I have come to ask a boon of him and would not press him to do aught that he is too feeble to—"

"Feeble?" Her lips twitched in a near smile, and as she turned away, she said over her shoulder, "He came to us because, having learned of trouble stirring in our area, he wanted to look into its cause. However, my mother does hope that my father and brothers will return soon. See you, my grandfather trusts my father to deal with any problem we might face, because he is our Clan Chattan war leader."

New tension gripped him. Quietly, he said, "Who *is* your father, lass?"

"Shaw Mackintosh, Laird of Rothiemurchus," she said.

"Before he married my mother and took the name Mackintosh, men knew him as Shaw MacGillivray."

Stunned, Fin stopped in his tracks.

Shaw MacGillivray was the Clan Chattan war leader he had sworn to kill.

Chapter 2 _____

Noting the sudden silence behind her, Catriona turned, saying, "What is it?"

"Nowt," Fin of the Battles said—rather curtly, she thought.

She frowned. He seemed paler than before. "Are you dizzy again?" she asked.

Rosy color tinged his cheeks, telling her that he did not like the question. But she thought she detected relief in his expression when he said, "Aye, now and now."

Clearly, like her brothers, the man hated admitting any weakness.

To prove that to herself, she said, "We'll reach the boat soon. Crossing takes just a few minutes, and then I'll take you inside where you can rest."

Still watching him, she saw a flash of consternation rather than the annoyance she expected from a man reminded of his need to rest.

His gaze met hers. In the open, she saw that his light gray irises would have blended right into the whites were it not that they darkened slightly at the rims. The length and thickness of his lashes now seemed protective rather than just unfair.

Standing close to him as she was now, she realized that the top of her head barely reached his chin. And as she continued to meet his steady gaze, she felt a prickling in her skin that radiated warmly inward.

As she struggled to collect her wits, she sensed new hesitation in him, a stronger reluctance. She felt as if he might say that he had changed his mind and would go on without stopping at Rothiemurchus.

But then he said firmly, "Lead on, my lady. I am eager to speak with your grandfather if he will receive me."

"He will," she said as she gestured for Boreas to precede them.

Following the dog, she became more conscious than ever of the man behind her and tinglingly aware of each firm footstep he took.

Fin wondered if the Mackintosh customarily let his granddaughter roam the woods at will, or if she might face rebuke for bringing a stranger home with her. He hoped not, because it would complicate a matter that was complex enough already.

Considering the dilemma that he faced with regard to the lass's father, Shaw MacGillivray, he wondered next at his own motives. The Clan Chattan war leader's name had haunted him for nearly four and a half years. That he was about to enter the man's stronghold produced a host of conflicting thoughts and emotions.

He would be accepting Shaw's hospitality, so the voice in Fin's head shouted that he should seek shelter from anyone but the man he had sworn to kill. Highland law forbade harm to anyone who sought hospitality or *provided* it.

His original plan had been to pass through Strathspey into the mountains to the west and reach Castle Moigh quietly. To that end, he had traveled cautiously, and after parting from his squire and his equerry, he had traveled alone.

The fact was that he was in enemy territory. To be sure, a truce had existed since the great clan battle. But truces could evaporate overnight, especially in conflicts over land. And when a feud had gone on for decades, as the Cameron-Mackintosh feud had... Had whoever shot him known he was a Cameron?

Fin knew that he had kept up his guard. Although he had seen crofts and cottages along the way, he had not wandered near enough to draw undue notice.

After entering the woods where the lass found him, he had felt safer. But although the forest provided more cover for a traveler than open glens and hillsides did, the unseen archer had shot him. And no man shot without seeing his target.

Without the lady Catriona's timely arrival, the villain might have killed him. In return, he was about to accept her hospitality despite his fell intent toward her father.

She led him downhill at an angle, past the islet, to a granite slope on which a flat-bottomed boat lay beached. As she dragged its oars from nearby shrubbery, Fin said, "Do you expect that wee coble to carry us *and* the dog all the way to yon islet?"

Turning to face him—chin raised, eyes flashing—she stood her oars on the ground with their blade ends against one shoulder. "I do expect that, aye. Art so cowardly, sir, that you fear I shall *not* get you safely across?"

Disliking both the word and her tone but determined not to rise to such obvious bait, Fin noted absently that her eyes were not light brown but golden-hazel. When she glared at him again, he said, "I do wonder, Lady Imperious, if you habitually speak so to men. But, frankly, I'd not trust anyone except myself to row such a craft, overladen as it will be. But the dog and I can swim, and a ducking will do you no harm."

When her hand shot up in response, he caught her wrist and held it.

What, Catriona wondered, had come over her to dare such a thing?

His grip would leave bruises, she knew. She also knew that had she dared to taunt either of her brothers so, let alone tried to slap him, he would have flung her into the icy loch if not right over his knee. Worse, Fin was injured, albeit evidently recovering quickly, and he was about to become a guest of her father's household.

Still annoyed that he had doubted her skill but tingling now in a different, more unusual, and intriguing way in response to the stern look in his eyes, she did not fight his grip or answer his question. Nor would she look away until he released her.

When he did, she put her oars in the boat and began to tug it toward the water. She had not got far before he grabbed the other side to help her.

If he still suffered from dizziness, the speed at which he had caught her hand belied it, as did the ease with which they dragged the boat to the water. Still silent, she gestured to Boreas, and while she and Fin steadied the boat, the dog stepped gingerly into it, then over the oars and the midthwart to curl up in the stern.

Fin continued to eye the boat askance. "Mayhap I *should* row," he said.

"With you in the middle and Boreas at the stern, the pair of you would likely weigh it under whilst I was still trying to launch it and climb into the bow," she retorted. "However, you have clearly recovered enough to launch us, and I expect you are agile enough to jump in without getting your feet wet if that concerns you."

This time when his gaze met hers, something in the look he gave her shot a sense of warning through her. But he said only, "Get in, lass."

Wondering what demon had possessed her to tease him again, she obeyed at once and took her seat. Facing the stern and Boreas, she freed her kilted-up skirts for propriety's sake and adjusted the arrow at her girdle more comfortably. Then, taking up her oars, she steadied the coble while Fin of the Battles launched it.

When he swung himself into the bow, water sloshed over the port side, but it was not enough to endanger them. The boat had less freeboard than she liked, but the loch was calm, and she was skilled with the oars.

Glancing over her shoulder, she had to lean and look past her large passenger to be sure she would not hit a rock as she backed away, then turned the bow toward the island. She noted that he watched her narrowly as she wielded the oars. By the time she had executed her turn, he had visibly relaxed. But he did not apologize.

When she was facing away from him again, he said, "You never answered my question about how your people usually treat strangers. However—"

"We treat them civilly, of course, unless they prove uncivil."

"Then we treat people alike, lass. Moreover, before we met, I had talked with no one since this morning, so I can scarcely have offended anyone."

"Mayhap whoever you were with this morning took offense at something."

"Nay, for I was with my own lads, riding from Glen Garry northward."

She glanced over her shoulder again. "You rode with a tail of men?"

"Two lads only," he said with a shrug slight enough to show that he still distrusted the coble's stability.

"Where are they now?" she asked.

"Knowing that the mountains west of here are easier penetrated on foot than on horseback, as we were, I chose to walk on ahead of them."

"But why did they not just come with you? And where are your horses?"

"I sent the men on an errand, and they were to stable the horses until our return from the mountains. They expect to meet me at Castle Moigh, though."

"Mayhap *they* attracted attention. Or mayhap you did without knowing that you had. I did ask you earlier if you had enemies hereabouts," she added. "You said only that you had not passed this way before."

He was silent long enough for her to take two strokes with the oars and for that odd prickling awareness of him to stir again before he said, "By my troth, lass, I have *not* passed this way before. I have heard, though, that rather than enjoying a repute for civility, the men of Clan Chattan are a fractious lot. Also, you did mention trouble brewing. It seems logical that my mishap may have resulted from that."

Noting that he still had not said whether he had enemies in the area, Catriona nibbled her lower lip, thinking. She could not refute his logic, for it was excellent. But she was reluctant to discuss the irritating Comyns with a stranger.

"I see," he murmured provocatively.

"*What* do you see?"

"That I may be right," he said. "Just who is stirring this trouble of yours?"

Grimacing, she said, "'Tis only the plaguey Comyns. I cannot think why they would trouble you, though."

"Comyns? I thought that clan had nearly died out."

"Aye, but they were once lords of Lochindorb Castle, which lies near here and is now home to the Lord of the North. The Comyns seek to grow strong again."

"Do they hold a grievance against your confederation, then?"

"Nay, they act in response to imagined complaints and their own arrogance," she said. "Much of their sense of ill-usage arises, as most such conflicts do, from land that they think should be theirs but which is and always has been Mackintosh land. Except for Lochindorb and all of its estates," she added conscientiously.

He was silent. Glancing back again, she saw him frowning. When she rested her oars and gave him a quizzical look, the frown eased and he said, "How quickly did you come upon me? Do you recall?"

"Not exactly," she said, returning to her rowing. "Does it matter?"

"It might," he said. "The trees in those woods were too far apart for me to miss seeing an archer who stood near enough to shoot me from point-blank range. But I could have missed seeing one who shot from a greater distance."

"Mayhap something distracted you, kept you from seeing him."

"I doubt it. I don't recall what I was thinking when the arrow struck. But being alone in unknown woods as I was, I was not careless. Nor was that shot an accident. Might a Comyn have had cause to shoot a stranger here on any other account?"

Resting her oars again, she shifted enough on her seat this time to look at him without getting a crick in her neck. "We have not agreed that the archer was a Comyn," she said. Her tone, she hoped, had been matter-of-fact, but his eyes had narrowed. Hastily, she added, "He could as easily have been a poacher who missed his shot as an archer performing some great feat of archery."

She could feel her cheeks burning and turned back to her rowing, fearing that he had noticed her increased color and hoping he would not quiz her about it.

He said evenly, "Such a bowshot in the open may be easy for most archers. But one from the distance and with the concealment necessary to prevent my seeing the archer is not. And whilst we have *not* determined that the shooter was a Comyn, *you* have not yet said whether some Comyn or other might think that he had cause."

"One cannot know *what* such a man may think," she replied. "Earlier, you mentioned the noisy jay. I thought he'd got noisy because of your mishap, but—"

"Jays are noisy by habit," he interjected.

"They are, aye," she agreed. "But they are also noisy when predators invade their territory. The squirrels were noisy, too. Also, the ravens."

"Ravens?"

She nodded. "They must have scented fresh blood,

just as Boreas did, and hoped to feast on whatever they found."

"We can forget the ravens, since there was no blood before the arrow struck me. But someone else *was* in those woods. If you did not see anyone..."

"I did not see or *hear* anyone," she said when he paused. "We were upwind of you, sir, and thus, too, of whoever shot you. Boreas scented naught until the breeze dropped, and we found you shortly after that."

"Wolf dogs do catch scent on the air," he said thoughtfully. "Surely, though, if a stranger had been nearby, he'd have caught wind of him then, too."

"One would think so," she agreed. "But it did take some time to reach you. And the ravens had got louder. Mayhap the man who shot you took advantage of their racket to run away, or mayhap the stronger scent of blood hid his scent from Boreas. In any event, we do not know who it was."

"Nay," he said. "Nor do we know why he shot me."

Catriona glanced over her shoulder and saw with relief that they were nearing the island. The castle's stone curtain wall rose from just above the high-water mark on the gentle slope. The heavy gate stood ajar.

Everyone would know by now that she was bringing a stranger home. Had her father and brothers been there, they would be waiting at the landing. As it was, their welcoming committee consisted of two stalwart men-at-arms and one grinning boy.

⁓

Eyeing the two men-at-arms who approached from the gateway, Fin wondered if he had been foolhardy to accept the lass's invitation. Belated memory of Clan Chattan's motto, "Touch not the cat but with a glove," suggested that he *was* a fool.

But he had had no other choice.

His orders had been to persuade the Mackintosh to accept a role that the man might be reluctant to play. And the Mackintosh was on the island.

However, accepting hospitality at Rothiemurchus still presented sufficient difficulty to give Fin's conscience another twinge.

In truth, no actual law forbade dispatching one's erstwhile host *after* having accepted his hospitality... as long as one waited until one was no longer under the man's roof. Moreover, if he were to decide now against staying, he would stir the lady Catriona's curiosity if not her outright distrust. As to his honor...

That half-thought had only to enter his mind to produce a mental image of his powerful, exceedingly volatile master that made him speedily collect his wits. Whatever his personal dilemma was, he had a duty to execute, and simply put, the Mackintosh was here. All other concerns must surrender to that one.

The coble's bow scraped bottom, diverting his attention. When the boy who had accompanied the two men-at-arms splashed into the shallows and tried to pull the craft ashore, Fin jumped out to help him.

His rawhide boots got wet, but he did not mind. He'd worn them to protect feet that had lost their Highland toughness after years of riding in the Borders and lowlands, instead of walking barefoot everywhere, as most Highlanders did.

"The Mackintosh would see ye straightaway, m'lady," one man-at-arms said when Fin and the lad had beached the boat. "He'll be in his chamber, but Lady Annis and your lady mother be in the great hall. They want tae see ye, too."

Fin extended a hand toward Catriona, but she stepped ashore on her own and with a grace that surprised him. Few could emerge unaided from such an unstable craft with anything but awkwardness.

He had seen from the hilltop that the fortress covered most of the island, except for its wooded northern end. When they reached the gateway and passed through it into the yard, he saw that a four-story keep formed the southwest angle of the curtain wall. The fortress boasted two other, smaller towers, one at the north end near the gateway, the other at the southeast corner. One man stayed by the gate.

"Tadhg," the lady Catriona said, addressing the small gillie, "prithee, run ahead and tell the cook that Boreas will soon want his supper."

"Aye, sure," the lad said cheerfully. Raising a hand to pat the big dog's withers as if to reassure it that it would not starve, he dashed off toward the keep.

Boreas continued to trot alongside Catriona and the remaining man-at-arms.

As they hurried across the rocky, hard-packed-dirt yard toward timber stairs leading to the main entrance, they passed an alcove between the keep and the row of wooden outbuildings against the curtain wall. Fin saw a path leading to a lower entrance, and when Tadhg pulled open the door there and disappeared inside, he decided that it likely opened into the scullery and kitchen.

He followed the others up the timber stairs and inside, then up more stone steps and through an archway into the great hall. It felt chilly despite a roaring fire in the huge hooded fireplace that occupied much of the long wall to his right.

He saw three women standing halfway between the fire and the dais at the other end of the hall. One was thin and elderly, the second a young matron, and the third fell between them in age. She was more attractive than the other two and a couple of stones plumper. Their veils and gowns proclaimed them all noblewomen.

"There ye be, Granddaughter," the oldest of the three said in a high-pitched voice that carried easily, although she did not seem to have raised it. "Ye've been gone an age, lass. I hope ye did not roam too far afield."

The young matron looked disapprovingly at Catriona but kept silent.

The plump, attractive lady smiled warmly.

"I did not go far, madam," Catriona said to the eldest as she went to them and made her curtsy. "Nor must I linger here now, because my lord grandfather has sent for me. Before I go to him, though, pray let me present to you this gentleman whom Boreas and I found injured in our woods."

"Mercy, dearling, I wish ye would no ramble with only that great dog to guard ye," the plump lady said. "A body might meet *any*one these days."

"In troth, you might," the younger matron said. "Why, you ken fine that—"

"Never mind that now, ye two," the old woman said, holding Fin's interested gaze. "Do present your new acquaintance to us, Catriona."

"He is called Fin of the Battles, madam," the lass said as Fin made his bow. "This is my grandmother, Annis,

Lady Mackintosh, sir." Gesturing to the others, she said, "This is my mother, the lady Ealga, and my brother James's wife, Morag. Fin of the Battles came into Clan Chattan country to speak to the Mackintosh," she added.

"Then, ye must take him to your grandfather straight-way," Lady Annis said. "But I would ken more about ye, Fin of the Battles. Ye'll join us for supper."

"With the Mackintosh's leave, I will be pleased to do so, your ladyship," Fin said. He saw that the "great dog" had flopped near the fire and closed its eyes.

When Catriona turned toward the dais end of the hall, her grandmother said with a gesture to the man-at-arms who had come with them from the shore, "Take Aodán in with ye, lassie. The Mackintosh may have orders for him."

Fin's lips twitched in a near smile. Lady Annis was too polite to insult him by demanding that he leave his weap-ons behind. But she evidently believed that one guard could protect the Captain of Clan Chattan if the need arose.

There would be no such need, which was just as well. Wounded or not, Fin knew that he could win a fair fight against any single opponent.

"This way, sir," the lass said, gesturing toward the dais. "In Father's absence, my grandfather uses our inner cham-ber." Then, quietly enough to keep anyone else from hear-ing but with the note of humor that he had heard before, she added, "I warrant he will occupy it after Father comes home, too."

"The Mackintosh likes to get his own way, too, does he?" Fin murmured.

Her twinkling gaze met his. "All men expect to get their own way."

"Women do, too, do they not?"

She shook her head. "Women may hope to do so in some things. But, surely, you know that when heads knock together, men *usually* win."

"Not always?"

This time, she chuckled. "Nay, as you did see for yourself."

He hid a smile of his own but let her have the last word, for now.

A gillie appeared from an alcove at the end of the dais to Fin's right and hurried to open the door at the rear of it for them. Catriona stepped into the room beyond with Fin at her heels and the man-at-arms, Aodán, behind him.

"Sakes, is this an invasion?" a gruff voice demanded, drawing Fin's gaze from the huge bed in front of him, where he had expected to see the Mackintosh, to a table at the far right of a room that looked to be the same width as the great hall.

The Mackintosh sat in a two-elbow chair behind a table laden with scrolled documents. And Fin saw at once that the lass had been right.

Although her grandfather had long since passed what many tactfully called the age mark, from middle to old age, his shoulders and arms still looked muscular enough to wield the huge sword that had made him famous in his youth. The old man's scowl was piercing, with a strong glint of intelligence behind it.

Fin realized that he had based his earlier opinion solely on the fact that four years before, Clan Chattan had declared the old age and infirmity of their captain as the reason that his war leader had led them at the clan battle in his stead. No man had questioned the reason, because all there had known that the eighth chief of Clan Mackintosh had already been Captain of Clan Chattan for more than three decades.

"This is no invasion, my lord," Catriona said, ignoring her grandfather's scowl and smiling as they approached his table. "I come at your command, as you ken fine, and beg leave to present our guest to you." She gestured gracefully toward Fin.

As he stepped nearer to make his bow, she added, "I found him in the woods beyond the west ridge, injured as you see. When I learned that he was heading for Moigh to speak to you, I brought him here."

"How came ye to be injured?" the Mackintosh demanded of Fin.

"Evidently someone shot me with an arrow, sir," Fin replied.

"I found him unconscious with that gash on his forehead," Catriona said. "Boreas found the arrow in nearby shrubbery with the blood on it still tacky."

"Is that the arrow at your waist, lass?"

"Aye, sir," she said, pulling it free of her girdle and laying it before him.

"Had they not found me when they did, sir, I suspect I would be in no case now to accept hospitality from anyone," Fin said as the old man examined the arrow.

"Ye suspect someone of murderous intent then, do ye?" He glanced at his granddaughter, and Fin noted silent communication in his expression. He could not observe her response without turning his head, but the Mackintosh added, "I must ask ye to curb your wandering for a time, lass. Things being as they are..."

Without looking at her, Fin sensed her resistance. But she did not argue.

The Mackintosh added, "Ye'd better go away now and let me talk with him."

"When you are finished with him, sir," she said, "I will show him to a chamber so that he may rest."

"Aodán, ye go along, too," the Mackintosh said. "I'll have nae need of ye."

Their footsteps—hers light, the man-at-arms's plodding and heavy—sounded behind Fin as they crossed the floor. Related noises followed as the man opened the door for her and shut it behind them.

In the silence that fell, the Mackintosh said, "Who are ye, then, that ye call yourself Fin of the Battles? I must say, ye've a certain look about ye that I find familiar. But my memory nae longer serves me as well as it once did."

Although he had been expecting a demand for his antecedents, Fin realized as he met that fierce gaze that he had no ready answer. He knew that he resembled his famous father, but due to one thing and another, many others in Lochaber also resembled Teàrlach MacGillony.

At last, he said, "I bear safe conduct from Davy Stewart, Duke of Rothesay and Governor of the Realm, my lord. He would ask a boon of you."

"Would he?" the Mackintosh said dryly. "We'll need whisky then, I trow."

Chapter 3 _____

Catriona would have liked to change her clothing. But when she emerged from the inner chamber, her mother, grandmother, and good-sister were on the dais just outside it. And she knew from the curiosity on all three faces that she would be wearing her old kirtle for a while yet.

"Who *is* he, my love, and why does he call himself 'Fin of the Battles'?" Lady Ealga asked. In much the same breath, Lady Annis snapped, "Where does he hail from, Granddaughter? Who are his parents?"

Stifling a sigh, Catriona said, "I wish that one of you had asked him, because I ken no more than what I've told you. I was walking with Boreas when we found him. In troth, I worried more about the man's injury than his antecedents."

"In faith, Catriona, you should take more care," her good-sister said sternly.

"Aye, Morag is right," Lady Annis said. "One should always ken a man's roots before approaching him. Sithee, Granddaughter, one day your impetuous nature will land ye deep in the suds."

"He *is* handsome, is he not?" Ealga said. "It would have been hard to leave him lying on the ground without trying to aid him—sadly inconsiderate, too. And whilst I might have been too cowardly to help him, Annis, I believe that *you* would have done just as our Catriona did."

"If I did, it would be because I ken fine that I can defend myself. Can you say as much, Catriona?"

Lady Ealga said, "You do have your wee dirk, do you not, my love?"

"I do, aye," Catriona said, slipping her right hand through the slit—or fitchet—in her skirt, which let her take the weapon from the sheath strapped to her thigh. Seeing her grandmother's eyes widen, she said, "My brothers taught me to use it, madam, and said to do so only if I feared for my life. I did not need it."

Morag shook her head, ever disapproving, and Lady Annis pressed her lips together. Then a twinkle lit the older woman's pale blue eyes, and she said, "I am not surprised that ye carry a weapon, dear one. And it was both wise and kind of James and Ivor to teach ye to use it properly. However, in my experience, guile and her own claws make better weapons for a woman than aught else."

Catriona's mind offered an instant image of her attempt to slap Fin, and she could think of nothing to reply. Despite her grandmother's own words, Lady Annis would instantly condemn such rudeness to a guest—and rightly so.

Tactfully, Ealga said, "Ye'll want to change that dress afore we sup, my love."

"Aye, Mam, but I doubt that our guest will trouble Granddad much longer. I said I would show him to a chamber when they have finished talking."

"Ye go and change," her mother said. "Aodán can put him in that room across the landing from the one I am using at present. Will he stay just the one night?"

"I had to persuade him to stay at all," Catriona said. "But that was before I learned that he was seeking the Mackintosh. When I told him that Granddad was here, he agreed to come. But he gave me no more information."

"Ye may be sure that I will learn all he can tell us about himself," her grandmother said. "I want to know who his parents are and much more, forbye."

Determined to witness that confrontation, Catriona excused herself and hurried upstairs, calling for her maid-servant as she went.

At the Mackintosh's command, Fin took a jug of whisky and two goblets from a niche, poured whisky into each goblet, set one before his host, and left the other where it was. "Shall I put the jug back, my lord?" he asked.

"Nay, we'll have need of it. Just pull up yon stool and tell me what the devil Davy Stewart means by disturbing an old man's peace with his royal affairs."

"He prefers to be known as Rothesay, sir, and he spoke not of your age but only of your power. *That*, he assured me, is vast enough to serve his ends."

"Ye'll no be telling me that he thinks my power exceeds his own."

Knowing it would be tactless if truthful to say that Rothesay believed *no* man's power exceeded his, Fin said, "As heir to the throne and now Governor, he is well aware of his power, sir. He is also aware that he has powerful enemies."

The Mackintosh cocked an eyebrow. "One in particular, I warrant."

"Aye, for when Parliament and the King agreed on Rothesay's coming of age that he should assume the Governorship for three years in the Duke of Albany's stead, to show that Rothesay *can* govern, Albany was most displeased."

"Ye're being diplomatic, lad. I heard that he was infuriated. But I've nae patience with all these new dukes of ours—like the devilish English. Faugh, I say!"

"Scotland still has only two dukes," Fin assured him. "Rothesay and Albany."

"Aye, well, Albany was dangerous enough whilst *he* governed in the King's stead. To my mind, a man who has no interest in ruling shouldna *be* King."

Fin said, "Rothesay will be a much stronger ruler than his father, sir."

"That will not be hard, if Albany lets the lad live that long," Mackintosh said. "And if his reputed recklessness and profligacy are overstated. Sithee, Davy Stewart is Albany's own nephew, but Albany is evil. Auld Clootie put the mark of his hoof on him in the cradle. And the older he gets the plainer it becomes that he'll ever be the devil's own. Even so, he wields nae power here in the Highlands or in the Isles."

"Just so, sir, although he did name his own son Lord of the North."

"Aye, sure, when he was Governor. But he kens fine what will happen if that whelp of his ever tries to seize the Lordship from Alex Stewart," Mackintosh snapped.

"Alex does hold the Lordship close," Fin agreed.

"Aye, he rules from Lochindorb as strongly as ever his own sire did."

"I should tell you that Rothesay also sent word to Lochindorb," Fin said.

"That castle lies but fifteen miles north of here," the

Mackintosh said. "But if Davy...if Rothesay hopes for his message to reach the Lord of the North, he's missed his mark. Alex is in the Borders with my own people, aiding the Earl of Douglas."

"They will soon return," Fin said. "Douglas is still the most powerful lord in the Borders. And, thanks to such aid from many powerful nobles, he has routed the English again. My men carried the message to Lochindorb, so I could go on to you at Moigh. But after we parted, whilst seeking a path into the mountains west of here, I walked farther south along the Spey than I'd intended without finding a ford—"

He broke off when the Mackintosh chuckled.

"Sakes, lad, we take good care to create no tracks through our mountains east or west," he said. "If a man does not ken his way, he'll not find it without help."

"One of my men knew the way to Lochindorb," Fin said. "And I ken the Great Glen fine and can reach it from here just by going west." To avoid further discussion of his error, he added, "Rothesay also sent a message to the Lord of the Isles."

"So he seeks allies amongst his uncle's enemies, does he?"

"He does, aye."

"What does Davy expect from us...from me, especially?"

"He wants you to host a meeting for him at Castle Moigh with the Lord of the Isles and the Lord of the North."

"To what purpose?"

"To keep Albany's ambition in check, he said. Beyond that, I cannot tell you. I do not know his exact intent."

The Mackintosh said thoughtfully, "His provisional term as Governor ends in January. So I'd wager that he wants to be assured of their votes when Parliament meets to consider whether they will extend it or give it back to Albany."

"I would not bet against your wager, sir. But my orders are to deliver his message and send word to him at Perth if you agree to host the meeting."

"I see. Then, before I trust your word on this, I would ken more about ye."

Having hoped that he had diverted the old man from the business of antecedents and fervently hoping that Mackintosh would not detect his uneasiness now, Fin drew a breath and reached for his goblet.

"Help yourself to the whisky and ye need to compose your thoughts," the Mackintosh said amiably. "But, I'd warn ye, lad, do *not* lie to me."

The emphasis in his words forcibly reminded Fin that the Mackintosh held the power of the pit and the gallows. Hanging Davy's messenger might annoy Davy, but Fin doubted that the old man would spare that a single thought.

With her maidservant Ailvie's help, Catriona changed to a more becoming moss-green gown and matching silk slippers. Then, curbing her impatience, she let Ailvie brush her tangled hair and plait it into a smooth coil beneath a white veil.

Returning to the great hall, she noted her mother's approving smile and saw that servants in the lower part of the hall were setting up for the evening meal. Food would not appear for another hour, but her grandfather liked his meals on time, so there must be no delay unless unexpected guests arrived or if, by some stroke of fortune, her father and brothers returned in time to sup with them.

The likelihood of that event was small. When Shaw and his sons entered the Highlands, word would reach Rothiemurchus hours if not days before they did.

"I've not seen that gown afore," Lady Annis said. "It becomes ye well."

"Her gowns all become her," Ealga said. "Morag's become her, too."

"Thank you, madam," Catriona said. "I never look as tidy as Morag does, though," she added, smiling at her good-sister.

"You never take the pains to do so," Morag said.

"'Tis youth that becomes them, Ealga," Lady Annis said. "Catriona," she added, "your injured gentleman has not emerged yet, so he'll get nae rest afore we sup. We must hope that the arrow, in striking his head, did not curdle his brains."

Catriona chuckled. "If it did, I saw no sign of it. Nor, if he were addled, do I imagine that Granddad would tolerate his presence as long as he has."

"Let us adjourn to my sitting room whilst they finish setting up the tables," Lady Ealga suggested. "I told Aodán to show our guest to his room when he does emerge. He will want to refresh himself before facing us again."

"Before facing Grandame, you mean," Catriona said, tossing that lady a grin.

"Aye, laugh," Lady Annis said with a piercing look from under her thin, gray eyebrows. "But know this, impudent one. Ye've taken your temperament from me rather than from your gentle mam, so ye'd do well to take a bit o' my good sense as well. Ye're impetuous as well as impudent, lassie, and ye can be willful withal."

Catriona knew better than to return a saucy reply to that observation, especially since it was true. She said coaxingly instead, "You turned out well, Grandame. And I do have you to show me how to go on."

"Ye do, aye, if ye'll but listen to me. Now, do we go upstairs, or not?"

Still reluctant to risk declaring himself a member of Clan Cameron, which, truce or none, would likely prejudice his host against him, Fin said, "I will gladly tell you about myself, sir. But I must warn you, I am not at my best and might do better to ascertain first if you have questions about hosting Rothesay's meeting."

"I will stay here until Shaw returns," the Mackintosh replied. "If Davy Stewart wants his meeting before then, we'll hold it here. Rothiemurchus was my seat until just a few years ago and is as safe as Moigh would be for such a meeting."

"It does seem safe enough," Fin agreed. "But the lady Catriona did speak of trouble hereabouts...enough to draw you here from the peace and safety of Castle Moigh. Should Rothesay be wary of such trouble?"

Mackintosh snorted. "Wary of the worthless Comyns? Why should he be? That clan clings to its very existence whilst claiming title to land that has been in Mackintosh hands for a century. They are nobbut a nuisance. One of them has even dared to offer for our Catriona. And some, including my grandson James, do say that we might lay the troubles to rest were her father and I to agree to the match."

The notion of the forthright lady Catriona involved in such a marriage seemed preposterous to him, but Fin said only, "Such weddings can sometimes succeed in allying otherwise unfriendly clans."

"Aye, sure," Mackintosh said. "But Rory Comyn is a lackwit too full of himself for his own good or anyone else's and too quick to seek offense where none is meant. Moreover, the proposed alliance would benefit only Clan Comyn, because they want Castle Raitt added to Catriona's tocher, which is a thing I will *not* do."

"So Raitt sits on the land that the Comyns claim."

"It does, but we drift from the main subject, lad, so tell me more about Davy Stewart. I'll admit that Scotland has seemed more peaceful since he took on the Governorship." With a chuckle reminiscent of his granddaughter's, he added dryly, "I doubt that the King's life is more peaceful, though."

"There have been ructions," Fin admitted. Knowing that it would be unwise to add that the ructions had occurred most often with men whose pretty wives had caught Rothesay's eye, he said, "Doubtless that is one reason he seeks allies who will at least give an appearance of supporting him against Albany."

"Aye, well, I want to think a bit more on the matter," Mackintosh said. "Sithee, the lad does be one to reck nowt, and he is headstrong. But drink up now, Fin of the Battles. They'll be serving supper after they ring yon bell for vespers."

"Do you keep a chaplain here, sir, or do you lead a service in the hall?"

"Neither. I leave Kirk matters to parsons, bishops, and the like. But I do want to ken the time of day. They'll be ringing that bell soon, though, and I warrant ye'll want to have a wash afore our ladies see ye again."

"I would, aye," Fin said, feeling a rush of relief at the respite.

"Ye'll not have time to go upstairs, so just use the ewer and basin in yonder corner," Mackintosh added, pointing. "The jib door beside the washstand opens on the service stair. If ye want the garderobe, it lies three steps up on your right."

Realizing that he would be putting off the inevitable if he delayed further, Fin said, "You did say that you wanted to know more about me, sir."

"I did, aye, but I want to think now. Forbye, the women will ask ye all that at supper, and I'm thinking I have nae need to hear ye spit out the details twice."

Having returned to the hall with her grandmother and mother while Morag ran up to get a shawl, Catriona had just begun to think that her grandfather might have ordered supper put back when the inner chamber door opened and he stepped through the doorway. Fin followed him, looking freshly scrubbed but tired.

Immediately feeling guilty again about trying to slap him, Catriona smiled and felt a rush of pleasure when he smiled back. The smile was not the small one she had seen on the hillside earlier but wider and more natural, lighting his eyes and revealing his even white teeth.

The Mackintosh strode to the central chair at the long high table, facing the lower hall, and gestured Fin to the seat at his right. Morag hurried in as the other three women took their places. Lady Annis sat at her husband's left with Ealga next to her, Morag next to Ealga, and Catriona at the end.

For some time, everyone's attention fixed on servers who proffered platters of food and jugs of whisky and claret. But when Lady Annis had accepted all that she wanted, she leaned forward and said across her husband to their guest, "One trusts that ye've found all ye need, sir. Did they show ye to your chamber?"

"Not yet, my lady," he said. "We talked too long."

Catriona had leaned forward when her grandmother did, and his gaze caught hers long enough for her to smile before he shifted it politely back to Lady Annis.

"What did ye talk about?" her ladyship demanded of him.

If the question disconcerted Fin, he did not show it. But the Mackintosh said curtly, "What we discussed concerns others, my lady, and *will* remain between us."

The emphasis on that single word made Catriona look to her mother, hoping that Ealga might understand what he meant. But Ealga watched her own mother.

Lady Annis kept a gimlet gaze on her husband but turned it at last to Fin and said, "Do such concerns include where ye hail from, Fin of the Battles?"

"At present, my lady, I come from the Scottish Borders," he said.

"Ye're not a Borderer by birth, I trow," she said. "Ye lack the sound and manner of such. Ye sound like ye hail from a place nearer to Glen Mòr."

"I have lived in the Borders for years, but I do know the Great Glen," he said. "I spent my childhood in Lochaber near the west shore of Loch Ness. I regret to admit, though," he added glibly, "that I never saw the monster that dwells there."

Ignoring that gambit, if gambit it was, Lady Annis said, "My father was Hugh Fraser of Lovat, on the east shore of Loch Ness. I ken most folks fine from Inverness down both shores to Loch Lochy. Who are your parents?"

"My father was known as Teàrlach MacGill, my mother as Fenella nic Ruari," he said. "I also spent some years in Fife, madam, near its eastern coast."

A movement from her grandfather—almost a start—diverted Catriona's attention as Fin spoke. But she could not read the Mackintosh's expression, because he had fixed his attention on Fin and did not say a word.

Her grandmother said, "Your father's name does sound as if I ought to know it, but MacGill is a general sort of patronymic, is it not? I expect that your business with the Mackintosh pertains more to your having come here from the Borders. Still, I suppose I must not question you about what you did there or..."

She paused, clearly hoping that he would invite her to question him. But Fin just smiled as if he were waiting for her to finish her sentence.

Sighing, she said, "What did your father do in Fife that required him to take your family so far from Lochaber?"

Fin looked startled then, as if he had not expected the question, but Catriona could not imagine why he would not, since he had mentioned Fife himself. Evidently, they were not to pursue the subject, though, because the Mackintosh said, "Bless me, lad, if I did not forget to ask ye how soon ye'd be expecting your men to join ye."

"His men?" Lady Annis shifted her attention to her husband again and then back to Fin. "Ye've men of your own hereabouts, too? Where are they?"

"I can boast of only two, madam, and they should rejoin me tomorrow or the next day. But now that you bring them to mind, sir, it occurs to me that they'll seek me at Castle Moigh unless I can get word to them to come here instead."

The Mackintosh laughed. "By morning, there won't be a man in Strathspey who does not ken that Catriona brought ye here. I'll put out word for our people to watch more keenly than usual for strangers, but I trow that your lads will find ye."

Conversation became desultory after that, although Catriona had hoped that her grandmother would press Fin harder for information about himself and his family, because she had sensed soon after meeting him that he was keeping secrets. Moreover, although his antecedents sounded common, he had traveled more than most Highlanders did and spoke better than most other noblemen.

And his sword was that of a warrior.

However, the Mackintosh bore him away to the inner chamber again when the two had finished eating, saying cryptically that he had made his decision.

The statement stirred her curiosity. What decision, and why not share it with all of them? They would doubtless learn of it in time, but she wanted to know now.

⁓

Following the Mackintosh into his chamber, Fin was glad to see that he did not reach for the whisky jug. His head ached, and he was sure that it ached as much from the whisky he'd had before supper as from the gash suffered earlier. The ache had a familiar dullness about it and a depth that reminded him of mornings in his youth that had come too early, after he had imbibed too freely of the potent stuff.

He would have liked a mug of spring water. But he decided that, rather than troubling his host, he would ask a gillie to fetch some for him when he retired.

Mackintosh returned to his chair but gestured Fin to remain standing. "Ye look as if ye'd do better to take to your bed, lad, so I'll not keep ye," he said. "I do agree to host Rothesay's meeting here with the lords of the Isles and the North."

"Thank you, my lord."

"Aye, well, I ken them both. Donald of the Isles and Alex of Lochindorb are both men of their word, so I'll grant them safe conduct to come here. But I'll want their word, *and* Davy Stewart's, that they'll come here without great tails of men."

"Rothesay told them the same, sir, because he does not want them to draw notice, as they would with their normal entourages. But Donald will need your safe conduct, since he is not welcome in the western Highlands, where he covets much land. When my lads arrive, I'll send one to Perth to tell Rothesay you have agreed."

"Aye, good. Now, just shout up yon service stair for my man, Conal, and ask him to show ye to your chamber. He'll ken where they've put ye, and that way ye'll not have to talk more with the women but can get right to sleep."

Fin, feeling his weariness again, was more than willing to obey.

Stirling Castle

Robert Stewart, erstwhile Earl of Fife and now Duke of Albany, looked up from the document he had been reading when, with a single sharp rap, a gillie opened the door to his sanctum and stepped back to admit a visitor.

Still lanky and fit in his sixty-first year, his dark hair streaked white in places, but otherwise showing few signs of age, the duke continued as always to favor all-black clothing and obedient minions. In his usual curt way, when the gillie had shut the door again, Albany said, "What news have you, Redmyre?"

"We ken little of note yet," Sir Martin Lindsay of Redmyre said. "He is still in Perth, but I have found someone from the area in question to aid us."

"You may speak freely here," Albany said, pouring him a goblet of claret.

The two men had known and trusted each other for years, because although the stocky Redmyre was younger by more than a decade, they shared like views on Albany's right to power. They also shared a loathing for the heir to Scotland's throne.

Redmyre accepted the wine, saying, "Right, then. I've found a man to watch Rothesay if he heads into the Highlands. And my chap, Comyn, has kinsmen who will aid us if it means stirring trouble for the Lord of the North. I ken fine that you have men listening everywhere, but are you sure Rothesay will make for Strathspey?"

"I am, because Davy drinks too much and then talks too much."

"Aye, and wenches too much, by God," Redmyre growled.

"Just so, but your sister is safe now, and her husband won't dare to abandon her. I do not know that Davy will go to Lochindorb, but he does want help from Alex. In any event, Davy is unfit to rule this realm as Governor, and must be unseated."

"Aye, then, we're in agreement. I'll report to you when I learn more."

Albany knew that he would, and that Redmyre would exert every effort to bring Rothesay to book. There were others like Redmyre, too, who would help.

⁓

When Catriona, her mother, and Morag went upstairs to their bedchambers, they went together as far as the landing outside Lady Ealga's room. Noting that the smaller room across from it showed no candlelight under the door, Catriona hoped that her grandfather had sent Fin to bed. He had looked woefully tired.

When she and Morag had bade Ealga goodnight and continued up the stairs, Morag muttered, "I hope your mam will be safe with that man sleeping there."

"God-a-mercy, why should she not be?" Catriona said. "He is injured and exhausted, so I warrant he wants only to sleep."

"Doubtless, James would agree with *me*," Morag said stubbornly.

"Then I wish James were here, because if he *was*, mayhap you would cease to be so glum all the time," Catriona replied, and was instantly sorry.

Her good-sister was not a close friend, but Catriona knew that Morag was unhappy at Rothiemurchus. Indeed, her unhappiness had long since persuaded Catriona that *she* never wanted to marry and have to live among strangers.

"I apologize, Morag," she said sincerely. "I should not have said that."

"Nay, you should not," Morag said, passing her to go to her own room.

Letting her go, Catriona went to bed and lay contemplating the man she had met that day, wondering how it was that, having known him such a short time, she could feel as if she knew him well one moment and not at all the next, and how he had so easily stirred a temper that she thought she had learned to keep well banked.

She slept at last, and when she awoke, the sky outside her unshuttered window was gray. From her bed, it was hard to tell the hour, but it seemed earlier than usual, so she got up, wrapped her quilt around her to keep the chill off, and went to the window.

Her view extended over the wooded north end of the island to the loch, and she could see over the wall to the northeastern shoreline beyond it to her right.

A figure walked there, a well-shaped masculine figure, completely naked. Feeling chillier just watching him, she drew the quilt closer. He turned then and raised his face toward the gray eastern sky. She had suspected who it was the moment she saw him, but there could be no mistaking him now.

As she watched, he looked from the gray sky back to the equally gray water before him, took a few running steps, and dove in.

Flinging the quilt aside, Catriona snatched her old blue kirtle from the hook where Ailvie had hung it, threw it on over her head, pulled the front lacing tight, and tied it swiftly. Without a thought for her hair, let alone for washing her face or hands, she flew barefoot down the stairs and past the great hall to the main entry.

There she paused. Drawing a deep breath, she pulled open the door and went with more dignity down the timber stairs and across the yard to the gateway.

Chapter 4 _____

The water was so cold from its snowmelt tributaries that it took Fin's breath away. He felt an intense urge to shoot straight back up and out, as if he could then run back across the water to where he'd left his tunic and braies on the rocky shore. So great was the icy shock of diving in that it almost made such a feat seem possible.

When he did surface, gasping, he began to swim hard and fast.

Reflecting the gray dawn light as the loch had, with the spectacular, knife-edged, still snow-covered granite ridges and peaks of the Cairngorms providing a backdrop to the east, the water had looked so silvery and serene that he had felt guilty even to think of disturbing its calm. But he wanted to feel clean again and to see if the water would reopen his wound.

Soon he felt the agreeable awareness of exploring virgin water, and his sense of humor stirred. He was putting his mark on the loch, conquering new territory.

If his wound had opened, the cold water numbed any indication of it.

The lass had said no more about stitching the gash, but when they'd reached Rothiemurchus, her family had given her precious little chance to say anything to him. In truth, though, he did not think it necessary for anyone to sew him up.

The very thought of her sticking a needle into his aching forehead...

Briefly, he shut his eyes.

Focusing again, and warmer, he took powerful strokes toward the eastern shore, less than a quarter-mile away. Despite the water's hitherto calm appearance, he felt a current trying to tug him toward the north end of the loch. It did not pull hard enough to worry him, only to make him work harder. He would explore later and see where the water spilled out of the loch. It might provide a good waterfall.

He was partial to falls, especially when they were as full as any in that area should be at that time of year, when the snows were still melting.

He had warmed up enough to breathe normally and know that he was not going to freeze. So, when he neared the eastern shore, he turned back toward the castle without pausing. Continuing his fast, powerful strokes, he took pleasure in the exercise until he realized that he was nearing the island shore again. He knew that if he were careless, he might hit a rock with a foot or his fingertips.

Looking ahead to judge how much nearer he could safely swim before feeling for the bottom, he saw Catriona walking with her wolf dog on the shore. She was looking down, watching the ground in front of her.

She had walked confidently with her head up the previous day, despite rougher terrain, so he wondered if she was upset about something. Or, perhaps she had seen him, noted his nudity, and was shy of letting him know that she had.

He had a sudden desire to test that possibility.

She wore the same old blue kirtle that she had worn kilted up the day before. So, either she enjoyed early-morning rambles, as he did, or she had come outside in haste because she had seen him swimming or walking naked on the shore.

The dog glanced his way but stayed at her side.

Her confidence in rowing the overladen boat had assured him that she could swim, because he, too, had spent his childhood on an island in a loch. He and his siblings had learned to swim like fish almost before they could walk. He supposed that she had enjoyed similar training for safety's sake if for no other reason.

In any event, she had shown no fear of the water.

"Good morning," he called as he drew nearer.

By then he was certain that she either concentrated harder on her thoughts than any woman he had ever known or purposefully avoided looking his way.

She turned when he called and walked to the water's edge with the dog at her heels. Returning his greeting, she added, "You are up early, Fin of the Battles. At this season, only osprey and fish swim so early. Is that why they call you Fin, because you swim so well?"

"Nay, they call me so because my name is Finlagh," he said. Then, because she still watched him, he added, "I'm coming out, lass. If you are going to look, then look. But if you want to protect your modesty, you had best turn away. My clothes lie yonder by that boulder some yards to your right."

"Shall I fetch them for you?" she asked demurely.

He chuckled, swallowed water, and kicked hard for the shore. Moments later, he touched a granite slope that provided traction enough for him to stand waist deep without incident. He did not want to slip awkwardly back in while she watched.

Shaking water from his head and slicking his hair back with both hands, he walked out of the water, wondering how long she *would* watch.

In most Highland households, women assisted male guests with their bathing if the men had not brought servants with them. But women who did were usually married servants, not noble granddaughters of confederation captains. He noted with a grin that Catriona looked hastily away before he fully exposed himself.

Still, she had two brothers as well as a father and grandfather, so he suspected that the male anatomy was no secret to her. Her modest demeanor amused him.

Boreas had moved to the water to lap.

"What are *you* doing out so early, lass?" Fin asked her as he pulled his tunic on over his head. Reaching to his knees, it covered him enough for modesty's sake as he reached for and pulled on his braies. "Methinks your family would not approve."

"Aye, they would, though," she said without turning. "I came out to apologize for...for trying to slap you yesterday."

"Forgive me if I doubt that they even know about that," he said. "Don't fret about it, but don't try it again, either. Such behavior is always unwise."

His rawhide boots lay nearby, because he had worn them downstairs and across the rocky yard to the shore. But he decided to leave them off. After wearing boots and shoes for so long in the lowlands, his feet needed toughening. Moreover, the boots were still damp from the day before. Leaving them where they lay, he ignored the pricking of numerous small stones as he walked toward her barefoot.

When she turned at last, her eyes widened. Their pupils expanded so much that her irises looked black rather than golden-hazel.

"God-a-mercy!" she exclaimed. "You are not even... uh...shivering!"

～

Catriona had not noticed his clothes before he had mentioned them, but she had expected him to have brought his plaid, at least, for warmth. Instead he wore only a thin saffron-colored tunic and thinner linen braies. So he had covered himself from shoulders to knees. But with his body still so wet, the garments hid nothing.

Knowing he could not help but notice where she was staring, and not wanting to reveal how impressed she was with his muscular, well-hewn body, she had hastily commented instead on his lack of reaction to the shockingly cold water.

His eyes twinkled when he said, "In troth, I feared that I had plunged into a half-melted block of ice. But, with exercise, the water soon grew bearable. I felt a current though. How far is it from here to the burn that runs out of this loch?"

She shrugged. "A half-hour's walk along the west shore. Or one can row there *with* the current in the coble. It would take much longer to return against it."

"Does the outflow produce a waterfall?"

"Nay, just a tumbling burn that joins the Spey north of here. You must have forded it to get to where I found you, unless you entered the woods from the south."

"We did come into the Highlands through Glen Garry, but I turned back when my lads and I parted miles north of there," he said. "I did not realize that I would not find another ford on this side. I do recall fording numerous burns and rivulets, but only the Spey seemed tumultuous enough to produce any good falls."

"I know of a fine one on the way to Castle Moigh," she said. "If you should go on to Lochaber from here and take the right path, you will see it for yourself."

"I still want to see the burn spilling out of Loch an Eilein," he said. "I like to explore the landscape wherever I am. Will you show me the way after we eat?"

Cocking her head, she said, "You do not need a guide to find that burn. If you just follow the loch shore northward, it will take you there."

"But your grandfather is more likely to let *you* take the wee coble. I don't want to have to swim ashore and back again."

"The distance from the island to the west shore is less than half the distance you swam just now," she pointed out, meeting his gaze and instantly feeling the same prickling sense of warmth flowing inward that she had felt the day before.

"I'll need dry clothes when I get to shore," he said without looking away.

"Then ask a gillie to row you across and collect you when you return."

"I don't want a gillie. I'd rather go with a fine-looking lass and her dog."

Aware that she was blushing but determined to win, she said, "My grandfather would be even less likely to let you take *me* with you than his boat."

"The Mackintosh kens fine that he can trust me with you, for he said nowt about our being together so long yesterday. He might not be so sure about the boat. Sithee, he kens its size and mine. He'd fear that I'd sink it if I treated it carelessly."

"He would likewise think a dousing no more than you'd deserve for your carelessness," she retorted. "It would be, too."

"Would it?" he asked, stepping closer, and holding her gaze as he did.

Swallowing, feeling new heat surge through her body, Catriona fought to ignore the sensation. When he put a hand on her shoulder, she managed to collect her wits enough to say, "You go to him just as you are, sir. Ask *him* what he thinks of your plan. Even if you change first and dry yourself, you'd best hope that no one who sees us out here tells him how you look now."

He looked down at himself and chuckled. "You're right about that, lass. I warrant he'd have a few things to say to me. Still, if he grants us permission, will you walk with me to that outlet?"

"Aye, sure, *if* he gives permission." As she said the words, she wondered at his confidence. Perhaps he had not taken her grandfather's full measure yet. But if he thought he could act so audaciously with the Mackintosh's granddaughter, he would soon learn his error whether the Mackintosh took exception to it or not.

The lady Catriona's blushes became her, Fin thought. She was enticingly unlike the women he'd met in Rothesay's company. Most of them were more skilled at the art of dalliance than Fin had been when he had entered Rothesay's service.

Before that day, Fin had believed himself *well* experienced. He was three-and-twenty by then and had not lived as a monk. But few would debate the Mackintosh's opinion that the young Governor of the Realm was a profligate and reckless, withal.

Rothesay was the same age now as Fin had been then, but wherever Rothesay went, he assumed that any female he met would welcome his attentions—that noble or not, married or not, she would welcome him in her bed or elsewhere. So far, he had been right most of the time, even when the lady's husband chanced to be at home. Such was royal privilege, as Davy Stewart himself frequently declared.

Although many knights who served him were years older than he was, they quickly learned that he did not welcome friendly teasing, let alone warnings away from his prey. But most people liked him despite his behavior. He had inherited all the Stewart charm that his uncle Albany lacked, and more.

That females submitted to Rothesay's slightest smile had often made Fin wonder at such females. However, he had never professed to understand women. His sisters had been mysteries to him, and by the time he might have been old enough to figure them out, he had left home for schooling at St. Andrews.

Catriona kept silent while he collected his boots, and remained so when the two of them turned toward the castle gateway.

"What are you thinking, lass?" he asked.

"I was wondering what my grandfather might say to you," she said.

"He will give me permission to walk with you round the loch," Fin said.

"You are exceedingly confident," she said tartly.

"Will he have broken his fast yet?"

She glanced up at him. "Do you think I ken his every move?"

"I think that a man who has bells rung to tell people when to eat will likely be most regular in his habits. He did not strike me as a slug-a-bed."

Her eyes twinkled, and she looked away as she said, "Nay, he is not."

"Then I will don proper clothing and approach him at his breakfast table."

They parted at his door, and she went to her room, telling herself that Fin of the Battles was about to lose one and wondering why she felt less than certain of that.

Ailvie awaited her with a fresh kirtle of yellow camlet in hand. "Where ha' ye been so early, m'lady?"

"Outside, walking on the shore," Catriona said as she cast off her blue kirtle and accepted the yellow one. "Just brush my hair, Ailvie, and confine it in a net," she added. "I've not yet broken my fast."

When the maidservant had finished, Catriona hurried back downstairs. Her mother and grandmother were at the high table, as was her grandfather.

Fin entered shortly afterward and paused to speak briefly with one of the gillies before taking his own place.

Noting the speculative look that her grandfather shot him, Catriona suspected that the Mackintosh knew that they had met on the shore.

She settled herself to await events.

As Fin approached the dais, he also eyed the Mackintosh, trying to gauge the older man's mood without blatantly staring at him.

"Good morrow, my lord," he said when he reached the dais. "I hope I have not overstepped my role as a guest. I asked yon gillie to fetch me a mug of Adam's ale instead of the ale and whisky that he said the jugs on this table contain. In my experience, such beverages do naught to aid an aching head. And although mine is fast mending, it does keep reminding me that healing takes time."

"Sakes, lad, in *my* experience, good whisky will heal aught that ails a man. As for water, for all that they may call it Adam's ale, it did nowt to keep Adam in his garden, now, did it?"

Smiling at the old sally, Fin said, "As you say, sir. I trust you slept well."

"Longer than ye did, I'm told," Mackintosh retorted.

"Then you have heard about my swim," Fin replied as he sat and his host signed to the gillies to serve him. "Your loch is wondrous refreshing."

"As was your conversation with our Catriona, I trow."

"That was also pleasant," Fin agreed. "She was kind enough to tell me something about the loch, and she agreed to show me more of it. Just nearby and with the dog to guard her, as I am sure you would demand. She did say that we required your permission, sir, but I'd have asked you myself, come to that."

Mackintosh looked at Catriona. "Be ye willing to take him about, lass?"

Fin could tell that she had not expected the question,

because her eyes widened. She kept them fixed on her grandfather and did not even glance at Fin.

"I'd be fain to show him, sir, if you do approve such a plan. He wants to see the burn that runs out of the loch. We would take the coble across to the landing."

"D'ye trust yourself not to overturn it with the man and the dog?" he asked. When she nodded, he said, "I did hear that ye'd brought the two of them over in that wee thing. I'll own I was surprised ye did not sink it. Ye might take one of the bigger boats an ye let a pair of our gillies row it."

"I don't mind the rowing, and all three of us can swim," she said, confirming Fin's earlier deduction.

Mackintosh turned to him. "Can ye no manage a pair of oars yourself, then?"

Fin smiled. "She would not let me."

She said, "With Boreas in the stern, as he must be, Fin is too heavy to—"

"Ye should properly call the man Sir Finlagh, I'd wager," Mackintosh interjected, turning back to Fin. "Ye *have* won your knighthood, aye? As puffed up as your master is in his own esteem, I doubt he'd trust any lesser man with his messages."

"Who is this puffed-up master of his?" Lady Annis asked her husband.

"I'll tell ye that later an I tell ye at all. Now whisst, and let the man talk."

"I do have the honor to hold a knighthood," Fin admitted.

"And, nae doots, ye won that honor on the battlefield," Mackintosh said. "Thus earning the name by which others do call ye."

"That's right, sir," Fin said, wondering if the old man would demand a list of the battles he had fought. He devoutly hoped that he would not.

Before the Mackintosh replied, Lady Ealga said, "If you two mean to walk the shore of the loch, you should tell someone to fetch some apples and other food to sustain you until our midday meal. One always gets hungry, rambling about."

"I havena said that I approve this outing," the Mackintosh reminded them all.

To Fin's surprise, Catriona said, "You do know that you can trust Boreas to protect me, sir. If Sir Finlagh should prove dangerous, that is."

Mackintosh chuckled. "Faith, ye do well enough protecting yourself. Ye may go, aye. Just bear in mind, lad, that I see more and ken more than ye think I do."

"I had deduced as much, aye, sir," Fin said with increasing suspicion that the old man *did* know exactly who he was.

Mackintosh said, "I've put out the word to send your lads here when they show themselves. Nae doots, they'll arrive by suppertime if not afore then."

Fin thanked him and returned his attention to his food.

While he finished his meal, he tried to recall all that he had heard about the Captain of Clan Chattan. Men had called him canny and shrewd. Others spoke highly of his integrity. All said that his word was his bond and that no one had known him to break it. But the same was true of most Highland lairds.

A Highlander who broke his word lost the trust of neighbors, friends, and family, let alone that of any enemy clan with whom he might have to parley.

No one had suggested, either, that the Mackintosh played the verbal games that some men played when they did give their word, such as arranging their words with care so they could draw on that phrasing later to prove that what *seemed* to be breaking a promise was not. Such men were likely to earn more scorn than respect.

Fin decided that Mackintosh would be fair with him when he learned that he was a Cameron. If he was fair, he would not erupt in fury or order Fin hanged or thrown into a pit (doubtless water-filled if it lay in a dungeon at Rothiemurchus).

Recalling his safe conduct from Rothesay, Fin sighed. He would do better to depend on the old man's reputation, considering what Mackintosh thought of Davy.

"Do you want to go at once, Sir Finlagh?"

Lost in thought, aware of little beyond a hum of low conversation, Fin started at the sound of Catriona's voice. He had not realized that she had risen from her stool and walked behind the others to speak to him.

He said, "I must fetch my sword. Have you aught to do before we go?"

"Just to fetch some apples and Boreas. He'll be in the kitchen, because our cook is his most favored friend. But I've only to shout down the stairs for him."

"That thin dress won't keep the chill off," he pointed out. He noted that the cheerful yellow kirtle fit her body sleekly and looked soft to the touch. It delineated her delightful curves even better than her moss-green gown had the evening before.

"'Tis camlet, sir, fine wool," she said. "I'll send for a shawl though. It may grow windy." As she spoke, she gestured to someone in the lower hall.

Collecting his sword and sword belt from his room, Fin went down to the entryway but found the young gillie Tadhg waiting there instead of Catriona.

"I thought ye might need me tae help look after the dog, sir," Tadhg said. "See you, I mean tae be a knight one day m'self. I can swim, and I'm a fine runner, and I mean tae be a great swordsman, too. Ye could teach me much, I wager."

Fin smiled at him. "You need to grow a foot or two first, lad."

"Aye, sure, I will. And Sir Ivor says I ha' tae learn tae use me head, too."

Recalling that Ivor was Catriona's brother, Fin said, "He is right about that, laddie. You cannot come with us today, but we'll talk more of this anon."

Grinning, Tadhg dashed off, and Catriona soon joined Fin. Launching the boat as they had the day before, they laughed together at the audible sigh that Boreas gave as he curled himself in the stern and laid his head on his forepaws.

Once ashore, Fin slung on his sword belt so that the weapon lay across his back in its sling. Then he and Catriona strode northward along the track.

He smiled when she raised her face to the cloudy sky and drew a long breath. Despite her smaller size, he barely had to shorten his stride to accommodate her. Moreover, much of the track was wide enough for them to walk abreast.

"Do you know the Cairngorms?" she asked ten minutes later.

"We caught glimpses of them on our way here," he said. "I cannot say that I know them, but they do look as forbidding as men say they are."

"They can be gey dangerous, aye," she said. She was silent again for a time. Then, she said, "I want to ask you something else."

"Ask me anything," he said rashly. "If I can answer you, I will."

"You mentioned Lochaber yesterday and told my grandmother that you spent your childhood there. The first seat of the Mackintosh lies in Lochaber, albeit at a distance from Loch Ness. Do you know of Tor Castle?"

"Aye, sure," he said, hoping that his tone concealed his reluctance to discuss that topic at any length yet. "I'd wager that anyone from Lochaber has heard of Tor Castle, although it lies high in the mountains, in Glen Arkaig."

"My grandfather wants to be buried there. He goes there every Christmas."

Fin nearly admitted that he knew that, too. But he managed to hold his tongue. After a period of silence, he told her about meeting Tadhg and what the boy had said.

She chuckled. "Aye, Ivor says he'll make a fine knight. But if he doesn't, Tadhg has declared that being a running gillie would be almost as good."

Fin laughed. "I doubt he'd find carrying messages as much fun as a tiltyard."

She smiled again, and the sun had come out. It was a fine day.

Boreas trotted ahead of them. Carrying his snout high, the dog ranged back and forth from one side of the trail to the other, taking scents from the air.

They approached a narrowing of the track where dense shrubbery closed in on both sides. On the landward side, the shrubs covered much of the steep hillside until woodland took over. Fin slowed to let Catriona go ahead of him.

As she did, Boreas stopped and turned to look uphill, sniffing, ears aprick.

Catriona halted. Fin, perforce, did likewise.

The dog's growl started low and deep in its throat. But it was loud enough for Fin to hear. Putting a hand on each of Catriona's shoulders and feeling her start at his touch, he murmured, "Let me by, lass."

So intently had Catriona concentrated on Boreas that she had not sensed how close Fin had come. When his warm hands grasped her shoulders, although she started, she felt an immediate sense of safety.

"Prithee, sir, stay as near the downhill shrubbery as you can when you pass me," she said quietly. "I need to watch Boreas, so I can command him if need be."

She was pleased when he did not question her or ignore her request as many men would have. He just shifted his left hand to her right shoulder and eased past her, pressing into what, on him, was waist-high shrubbery.

His body brushed against hers, so near that he pressed the sheathed dirk she wore under her skirt into her hip and thigh. Only after he had moved ahead did she see that he had drawn his own dirk. His sword remained in its sling.

Boreas blocked the path, his head still high.

Snapping her fingers twice, Catriona watched the dog shift body and head until both aligned with the direction of the disturbing scent.

When Fin glanced back at her, lifting an eyebrow, she murmured, "Whatever he senses is directly ahead of him."

"Man or beast?"

"I cannot say for sure, but human, I think. Were it a wolf or a deer, he would show excitement rather than wariness. He looks much as he did yestermorn, with you, although he showed more intensity then because of the blood. Likely one man, or more, lurks ahead. Were they in the open, fishing or the like, Boreas would not be so wary. His behavior indicates that he is curious but also protective."

"So he does not trust me to protect you. Is that it?"

"He is not thinking about *you*, only of what lies ahead of him, and of me."

"Then we'd best find out what it is," Fin said.

As she watched him stride toward the dog, Catriona reached through the right-hand fitchet in her kirtle to grip the handle of her dirk. Their apples, in a small cloth sack with its long end wrapped around her linked girdle, were out of her way.

Boreas had not moved. But as Fin neared him, Catriona put two fingers to her mouth and gave a low whistle. At the signal, the dog began loping up the hill, ranging back and forth and barking deeply.

If archers lay in wait there, they might shoot. But the weaving dog made a poor target for any man concealed in woodland or shrubbery.

Fin made a better one.

She was about to shout that he should beware when a man stepped out of the shrubbery. Pulling off his cap to reveal thick, curly red hair, he shouted, "Call off yon blasted dog, lass! 'Tis only me!"

Chapter 5

Fin glanced back at Catriona, who looked annoyed.

When she eased her hand free of the slit in the yellow kirtle, he wondered if she carried a weapon. He had not considered that possibility, but it would help explain her confidence the previous day when she'd had only Boreas for company.

She did not speak as they watched the redheaded man bound down the hill toward them, leaping over bushes as he made his way to the track.

"Who is that?" Fin asked.

"Rory Comyn," she replied, her eyes never leaving the other man. "Boreas," she said then so quietly that Fin barely heard her, "to me."

The dog loped back. Just before it reached her, she made a sweeping gesture with her right hand. Stopping, the dog turned, fixing its gaze on Rory Comyn.

"Stop there," Fin said when the man reached the track ten feet ahead of him.

Comyn snatched his sword from the sling on his back and held it at the ready, snapping, "Who *are* ye, and where d'ye think ye be taking her ladyship?"

Fin watched every move but did not reach for his own

sword and held his dirk low. A fold of his plaid hid it from the other man.

Comyn was some inches shorter than Fin was, although he was as broad across the shoulders and thicker at the waist. He wore a green and blue plaid, kilted at his waist with a wide leather belt, and rawhide boots to his knees. He held his sword steady. His dirk remained sheathed at his waist.

In reply to his question, Fin said quietly, "They call me 'Fin of the Battles.'"

Comyn's eyebrows shot upward, suggesting that he recognized the name. But he said with a cocky grin, "Do they now? Do they also give ye leave to take liberties with other men's women?"

"I am *no* man's woman," Catriona snapped from behind Fin.

"Aye, well, ye *will* be mine, lass, just as soon as we get matters sorted."

"Nay, I will not."

"Just ye wait until James and your father return, lassie. Then we'll see."

Having noted that Comyn had addressed them both as if they were inferiors, Fin said, "You would be wise to address her ladyship more courteously, sirrah."

"I'll address her as I please," Comyn said, spreading his feet and extending his sword toward Fin. "Or d'ye think ye can *make* me speak doucely?"

"I think you had better not try me," Fin said.

"Sakes, I've heard of ye, but now that I see ye, I'm thinking someone has already tried to teach ye your manners. It doesna look as if ye bested *him*."

The smirk on his face spoke volumes. Fin hoped that if

Catriona deduced the same thing from it that he did—that Comyn had shot the arrow himself or had ordered someone else to shoot it—she would keep silent.

It was always wiser, he believed, to let an enemy think that you knew less than he did until the time came to reveal his error. He suspected nonetheless that Comyn was the sort who always pretended to know more than he did.

Catriona remained quiet, and Fin held his tongue, too, to see what Comyn would say or do next. For a time, tense silence prevailed.

Comyn took two steps forward.

Then, from behind Fin, came a disturbance of pebbles and a low growl.

Catriona said, "How many men did you bring with you, Rory Comyn? Are they such cowards that they dare not show themselves, or did you order it so?"

So the dog had sensed more men above, had it? Fin wondered if the men on the wall at Rothiemurchus could see them or would be much help if they could.

Comyn said, "Ye ken fine that your own brother James said that it be time and more for ye to wed, lass. I dinna ken if your da agrees with him yet that I should be your man, but James wields strong influence with Shaw MacGillivray."

"Do you think so?" Catriona said. Her flat tone gave no indication even to Fin if her brother's possible influence over her father disturbed her.

With a crack of laughter, Comyn took another step forward, saying, "Ye're a one, lass. But ye'd do better to speak wi' more warmth when ye talk to me."

Fin said, "Call out your men, Comyn, or depart with them. You choose."

Comyn grinned. "Or what? D'ye think ye can take on all of us, man? Sakes, ye've not even drawn your sword."

"You should be glad of that," Fin replied. "Whether I can take you all depends on how many you have with you. I do know that I can kill *you* before any other man reaches us. Nay, don't move," he added, hefting his dirk.

"*That* against me sword? Ye're daft!" He took two more steps toward Fin.

"If you look toward the island, Rory Comyn," Catriona said in a tone as calm as Fin's had been, "you will see two boats setting out from Rothiemurchus. You do yourself no good by threatening a guest of our household."

A piercing two-note whistle sounded then from above them on the hillside.

As it did, Comyn leaped forward, clearly intending to cut Fin down.

Fin's sword was out in a trice. Deftly parrying the blow, he sent the other man's weapon spinning up high and far out into the loch.

Staring in shock at the flying sword and then at Fin, Comyn reached for his dirk.

"Nay, lad, don't be a fool," Fin said, smiling. Without taking his eyes off him, he added, "Your blethering is over for today. Look yonder on the hill."

Comyn frowned and glanced over his shoulder at the hillside, where two men were coming out of the woods at nearly the same spot that he had. However, each had his hands clasped atop his head, and two other men followed, dirks in hand.

The younger and taller of the two armed men shouted in broad Scot, "We found these lads lurking yonder, sir, watching you!"

"Who the devil are *they*?" Comyn demanded.

"My men," Fin said. "But I tell you without boasting, sirrah, that if *that* is your army, dispatching the three of you would have been but mild exercise for me."

Comyn grimaced and looked again at the loch, where ripples still flowed from the spot where his sword had splashed into the water.

"'Tis true, that," Fin's wiry equerry, Toby Muir, said gruffly in Gaelic. "These two be worth nowt, sir. They didna take their eyes off ye, even to look behind them, till our Ian here asked them, gentle like, if they'd like to meet wi' their Maker today."

"You searched them, of course," Fin said.

"Aye, sure," Toby replied. "*And* took away such weapons as they had."

"Ye've nae right to take our weapons or to threaten us!" Comyn snapped.

"Take your grievance to the Mackintosh," Fin said. "It means nowt to me."

"I'll talk anon wi' Shaw MacGillivray. Then ye'll see."

Provocatively, Catriona said, "Come back with us, Rory Comyn. The Mackintosh is at the castle, so you may make your complaint to *him* now."

"I ken fine that he's there. But I've nae wish to fratch with him. I'll bide my time till your da returns. Tell your friend here to give my men back their weapons and we'll go. Ye'll owe me for mine," he added with a challenging look at Fin.

"You should be grateful that I was willing to spare her ladyship the sight of your blood," Fin said. "You all lost your weapons through your own folly. So let it be a lesson to you. But get hence now, the three of you."

"Aye, go, Rory Comyn," Catriona said. "If my father wants you, he'll send for you. He'll not be pleased to hear that you attacked a guest of his at Rothiemurchus."

"We'll see about that," he said. But after another glance at Fin, he gestured to his men to follow and strode angrily back up the hillside from whence he had come.

Returning his sword to its sling, Fin clapped each of his men on a shoulder as he said, "You timed your arrival well, lads. Lady Catriona, pray allow me to present to you my squire, Ian Lennox, and my equerry, Toby Muir. Ian speaks little Gaelic."

"I can get by if you speak slowly," Ian said as he made his bow.

Catriona greeted both men with her customary grace, but Toby was watching Boreas narrowly. "Wi' respect, m'lady, be that great beast friendly?"

"Aye, he is," she replied, smiling. "Boreas, give the man a paw."

The dog sat, tail thumping, and raised a forepaw to the grinning Toby.

Fin looked toward the loch. "Do we wait for your boats?"

"Nay, I'll wave them off unless you want to go back," she said.

"I want to see that burn," he said. "My lads could follow us, but we won't all fit in your coble when we return. Still, I expect they can swim to the island."

"Nay, then, master, unless ye've acquired a taste for wet clothes," Toby retorted. "We left our sumpter pony laden wi' your gear in yon woods above."

Laughing as she raised a hand, Catriona said, "They will want food and rest in any event. Our men can take them across now with your gear, sir."

"That suits me," Fin said. Looking thoughtfully from Ian to Toby, he added, "Toby, after you rest I'll want you to return to Perth. The Mackintosh has agreed to the request but bides here at Rothiemurchus and will for some weeks yet, I trow."

Doubtless noting Catriona's curiosity, Toby glanced at her and back at his master before giving a nod. He asked no questions, but Fin had expected none.

⟳

"What was that about?" Catriona demanded when she and Fin were out of earshot. They had not waited for the others to deal with the pony and the baggage.

Fin said evenly, "Now, lass, if I could tell you that, do you not think that I'd have spoken more plainly to Toby?"

Catriona was accustomed to men who kept secrets, but custom made them no more acceptable. Grimacing, she said, "I'll find out, you know."

"You will, aye, but not until you must. And before you assure me that I can trust you to keep silent, I will tell you that I do believe I could. But I dare not risk even a slight possibility that you might be a prattler. Moreover, you are sensible enough to admit that if I did risk it, *you* might think me one who trusts too easily."

She had been poised to tell him curtly that she was not a prattler, but his last statement silenced her. She *might* say or think such a thing of him in such a case.

Had he just manipulated her feelings to make his silence seem right?

"Do you mean for us to stroll all the way?" she asked. "Or may we go faster?"

He gestured for her to lead the way. When she obeyed,

sending Boreas to range ahead of her, Fin said, "I hope you do mean to refuse that churl Comyn."

"I do. In troth, though, I don't mean to marry any man yet, if ever."

"Why not? Most lasses want to marry as soon as they can, do they not?"

"Perhaps, but even if I were willing to leave here, I've known too many young men who have died—three cousins and an uncle in just the last two years. And four and a half years ago, the wretched Camerons killed eighteen of Clan Chattan's finest in one battle alone, at Perth. Mayhap you heard something about that, sir."

"I did, aye," he said quietly. "A terrible affair."

"Aye, well, no worse than others. But I love my family. And I *don't* want to live as a stranger in another one, being as miserable as my good-sister is. In troth, though, if I find a man lacking all eagerness for battle, I might well marry *him*."

"You would?"

She smiled wryly, knowing that he could not see her face. "When I am lying in bed at night, imagining a perfect life, I do like to think that I would."

"But?"

"In troth, I admire bravery and would likely think that such a man was a coward," she said. "Sithee, the plain fact is that I like making up my own mind and acting on my own thoughts. And I hope to go on doing so for a long while yet before I must subordinate my wishes to a husband's commands."

"But your family cannot mean for you to marry *Comyn*."

She wished she could reply to the statement as fiercely as he had declared it. Sighing, she said, "I won't do it, but

Rory Comyn was right about one thing. My brother James has said that it is *more* than time that I married. Before he and the others left for the Borders, he threatened to arrange a marriage for me himself."

"But surely your father—"

"He *is* the one who matters, aye. And he *can* be more indulgent, but..."

"How stands your other brother?"

Smiling again as the younger of her two brothers leaped to mind, she said, "Sithee, Ivor calls me Wildcat, so he just laughs at James and says that until they find someone who can tame my wild ways, any such effort must end in disaster."

"So, you are wild then and not just possessed of an independent mind?"

Nibbling her lower lip, watching her step, and wondering why she was telling him so much about herself, she said, "Some do call me wild, aye."

"I have seen how fond you are of roaming the woods alone, even when you must know that such woods harbor villains," he said.

His tone of voice sent a shiver up her spine and reminded her of how swiftly he had disarmed Rory Comyn—almost as swiftly as Ivor might have. The edge in his voice reminded her of Ivor, too. Hoping to turn the subject from herself, she said, "So you suspect, as I do, that Rory Comyn or one of his men shot that arrow."

"That smirk of his made me sure of it," he said. "Does it not occur to you that if he *has* been lurking about, watching Rothiemurchus, he or one of his lads might have seen you row across the loch yesterday and followed you, taking care to keep the dog from catching his scent? If, in doing some such thing, your Comyn saw me, might he not have suspected that I had come to meet you?"

"He is *not* my Comyn," she retorted.

"He thinks he is."

"Well, he's not! Faith, you don't think I was going to meet *him*, do you?"

Fin did not reply, so she whirled to face him, to make sure that he understood her loathing for Rory Comyn before they took another step. Having assumed that he had dared to disbelieve her, she was astonished to see him smiling.

Her hand, with a mind of its own, had risen to strike. She quickly lowered it.

⟳

Her reaction told Fin that his silence had somehow sparked her temper. But her flashing eyes and glowing cheeks stirred only a strong urge to kiss her, despite certain rules that applied to knights who escorted young noblewomen. The first and foremost rule forbade the knight to take unfair advantage of the lady.

And, too, a wise man would first consider her grandfather... and Rothesay. Alienating the Mackintosh or infuriating the prince would be imprudent at best.

There was also the fact of his being one of the "wretched Camerons."

Her lips parted, and Fin felt his cock leap in response.

Anger stirred then, at himself. How could he even be thinking of her in a sensual way when he had sworn to seek vengeance against... nay, to *kill* her father?

"Is aught amiss, sir?" she said. "You were smiling and now you frown, but I don't think that you are angry with me. Does your head ache again?"

Her concern awoke a long dormant sense of warmth inside him. He tried to recall the last time someone had made him feel so. Wishing that he deserved her disquiet, he said gently, "My head is fine. I was wondering if your love of wandering or your quick temper had led you to think of yourself as a wild creature."

Looking relieved, then rueful, she said, "As you have just noted for yourself a second time, sir, my temper does inflame quickly. My brothers tease me about it. Ivor says I spit like a fierce kitten. But in troth, I just say what I am thinking."

He nodded. "I have seen that, but a lass's temper rarely troubles me. It troubles me more when she risks her life or her safety foolishly. I trust that you will heed your grandfather's command to end your solitary roaming until we can be sure that your woods are clear of Comyns and any other such vermin."

"Aye, sure," she said. Then she grinned. "Granddad has a temper, too. He is the embodiment of our clan motto: 'Touch not the cat but with a glove.'"

Satisfied that he had made his point, he said, "I will try to avoid stirring coals with either of you. Shall we walk down to yon burn now?"

Nodding, she led the way again.

As they walked, he added, "I doubt that I will be giving away any great secret if I tell you that your grandfather seems unlikely to support Comyn's suit."

She glanced back at him. "God-a-mercy, I know he has little use for Comyns in general, and he will not allow any Comyn—even one married to me—to live at Castle Raitt, which is what they really want. Also, Rory's behavior today will irk him. But Granddad does favor peace, so how can you be sure of what you say?"

"Because yestereve, when he and I talked, I recalled that you had mentioned troubles here and asked him about them. In describing the Comyns, he called Rory a lackwit. I'd wager that the notion of uniting you with any lackwit displeases him."

"I hope you are right, for whatever you may have thought earlier, I loathe Rory Comyn. Granddad will not shove his oar into what is more properly my father's business, but my father is bound to ask for his opinion."

"Lass," he said, "I never thought you were in those woods to meet Comyn."

"That's good, too. Here is the outflow. Shall we follow it for a time?"

He agreed, and they started downhill beside the rushing burn in silence. The pebble-strewn path was steep and narrow, requiring close attention.

Fin saw that the swift, roaring water had carved a deep cleft between two of the steep hills that formed the loch basin. Although the spewing outflow did not produce the sort of waterfall he admired most, the burn leaped noisily over boulders and was soothing and beautiful to watch. "Do you get salmon up here?" he asked.

"Nay, we are too far from the sea. They swim up the Spey only to Aviemore. But brown sea trout do sometimes reach Loch an Eilein. The osprey catch them before the men can, though—or so Ivor tells me. Are you ready to go back?"

"I want a drink first, and an apple, don't you?"

"Aye, sure," she said, kilting up her skirt and making her way to the water's edge. Kneeling with a hand on a boulder to balance herself, she bent low and used her other hand as a cup to scoop water to her mouth and drink it.

When she stood and wiped her wet hand on a skirt already damp from the splashing water, drops beaded on her lips and cheeks. Brushing a hand across one cheek, she grinned, looking like a merry child although she was not childlike in any other way. She was utterly *un*childlike, a woman grown, a woman who could stir...

Fin looked away, strode to the water, and knelt to get his drink. He splashed icy water on his face, although it was *not* the part of him that most needed cooling.

She handed him his apple when he rejoined her. But, as they headed back up the hill, munching their apples, he saw her pause to hitch her skirt higher under her linked girdle to leave both hands free as she trod the rocky, uneven path. He marveled at her ability to walk barefoot on such a path but remembered when he could do so, too.

Into that amiable silence, a less amiable memory intruded of the day he had flung himself into the Tay. His dilemma remained unresolved, and at any such quiet moment it could step into his mind as if it had a mind of its own. He had discussed it only with a priest, who had told him to pray for guidance and assured him that God would answer him or that he would, in time, find the answer in his own thoughts.

God had not answered him yet, and as for his thoughts—

"If you came here from the Borders," she said, "what were you doing there?"

"Fighting much of the time," he said, tossing his apple core up the hill where birds would make quick work of it. "King Henry of England invaded again and tried to take Edinburgh, as you must ken fine."

"Aye, sure I do. 'Tis why our men are still in the lowlands, because although the English left when their

supplies failed, they may return. You are gey quick and
deft with a sword, as I saw for myself. Do you enjoy
fighting?"

"I do enjoy the challenge, I expect, but no one likes..."
Remembering what she had said about the imaginary
chap she had thought she might marry, he said, "Do you
really think that any man who hates war is a coward?"

"Not for hating it," she said. "All sensible people hate
war, as I hope you were about to say. A man who refuses
to defend what he loves *must* be a coward, though. Sakes,
I'd think the same of any woman who did not at least *try*
to protect her own."

"Sometimes, though, people say or do things hastily
without knowing why."

"Sakes, people *often* behave so, all of us. It is called
acting without thinking first and is generally not to be
encouraged."

"Sometimes one has no time to think."

"One always has time to think," she said. "Sometimes
one just has to think faster than other times."

"But if a person thinks *too* fast, his thinking gets mud-
dled or he neglects to consider all the likely consequences
of his actions or his words."

She had reached the top of the hill where the path widened, and as she moved aside to make way so they could
walk abreast, she gave him a shrewd look. "This is an
interesting subject for discussion, sir. But I'm beginning
to wonder if it might have aught to do with why you came
here."

Fin searched his thoughts for a reply that would be
true without revealing more than he yet wanted to share
with her.

Into that silence, she said, "Did some such thing happen to *you*, something that troubles you now?"

Fin's silence told Catriona much about his thoughts. Doubtless, he thought his face was inscrutable, a warrior's face. But her brothers, father, and grandfather were all warriors, and she had learned from childhood to read certain signs.

She could tell when they had secrets, when they were preparing for war, when they were angry, and when they simply did not want to talk.

He seemed to show consternation now, as if he had not realized that she might draw such a conclusion from his comments.

Casually, she said, "If you go to Lochaber from here, remind me to tell you where to find that splendid waterfall along the way."

"I don't recall suggesting that I might go to Lochaber."

"Perhaps not, but it was your childhood home, so I assumed you must have family there and would visit them whilst you are in the Highlands. And we did talk of waterfalls yesterday," she reminded him. "Sithee, I just thought, from your reaction to my question, that you might prefer a change of subject."

"Sakes, lass, we were just making conversation," he said. "I like to discuss matters on which people have differing views and was but seeking to learn some of yours. I cannot think why you might think me troubled. I just wanted to know if you agree that certain events might occur so fast that one does not have time to consider all that one should before acting ... or speaking."

"I see."

"Then what would you say?"

"Without a specific event to consider, it is hard to imagine how one could lack time to consider at least the *likely* consequences of any act."

"Aye, well, you live a more peaceful life than most men do," he said. "I can tell you that in the pitch of battle, a man has *no* time to think. Merely to survive, he must act quickly, relying only on instinct and his training."

"Is one's training not what creates those instincts?"

"Not always. In troth, sometimes one's training, even one's loyalties and sense of duty, can obstruct rational thought. For example, men often obey blindly, without thinking, when a superior gives an order. Or one agrees to something simply because one respects and trusts the one demanding agreement."

He reached to cup her left elbow as the trail plunged into a declivity. The warmth of his touch through the thin camlet sleeve sent a tremor up her arm and a warmer sensation through her body that reached places never touched so before.

She turned to him. "Did you fear that I might trip over my feet?"

He did not answer but continued to support her elbow as he put his left hand gently on her right shoulder and continued to hold her gaze. The sensations roaring through her body now were disturbing, and so was the look in his eyes.

She knew exactly what he would do next.

⁓

Fool! The word exploded in Fin's mind but had no effect on his body's response to her. She was too close to him, too desirable, and too enticing. Moreover, she was too quick to read the truths in his words and *much* too easy for him to talk to.

She had said that she tended to speak her thoughts aloud. The idea that such a thing might be contagious disturbed him. He had rarely revealed his thoughts even as a child. And, later, he had learned that it was safer to keep them to himself.

For one thing, he served a powerful royal prince who did not take kindly to having his actions or words discussed outside his presence. For another, his equally powerful enemy had ears in unexpected places, so one did not discuss one's plans or anything else of import even in pleasant company unless one trusted the companion.

But now, Fin had a strong urge to tell her exactly what he was thinking and an even stronger one to kiss her thoroughly. He settled for kissing her cheek.

Her eyes widened as he did it, but he detected regret, too. The combination sent a surge of satisfaction through him, and something else, less pleasant.

"Don't look at me like that, lass," he said. "In troth, I've wanted to kiss you ever since I came out of the water this morning. But I should not have done it."

"Well, don't do it again!" Then, more gently she added, "I've enjoyed this walk with you, sir. But if my grandfather should hear even a hint of misbehavior on our part, he'll not let me out of his sight again until you are safely gone."

The dangerous moment had passed. He could not burden her with his problem, nor did he want to, but he felt no relief. Instead, a strong notion struck him that before long he would have to tell her the truth.

She would call him a coward when she learned that he had swum away from the battlefield at Perth, because anyone of sense would call him so.

At least, if she scorned him then, he would never have to reveal to her the sacred bequest that he had sworn to accept.

*Chapter 6*_____

When they returned to the castle, the midday meal was over and hours still remained until supper. Parting with Fin at the entrance and believing that he must be as hungry as she was, Catriona went down to the kitchen. Boreas followed her.

Because her rambles nearly always ended the same way, the cook was accustomed to her raids on his kitchen. He provided a sack with succulent slices from a leftover roast, two manchet loaves to eat with them, and scraps for Boreas.

Thanking him, she said, "This should stave off starvation till supper." Then seeing Tadhg poking up the kitchen fire, she said, "Run up to the hall, lad, and tell Sir Finlagh that I have food if he is hungry. He'll find me in the woods to the north."

"Aye, I'll tell him, m'lady," the lad said, brushing ashes off his breeks. "Did they tell ye above that someone special be a-coming here anon?"

Hope leaped within her, "My lord father and my brothers?"

"Nay, nay, it be someone else," Tadhg said. "Everyone be all secret-keeping about it, but he'll likely be coming shortly, they say."

"Do they say aught else about him?" she asked, amused by the lad's ability to glean knowledge that he was not supposed to have.

"Aye, sure," he said. "He comes from Perth and a host o' men wi' him. That will no please Himself, they say, 'cause he said the man shouldna bring so many."

"Then is the one who comes here an enemy?"

"Nay, for the lads do be stirring their stumps so much to tidy up the place that ye'd think his grace the King were a-coming. But I asked, and he isna the one."

Smiling, she thanked him, but he had stirred her curiosity. Recalling that Fin had ordered his equerry to Perth with a message, she suspected that his man must have let something slip. In any event, she was sure that Fin knew who was coming.

Clicking her tongue twice, she summoned Boreas, who hastily finished the last scrap the cook had given him and trotted after her.

⁓

"I have met your two men," the Mackintosh said when a gillie admitted Fin to the inner chamber. "Your Ian Lennox told me that ye've a new tale to unfold."

"Did he, sir?" Fin asked, drawing the stool up to the table, where the Mackintosh sat as he had before.

"Aye, but he said that the tale was not his to tell me. And since he did say that our Catriona was safe and I ken fine that two boats set out after men on our wall saw visitors approach ye, I'd wager that the pair of ye had an adventure."

"We met Rory Comyn and two of his men," Fin said. "He was displeased to find me with her ladyship and foolish enough to draw his sword."

"I did tell ye that the lackwit expects to wed with her."

"She says she won't have him."

"She says that, aye," Mackintosh said. "But a lass does not always get her say-so, even an she declares it as frankly as our Catriona does."

"So I told her," Fin said, watching him carefully.

"'Twould be a foul thing to wed that saucy lass with a lackwit, though."

"It would," Fin agreed, satisfied that he had read him correctly earlier.

"Ye did not kill him," Mackintosh said. "I warrant he'd have liked to put that sword of his through ye, though."

"He might have liked to do that. But I knocked it into the loch. Then my equerry, Toby Muir, and Ian Lennox arrived with Comyn's men in tow. Toby said they were gey careless and easily caught. There is one other thing, too."

"Ye suspect that Rory Comyn had summat to do with your injury yesterday."

"I do."

"Aye, well, I suspected as much. He has shown himself on our land afore without invitation. But although he does delight in making trouble—"

"With respect, sir," Fin interjected, "if he has been troublesome before, why have you not kept her ladyship on this island rather than letting her wander the hills alone? If Comyn wants her, what is to stop him from taking her?"

"Knowing that Clan Chattan would wipe out every last Comyn if he dared such a thing," Mackintosh said grimly. "Their clan is weak, unprotected by any other. I've bided my time to see if our young Lord of the North would protect them, but Alex Stewart trusts them less than I do. Forbye, but ye need not worry about our Catriona. As long as she keeps Boreas close by, she's safe enough."

"The arrow that struck me could as easily have killed the dog," Fin said.

"I expect that it could have. But that just puts us back to the Comyns' weakness. They hope to gain power by allying wi' us. Sakes, if I thought they'd change their ways, I would welcome them, because a confederation that grows is stronger than one that does not. Ye do ken that fact for yourself, I warrant."

"Do I?" Fin asked, tensing.

"Ye do, aye. I have spent nearly every Christmas of my life at Tor Castle, lad. D'ye think I don't recognize the son of Teàrlach MacGillony when I see him? MacGill!" He snorted. "Your da would clout ye good, did he hear ye call him MacGill. What were ye about to be saying such a thing of him to my lady wife?"

"In troth, sir, I thought it unwise to reveal my full identity whilst I was here for Rothesay. It might have stirred up *our* old enmity and complicated his dealings with you. My presence is solely as his envoy and has nowt to do with Clan Cameron."

"But so ye would say, nae matter why ye had come here. Did Rothesay not consider the likelihood that your presence alone might complicate matters?"

That was getting to the core with a vengeance, Fin thought with reluctant admiration. But the facts would do. "Rothesay and I met when we were two of the winning knights at her grace the Queen's Edinburgh tourney two years ago, sir, not long after he'd gained his dukedom. He knows me only as Fin of the Battles."

"That be nobbut rubbish, that. Ye'll not make me believe that that canny young scoundrel did not demand every detail of your past afore he took ye into his service. He'd do it just to be sure his wicked uncle hadn't sent ye to spy on him."

"You underestimate Rothesay, sir," Fin said. "He knows some whom he *does* trust, and I was able to provide him with three such excellent references."

"If he did not question ye, they must have been good. Who recommended ye to him, then, whose word he did heed? I might like to question *them* myself."

"His grace the King, her grace the Queen, and his reverence the Bishop of St. Andrews were all kind enough to recommend me to his service."

Mackintosh raised his eyebrows. "Bishop Traill himself? *And* their graces?"

"All three, aye, by my troth, sir."

Mackintosh's eyes narrowed. "Which of them recommended ye first, then?"

"Bishop Traill."

"I see."

Meeting that intelligent gaze, Fin had the feeling that it saw too much. But he did not know how the canny old man could know more than Fin had told him.

"Ye've given me nae cause yet to doubt your word," Mackintosh said then. "But do not be thinking that the royal safe conduct Davy Stewart gave ye will protect ye against his uncle Albany if Albany learns what Davy is up to. Sithee, ye were right to say that Albany has nae scruples. But I have another question for ye."

"Aye, sure," Fin said, wondering what was coming.

"'Tis about our Catriona. For all her wild ways, she is

an innocent maiden. So I want to know if ye've spoken yet for any woman, elsewhere. Ye look to be about five-and-twenty, so it would be only natural if ye had."

"Nay, sir," Fin said, startled. "Nor am I on the lookout for a wife. I've not seen my own family for years, and my brother, Ewan, is our chieftain now. Until I see and talk with him, I should not be *making* any such plans."

"I was sad to learn of your father's death," Mackintosh said. "I met him several times at Tor Castle. But ye say your brother be head of the family now."

"He is, aye," Fin said, hoping he was giving no hint of his discomfort with the direction their conversation had taken.

The old man smiled. "I see that I have touched a nerve with my questions, lad, but I'm curious withal. I ken fine that I can trust ye with her, and I like ye."

Fin said nothing to that. If the old man trusted him with Catriona, it was more than Fin himself did. The lass was too enticing for any man to resist for long.

~

Catriona had gone to her favorite place, a tiny clearing just inside the woods at the north end of the island. A boulder there, perfectly shaped for sitting and leaning against, gave a splendid view of the north expanse of the loch and the lush green forest of pine, alder, and birch that covered the steep hills surrounding it.

Boreas lay curled at her feet, the clouds had gone, and the sunshine felt warm on her face. She loved to sit and rest her gaze on the water, turned dark green today where the woods reflected on its surface. She closed her eyes, opening them only when she heard Fin's approaching footsteps.

He had come quietly, so he was nearly upon her when she heard them. He stopped when she opened her eyes.

"I hope I did not wake you," he said with a smile that warmed her through.

Smiling back, she said, "Nay, I was just being lazy. I brought food, though."

"So the lad, Tadhg, did tell me. Does he truly run everywhere?"

"Aye, to build his wind, he says. He told me that some-one important is coming here from Perth. He did not know who it is, but I warrant you do. Tell me."

He frowned, obviously disturbed by her knowledge. "I cannot tell you who it is," he said. "Your grandfather knows, though, and approves. I was just with him."

"Did he mention our walk?" she asked as she opened the sack that the cook had given her and handed him one of the manchets.

"He repeated his low opinion of the Comyns," he said, accepting the bread.

"I have beef, too," she said, handing him some and watching as he rolled two slices together. "Was that all he said about our meeting them?" she asked a moment later when he took a seat on a flat-topped boulder and began to eat hungrily.

Pausing to swallow, he looked thoughtful. "He said more, but it meant much the same. We also talked some about trusting. He said he trusted me with you."

"God-a-mercy, did someone see you kiss me?"

"Nay, lass. He said nowt to make me think any such thing." As he said it, though, he looked as if he'd had a second thought.

"What?" she asked.

Added color in his cheeks made her even more curious, but he said, "'Tis just... He *may* have heard about it, but if he did, he doesn't mind."

"Even if someone did see us, I think we were too far away for him to be sure of what he saw," she said firmly. Still, she wondered if her grandfather might be thinking that Fin would suit her. If the Mackintosh thought so, and if he said as much to James or Ivor, or even to her father, she would never hear the end of it.

Dismissing the thought, she said, "What else did he say about trusting?"

"It was just a subject that came up, but it does remind me of that impulsive kiss earlier. I don't know why, since nowt more came of it, and he *can* trust—"

"Before you kissed me, you had been saying that men sometimes obey blindly... such as when they obey a superior officer giving an order or agree to something simply because they respect and trust the one asking them to agree."

"Especially when they lack time enough to think the matter through, aye," he said, remembering. "I... I do know a chap who got himself into just such a position amidst a battle. Sithee, he found his... his kinsman amongst the fallen, dying."

"How dreadful!"

"Aye, so when the kinsmen demanded that my friend swear vengeance against his killers, my friend was sorely grieving, as you might imagine."

"Aye, sure, and he was exhausted, too, I'd warrant."

⁓

"He was, aye," Fin said. Her sympathy made telling the tale harder than he had expected it to be. His intent had been to relate just the barest details. Not only was he reluctant to admit yet that the battle had been the one at Perth between her clan and the "wretched Camerons," but he also wanted her objective opinion rather than one colored by their growing friendship or their clans' longstanding feud.

"What manner of vengeance did your kinsman demand?"

"The usual sort," he said. "But everyone had sworn an oath at the outset to seek no vengeance afterward against any opponent. In his grief... aye, and in his exhaustion, as you suggest... my friend forgot about that first oath and swore to the second just before his kinsman died."

"But he could not have kept either oath without breaking the other, could he?"

"Nay, so what do you think he should have done?"

"For a woman, that question is easy to answer, sir. However, from knowing my father, my grandfather, and my two brothers as I do, I am well aware that men do not think as women do. Their daft sense of honor too often gets in the way."

"Honor is not daft," he said, more sternly than he had intended. "Honor is everything, lass, because without it, men could never trust each another. If a man sacrifices his honor, he loses his self-respect and everything else worth having."

"I know that men think that way," she said, nodding. "But I still think that your friend's dilemma is easily resolved. Life must always be more important than death, sir. And surely, a man of honor kills only in self-defense or defense of others, never out of spite or anger. An honorable man *cannot* kill just to protect his honor."

"All Highlanders do hold any such bequeathed duty of vengeance sacred, Catriona. Surely, you know that."

"I do, aye. But God-a-mercy, sir, in a civilized world, surely killing another human has naught of honor in it, whatever the reason."

"Suppose that Rory Comyn had killed the two of us this morning," he said. "What do you suppose the Mackintosh, your father, and your brothers would do?"

She shuddered. "They would kill him, of course, and likely kill off whatever is left of his clan as well. But that does not make it right."

"Does it not? Would not his clan do the same if you or I had killed him? You know that they would. And, before you say that you would look down from heaven and condemn your men for avenging you, tell me how you'd feel if they did not."

"Sakes, I'd be dead, would I not? How would I know what they did?"

"We don't know what happens on the other side. I like to think that my father watches over me. At times, I vow, I have felt his hand on my sword hand in the pitch of battle, guiding it."

"Have you?" Her eyes widened, and then she smiled and looked into his eyes. "How comforting that must be."

He had not thought of it as comforting, just welcome. It had happened at least twice since Teàrlach MacGillony had died, each time at just the moment that Fin had feared he would collapse from exhaustion. Each time, the sense of his father's hand aiding his had kept him fighting on to victory.

"You have not answered my question, lass. How would you feel? I'd wager that you'd expect someone to *want* to avenge you."

"Good sakes, I'm as quick as any to defend my family. We all are, so in my first feelings of rage at the person who killed me, I might well expect my father and brothers to avenge me. But if I had time to think on the matter, I hope I would be wiser. I do believe that life is preferable to death in *any* event."

Deciding that she simply did not understand about a man's honor, Fin was tempted to try to explain it more clearly. She did have a point about thinking first, though. Moreover, a chilly breeze had come up.

"Shall we walk to that point yonder and back again?" he asked her.

She agreed, and they strolled to the tip of the island. On the way, she showed him a log raft tilted on end against a tree and tied to it with a long rope.

"Ivor and James made that when they were young," she said. "We paddled often from here to the west shore and back, especially in summer, when we even took it out on calm nights. Calm produces a fine echo here, so we'd hoot to wake it up."

"Sakes, did that thing hold all three of you?"

She chuckled. "Usually, one or two of us would end up swimming one way or the other, because if anyone fell in, those on the raft would refuse to let him or her climb back on, lest all fall in. That is one reason we all learned to swim well."

They talked and laughed together as they walked. When it was time to go in again, Fin tried to recall the last time he had spent most of a day just walking and talking with a lass in such a casual way. He was not sure that he ever had.

Catriona watched Fin as they walked back into the castle to change for supper. He seemed to be deep in thought, and she was loath to disturb him. She had a notion that his friend was apocryphal. Ivor had often mentioned "friends" who had particular problems when the problem in question was his own.

She suspected that Fin had done the same thing, but she did not know him well enough yet to be sure. In any event, she did wonder what his "friend" had done in the end. Doubtless, she decided, he would tell her in his own good time.

Parting from him on the landing outside his door, she went up to find Ailvie ready to help her change her dress for supper.

"I were beginning to think that I ought to send someone to see if ye fell in," the maidservant said.

"I was with Sir Finlagh," Catriona said.

"Aye, sure, and who doesna ken that?" Ailvie said as she urged Catriona toward the stool so she could brush her hair. "I'll plait it and twist it up under your veil, shall I? What did ye talk about for so long?"

"Everything," Catriona said. "We seemed just to move from one topic to another as if we had known each other all our lives. He is an interesting man."

"Hoots, ye ought to ken all there is about him by now," Ailvie said.

"I'm sure I still know little at all. He likes to discuss things. That I do know, and he likes to debate things, even one's thoughts. He often contradicts me."

"Ay-de-mi, that sounds most discourteous, m'lady."

"I suppose, but it did not seem so at the time. It is as if he cannot hear an idea without hearing contradictions in his head. If I say the grass is green, he will say, 'Yonder, it seems yellow, but mayhap that is just new barley, turning early.'"

"He sounds a wee bit peculiar like," Ailvie said with a frown.

Catriona laughed. "I suppose he does, at that. I don't want that gray gown, Ailvie. Prithee, fetch out the pink one with the red braid on its sleeves instead."

⁓

Fin enjoyed a peaceful sennight while he waited to hear from Rothesay. He swam nearly every morning, often with Tadhg, who had flung himself in on the third morning and demanded to know if Fin could teach him to swim as well as he did.

Fin also walked several times with Catriona, albeit only on the island. They talked of many things, and comfortably, because to his surprise, she forbore to quiz him when he felt reluctance to explore a particular subject. He knew that she was curious, but she seemed to sense his reluctance and to respect it.

Oddly, her ability to do so increased his feeling that he ought to tell her everything. Believing she would no longer respect him if he did kept him silent but also created a new dilemma. His need for her to think well of him increased daily.

Word arrived on the ninth day of his visit, a Tuesday, that a large force from Perth had reached the Cairngorms to the east. Some said that must be the Lord of the North because he preferred the higher route to the less demanding one through Glen Garry, knowing well that the formidable, icy passes discouraged pursuit from the south. Others suggested that the army might be that of the King of Scots.

. Fin was sure that it was Rothesay, and that the Mackintosh was aware of the approaching army. But the old man had not expressed the irritation, if not outright anger, that he would surely feel to learn that Rothesay had ignored his wishes.

In an area where most people traveled afoot or on small Highland ponies, it surprised him that news of the army had reached them so far ahead of the army itself until he recalled how fiercely all Highlanders thirsted for news. Mendicant friars were welcomed everywhere simply because they brought news from elsewhere.

On Friday afternoon, Fin walked with Catriona to the north end of the island, which had become their favorite stroll. When they turned back, Boreas ranged ahead of them as usual until they emerged from the woods. Then, halting suddenly, the dog fixed its gaze on a point some distance out in the loch.

Fin stopped what he was saying midsentence. "What does he see, lass?"

Before she could answer, Boreas dashed into the water and swam toward whatever had caught his eye. Fin could see that something was out there, roiling the surface, but it was not large enough for him to guess what it might be.

When Boreas plunged his head underwater and flung it back upward, he had something in his mouth.

Catriona said, "It looks as if he found clothing or— Sakes, what *can* it be?"

When the dog emerged from the water, Fin saw that what it carried was a cloth sack that writhed furiously and emitted frantic squeaks.

Boreas set the sack gently on the ground and began to nose it, as if hoping it would open, only to rear back abruptly with a surprised yelp when it did.

Loudly hissing, a small feline head pushed through the opening of the sack.

Catriona knelt and jerked the sack open. Three gray kittens spilled out, the one still hissing angrily. The others scampered toward the open gate, and Fin grinned when both of them darted away to avoid a man-at-arms running toward them.

"Stop, Aodán!" Catriona shouted. "What *are* you doing?"

"I thought I were drowning kittens for the cook, m'lady. I dinna ken how them wee rascals got ashore again."

In a blink, Catriona was on her feet, and watching her, Fin decided that she needed only a lightning bolt in each hand to match any mythical Fury.

"That was cruel!" she said, confronting Aodán. "If the kittens cannot lap and no one wants them, you must drown them, to be sure. But *not* by flinging them into the loch to drown in terror. Use a pail next time, sirrah, and bury them decently."

"I'll have to catch them first, m'lady," Aodán said, turning away.

Boreas stepped in front of him, growling.

"Nay, let them be," Catriona said. "Those three will *not* suffer again. They do look big enough to lap, so tell Tadhg to find people willing to take them, but do not *ever* do such a thing again. Just imagine how terrified they must have been!"

Aodán looked at Fin, the look of one helpless male to another. But Fin was struggling to conceal his amusement and shifted his gaze back to Boreas.

The dog continued to take stern interest in the hapless man-at-arms.

Fin had never had to drown kittens, but he did know how easily a few could turn into hundreds of hungry cats on any estate, let alone on an island. The lass would not thank him for any comment he might make, however, so he held his peace.

Catriona, still angry, said, "Go now, Aodán, and tell Tadhg he must put out food for them until he finds good homes for them. He can ask amongst our people in the hills. Tell him to say that I will count such adoption as a boon to me."

"Aye, m'lady, I'll see to it," Aodán said, hastily making good his escape.

Catriona turned toward Fin then, her eyes still afire. "You!"

"Nay, now, don't fly at me," he said. "I had nowt to do with any of that."

"You thought it was *funny*!"

"Nay, now..." Seeing her lips tighten, he said, "Aye, well, in troth I did. The dog stepping forward to halt the man nearly did finish me off. Look yonder now," he added with a grin, gesturing toward the gateway.

Evidently pleased with the outcome, Boreas headed for the kitchen with the third kitten hurling itself at and between his legs in scrambling leaps and bounds.

When she laughed, Fin said, "That's better." He turned away long enough to pick up the wet sack, which still lay where she had left it after freeing the kittens.

"We should go in," she said. "Our visitors will arrive soon, whoever they are."

"You still have not learned who is coming?"

"Nay, although I did hear that it might be the Lord of the North returning to Lochindorb. But you *do* know who is coming." When he did not reply, she added, "I heard that they show no banner, sir. But no one seems to be alarmed."

"I told you, your grandfather is content to let them come."

"Aye, you did say that," she said, frowning thoughtfully at him.

Catriona knew that those her grandfather would most readily welcome were her father and brothers, but they would fly the Mackintosh banner, just as Alex Stewart would fly his own as Lord of the Isles. She was certain that Fin knew them, whoever they were, and that he had persuaded her grandfather to let them come.

After she parted from him, she found Ailvie and said, "I want a bath before supper, Ailvie, so prithee, order hot water for me."

"Aye, sure, m'lady. Then, I'll come up straightaway to help ye."

With Ailvie's help, Catriona washed her hair, bathed, and donned the air-freshened yellow camlet gown. When she went back downstairs, her hair still damp but neatly plaited under her veil, she learned that the Mackintosh, despite his usual punctuality, had ordered supper set back an hour in expectation of guests.

Deciding to dry her hair by the hall fire, she drew a stool up by the hearth, took off her veil, and undid her plaits. She was still running fingers through her hair to let the heat of the fire dry it when Fin found her there.

"I hear that the Mackintosh does expect visitors," he said. "Do you not fear that they may walk in and find you at your task?"

"Nay, for we will hear when they shout for the boats. The windows are unshuttered, sir, and such shouts echo long at this hour when the loch is calm."

"I think your grandfather already sent boats across to await them."

"Faith, why did no one tell me?"

Hastily, she began plaiting her hair again, aware that he watched closely as she did, because his gaze stirred the tingling sensation he so often stirred in her. It still surprised her how quickly and easily her body responded to his presence.

Hearing the first arrivals coming up from the yard, she twisted the two plaits together at her nape. She was pinning her veil into place when Fin stopped her.

"You've pinned it askew, lass," he said, reaching to unpin and tug her veil into its proper place. The air around them seemed suddenly to crackle, making it hard for her to breathe, and the great hall seemed smaller. She was conscious only of him.

"Thank you," she murmured to the air between them when he had finished.

But he did not reply, nor take his hand away. And the air, rather than crackling, filled with new tension. Looking at him, she saw that he stared toward the entrance, his face ashen. Following his gaze, she saw her father and James first, then Ivor. Other men were on the stairs behind them, but Ivor had stopped, blocking their way. The expression on his face reflected the one on Fin's.

"God-a-mercy, you know Ivor!" she exclaimed. "Why ever did you not *say* so?"

Chapter 7 ―――――――――

Having barely heeded Catriona's words as he stared in consternation at Hawk, Fin glanced at her, realized that he still had his fingertips on her veil, and drew his hand back as he said, "That man in the doorway is your brother Ivor?"

"Aye, of course it is. Don't pretend that you do not know each other, for it is plain to me that you do."

"My lady, I must leave you for a time," Fin said, collecting his wits when he saw Rothesay push past Hawk. "My own master is there, by your brother—"

"But why did you not tell me that you know Ivor?"

"I will explain everything as soon as I can, but prithee, do not make a song about this. Your brother will not thank you for it any more than I will. You may even put one or both of us in danger."

"Give me your word that you will explain this to me, or by heaven, I will tell my father about it just as soon as he comes near me."

"I will explain as much to you later as I can. But curtsy now, lass, and right swiftly, for the Duke of Rothesay approaches."

"Davy Stewart? The Governor of the Realm and heir to Scotland's throne? *He* is the man you serve?"

"Aye," Fin said, making his bow to Rothesay, who bore him away at once.

The younger man had the fair, blue-eyed Nordic good looks of nearly every Stewart, the prime exception being his uncle Albany, who was as dark, some said, as the devil's own. Men had often suggested that since Albany looked so unlike his kinsmen, mayhap he was no Stewart at all but a changeling, or worse.

No one said such things of Rothesay, although he was certainly the subject of much gossip. He looked much as his grandfather, Robert II, had in his prime, and Rothesay seemed determined to outdo his grandfather in bed. The late King had sired more than twenty illegitimate offspring and nearly as many legitimate ones.

So far, though, Rothesay had sired no legitimate children.

"A beauteous lass, that one," he said to Fin in Scot when Catriona excused herself and walked off. "Prithee, tell me she has a fondness for flirtation and that you've cultivated her acquaintance for me. I've had a devilish few days till now."

"Have you, my lord?" Fin replied. "I thought today was a fine day."

"Have you *seen* those damned Cairngorms?" Rothesay demanded without bothering to lower his voice. "I tell you it was cruel to put horses to them. But it was gey worse to make me walk here from the turning-off to Lochindorb."

"They must have offered you a Highland pony to ride," Fin said.

"Aye, sure, a garron they called it and assured me it was gey sure-footed. But my feet nearly dragged on the ground, Fin. I *preferred* to walk."

"How did you meet the Laird of Rothiemurchus?" Fin asked.

"Shaw and his men were with my cousin Alex, Lord of the North, when I met them in Perth. They had traveled north together from the Borders. My lads and I joined their party, so that I could enter the Highlands without making a noise."

"Where is Alex now?" Fin asked.

"He rode on to Lochindorb, taking our horses with him, rot the man. He said we'd do better here without them. But he should arrive tomorrow."

"That explains why rumors of an army coming here did not disturb the Mackintosh," Fin said. "He must have known that you had joined Alex. See you, he'd made himself clear about you and the others' bringing only a few men to this meeting. So I feared that he might be wroth if you *were* bringing an army."

"Shaw said the same thing. In troth, he sent half of his own men or more home to their families, saying he would not need them for a time. Alex is doing the same and will bring few with him. But if my uncle Albany should get wind of this meeting, we'll need every man they've sent home, and right quickly."

"Aye, perhaps, but the custom here is much as it is in the Borders. If need be, Highlanders light signal fires or send running gillies to summon the clans. And the Mackintosh men *have* been away from their families for months, have they not?"

"Aye, sure, but so what?" Rothesay looked toward Catriona, talking with her mother and grandmother a short way away. Her good-sister, the lady Morag, spoke to her husband, James, beyond them with more liveliness than Fin had yet seen in her.

He said quietly, "The lass who attracts you is the lady Catriona Mackintosh, my lord. She is the Mackintosh's granddaughter and Shaw's daughter."

Rothesay's blue eyes gleamed as he said, "Is she now, in troth?"

"Aye, sir, and a maiden. The two ladies with her are her grandmother, Lady Annis of Mackintosh, and the lady Catriona's mother, Lady Ealga."

"I don't care about the others, Fin. But since you *will* present the lass to me, I expect you had better present all three."

Fin had begun to feel the uneasiness that he frequently felt in the younger man's presence. Moreover, he realized as he scanned the other men in the hall, although Rothesay had brought two noble sycophants with him, he had brought no one who had the knack, if anyone did, for keeping him out of trouble.

"I don't see your usual keepers," he said with a smile.

"You do not, nor will you," Rothesay said curtly. "Whilst my good-father lived, I had to put up with them. He's dead now, so I no longer do."

Fin had respected both of the so-called keepers *and* Rothesay's good-father, Archie "the Grim," third Earl of Douglas. He had agreed with Archie that, having married Archie's daughter, Rothesay ought to honor his vows to her. And, lacking the keepers' ability to curb his impulses, he regretted their absence now, because Rothesay had made it clear that he meant to have things *his* way at Rothiemurchus.

With a mental, if not audible, sigh, Fin said, "I will present all of the ladies to you, my lord. But mayhap I should first take you to meet the Mackintosh."

"Where the devil is the man? I expected him to be at the landing."

"Would you meet *your* guests at the landing, sir?"

"Nay, I would not! But *I*—" He broke off, grinning. "You mean to say that the Mackintosh is as arrogant as I am, don't you? Damn your impudence, Fin."

"Aye, sir. Shall I take you to him, or do you want me to tell him that you have summoned him here to greet you."

"Nay, nay, you made your point. I don't want to come to cuffs with the old man before we begin this meeting. I want him on my side, so take me to him without delay, if only so that you can present that beauty to me the sooner."

"Aye, sir," Fin said, and led the way to the inner chamber. He glanced back as Tadhg ran to open the door for them and saw Catriona still chatting with members of her family. She stood by her dark-haired father and near the tawnier-headed Hawk—Sir Ivor, as he must call him now, at least when they were with others.

He wondered if Hawk would tell her about their meeting at Perth before *he* had a chance to do so. And, if Hawk did tell her, would she, with her quick wits, put that information together with what Fin had told her about his "friend's" dilemma and thereby deduce more than he wanted to discuss with her yet?

Reassuring himself that if Hawk had not spoken of the incident in four years he was unlikely to do so immediately, Fin stood aside and let Rothesay precede him into the chamber to meet the Mackintosh.

⁓

Catriona, although engaged in an agreeable family reunion, watched Fin follow Rothesay into the inner chamber.

When she turned back to her family, her gaze collided with Ivor's far more intense one.

She opened her mouth only to close it again at a slight shake of his head. Returning her attention to the others, she engaged in the general exchange of news.

The Mackintosh, his royal guest, and Fin emerged from the chamber shortly afterward. Those near the fire who were to sit at the high table began to make their way toward the dais, and Ivor joined Catriona.

Offering her his arm, he bent his head toward hers and said, "I see that you have found yourself a new laddie to charm, my Catkin. But you should not let him play so impudently with your veil where others can see. 'Tis most unseemly."

"Don't play the dafty, sir. I saw from the way that you looked at him, and he at you, that you know each other. Prithee, tell me all about him."

"Nay, lass, the boot is on the other foot. I want you to tell *me* about him."

She stared at him, saying, "Ivor, if you do not stop behaving as if I had no wits at all, I vow that I shall—"

"Speak softly, my wildcat. Recall that the laird, our father, is behind us. After our long day, he is of no mind to stand for any fratching. Nor am I, I should add. I may be a right merry soul when I'm pleased, but—"

"But you are a devil when you're angry, just as Father is," she interjected. "I ken that fine, sir. Even so—"

"Enough, Cat. We will continue this discussion later and not whilst our family and guests surround us. I must speak first with Lion—"

"Lion! What manner of name is that?"

"Hush. 'Tis the only name I know for him, and that is

all I'll say. We'll explain more later. That is, I think we will. First, I must learn why he is here."

Keeping her voice low, she said, "When I met him, he said he had come to talk to the Mackintosh. And tonight he told me he serves Rothesay. So I'd wager that the duke's coming here is a result of that talk your Lion had with Granddad."

"No more now," Ivor muttered hastily as James approached them.

"Art telling secrets, my bairns?" the older of Catriona's two brothers said. "Only think what our grandame will say if she catches you. Manners, manners! Who the devil is that fellow who carried Rothesay off so swiftly, Cat? Morag tells me that he has been taking liberties with you. Have you an interest there, lassie?"

"I was just asking her about that," Ivor said, giving her a warning look.

"And, as I was telling you," Catriona said sweetly, "I know that men call him 'Fin of the Battles.' But Granddad made him admit that he is *Sir* Finlagh, and our grandame did learn that he is a MacGill. He told us that he lived in Lochaber as a child and then in eastern Fife. Also, he came to Rothiemurchus from the Borders."

"I have heard of 'Fin of the Battles,'" James said with increased respect. "They say he is one of the finest swordsmen in Scotland and a fine archer as well. I did not know that he was Rothesay's man, though. He lived for a time in eastern Fife, you say?" James added, shifting his gaze from Catriona to Ivor.

Ivor met that shrewd look unblinkingly. But although Catriona's ever-ready curiosity stirred, she devoutly hoped James would not quiz her more about Fin and therefore did not urge him to tell her why Fin's time in Fife seemed so important.

Something unusual was going on, and although she believed that Fin could defend himself, she did not want to make things more difficult for him by trying to explain him to her brothers. If she tried, she would inevitably land herself or Fin, or both of them and perhaps Ivor, too, in the suds.

When the two groups met on the dais, the Mackintosh presented his ladies and Morag to Rothesay, who nodded with a smile and a pleasant word to each of the older women. Then, greeting Catriona, he grinned, and she saw why others called him charming. He had an attractive air about him, but he was not as tall as Fin or as broad across the shoulders. His eyes twinkled but were an ordinary blue.

"I can see that my visit will be most enjoyable," he said, still smiling as he aided her to rise from her curtsy. Without releasing her hand or shifting his warm gaze from hers, he added, "I thank you all for your hospitality."

Feeling her grandmother's prodding fingers at her waist, Catriona gently withdrew her hand and turned obediently to take her place at the high table.

As she stood beside Morag, she heard the Mackintosh invite Rothesay to take the central chair, reserving the seat at the prince's right for himself. Next, he directed Shaw to the seat at Rothesay's left, adding glibly that the ladies would not mind sitting one seat farther down than usual to make room.

"Sithee, there be only the four of ye," he said to his lady wife, "whilst we have more than a few extra men. Moreover, we men want to talk." Then, as if clinching the matter, he added, "Also, it be Shaw's right as much as me own to sit alongside of his royal guest. Rothiemurchus does belong to Shaw, after all."

Rothesay bowed to Lady Annis and said with his twinkling smile, "I will say, your ladyship, that under any other circumstance I would strongly object to being deprived of your charming presence beside me. You and I must talk later."

With a wry smile of her own, she said, "I look forward to that, my lord."

As Catriona moved to allow for the change, she wondered if her father's return would put an end to her walks with Fin. She enjoyed them, and the sudden awareness that Shaw might henceforth forbid them made her realize just how much she did.

When the gillies began presenting platters of food, Ealga leaned closer to Lady Annis. Nevertheless, Catriona heard her clearly when she said, "Do you think that young man always speaks to ladies in so familiar a manner?"

"I do," Lady Annis said, looking past her at Morag and Catriona. "I expect that you two heard that, did you not?"

"Aye, madam," Catriona said.

"I've noted that ye have quick ears, lass," her grandmother said. "I trust ye'll have the sense not to grow as friendly with Rothesay as ye have with Sir Finlagh."

"She must not be rude to Rothesay, Mam," Ealga said. "He is our guest."

"He is one who will assume encouragement whenever he likes," Lady Annis said, looking sternly at Catriona. "If ye're wise, ye'll not give him *any*. Nor will ye, Morag. Dinna be thinking that your being James's wife will dissuade *that* lad."

"Faith, Mam," Ealga said. "You make it sound as if Rothesay would behave improperly to them. Surely, he would not do so in our own castle!"

"Piffle," Lady Annis retorted. "That young rascal dared to flirt with me, did he not? They say he'll flirt—aye, and much more than flirt if he's of a mind—with anyone who wears a skirt. Ye'll heed my warning, Catriona. Ye, too, Morag."

Catriona was glad that her father was talking to her grandfather just then, but in chorus with Morag she said obediently, "I will take care, madam."

Supper was overlong, although she knew that that was only because they had more men to feed than they'd had for months.

With Rothesay's men and her father's in the lower hall, and her brothers and Rothesay's nobles at the high table, the din of conversation made it hard for the four women to hear each other. Her grandfather, in particular, had a booming voice.

Hearing it raised then, Catriona remembered with a smile that Fin had thought that the Mackintosh must be decrepit. She wondered what had given him that notion.

~

Fin had hoped to find opportunity to talk with Ivor while they ate, but James had invited him to sit between them instead, with Ivor at Fin's right.

"Sithee," James said, "our grandfather will want to talk with Rothesay and also to ask my father about all we've been doing in the south. So, this is a good time for us to learn about you. My sister said that you hail from Lochaber. What part?"

From Fin's right, Ivor said, "Sakes, James, don't quiz him whilst he's trying to eat. You'll soon have Granddad complaining that he can't hear in this din, and as you're sitting next to him..." He grinned.

"Aye, that's true," James said to Fin. "Granddad likes to bellow now and again, and one takes care not to be the nearest target. We can talk swordsmanship. I've heard men talk of your prowess in both field and tiltyard, Sir Finlagh. Were you not one of the twelve knights selected with Rothesay for the Queen's tourney?"

That gambit was one that Fin was accustomed to deflecting by taking the first opportunity to shift discussion to other men's skills. Since the other two had fought in the eastern part of the Borders with the Earl of Douglas, while Fin had spent his time with Rothesay near Edinburgh or Stirling, they had much to discuss.

At one point, James said, "I can see why we never met in the Borders. Rothesay takes good care to keep out of the Douglas's way, does he not?"

Fin was adept at avoiding that topic as well. Archie the Grim's son, the fourth Earl of Douglas, being Rothesay's good-brother and fond of his own sister, lacked even their late father's scant tolerance for Rothesay's profligate ways.

Fin said quietly, "Rothesay is his own man, sir. One in my position does not question his motives or discuss them, as I am sure you will understand."

"I do, aye. I've heard he has a fiendish temper. I have also heard that we are to be his hosts for some time longer."

"If you expect me to tell you how long, I cannot oblige you," Fin said with a smile. "He rarely shares his exact intentions."

They talked desultorily until the Mackintosh indicated that the meal was over and suggested that Rothesay and Shaw join him in the inner chamber.

When Shaw gestured for James to go with them, Ivor said in an undertone to Fin, "Don't you dare go anywhere until we have talked, my lad."

"I was just going to say the same to you, albeit more courteously," Fin said with a rueful smile. "I am, after all, enjoying your family's hospitality."

"If that was meant as a comment on my manners, we can go out to the yard to discuss which of us has got better ones," Ivor retorted with a glint in his eyes.

"Hawk, I have already deduced where your sister got her temper," Fin said. "You needn't remind me."

"Just what did you do to learn that she *has* a temper?" Ivor demanded.

"Nowt to raise a brother's hackles, as you who know me better than anyone should know," Fin replied calmly.

"I may have known you once, *Lion*. But I did not know your true name even then. And, for all I know now, events may have altered you beyond my ken."

"I could say the same of you," Fin said, glancing around to be sure that no one else had wandered near enough to hear what they said. In a lower tone, he added, "Would it not be better to talk in the yard or elsewhere?"

"We'll go to my chamber," Ivor said. "'Tis nobbut a hole in the wall. I shared a larger one with James before he married and that option vanished."

"I should hope so," Fin said, grinning. "Lead the way then."

Despite Catriona's relief that the meal had ended, she was annoyed to find herself relegated to the company of women and more so to see Ivor bear Fin off and up the stairs without as much as a word from either one of them to her.

She saw that Morag was just as peeved when James followed their father into the inner chamber but found no solace in that.

Although Catriona wanted to know what Rothesay sought from her kinsmen, she cared more about what Fin and Ivor were saying. Both having agreed to explain their relationship, she had hoped that they would do so together.

"I'm going to bed," Morag stated to all generally. "If you see James, prithee be so kind as to tell him that I shall be eager to welcome him when he comes to me."

Catriona nodded but had no intention of waiting for James to reappear.

Believing that Fin would seek her out later if Ivor did not, she tried to think how she could avoid spending the time until then stitching or tatting in the ladies' solar with her mother and grandmother.

Should that be her fate, she knew that with so many more men at the castle, the older women would insist that she go to bed when they did.

Her excuse to evade that had to be plausible, though, and she dared not lie to them. It would be unwise, for example, to say that she was going to bed if she meant to slip out the postern door to gaze at stars as she frequently did. Not that doing so would be wise in any event that night. Her father had brought enough men with him to fill two lower-hall trestles at supper, and many would sleep in the yard.

After months of feeling nearly empty, the castle now felt full to overflowing.

~

Hawk was right. His chamber was too small, and it felt even smaller when he turned toward Fin after lighting a number of candles.

He still held the taper that he had taken from a box at the foot of the stairway and lit from a cresset in one of its niches. Extinguishing the taper now, he looked long and thoughtfully at Fin, and sternly, as if Fin were an errant squire.

Fin met the look silently until Hawk grabbed his shoulders and squeezed them hard, saying, "It is *good* to see you, Lion. I cannot describe how I felt when I saw the river Tay swallow you and sweep you off toward the sea. When you went under…"

He turned away and fiddled with the nearest candle as if it had sputtered.

Fin knew that it had not. "I let the current carry me for a time, lest someone pick up a bow and finish me off."

"Sakes, you don't think—!"

"Nay, nay, although you *are* the only man I know who could have made such a shot." A sudden memory of Catriona, boasting, made him chuckle.

"What's so funny?"

"Your sister told me that her brother Ivor was the finest archer in all Scotland, and I informed her stoutly that I knew a better one. Mayhap I should have suspected the truth then. After all, you were fighting with Clan Chattan against us."

"I was, aye. But I don't believe that either of us was thinking much by the end of that battle. A dreadful affair it was."

"Aye, and all Albany's doing, according to Rothesay," Fin told him.

"Father suspected that from the outset, for all that his grace the King issued the command to trial by combat. Albany does not like us here in the north, especially Clan Chattan. We were allies of the last Lord of the North, after all. And we have refused to let Albany's worthless son succeed him in place of his own son."

"'Tis true, aye. No one in the north could want Murdoch Stewart to take Alex's place at Lochindorb. By all accounts, Alex is a better man *and* warrior."

"Donald of the Isles might prefer Murdoch for being the weaker," Ivor said. "But never mind that, Lion. Where did you go when you climbed out of the Tay?"

"Where do you think?"

"St. Andrews?"

Fin nodded.

"I see. You saw his reverence then. Did you tell him what had happened?"

"I did, aye. At present, he is the only man save yourself who can identify the coward who left the field by flinging himself into the river."

Shooting him a grim look, Ivor said, "Did you tell him that I *told* you to go?"

"Nay, I was sure that you'd tell him yourself if you wanted him to know."

"I thank you for that, I think. It raises another issue,

though. Sithee, I have served Alex Stewart just as you serve Rothesay, and whilst we were in the Borders, Traill sent for me. He gave me a message for Alex to go to Moigh, saying that he dared put nowt in writing for fear it would end up in the wrong hands. When we met Davy in Perth, someone had just told him that we were to meet here instead."

"That was my man, Toby Muir," Fin said. "Rothesay sent me to persuade your grandfather to host the meeting, and the Mackintosh wanted it held here. I also sent a message to Lochindorb in the event that Alex should return meantime."

"Traill must be heavily involved in this then, must he not?"

"Aye, for he sent me to serve Davy two years ago," Fin said.

A loud double rap on the door diverted them both.

When Ivor snapped, "Enter," the door swung open to reveal Catriona with a jug and two goblets in her hand.

"Grandame thought that the two of you might like some wine," she said, smiling mischievously. "I have carried it all the way up here to you myself, to preserve your privacy. Does not such an effort deserve proper payment?"

*Chapter 8*_____

Catriona watched warily as Ivor took the jug from her, trying to decide if he was angry or amused. Either mood would annoy her, but the latter one was safer.

He said, "Come in, Cat, so I can shut the door. But I warn you, you may not learn all that you want to know. Some things are not for you to hear."

"Sakes, you of all people should know that I can keep a secret," she said. "I'll hold my tongue about the two of you knowing each other," she added when he frowned. "But only if you will tell me how that came to be so."

"I hope that is not a threat," Ivor said, his tone sending a shiver up her spine.

"Don't scold her, Hawk," Fin said. "I've already promised to tell her what I can, but I did want to discuss things first with you."

"Aye, well, we met at St. Andrews," Ivor said, taking the jug from her and pulling out its stopper. As he poured wine into one of the goblets, he added, "You will recall that Granddad and Father sent me to the bishop there some years ago."

"To study, aye," she said, trying to remember what she

could of those days. "I was no more than a bairn when you left, being six years younger than you are."

With the quick, unexpected smile that often surprised her after she had irked him, he held the goblet out to Fin and said, "I do know that, lass."

"I just meant that you cannot expect me to recall much about those days. I must have been about four when you left. And although you came back each year for a visit... long enough to teach me things such as to paddle our raft and to swim... you were away much of the time until I was nearly ten. I don't know anything about St. Andrews except that you learned to read well there."

"We did, aye, and learned much else forbye," Ivor said.

"Also, you did teach me my letters and numbers."

"Bishop Traill believes in educating anyone who wants to learn, and many who do not," Ivor said with a wry look. "He believes that if men learn the history of places beyond their ken, and about each other, they will better understand themselves and other men—other countries, too, such as England and France, come to that."

"But if you were a student with Fin... with Sir Finlagh," she amended hastily, "then why did you not know his name?" She glanced at Fin, but he kept silent.

"For the same reason that he did not know my name," Ivor said. "Traill's students study at St. Andrews by invitation. He chooses mostly younger sons of powerful nobles and clansmen, as well as other lads who show promise in their studies, or with weapons, or in other ways."

"What other ways?"

Ivor smiled again. "One friend of ours had already gained much expertise in sailing ships and galleys when he joined us."

"I can see how ships might help the bishop spread understanding, if that is what he was to do. But why would a man of the Kirk teach you skill with weapons?"

"Because, in our world, such skill earns respect," Fin told her. "And when a man commands respect, others listen to him. If he doesn't, they don't."

"Why younger sons, then?" To Ivor, she added quickly, "In troth, sir, I'd think that James would command respect more easily because he *will* inherit Rothiemurchus. He might even inherit the captaincy of Clan Chattan."

"Aye, sure," Ivor said. "But Traill prefers to teach men more likely to go into the world. Sithee, lass, although some eldest sons do achieve knighthood, all who survive long enough eventually have to tend to their estates and their people."

"Bishop Traill told us much of this over the years," Fin said. "He also seeks lads who are less likely than eldest sons to be thoroughly steeped in their clan's rivalries. The reason that your brother and I did not know each other's names is that as soon as we arrived at St. Andrews, we received our student names—"

"Hawk and Lion," she said, remembering that Ivor had called him Lion.

"Aye," Fin said. "And the others had similar ones. We had to swear by our honor not to seek information about other students, their clans, or their homes. Our world whilst we lived at St. Andrews had to *be* St. Andrews, because we came from all over Scotland and his reverence did not want clan war to erupt at the castle."

"I fear that I would have tried to find out, anyway," Catriona said.

Fin's smile warmed her. "The bishop made it a matter

of honor, my lady, and all of us yearned to seek knight-hood. We knew that if we sacrificed our honor to satisfy mere curiosity, that goal would fly beyond our grasp. Traill also believes in chivalry. *And* he had a strong right arm with a switch or a tawse."

"So you and Ivor have not seen each other since then, until now?"

The two men looked at each other.

"You have!" she exclaimed. "Did you not learn each other's names then?"

Understanding from Ivor's expressionless face that he'd leave it to him to answer that question, Fin said, "We have seen each other once since then. But only once and in circumstances that allowed for only brief conversation."

She met his gaze and seemed to study him for a long moment before she said, "You are not going to tell me more than that, are you?"

"Not yet," he said. "Your brother and I must talk more before we do."

"So, despite all our talks together, you still do not trust me to keep silent."

He hesitated and, by the look on her face, knew that he had hesitated too long. A glance at Hawk...Ivor...told him that he would get no help there, so Fin caught and held Catriona's gaze as he said, "I told you that I would reveal what I could, and I have done that. By my troth, although there is more to tell, my *not* telling you has little to do with my trust in you and much to do with the fact that we do not yet know whether the information may endanger you or even ourselves."

"But—"

"That will do, Cat," Hawk said. "You have known the man for little more than a sennight, so you cannot expect him to trust you all in all. Such trust does not bloom so quickly but must grow over time. Moreover, if you expect him to trust you, you need to exert yourself first to trust him. Think, lass! This matter is one about which he—and I, too—know much more than you do. If we tell you that it may be dangerous for you to know too much, you should trust us."

Fin could tell that she was reluctant to accept Hawk's argument. So, when she shifted her gaze to himself, he met it and held it until she quirked her mouth wryly and sighed. He knew then that she would yield.

Tempted as he was to promise that he would tell her everything as soon as he could, he would not do so without knowing that he could keep that promise. He would talk to her later, more privately, and if she wanted to fratch with him then, she could. He could tell from Ivor's expression that he would not extend the discussion to soothe her temper and that Ivor still had more to say to him.

The silence lengthened for another beat or two before Ivor said lightly, "I could tell you some fine tales about Fin's days at St. Andrews, Cat. But I fear that he may have worse ones to tell about me."

She smiled then. "I'll coax those tales out of both of you one day."

"Aye, sure, you will," he said. "For now, though, you must leave us to our talk. We do thank you for the wine, although I have a strong suspicion that it was your own notion and not Grandame's to bring it to us."

Chuckling, she bade them both goodnight and left the chamber.

Ivor said, "Don't imagine that you are going anywhere, my lad."

"I don't," Fin said, holding out his goblet. "But I want more wine."

Ivor refilled both goblets, saying, "It occurs to me that I still don't know exactly who you are. Don't you think that it's time you told me?"

"I do, aye," Fin said, as several ways of saying it flashed through his mind. Opting for bluntness, he said, "My father was Teàrlach MacGillony."

"The king of archers, who died at Perth. He must be the man by whom you were kneeling when I saw you. I wasn't sure then that it *was* you, not until you stood up. So you are a full Cameron then and not from one of the minor tribes. Have you revealed that interesting fact to my grandfather?"

"I didn't have to. He said that I look just like my father and took me severely to task for telling Lady Annis that his name was Teàrlach MacGill. Said my da would have clouted me good for saying such a thing. He would have, too."

"That was a terrible day, that battle at Perth," Ivor said soberly. "We're going to have to make a clean breast of it to them, you know."

"What do you mean?" Fin asked, hoping that his own deeper thoughts about vengeance and sacred oaths had not revealed themselves. "Did you not—?"

"I fear that I was not entirely truthful afterward with my father and others of Clan Chattan, and James was not there. He wields a sword skillfully, but he has not won his knighthood. And, as you will recall, the royal command was for thirty champions on each side that day."

"So you are a better swordsman than James. That does not surprise me, Hawk. You are more skilled than most, albeit not as skilled as you are with a bow."

"Not skilled enough with a sword to defeat you, Lion. Sakes, though, I expect that we'd better start calling each other Fin and Ivor now."

"What *did* you tell your people?"

"After you dove in, Father asked what you had said to me. That was easy enough, since neither of us had said much of consequence."

"I said your name," Fin told him. "I don't recall what I said after that." Then he did remember more. "I said that they'd flay you, but you told me you'd be a hero. Not until afterward did I realize that you had meant that they would call me coward. And so I was, I expect. But I could not fight you."

"Don't be daft, man. Would you have gone into that river had I not urged you to go? And don't pretend that I did not. You heard and understood me plainly."

"Did I? I doubt that I was thinking at all by then."

"Would you say to my face that I had nowt to do with your departure?"

Fin shook his head. "You know I won't do that. But neither do I agree that you should tell them that it was your idea. I made the choice, my friend."

"Are we still friends then? Nowt has changed?"

"As far as I am concerned, you and I are still as close as brothers. Sakes, I feel closer to you than I ever felt to Ewan." Memory of the vengeance that he had sworn to claim stirred then so harshly that it was all he could do not to wince in response to it. But how could he ever kill his best friend's father, Catriona's father? He heard her voice then in his mind: *"Life is always more important than death,"* she had said. *"An honorable man cannot kill to protect his honor."*

"What is it?" Ivor asked him.

"Nowt," Fin said. "If you did not tell them the truth, what *did* you say?"

"I told them the same thing I'd said to you, that I had had enough of killing for one day and thought that someone from your side ought to stay alive to tell his version of the tale. Father was sure that you must have drowned, but we'll have to tell him and Granddad the truth—aye, and James, too."

"And Catriona," Fin said. "I don't look forward to that."

"So you haven't told her yet about Perth. Not even that you were there?"

"I haven't mentioned Perth to her." It occurred to him that, at St. Andrews, Hawk would have been the first person to whom he would have confided his dilemma. They would have talked it over until both had agreed on what the best course of action would be. That he could not do that now added to the pain that his indecision had cost him over the years.

"You must tell her," Ivor said. "But stand back when you do. We don't call her Wildcat without reason. She has claws, sharp ones, and although she keeps them sheathed most of the time, she does not hesitate to use them when she's angry."

"As I said earlier, I have seen that she has a quick temper, but she seems usually to keep it under control," Fin said.

"Just wait," Ivor warned him with a grin. "Now, I keep

a dice cup in here. Are you of a mind to throw against me for a while?"

"Aye, sure," Fin said, drawing up a stool while Ivor moved a table close to the narrow bed and then sat on the bed.

As he did, Fin had a sudden stray notion that Hell might just be a place where every resident faced a dilemma like his, and where the only way out was to find the right answer to an unanswerable question.

～

Catriona had paused outside Ivor's door, because as she had closed it, she'd heard Ivor say, "Don't imagine that you are going anywhere, my lad."

But once the heavy door had shut, she could hear only the hum of their voices. She could tell Fin's voice from Ivor's but could not make out their words.

Moreover, she knew that it might occur to Ivor that she would try to listen. If he caught her, she did not want to think about the consequences.

She did not want to go to her own room, because she was not sleepy and Ailvie would be there. Nor did she want to rejoin the older women. She wanted to think, which required solitude, so she made her way quietly down to the kitchen.

It was dark, except for the glow of embers in the huge fireplace. But the embers cast enough light to show her the way to the scullery and to reveal Boreas curled by the hearth with the kitten that had adopted him sprawled across his neck. Boreas opened his eyes, then shut them when Catriona signaled him to stay.

Lifting the bar from the scullery door, she eased it ajar and stepped outside. Then, leaning against the wall, she inhaled the crisp night air and relaxed, gazing up at the thick blanket of stars in the moonless sky while she considered what Ivor and Fin had told her and tried to imagine their life at St. Andrews.

As she did, she realized that the two men had much in common. Both had an air of easy confidence, and from what she had seen of Fin's skill with a sword, he was almost as fine a swordsman as Ivor was. She smiled, realizing that they must both have been thinking of Ivor when they'd argued about great archers.

She had always thought Ivor easy to talk to, and by comparison with James, he was. Fin was even easier to talk with, because Fin expressed more interest in what she said. Ivor was impatient and less likely to listen as carefully or discuss things as thoroughly as Fin did. And Ivor had never stirred her senses the way . . .

Feeling fire surge into her cheeks at the direction her idle thoughts had taken, and imagining Ivor's outraged reaction to such a comparison, she realized that Fin outdid him in another way. Although she had always tried to avoid arousing Ivor's quick temper, the very thought of angering Fin disturbed her more.

Where Ivor raged and might even wreak vengeance, Fin had only to look at her to make her feel his displeasure. Thinking then of what else Fin could make her feel, she let her imagination linger on those thoughts.

Realizing abruptly that the longer she stayed the more she risked discovery, she went back inside and replaced the bar across the door, hoping she would not meet her father on her way upstairs. With so many extra men at the castle, Shaw would not accept the excuse that she had just sought solitude and fresh air. Wincing at the thought of his most likely response—that he would give her all the solitude she needed by confining her to her bedchamber for a sennight—she went quickly.

～

"There is one other thing I'd like to ask you," Fin said after he and Ivor had cast dice for exorbitant, albeit imaginary, wagers for a time. "Sithee, I've been thinking more about Bishop Traill and our meeting here as we did."

"I have, too," Ivor said, scooping the dice up into the cup. Covering a yawn, he added, "Traill may have *much* more to do with this business than we knew."

"I'm coming to think so," Fin admitted. "As Bishop of St. Andrews, he has the ear of the royal family, and thus wields influence over the King and the Queen, as well as Rothesay, so perhaps he influences Albany, too. And perhaps..." He paused. "Do you know yet who else will be attending Rothesay's meeting here?"

"I thought that it was to be just my grandfather, my father, Alex, and Davy's minions. Do you mean to say that someone else is coming?"

Fin nodded. "The Lord of the Isles."

"Donald? But everyone in the Great Glen—aye, and west of it, too—would do all they can to keep his ships from touching shore, let alone allow him to cross their lands with his army to get here. Sakes, everyone knows that he covets control of the western Highlands, and more. How the devil will he get here?"

"He'll carry safe conducts from Rothesay and the Mackintosh, and he brings no army but only a small tail of men, as Alex will," Fin said. "Sithee, Rothesay needs them both to stand with him against Albany. The Mackintosh suggests, and I agree, that Davy likely wants them both to promise him their votes when his provisional term as Governor of the Realm expires in six months. After all, if they will agree to that, most men who support *them* will also support Davy."

"Then it is possible that someone else from our group is serving Donald, as I serve Alex and you serve Davy. Any number of us may be mixed up in this."

"Aye," Fin agreed. "And if so, we become part of a much greater conspiracy against Albany, do we not? My concern is that the more people Davy involves, the greater the risk grows that Albany will learn of it."

"I'd wager that he already has. Does Davy understand the danger *he* is in?"

"He knows that Albany wants to take the Governorship back into his own hands. In troth, Davy believes that his uncle covets the throne."

"Albany is not next in line," Ivor pointed out.

"Nay, but Davy's brother, James, is just seven, and Albany is next after him."

"Some would say that Albany is better suited to take the throne than Davy is. Many more agree that Scotland does need a stronger king."

"Aye, but Davy is the heir, and I believe that he will be a strong king. Sithee, he believes in the people. Albany believes only in acquiring power for Albany."

"We'll have to wait, then, and see who triumphs, won't we?"

"Aye," Fin said. But he felt a chill shoot up his spine as he said it.

"I'm for bed," Ivor said. "I've not slept a full night in four months."

"I'll leave you to it then," Fin said, putting out his hand. "'Tis glad I am to have you as my friend, Hawk, and to be talking things over with you again."

Firmly grasping his outstretched hand, Ivor shook it, saying, "I, too, Lion."

Fin left then, hoping that they would still be friends when the events they had set in motion had played themselves out.

As he rounded the torchlit curve before his landing, he met Catriona hurrying upstairs. She stopped, staring wide-eyed at him, her cheeks suffusing with color.

Amused, he said sternly, "And just what mischief have you been up to, my lass, to put such fire in your cheeks?"

～

Catriona gaped at Fin, feeling his gaze with every fiber of her being.

Standing two steps above her, he looked taller and larger than ever, and he filled the stairway so that she knew she would have to brush against him to get by.

She felt the heat in her cheeks spread elsewhere when the thought of pressing against him grew to a mental image that included his arms slipping around her and pulling her close. She drew a sharp breath but could not think.

"Cat got your—" He broke off, chuckling. "I expect that that old saw does not find much favor with you, does it?"

"It does not, although my brothers have long delighted in finding new ways to say such things. One of James's favorites was always to promise that he would do something before Cat could lick her ear."

"Is that your tactful way of saying I'd be wiser not to call you Cat as they do?"

"I did not mean that, nay." Aware that she was standing outside her mother's room and wondering if the other women had come upstairs, or the men, she glanced warily at the closed door.

Apparently oblivious to her concern, he said in a normal speaking tone, "You still have not said what happened to put such color in your cheeks."

"Perhaps you do not know that you are blocking my way."

"Am I?" He stepped down a step.

Tension filled the air around her, raising the hairs on her arms and drying her lips. Wetting them with the tip of her tongue, she glanced again at the door of her mother's bedchamber and listened for footsteps that might be her father's coming up the stairs. Looking up at Fin, she muttered, "You know that you are."

His eyes twinkled. "Nay, then, why should I? Nervous, lass? I'll wager that you *have* been up to mischief, then. If so, and if I am to let you pass, I believe I should collect a toll as a small penalty for your misbehavior."

"I have not misbehaved."

"Ah, but you have. Why else would you keep looking at that door as if you expect it to open and an ogre to leap out and call you to account for yourself?"

"Prithee, sir, keep your voice down. Anyone on this stairway will hear you." But she looked at the door again, sure that it *was* about to fly open.

"If you fear discovery, you had best get upstairs, had you not? I'll just tell anyone who comes that I was flirting with a maidservant who has since fled."

"Good sakes, *do* you flirt with maidservants in other people's households? I thought that only your royal master did such things. I expect I should have known that you would be just like him, though."

His eyes narrowed dangerously, but before she had time to realize that the feeling that raced up her spine was not fear but delight at having stirred him to such a look, it vanished. He said, "Art going to tell me where you have been or not?"

Pretending to consider which answer she would give, she said, "Not, I think. Why should I trust you with such a confidence when you do not trust me?"

"So that still rankles, does it?" He stepped down again, so that he stood on the landing with her, crowding her as if to see if she would step back.

She did not, but her body hummed at his nearness.

"I won't insist that you tell me," he said quietly. "But, as Ivor and I told you, if word of what we discussed drifts beyond these walls, it could put others at risk. I'd wager that you would put only yourself at risk by answering *my* question."

"Perhaps," she said. "But you do want to know, and that makes us even."

"Does it?" He put a finger under her chin, tilting her face higher. Moving his own face close enough so that she could feel his breath on her lips, he said softly, "Art so sure now that we are even, little Cat?"

That single fingertip seemed to burn into the soft skin under her chin, and she could smell the subtle essence of wine on the breath that caressed her lips. Without conscious thought, her lips parted.

He bent nearer, slowly, so slowly that she could not

think, could not even breathe. She could only anticipate the moment when his lips would touch hers.

The moment stretched until her whole body tingled and warmed, and then his mouth brushed hers... lightly and so softly that it was as if no more than a warm wind had followed his wine-scented breath to caress her.

He did it again, and she was concentrating so hard on what he would do next with his mouth that when his hands touched her shoulders and stroked lightly downward, she gasped and leaned toward him on tiptoe, pressing her lips to his.

His felt warm and soft, but she scarcely had time for that thought to enter her mind before he slid his arms around her and his right hand moved gently up her back and under her veil until his fingers could weave themselves in the plaits at her nape. He held her so, kissed her, and tasted her lips with his tongue, gently at first and then more urgently until she parted them, and he slid his tongue inside.

The hand that had remained on her shoulder moved slowly, tantalizingly, to the small of her back, teasing her senses as it moved. Then he pressed her closer to him until she felt his body move against hers. His mouth moved more possessively as his tongue explored hers, and she could feel her breasts swelling against him. They had come alive when he touched her, in a way she had never known before.

With a sigh, he gave her a last soft kiss on the lips and then set her back on her heels. Somehow his hands came to rest lightly again on her shoulders.

She blinked and looked up at him, wishing that he had not stopped.

"You go up to your chamber now, lass. But we must

talk more. Will you walk with me on the shore again in the morning, early?"

She stared at him, wondering what had come over her...sakes, over him! Was he imagining that one such kiss meant that she sought more? What was he thinking?

Striving to sound as if she were in full possession of her senses, she said, "Ailvie will have to come with us. My father would dislike it otherwise."

He frowned. "I don't want to share what I have to say to you, lass. Would it suffice if she walks far enough behind to see us without hearing us?"

"Aye, I'll tell her."

"At dawn then," he said. "Now go."

Chapter 9

Fin waited until Catriona had disappeared around the curve of the wheel stair before he opened the door to his chamber. Warm candle glow greeted him.

As he had expected, Ian Lennox was waiting to assist with his ablutions. The brush and breeks he held told Fin that Ian had been seeing to his usual chores.

When Ian looked up at him with a smile, Fin shut the door and said bluntly, "How much could you hear just now of what took place out on the stairway?"

Ian's smile vanished. "Only enough to know that one voice was yours, sir. I heard nowt of the other person and could not make out even if you spoke the Gaelic or Scot. You ken fine, though, that I'd never repeat aught that I'd heard."

"I do know that, Ian. But whilst we are here at Rothie-murchus, I want you to keep an even closer guard than usual on your tongue. Also, I want you and Toby to learn all you can from others in the yard and in the hall. Practice your Gaelic, for enemies may soon surround us despite Rothesay's hope of finding allies."

"Enemies, sir? More than just the Duke of Albany?"

"The Lord of the Isles will be here. He has no love for

the Lord of the North and less for Highlanders who resist his own insatiable thirst to add them to his realm. In troth, Donald would control the Highlands from the west coast to Perth."

"What about the Lord of the North, sir? I ken nowt o' the man save that his father's numerous offspring were all bastards."

"You'd be wise not to prattle about that here, I think," Fin said.

"I don't prattle," Ian said. "Be there more I should know about the man?"

"I doubt that he covets more land, as Donald does. Alex assumed the Lordship of the North despite Albany's having named his own son to inherit it. But the people hereabouts are doubtless grateful for that. They seem to like Alex."

"I do know Albany's son," Ian said, setting the well-brushed breeks aside. "A soft-living, preening coxcomb, I'd call him, not a man of knightly skills."

"He has none," Fin agreed. "Sakes, Albany himself despises him."

Ian chuckled. "The new Earl of Douglas is the same. Men called his father Archie the Grim, but they call the son 'the Tyneman' because he is such a bad leader. Why is it, do you think, that powerful men so often beget weak sons?"

"I can tell you only what my father said about it," Fin said. "He was a clan war leader, so he saw what happened with other such men. He said most powerful men trust only themselves to resolve problems properly. So, they constantly correct their sons, trying to teach them to think as *they* do, rather than how to make good decisions. The result, he said, was that they teach their sons instead to have little or no confidence in their own opinions—the opposite of what most fathers seek to do."

"But is that not how any father teaches a son, by correcting his errors?"

"A wise father acts otherwise," Fin said. "Or so my own told me. He said it is more important that a man learn to trust his own instincts and his own decisions than to believe that he must try to pattern them after someone else's."

"Sakes," Ian said, "how do you teach anyone *that*?"

"The same way that I hope I am teaching you," Fin said. "By letting you make decisions whenever it is safe for you to make a mistake, so that you can learn from those mistakes. A mistake that a man can see and measure for himself—if it does not kill him—will teach him more than any parent or superior can."

"But you do tell me when I err," Ian said with an almost comical grimace.

"Aye, sure, I do. That is one consequence of your mistake. But you will note that I rarely intervene beforehand to prevent you from *making* the mistake."

"In point of fact, sir, I have noted that and cursed you for it more than once when I thought that you *might* have warned me," Ian said dryly. "It occurs to me, however, that you have not given me a clout for some time now."

"Your decisions and judgment have improved, lad. And you have gained more confidence withal. The result is that you think and act more swiftly and more decisively, which gives the men that you command more confidence in you."

"They don't always show it."

"What do you do when they don't?" Fin asked him.

Ian smiled. "I seek advice from you, of course."

"Then you and I discuss the matter privately between us, aye. But, sithee, if a man is always wondering what a mentor would say or do, he slows down the whole process of deciding, which would be fatal error in battle. But by watching and learning from others' mistakes and talking over things that don't go as you thought they would, you also learn just what sort of leader you *want* to be."

"I think I ken that fine now, sir," Ian said with a direct look.

"Aye, well, we'll see. Meantime, I will not need you in the morning, so you may catch up on your sleep unless Toby can use your help."

Ian nodded and ten minutes later, Fin was alone in the dark room.

It was some time, though, before he slept. He could still taste Catriona's lips and feel her supple, curvaceous, warm body in his arms. That feeling faded, though, as his thoughts about her took him in another direction.

Having concluded that he had to tell her about his part in the battle at Perth and what happened there, he tried to imagine how to tell her the truth in a way that would not make her loathe him. As he did, it occurred to him that the minute he told her that he had been at Perth, she would know that that was where he and Ivor had had the one meeting that they had admitted having since their St. Andrews days.

Strangely, the urgency of resolving his dilemma had faded.

He no longer felt it looming, waiting for his guard to fall so that his conscience—or the presence of his father that he felt so often in his mind—could pummel him for failing to fulfill his sacred bequest.

At first, while he had spoken so loftily to Ian about learning to make good decisions, he had felt as if Teàrlach MacGillony's ghost were waiting to leap to life and fling lightning bolts at him by way of reproaches.

Instead, that talk seemed to have eased his sense of urgency more.

⁓

After Ailvie had retired to her own cot, Catriona lay in bed trying to sort out her thoughts about Fin. For a time, she let herself dwell on memories of their kiss and thoughts of where he might be imagining it could lead. Was that why he wanted to walk with her? Did he think that she would marry him and let him take her away, only to leave her in Lochaber with his people when he rode off to knightly duties?

What manner of man was he, exactly?

Thinking again of what he and Ivor had said about St. Andrews, she decided that the information was of no aid to her in figuring out what was going on at Rothiemurchus. They had been boys then, not men involved in dangerous acts.

Both were knights, experienced in battle. And they had met once since St. Andrews under circumstances that kept them from learning each other's true names.

Her next thought followed easily but startled her so that she could scarcely think beyond it. She could imagine only one event that might have allowed such a meeting, and if it had, no wonder they did not trust her to keep silent.

If they had met in battle and Fin had tried to kill Ivor, or Ivor to kill Fin...

What would her father or mother think of that? Or her grandparents!

But if the two men had forgiven each other...

She tried to think more about that, but her thoughts drifted ahead to the morning walk she would have with Fin. She wondered if he would swim again. That thought stirred the sensations she had felt when he kissed her on the stairs, and she let her thoughts linger again on the image of him walking naked on the shore.

She wondered how it would feel to swim with him, to hug him underwater, to feel his skin all damp and slick, to touch him all over and let him touch her.

Familiar scratching at the door rudely jerked her from her fantasy.

Getting up, she let Boreas into the room, chuckling at the sight of the tiny shadow scrambling onto the landing behind him and dashing after the dog into the room. By the time she had climbed back into bed and blown out her candle, both were lying beside the bed, the dog curled around the kitten, the kitten expressing its satisfaction with a purr much louder than its size seemed to warrant.

Catriona shut her eyes to return to her fantasy only to awaken earlier than usual with a start and an exploding fear that she was late, that Fin would already have gone out and come back in. A look out the window reassured her.

The sky had lightened, but the sun had not peeked over the mountains.

Flinging on her blue kirtle, she decided not to waken

Ailvie but whisked her shawl across her shoulders and hurried out to the yard with Boreas and his tiny friend following in their own fashion. They crossed the yard, and when a man-at-arms stepped forward, she said, "Prithee open the gate. I am going for a walk."

"Aye, sure, m'lady. With all these other louts about, ye should ken that Sir Finlagh be out there somewhere. Likely, he'll keep an eye to your safety."

Until he spoke, she had not considered that he might try to stop her, but she knew she ought to have brought Ailvie. Her father would say so. But her grandfather had let her walk outside the wall with Fin, so perhaps Shaw would not object.

Fin was but one man, after all. And she could take care of herself.

Boreas loped past her, and as her gaze followed him, she saw Fin striding toward her. An urge stirred for her to run to him. To stifle it, she reached down for the kitten, but it eluded her grasp and darted madly after the dog.

Grinning, Fin stopped to watch them, and as she approached him, he said, "I have seen odder friends, I expect. But Boreas does seem to take adoration in stride."

"He does, and at times to the kitten's grief. It likes to chase his feet and when it darts after his forepaws, it sometimes gets kicked by the hind ones and goes flying."

"I trust you slept well," he said.

Remembering her fantasies before she slept and the lingering remnants of at least one dream, she felt heat flood her cheeks as it had the night before.

To divert his attention, lest he ask again about the fire in them, she said, "Did you and Ivor meet in battle, sir? Is that why you would not tell me more about it?"

Fin decided that the lass was either a witch or far too observant and quick-witted for any man's peace of mind.

That her blushes had made him want to grab her and kiss her did little to ease his disquiet. He had not meant to begin his explanation with the battle.

To gain time, he said, "What makes you think that?"

"She cocked her head. "You are called Fin of the Battles, are you not? And both of you are knights. Moreover, you said that the place and time precluded your learning each other's true names. What is more likely than that you met in battle?"

Resigned, he said, "We did meet in battle, aye, at the end of it to be precise."

"Faith, did you fight each other?"

"We did not."

"But if you were fighting on the same side, then surely—"

"We were not on the same side," he said. "Let us walk farther from the castle, lass. If we are going to fratch over this, I'd liefer not do it before an audience of your father's men on that wall."

"Are we likely to fratch?"

"I don't know. You will decide that."

She nodded, and they walked in silence until they reached the woodland.

Then he said, "Since you apparently forgot to bring your maidservant, should we stop where they can still see us, or may we enter the woods?"

"We can go into the woods," she said. "My grandfather trusts you, and I expect my father has decided to trust you, too. Sithee, the guard at the gate told me that despite the extra men at the castle, I would be safe out here with you."

"Did he, in troth?"

Nodding again, she led the way into the woods and along the path they had taken before. As they walked, he wondered what sort of game the Mackintosh and Shaw might be playing that they would allow him such liberty with her. Did they put so much faith in the truce between the two confederations?

That they trusted him at all was disconcerting, since the Mackintosh knew his identity and had surely told Shaw at the first opportunity. In Fin's experience, other people's trust often created a strong and, at times, even burdensome sense of responsibility. In light of the dilemma he had long carried, however, such trust from the Mackintosh men would, he knew, be a heavier burden than usual.

When he and Catriona came to the old raft leaning against the tree, she stopped and faced him. "Now, sir, prithee explain yourself."

He raised his eyebrows, but she met the look steadily.

"Shall we sit?" he asked, gesturing toward a fallen tree with a trunk thick enough to let them both sit easily.

"Just tell me when and where you and Ivor met."

"Nay, now. I'll tell you, but I'll tell it in my own way. By my troth, I meant to tell you, in any event. 'Tis the reason that I asked you to walk with me today."

"It is?" She eyed him narrowly. "*That* is the reason?"

He returned her look with one of his own. "Sakes, what else did you think? I told you I'd explain it when I could, that I just needed to talk more with Ivor first."

"Some might think that you two just needed to get your story straight."

"*Might* they? Then I am glad that you do not number amongst them."

"What makes you think I do not?"

"People who leap to such conclusions are usually not trustworthy themselves, lass. Since you insist that you are entirely trust—"

"Enough, sir. I should not have said what I did. I just did not want to tell you what I'd thought. But neither will I let you divert me further from the point."

"Aye, well, I won't press you then," he said. "But I do think that we will be more comfortable if we sit."

"I don't *want* you to be comfortable. I want to know."

"Aye, well…" He paused. "Sithee, the Bishop of St. Andrews—"

"Bishop Traill."

"Aye. He taught us more than our numbers and letters."

"You told me that. He and his minions also taught you weaponry."

"Aye, and tactics of war from Roman times onward. But more than any of that, he taught us the great and lasting value of strong friendships."

"Such as the friendship that you have with Ivor?"

"Aye," he said and saw her relax as he said it. "Now sit, lass, do. I'll tell you what you want to know, but I can tell it more easily—aye, and more clearly, too—if you do not quiz me or eye me like a wildcat about to seize its prey."

She chuckled then and moved to sit at the far end of the log, where she could lean against an upturned limb. As she did, she said, "I'm thinking this may have to do with the talk we had about blind obedience the first day we came here. Does it?"

Having expected her to question him more about what

he had said that day, Fin had decided that since she did not understand about honor, she had dismissed all he had said then as just another knight's tale. Doubtless she had heard many such from the men in her family, because tales of combat were common at tables and feasts throughout the Highlands and had been since their earliest days.

To learn that she remembered what he had said about blind obedience gave him pause, because he'd forgotten exactly what he had said then. They had talked both while walking to the outflow and later there in the woods. Remembering, he said, "It does relate to that talk, but there is much that I did not tell you."

"One thing in particular that you did say has remained with me."

"What is it?" he asked with a sinking feeling.

"You said that sometimes one agrees to something just because one respects and trusts the person asking him to agree. Did you mean that a man might, in such a case, agree to do something that otherwise he would *not* do?"

Certain now that she had put blind obedience together with the dilemma he had described to her that day, Fin looked skyward. But he saw no answer there.

Meeting her calm gaze, he said, "This conversation is not going as I had hoped. Nay, do not speak yet," he added hastily when her mouth opened. "Sithee, I can imagine what will happen if I try to answer your questions as they occur to you. So I would ask a boon of you, one that I am not sure you are even able to grant me."

She cocked her head. "What boon?"

"That you will let me explain the matter in my own way first, without interrupting, and then—"

"But—" When he held up a hand, she broke off, smiling ruefully. "I am not good at holding my tongue when I want to know something," she said.

"Doubtless, nearly anything I tell you now will stir questions in your mind," he said. "So, prithee, let me have my say first. By the time I've finished, I'll likely have told you most of what you want to know."

"What if I don't understand something that you say?"

"If I truly confuse you, tell me. But if you keep stopping me with questions, I'll be unable to explain the thing clearly and we'll just fratch over one thing or another. Then, I'll get angry, or you will get angry with me."

Her mouth twisted wryly before she said with a sigh, "I will try, sir. But that is all I can promise."

"'Tis enough, lass. I know that I can trust you to hold your tongue unless you simply cannot bear to do so any longer."

Her eyebrows shot upward. "Some people would call that statement no more than a sop to ensure that I keep silent."

"Would they?"

"I think you know gey well that *I* think so, aye."

"Shall we see if it works?"

Chuckling again in a way that both relieved his mind and made him want to snatch her off her log and hug her, she settled back and was silent.

Still on his feet, he said, "Since you deduced that Ivor and I met during battle, I will begin with that, although our meeting did not redound to my credit. Sithee, we were still standing but few others were. I was the only one, in fact, on my side."

Her lips moved as if she would speak, but she pressed them hard together.

Drawing breath, he said, "Ivor left his people and came

toward me. He told me last night that he was unsure then of my identity but suspected it and recognized me before he got close. I expected to have to fight him…sakes, to fight all of them who were still able to wield a sword or a dirk. Instead, he told me to leave."

Her mouth opened, but she clapped a hand across it.

Amusement stirred at such determination but quickly died. He had come to the point where he must face her reaction to what he had done.

"I dove into the river and swam away." He made the admission, forcing himself to meet her gaze, trying to prepare himself for the scorn he would see.

She continued to gaze steadily at him over the hand at her mouth.

He waited. His stomach clenched. He shifted his feet.

The silence lengthened beyond bearing.

At last, she lowered the hand that had covered her mouth. "Is that all?" she said. When he nodded, she said, "But where did you go?"

"To St. Andrews."

"Why?"

Not so easy, that question. The truth was that he had gone to Bishop Traill, hoping that Traill would tell him what he must do to find an honorable answer to his dilemma. But Traill had failed him.

He knew that he could not explain all that to her, just as he knew that he had already—albeit without knowing as much—decided that he could *not* kill her father.

Shaw was not only the Clan Chattan war leader. He was also her father and Hawk's. All that Fin had heard about Shaw, and what he had seen of him so far, he respected. He respected the Mackintosh, too. Moreover, both men had trusted him with something very precious to them, Catriona herself.

Since he was explaining any of it, part of him insisted that he ought to tell her everything. As he tried to imagine how he could best describe the dilemma he had faced, another, perhaps wiser voice suggested that he would simply be sharing a burden with her that was his alone to carry. The voice was so strong that he decided to heed its counsel long enough to consider longer before he told her.

She was frowning, waiting for him to explain why he had gone to St. Andrews. But that only made it more difficult, because he did not want to lie.

Suddenly, her brow cleared. "God-a-mercy!" she exclaimed. "*That* is why you asked if I thought a man who hated war must be a coward. *You* acted without thinking, and now you think that the act was cowardly! But you fled because Ivor told you to, so *that* is what you meant about agreeing to an act simply because you trusted the one who had told you to do it!"

Fin could not speak. He had not meant that at all. He had been trying to admit that the dilemma he'd once described to her was his own and explain that he had sworn to the second oath because his dying father had demanded it. But he realized as emotions surged through him that he could not tell her she was wrong. She wasn't. He *had* left when Ivor had said to go because he had trusted Ivor.

But that did not alter the fact of his having left the field as he had.

He looked so shocked that Catriona could not bear it. "Ah, poor laddie," she said then, softly. "You do believe that your leaving in such a way was cowardly. That is why you wanted to discuss war and cowardice."

"You don't understand, lass," he said. "Leaving in such a way *was*—"

His voice cracked, revealing the emotion he felt over what he had so clearly feared was an issue she believed that only a man could think was important.

Still speaking softly, because she knew how important the subject was to him, she said, "Men often say that women don't understand them. But I do understand about men and cowardice, and even about their sometimes strange notions of honor. You should think instead about what the outcome would have been had you not done as Ivor told you to do."

"I would have died, but I would have died honorably."

"Don't be stupid; dying is dying," she said, wishing she could hug him. "Had you died, you would not be here. Had you died, Rory Comyn would have found me alone on the trail that day." She nearly added that Boreas would have killed Rory, but that would not aid her argument. Standing, she moved closer to Fin. "Did I not say that life is always the right choice? Had you stayed, Ivor would have felt obliged to kill you. How honorable would it have been to put your good friend in *that* position?"

His mouth twitched as if he would protest, but he did not.

"What?" she demanded, confronting him toe-to-toe. "Are you now afraid to tell me what you are thinking?"

"Nay, but you won't like it. Honor would have demanded that I kill Ivor."

"You could not. He is a *very* fine swordsman. Moreover," she added as a clincher, "if you had killed him, the others would have killed you. Aye, and it has just occurred to me that this battle of which you speak is likely the clan battle at Perth, and Clan Chattan ended that battle with eleven men still living, did we not?"

"Eleven *living*, aye, but not—" He broke off when she put a finger to his lips.

"Hush now, for you will not persuade me," she said. "You could not have killed so many, nor must you forget that had *you* died that day, Rothesay would not be having his so-important meeting here now, and I would never have met you. To think that for years I believed I hated *all* Camerons. But I find now that I do not."

He caught hold of her hand, but he did not speak. He just gazed down into her eyes as if he might read more of her thoughts there.

"Just what the *devil* do you two think you are doing?"

Catriona whirled to see her brother James standing on the trail that they had followed from the castle. He stood with arms akimbo, looking very angry.

Chapter 10 _____

Fin took one look at James and stepped away from Catriona. As he did, he said quietly, "There is nowt occurring here to trouble you, sir."

"Faith, but you have drawn a conclusion that insults us both, James," Catriona said. "Did you come seeking us for any other purpose?"

Seeing fury leap to James's face, Fin set himself to intervene if necessary. But Catriona remained calm, clearly awaiting an answer to her question.

At last, after a measuring look at each of them, James visibly relaxed. "The lad at the gate said that you had come this way. I just wondered...that is, I thought you might have walked out with Morag, Cat. It surprised me to see you with him."

"The guard at the gate did *not* tell you that I was with Morag."

"Nay, nay," James protested. "I didn't say that. I never asked him about Morag. Sithee, I awoke and she was gone, but I did not want the lad thinking that summat was amiss with her, so—"

"Amiss betwixt the two of you is what you mean, I think," she said gently.

Fin nearly uttered a protest. That subject was not one that she should initiate in his presence.

James shot her a dour look, then turned to Fin and said frankly, "I do owe you an apology. I ought to have thought a bit before speaking so sharply."

Extending his hand, Fin said, "'Tis generous of you to apologize, sir. Had I come upon my sister in such a pose, I'd likely have reacted as you did. You have my word, though, that nowt was amiss."

Gripping his hand, James said, "I'll willingly accept it. My grandfather told me who you are, so I expect that you do understand my reaction."

Catriona said, "You say that as if you did not know his identity before, James. But I told you and Ivor about him soon after you arrived here yesterday."

"Ye did, aye," James said, his gaze locked now with Fin's. "But you told us his name was Sir Finlagh MacGill, lass. So clearly, you did not know everything."

Fin's glance flicked to Catriona, but she was still watching James.

She said, "I know all I need to know. He schooled with Ivor at St. Andrews and he fought on the Cameron side at Perth. He has not kept secrets from me, sir. I did used to think that being a Cameron must be a dreadful thing, but only until I came to know him. The truce between our two confederations still holds, does it not?"

"For the most part, aye," James agreed, meeting Fin's gaze again. "Did he tell you that his father was the Camerons' war leader at Perth?"

"Aye, of course, he did," Catriona lied stoutly. "Now, prithee, let be, sir. Come to that, if Morag is missing, you must find her."

"She makes it plain that she does not want to be found," James said bluntly.

"Nonsense, sir. No woman hides without wanting to be found, and Morag has missed you sorely. I fear she still feels like a stranger here, so she does not confide in us. Still, you must have done something to vex her. Do you know what it was?"

"Sakes, Cat, what man ever understands why a woman does such a thing?"

"Has she *told* you how much she has missed you?"

"Aye, sure, any number of times."

"How did you reply to her?"

James flushed and looked helplessly at Fin, but Fin knew better than to enter such a conversation without a stronger invitation than that.

The older man turned back to his sister. "Cat, we should not—"

"I do have reason for asking, sir. So, unless you said something dreadful..."

Shrugging, he said, "I told her I was doing my duty, of course. I explained that I'd had no say in how long I'd be away and would likely go again before long."

"I knew it!" Shaking her head at him, she added, "Dafty, you should have told her that you love her and missed her even more than you'd feared you would."

"But—"

"Nay, don't explain it to me. Go and find Morag. Talk to *her*."

"And say such mawkish things to her? Sakes, what would my men think?"

"Morag is *not* going to repeat to your men what you

say to her. But if you do not take more heed of your wife, sir, you may soon find yourself without one."

"Aye, well, you'd best come inside with me then, the pair of you," James said. "You'll want to break your fast, after all."

"I am getting hungry, aye," Catriona admitted.

Fin said, "We'll be along directly, sir. You won't want us at your heels if you should meet your lady wife, seeking you."

Catriona looked at him, and Fin knew that she had detected his annoyance.

The hard note in Fin's voice had startled Catriona, but recalling his strong sense of honor, she suspected why he had spoken so. She waited until James had vanished into the woods before she said, "I think I know why you are—"

"Don't lie for me again," he said curtly. "I did *not* tell you that my father was our war leader that dreadful day."

"Nay, but he had naught to do with your dive into the river, and I knew by your own words that you must be a Cameron, so I do not see that it matters."

"Even so, you must not lie to your brother, lass, and *never* to protect me."

"But I did not do it for you. I did it because I was sure when he apologized to you that he was going to start telling me that *I* should know better than to have come here *with* you. When he starts telling me how I should behave—" A thought struck her, making her grin ruefully. "Sakes, I expect that's just what I did to him!"

"Aye, it was," he agreed.

"Then I will apologize to you for making you a witness to what I said to him. But I assure you that had I admitted that you had *not* told me about your father, James would still be explaining at ponderous length why you should have done so."

"Mayhap he would," Fin said. "I would like to know, however, if you would have spoken as impertinently to Ivor as you did to him."

Feeling a sudden urge to laugh but aware that it might still be unwise, she said frankly, "I think you know very well that I would dare to scold Ivor so only if I were far enough away to escape to safety, and *never* this close to the water."

His eyes twinkled then, but he said, "I should perhaps warn you that I do not react well to such impertinence, either."

"Do you not? But then you have no right to treat me as Ivor would, do you?"

Meeting her gaze, he said, "I suspect that the men in your family would sympathize more with me than with you if you made me angry enough to toss you into that loch. Or do you think I'm wrong about that?"

Since he clearly knew that he was right, she said, "I'm thinking that if we do not go inside soon, someone will look for us."

When he chuckled, she stuck out her tongue at him.

～

Entering the hall with Catriona, Fin saw at once that the lady Morag sat at the high table with the ladies Ealga and Annis.

Catriona had also seen her good-sister and was frowning. He nearly asked why before he realized that James was nowhere in sight.

"He will think to look here eventually," he murmured to her.

"Do you think so? I can tell you, sir, men are rarely wise enough to look in the most likely places. Moreover, I'd wager that he looked here before he went outside, just as she knew he would."

"Is she so calculating then?"

"Faith, I scarcely know her. She and James have been married for nearly two years, but Morag does not talk much about herself. When she does, she talks most often about her home in the Great Glen, and her family."

"Have you tried to draw her out?" he asked.

"Aye, sure. That is, at first I did, and I do try to be kind. But she barely talks to me, or to anyone else, come to that. Surely, you have seen as much for yourself."

"Sakes, lass, I've taken no particular interest in the lady Morag. Only think how James would react if I did."

She shrugged. "In troth, sir, I don't know how he would react. But he would not react as Ivor would—or you, perhaps, if you were married."

"Most men react fiercely to those who show unseemly interest in their women," he said. "I doubt that James would behave differently."

"Do you?" She looked speculatively at Morag. "I think I should have a talk with her." Turning back to him, she added, "Thank you for telling me about Perth. Ivor would never have told me so much."

"I know that, aye. I also know," he added quietly, "that you might be wiser to let James and the lady Morag resolve their private differences privately."

"Wise or not, I do think she should know that James cares about her."

He shook his head at her, but even had he wanted to debate the point, Rothesay was on the dais beside their host, gesturing for him to join them.

Parting from Catriona when they stepped onto the dais, Fin went around the men's end of the table, past Ivor and Shaw, to the duke.

"Where the devil have you been?" Rothesay demanded. "Your wound looks to be nearly healed, but you vanished so early last night that I wondered if it was still troubling you. Your squire did say, though, that you had gone out this morning."

"I have recovered, sir, and I did walk about outside the wall," Fin said.

"Och, aye, I do recall now that you like to swim," Rothesay said.

"Did you seek me for a particular purpose, my lord?"

"Nay, I have these others to attend my needs, so your duties at present will be light. When Donald and Alex arrive—doubtless, later today—I want you to sit in on our talks if they keep their men with them. I trust both of *them* but not those who toady to them. So I'll want to know where to find you when I want you, Fin. Don't wander off again without letting me know where you'll be."

"Aye, sir," Fin said. Accepting a nod as dismissal, he took the seat that Ivor indicated beside him. Smiling, Fin said to him, "I trust that you slept all night."

"I did," Ivor said, giving him a shrewd look. "I begin to think that you and my irrepressible sister have grown to be fast friends. Is that so?"

"Do you wonder because we just now came into the hall together?"

"Nay, I wonder because you walked into the woods together."

"I see. You do know that she very likely saved my life, do you not?"

"I know that she found you bleeding all over the scenery in the upper glen and brought you home with her," Ivor said. "Art sure that she saved your life?"

"I am sure that it was a Comyn who shot me. I doubt that his arrow was a message of friendship."

"Rory Comyn?"

"Aye. Sithee, we met him on the loch shore the next day, and he's a smirker. So, if he did not shoot me, I'd wager that he ordered it done. What I do not know is if he did it out of a jealous belief that your sister was coming to meet me or because he knows why I came to the Highlands."

"He's a mischief maker," Ivor said. "He would need little reason."

Nodding, Fin changed the topic, saying, "Catriona and I met James outside, and he said that your grandfather had told him about me. Did he tell you as well?"

"We talked this morning," Ivor said. "He suspected that you'd studied with Traill when you told my grandame that you'd lived in eastern Fife. There is not much there, after all, other than St. Andrews—the town, the kirk, and the castle. So he did think that we might know each other. But I'd told him years ago that none of us knew which clans our fellow students hailed from, let alone their real names."

"I wonder if he will tell Rothesay. Sakes, mayhap Traill told him from the start. In any event, I expect he'll know one way or another soon enough."

"More to the point, my lad, since you've been serving Davy these past years, does this all mean that your family may not even know that you survived at Perth?"

Fin said, "I could say I've been too busy to travel so far before now. 'Tis close enough to the truth, but it is also true that I did not want to tell Ewan *how* I'd survived. I do mean to go home from here, though. So I'll have to tell Rothesay."

"If you'll take some advice..." Ivor paused.

"From you, always," Fin said.

"You will know how to tell your brother, but you should assume that Traill has told Rothesay everything. His reverence did not become Bishop of St. Andrews by keeping secrets from his royal patrons. He served as confessor for both the King and Queen, and doubtless for Rothesay and even Albany. I'd wager that Traill told Rothesay to make good use of you but otherwise to let you go your own road."

"You may be right," Fin acknowledged. "I own, I just assumed that Rothesay did not know, because he has always made a point of calling me Fin of the Battles and introduces me as such whenever he presents me to anyone."

"Aye, well, the one thing I do know about Davy Stewart is that he delights in secrets and can be gey good at keeping them. The only time he does not like them is when others act in secret against him."

"As Albany is doubtless doing now," Fin said.

⁓

Catriona took her place beside Morag, trying to decide if the older girl had been crying. Morag's expressions were so slight that it was always hard to read them.

Aware that Ealga was talking with Lady Annis, Catriona leaned close to Morag and murmured, "James is looking for you."

"Is he?" Morag said without looking at her. "He must know gey well that I come here to break my fast."

"Of course, he does," Catriona said, striving to conceal sudden impatience. "I'd wager that he looked here before he went out to the woods."

"*Did* he go outside the wall?" Morag signed to a gillie to pour ale into her goblet. "How do you know that he did?"

"I saw him, of course, and he asked if I had seen you. Look here, Morag, I know that you don't like me—"

"When did you come to think that?"

"Good sakes, you scarcely ever speak to me unless I speak first. And then you talk as if you are annoyed that I have disturbed you. What else should I think?"

Morag gave a shrug. "I expect you are right then."

"Are you angry with James?"

"Should I be?"

Catriona's temper stirred sharply. But courtesy and the present royal company required that she keep it in check. Forcing calm into her voice, she said, "He thinks that you are angry with him and do not want him to find you."

"I am a dutiful wife," Morag said. "A dutiful wife does not hide from her husband. Moreover, I should find it gey hard to do, since I cannot get off this island without permission from your grandfather, your father, or from James himself."

"God-a-mercy, you are furious. What did he do to deserve such anger?"

"Why nothing at all," Morag said. "How could he

have done aught to displease me when he stayed with the Mackintosh yestereve until long after I had fallen asleep? One assumes that they were drinking whisky with the other men."

"I see," Catriona said.

"I warrant you do. But James does not."

"Nay, for he told me what he said to you when you told him you had missed him," Catriona said with a sympathetic sigh.

"So he told you that, did he? Well, if he is going to share our private converse with you, there can be no need for me to tell you anything more."

"Morag, James is an ass, and so I told him. But he *does* love you."

Morag looked at her then, her pale blue eyes widening.

Catriona saw tears welling in them before Morag looked away again.

~

After they had broken their fast, Ivor said to Fin, "I mean to reacquaint myself with Strathspey today, and I'll take my bow. Do you want to come?"

Knowing that Rothesay would hold no meeting until Donald of the Isles and Alex of the North arrived, Fin accepted with alacrity.

As soon as he had spoken with Rothesay, the two friends took bows and quivers and rowed to the west shore. From there, they hiked to the river Spey and along its bank to a field where Ivor said they could get some good practice.

Returning to Rothiemurchus late that afternoon after exploring much of the countryside, they discovered that during their absence, Donald and Alex had both arrived.

To Fin's astonishment, it appeared that the burly, bearded, forty-year-old Donald and his companions had traveled on garrons through the west Highlands with a mendicant friar, all six of them dressed in robes similar to the holy man's.

"A good disguise, especially at this season," Ivor observed. "One hopes that Donald will not try to sneak in an army under the same guise."

Laughing, Fin pointed out that an army of monks might stir some curiosity. His leisure time had ended, though, because Rothesay had left word that he wanted to see him straightway. Fin found him alone in the inner chamber.

"You are to be another pair of eyes and ears for me," Rothesay said. "Donald did support my taking the Governorship when I did, and Alex has nae love for Albany. Still, I've learned that I can trust any man only whilst his future depends on my success. Donald did come here, but he is ever surly, and I need his ships to curb Albany in the west. As to Alex..." He shrugged.

"He did raise an army of his own from throughout the North to support yours in the Borders," Fin reminded him. "Forbye, sir, both men are your close cousins."

"Aye, sure, so they're bound to support me," Rothesay said confidently.

However, when the household gathered soon afterward for supper in the great hall, Fin noted few signs of good cheer between the cousins. Rothesay was amiable enough, but burly, dark-haired Donald of the Isles seemed dour, even irritable.

Alex looked enough like his fair, blue-eyed cousin to be Davy's brother but was quieter by nature. He remained reticent and watchful, albeit courteous.

Doubtless to cheer them all, the Mackintosh suggested that Catriona or Morag might sing for them after supper. But Donald declared when he had finished eating that he had endured a long, tiresome day and would seek his bed.

Rothesay was wide awake. But since he chose to entertain himself by flirting with Catriona, Fin would have preferred him to follow Donald's example.

He was grateful when the lady Ealga engaged him in desultory conversation but noted that James disappeared with Morag and Ivor moved to talk with Alex.

Looking toward the latter two a few minutes later, he saw that Ivor was grimly eyeing Rothesay and Catriona. Alex, also watching the pair, looked amused.

Fin was not. In the short time that he had been a guest at the castle, he had come to think of Catriona as more than just a good friend, and he did not want Rothesay to offend her. When her father joined them and spoke to her, Fin was relieved and felt more so when the lass made her adieux shortly afterward.

The next morning after breakfast, the three powerful lords met with the Mackintosh in his inner chamber. Alex and Donald insisted that their companions accompany them, and Rothesay kept his two and Fin with him. Shaw, Ivor, and James also attended, so the chamber was crowded.

After an hour of discussing past events—such discussion at times growing testy—Rothesay said, "Our uncle Albany, as you all ken fine, resents having lost the Governorship and its attendant powers. He wants them back."

"And your provisional term as Governor o' the Realm expires in January, lad," Donald said. "We all ken *that* fine. But what has that to do wi' me?"

Fin knew that Donald considered himself as equal, if not superior, to the King of Scots. The Lord of the Isles descended from a much older dynasty, owned many more castles and hundreds more boats, not to mention the great administrative complex at Finlaggan on the Isle of Islay, which boasted a palatial residence larger than any noble or royal equivalent on the Scottish mainland.

Rothesay eyed him measuringly. "You and Alex know as well as I do how Albany ruled when he was Governor before, by amassing power wherever and however he could. He holds the treasury, uses it as his own, and is greedy withal, which affects everyone in Scotland. I want to curb him wherever I can."

"As ye should, Davy," Alex said, nodding. "But ye ken fine how long I ha' been away wi' ye. I canna leave the North to look after itself again so soon, lest our uncle Albany swoop in with an army. Or someone else does," he added dulcetly.

Fin glanced at the Lord of the Isles, as did a few others, but Donald's thick beard concealed his mouth and thus much of his expression. The talking went on, but both cousins remained elusive, willing to talk but unwilling to speak plainly.

Some of their adherents seemed to Fin to be trying to stir dissension.

His thoughts drifted to Catriona, and he wondered what she might be doing.

Catriona was busy. The great lords had brought companions with them, but they had not brought the host of servants one usually expected with visiting royalty.

Each nobleman had a manservant. But they looked after only their masters and expected castle servants or womenfolk to attend to anything akin to menial labor. Thus it was that she and Morag were in the kitchen, aiding the cook's minions with preparations for the midday meal.

The two barely had enough time when they finished to run upstairs and change their gowns, but Ailvie was waiting for Catriona, so the change took little time. After a final look at herself in the glass, she hurried back downstairs, slowing only as she approached the landing between her parents' room and Fin's.

She told herself that she was just protecting her dignity and did not want to risk running full tilt into one parent or another on the landing. If her gaze lingered on the closed door of Fin's room instead of on the one opposite, no voice, including the self-critical one in her head, spoke up to chide her.

Entering the hall to see that people were still gathering at the lower tables and on the dais, she paused now and again to speak to those who greeted her. When she stepped onto the dais, her gaze collided with Fin's, and something in the way he looked at her warmed her through.

Movement to his right drew her notice to Rothesay, Shaw, and her grandfather as they emerged from the inner chamber with Alex Stewart and Donald of the Isles.

Rothesay caught her eye then, and if Fin's expression had been warm, *his* was searing. Aware that she was blushing and that her grandfather or Shaw would notice if she lingered where she stood, she moved hastily to the women's end of the table and took the place that a smiling Morag had left for her beside Ealga.

As soon as Donald's real mendicant monk had muttered the grace and everyone had sat down, Catriona said to her mother, "Do you ken aught of what happened this morning, Mam?"

"I do not," Ealga said. "You know that your father rarely confides his business to me. And you know, too, that when he does, I do not talk about it after."

From Catriona's right, Morag said, "James did tell me that he thinks they will talk long before they find consensus. There are issues, he said, which seem to stir much disagreement and men amidst them who seem to encourage it."

"God-a-mercy, *James* told you all that?" Glancing at her mother to see that Ealga had turned to talk with Lady Annis, Catriona said, "What else did he say?"

Morag looked self-conscious. "I should not tell you. But I did want you to know that...that he will not be revealing our confidences to you anymore. And I must warn you that I told him what you said about him being an ass. I expect that was as bad as his telling you what I had said and what he had said to me, but—"

A gurgle of laughter welled in Catriona's throat, and some of it escaped as she said, "You may repeat whatever I say if it will help bring James to his senses."

Morag looked relieved, but she said, "Sithee, I think he was irritated, so he may scold you. And when James scolds one, it is most unpleasant, believe me."

Catriona stared at her. "Good sakes, do you mean to say that he is brutal to you? 'Tis hard for me to believe that."

"James is not brutal, but I do not like him to be angry with me."

Catriona bit her lower lip and then decided to say what she was thinking. "Look here, Morag, have you ever seen Ivor in a temper?"

"Nay, I am thankful to say that I have not. I have heard others say that he does naught to restrain himself but flies into a fury."

"I can be much the same way," Catriona admitted. "But, by my troth, Morag, compared to either of us in a temper, James is . . . is most temperate."

Morag did not look convinced. But for once, she did not fall silent. Instead, she continued to talk affably with Catriona.

When everyone had finished eating, Mackintosh asked Morag to take up her lute, and Catriona excused herself, saying that she had promised to look in on the kitchen. But as she stepped off the dais, Rothesay approached her, moving with near feline grace, his long strides covering ground with deceptive haste.

When he could speak without raising his voice, he said, "Prithee, lass, say that you are not abandoning us already. I would speak with you again, for I vow, you are the most beautiful creature I have laid eyes on in a twelvemonth."

Although she smiled with ready delight at the unexpected compliment, she saw her brother Ivor and Fin not far behind him. Both of them were frowning.

Recalling what her grandmother had said about Rothesay, she said, "I fear that you flatter me, my lord, but 'tis most kind."

"I am never kind, lassie, and I do know beauty when I see it," he said with what in any man, including a prince of the realm, was an impudent grin. "Prithee, do not be so cruel as to say that you will not walk with me."

He was, nevertheless, not only a prince of the realm but also one of vast power and known to use it recklessly.

Evenly, she said, "I am never cruel, sir."

"Then you will be generous, my lady," he said, grinning confidently.

Glancing beyond him again, she saw that although Rothesay might call her generous, both Ivor and Fin had other words in mind.

Chapter 11 ————————

God's teeth," Ivor swore, glowering. "Under any other circumstance, I'd soon teach my sister not to smile at such a man."

"But this is here and now," Fin said. "And the man flirting with her is a prince of the realm. So you'd be wise to take that fierce look off your face, my lad, before he sees it. Others are already looking this way."

"Sakes, do you condone his behavior? No matter who he is, he has no business to be taking liberties with my sister. God rot the man! He's married."

"And treats his wife badly, though she is sister to one of the most powerful lords in Scotland, so he is unlikely to care about your feelings," Fin said. "As to my condoning what Rothesay does, it is not my business to condone or condemn it."

"Fiend seize you then. I thought you *liked* Cat."

"Don't be daft," Fin retorted. "Whether I like her or not has nowt to do with Rothesay. Nor would his knowing that I like her curb his impulses. Sakes, man, I serve him. He does not let powerful *husbands* interfere with him when he flirts with their wives—aye, and does more than flirt with most of them, come to that."

"So those tales are true, are they?" Ivor said grimly.

"He is the heir to the throne and dangerously personable," Fin said. "Women adore his handsome face and that devilish Stewart charm. I have never known one he favors to complain about his behavior in bed. On the contrary..."

Ivor made a sound perilously near a growl.

Glancing at the Mackintosh, Fin was surprised to see the old man eyeing him speculatively. Touching Ivor's arm, he said, "Your grandfather is watching us, and he will not thank you if you cause trouble with Rothesay. So control that temper of yours, my lad, and look elsewhere before you land us both in the briars."

"Wouldn't be the first time that happened," Ivor said, his lips twitching.

The bare hint of a smile was welcome and let Fin relax.

When Morag took up her lute, James joined them. "I have news," he said.

Ivor raised his eyebrows, and Fin said, "Would you like me to step away?"

"Nay, you should stay," James said. "'Tis just that I mean to take my lady wife home to visit her family. She misses them sorely and"—he looked at Fin—"she has missed me, as well. Father agrees that my presence or the lack of it cannot influence the outcome of these talks, and my grandfather said I'd do better to indulge my lady wife for a time whilst I can."

With a wry smile, Ivor said, "I'll admit, I'd go with you in a twinkling."

"Nay, you will not. Why should you?"

"Because today's proceedings bored me nigh to lunacy.

You'd think they were playing a game, each afraid that some other might gain a point."

"To them, it *is* something of a game," Fin said. "But before Rothesay can summon Parliament, he wants to know that he will retain the Governorship. To do that, he desperately needs Donald's support, Alex's, and the votes of every other lord in Parliament who supports either of them."

Ivor said, "I can see that Alex will play his hand as he always does, thinking only of keeping the Lordship of the North firmly in his own hands."

"But Donald wants more than keeping *his* Lordship, aye?" James said.

"Donald is a deep one," Fin pointed out. "However, we all know that he covets at least one vast area of the Highlands, and Rothesay has said that if Donald gets even a toe in the Highlands, he'll seek next to rule all of Scotland."

"You know Davy better than we do, Fin," Ivor said. "Do you trust him?"

Quietly, knowing that Davy had already annoyed Ivor and hoping Ivor would not take further offense, Fin said, "He has given me no cause to be disloyal to him."

"But you don't think he is always wise, do you," Ivor said, making it a statement rather than a question and watching him closely.

Fin did not reply.

Ivor nodded, satisfied.

To anyone else, Fin might have equivocated to protect the man he served. But he would not lie to Hawk.

As if to break the brief tension that had enveloped them, Ivor looked at James and said, "Do you and Morag leave straightway?"

"Granddad said that that would be rude, since everyone just got here. So I expect we'll wait a day or two. But my lass is eager to see her family, and I confess that I am just as eager to have her to myself. Granddad said that we should spend a night at Castle Moigh on our way."

They continued to chat until Ivor, who had been looking periodically around the chamber, suddenly swore under his breath.

Catriona was well aware of Ivor's black looks. At one time she had feared that Fin might be unable to restrain him, especially since Fin himself had looked rather peeved. Then James had joined them, and all three men immersed themselves in conversation. Only Ivor kept glancing her way.

She had ignored him, certain that he would cause no disturbance as long as the Mackintosh and her father were present. They, too, were talking, but neither one had heeded her for some time.

The other ladies chatted together, too. Morag seemed still cheerful, a fact that spurred Catriona to look at James again.

"Tell me, lass, do you often ignore your admirers, or is my tale boring you?"

Sure that she must be flushing to the roots of her hair, she looked hastily at Rothesay, smiled, and said, "I heard you plainly, sir. But you should be ashamed of yourself for telling me such a bawdy tale. I am, after all, a maiden whose ears have seldom been sullied so."

His eyebrows flew upward. "Seldom?"

Chuckling, she said, "I do have brothers, sir, and very sharp ears."

He laughed then, and she felt relief so strong that she wondered at it. Did she fear his displeasure so much that she welcomed his smiles?

He put a hand on her shoulder and bent near enough to whisper in her ear, "Your ears may be sharp, lass, but they are likewise beautiful—shell-like, soft, and pink. I would tickle them with my tongue and then kiss them thoroughly."

She'd stiffened immediately at his touch, but he pretended not to notice. Would he dare do as he'd said? She feared that he would if she did not stop him.

Glancing at Fin, she saw that he and Ivor were both looking her way, the latter with as black a look as she had ever seen on him.

Fin put a restraining hand on Ivor's arm, but Catriona could see that she would be wise to act before they did.

Accordingly, she said evenly, "Unless you want my father to send me to my chamber as he did yestereve, sir, you will take your hand from my shoulder. I do also suggest that you refrain from whispering such things into my ear...or any other things, come to that. My brother is already watching us, and his temper—"

Giving her shoulder a squeeze, he said, "I have heard of Sir Ivor's temper. It will not trouble me."

"Mayhap it will not, but he would be wroth with me. And my grandfather would flay me, my lord, if I should cause strife between you and anyone else in my family. If you look, you will see my good-sister coming even now to collect me."

Withdrawing his hand from her shoulder, he turned with his entrancing smile to Morag, but Morag was oblivious to it or trying to pretend that she was.

In any event, Catriona also noted that Shaw had joined Fin and Ivor.

Greeting Morag, she said to Rothesay, "I am sure you do remember my good-sister, Lady James Mackintosh, sir."

"Forgive me for intruding, my lord," Morag said as she curtsied, keeping her eyes downcast until she arose and looked at Catriona. "Your father did say that I should tell you it is time for us to retire from the hall, Catriona. Your mother and grandmother have gone to the solar. We are to join them there."

Relieved, Catriona curtsied and politely bade Rothesay goodnight.

As she arose, he leaned toward her with a merry smile and said, "I'll excuse you for now, lass. But I will look forward to seeing you again tomorrow."

Knowing that she was blushing furiously, and taking care not to look toward the men again lest she see her father's angry frown as well as Ivor's, Catriona linked arms with Morag and urged her to some speed.

"What were you thinking to let him flirt with you so?" Morag demanded as they headed for the main stairway.

"Sakes, one does not *let* the heir to Scotland's throne flirt with one, Morag. How would you suggest that I might have stopped him?"

"Why, by walking away when he takes liberties, of course, as one would with any impertinent young man."

"Is that what you would do?" Catriona asked her.

Morag opened her mouth as if to insist that she would. Then an arrested look told Catriona that her good-sister's thoughts had at last caught up with her tongue.

"You would not be so rude to any member of the royal family," she said.

"But James would say—"

"I ken fine what James would say and what Ivor *will* say as soon as he finds opportunity. But if they are so concerned about our safety, they ought to stay closer to us when we are in the hall. Rothesay is a prince of the realm, after all."

"Aye, he is, and I think the plain truth is that you were just flattered by his attentions. He is the sort who expects all females to swoon when he enters a room, and I have no patience with such. Thank heaven James is not like him."

"That is certainly undeniable," Catriona replied. Glancing over her shoulder as they reached the archway into the stairwell, she saw that while her father was talking with Ivor and James, Fin was looking at her.

He did not look angry, but nor did he smile. He looked stunned.

~

As Fin dwelt on a clear image of himself wringing Davy's neck, it abruptly dawned on him that he cared much more about Catriona than he had let himself believe. That he had no right to care so strongly struck him even harder.

He had concluded that he could not kill Shaw and that it would not be fair to tell her he had ever believed that he must. But to act on his feelings and leave the fact of the bequest unspoken would be the same as living with a lie between them.

What she would call his daft sense of honor would *drive* him daft under such circumstances. Even if he could tell her and make her understand, and if her family would allow him to court her, he would still have to face his own family's outrage.

That he had fallen in love with a Mackintosh might pale in minds reeling from the fact that of all the Cameron champions at Perth, he alone had survived, and only because he had fled the field. But surely, they would still forbid such a marriage.

There was also Catriona's likely reaction. She had made it plain that she did not seek marriage and would resist one that threatened to take her from Strathspey. Although she clearly accepted him as a friend, after seeing her smile at Rothesay, he suspected unhappily that she might have been flirting with him, too.

His fertile imagination suddenly presented him with a picture of how he must look as he stood staring at the now empty archway, transfixed by his own thoughts. He had no notion how long he had stood so, but when he looked for Rothesay, he saw that he was talking with the Mackintosh and Alex Stewart.

Donald of the Isles stood some distance away near the fire, looking grim as usual, and conversing with the two nobles who had come with him to the castle.

Shaw stood with James behind the Mackintosh, and Ivor was striding toward Fin, looking grimly rueful. Recognizing the look, Fin knew that Ivor was still angry.

"I think she's in for a warm few minutes with my father," Ivor said with satisfaction when he was near enough.

"I'll wager he did not spare you either," Fin replied.

Ivor grimaced. "He reminded me that royal blood courses through Rothesay's veins and...well, he suggested that I should cool my spleen lest I try to let some of that blood and find myself on a royal gallows. Forbye, though, I reckon Albany would save my hide and reward me for the bloodletting."

"Perhaps," Fin said, unamused.

"You don't approve of such talk, I know. But royal or not, Davy Stewart is two years younger than we are, and his behavior would try the patience of Job."

"I don't approve of his behavior," Fin said. "But he is not stupid. He will do nowt to offend the Mackintosh whilst he has need of him."

"Perhaps, but I shan't have to endure what goes on in that meeting this afternoon. Father asked me to supervise the peat cutting instead."

Fin raised his eyebrows. "Punishment?"

"Nay." Ivor chuckled. "The bogs are dry enough now to resist swallowing the men who cut the peat and stack it. Cart ponies can finally find good footing, too. And James wants to arrange for his journey to Inverness and his packing. Sithee, my father always likes one of us to be at hand because trouble may occur."

"The Comyns?"

"They do help themselves to peat that someone else cuts, aye, whenever they can. But they are not alone in that habit," Ivor added. "We'll set a guard on our stacks when men on the road can see them. As the peat dries, we'll cart it up here."

"Where are these bogs?"

"Near the river," Ivor said. "Why, do you want to come with me?"

"Just curious, and wishful. Rothesay wants me to sit in the meetings. But so far, he has not asked what I think of it all, which is just as well."

"Aye, but that may change," Ivor said. "My da told me that Donald is irked with the lack of progress. That he has contributed to it does not faze him, of course. In any event, I'd rather be playing in the mud with our peat cutters."

Fin smiled. Ivor's afternoon did sound more interesting than his would be.

⁓

Catriona had feared that she would spend the afternoon listening to Morag exchange commonplaces with the ladies Ealga and Annis. But her mood changed when Tadhg brought Lady Ealga word that Sir Ivor would be out all afternoon.

"Master James will be about though, m'lady, should ye ha' need o' him, and me, too. I'm tae run up and down to fetch and carry for him whilst he's packing."

"Where is Sir Ivor going, Tadhg?" Catriona asked.

"Only tae see tae the peat cutting, m'lady."

"Prithee, may I go with him, Mam?" she asked Ealga.

"If you can catch him before he leaves the island and if he will allow it, aye."

Praying that Ivor's annoyance with her had abated and taking no time to fetch her cloak, Catriona caught up her skirts and ran down to the yard.

Ivor stood near the gateway, talking with Aodán.

Hurrying toward them, she smiled at her brother, saying, "Mam said that I might go with you, sir."

Dismissing Aodán with a gesture, Ivor waited until the man-at-arms had walked some distance away before he spoke, thus warning her before he said, "I don't think so, Cat. Not today."

"I *would* like to go. I have not been off the island for days."

"Then consider it a penance for your behavior earlier. Now, I must go."

About to argue, she stopped herself, knowing that it would be useless and just as useless to try to explain that she had not purposely been flirting with Rothesay but could not just tell him to go away. Ivor might agree with the last part but would insist, as her father had, that she ought not to have stepped into Rothesay's path in the first place. She had not thought that she had done so, but that argument would fare no better with Ivor.

Going back inside, she found the stairway empty until she passed the hall. Then, rounding a curve, she nearly bumped into Fin, coming down.

"You should clomp more on these stairs," she said in a tone that sounded surly to her own ears. More politely, she added, "I vow, you move on cat's paws."

"And, for all the heed you were paying, I might have been anyone, my lady," he said, giving her a look of such intensity that she could feel it to her core.

That look, plus the formality with which he had addressed her, made her lift her chin higher as she said, "Are you vexed with me, too, sir?"

"Who else is vexed with you?"

She straightened, collecting herself before she said, "Ivor, of course. You were with him. You must know that Rothesay's flirting vexed him sorely."

"'Vexed' is not the word I'd have chosen," he said. "But I did see, aye, and I think that Rothesay was not the only one flirting. That is, I doubt that Ivor thinks so."

"But you *did* know that he is irked with me, too."

"I have not said that I *am*," he pointed out. "What makes you think that your behavior might have annoyed me?"

"I just thought you looked angry before, sir, when Ivor did. And I do think that you looked angry again just now."

"But I have no right to be angry with you, lass. If anyone angered me, it was Ivor by letting his temper show so openly to a royal guest in his house."

"I expect that is all that it was then. Will you let me pass?"

"I don't know," he said quietly. "Should I? You might meet someone else. You might meet an enemy on these stairs, or some other danger."

"There is no danger here," she said, trying to read his expression.

"Is there not, Cat?" he asked, his voice as soft now as soft could be and sending sudden tremors through her body as if he had touched her.

She swallowed hard and sought to find her voice. But it had deserted her.

He stood there for a long moment without speaking, then stepped politely aside and gestured for her to pass him. With a surge of unexpected disappointment, she knew that she had been hoping he would kiss her again.

Gathering the front of her skirt, she stepped onto the stair beside him, still hoping. Then she stepped to the one above it, still without incident. Abruptly, she turned, laced her hands through his hair, and forced him to turn his head toward her.

When he did, she kissed him hard on the lips, leaned away, and said, "You are the only danger here, Sir Fin of the Battles. And well do you know it."

As she fled, she heard his chuckle echoing up the stairs behind her. Grinning in response, she felt much better.

～

His spirits lifting, Fin continued downstairs, having gone up only to exchange his shirt for a lighter one. The fire in the inner chamber burned hot, and with so many in the room, it had grown stuffy during the morning.

The afternoon meeting was no more productive than the morning one had been, however, until Donald said gruffly, "As I see it, Davy lad, the risk of what ye're asking be far greater than any gain for me. Should we fail and Albany take up the reins of government again, we'll all likely pay with our lives."

Alex said with a deceptively lazy smile, "What d'ye *want*, Donald?"

Being a fellow Stewart, Alex spoke as to an equal, but Fin saw Donald's lips tighten and knew why. Alex, although likewise the King's nephew, was not only twenty years younger but bastard born.

Fin soon let his thoughts drift again to Catriona and her kiss on the stairs.

It had been all he could do not to catch her and hold her tight. Sakes, but he would have liked to take her right there against the stone wall of the stairwell.

Everything about her tempted him, and the strength of that temptation lingered. When she left after supper to go upstairs with the women, his thoughts continued to tease him, and they teased him even more in his dreams.

The next morning, he did not see her when he broke his fast with the men. But before the meeting had droned on long, the Mackintosh came to his rescue.

"Sithee, lads," the old man said, looking from one great lord to another. "Ye waste time with all this posturing! Whilst I did agree to host this meeting and can see that ye need me, I am no growing any younger by this. Forbye, Rothesay, I would ask that ye and these cousins of yours do choose a man each and sit the six of ye down with me.

Sithee, I'll stay and keep ye from murdering each other, but only an ye take me advice. So now, what d'ye say?"

Fin held his breath. Having feared that the old man had stepped beyond what Rothesay would stand, he nearly cheered when, with a curt nod, Davy said, "'Tis a good notion. I'll keep Havers with me. You other men may go."

Fin left at once to see if Ivor had yet departed for the peat bogs, where he was again to spend the day. Passing through the hall, he looked for Catriona but did not see her and then found Ivor at the landing, watching gillies launch a boat.

Fin thus spent a tolerably amusing day watching peat cutters and learning more than he had ever wanted to know about drying peat for fuel.

He and Ivor returned near dusk, sunburned, hungry, and thirsty. Shouting for bathwater, Ivor said, "We've got nobbut an hour to tidy up for supper, so hurry."

Fin obeyed, but when they gathered with the others on the dais, one look at Rothesay told him that he was in a dangerous mood and had already taken enough wine to make him reckless.

When Catriona entered with the lady Morag a few minutes later, Fin's breath caught at the sight of her. She wore a rose-pink velvet gown that hugged her figure from its low-plunging décolletage to her enticing hips, girdled now with a long, gold linked chain. Her skirt flared in soft folds that swayed as she walked.

Although the lady Morag walked beside her, had anyone asked him what she was wearing, he could not have answered without looking at her first.

Supper was long, and Donald kept up a tense, low-voiced conversation with Alex throughout. They both sat at Rothesay's right with Mackintosh and Shaw at his left, and the ladies beyond them.

Fin sat farther down on the men's side by Ivor, but he knew that Donald's conversation with Alex must be annoying Rothesay. And he could see that the lad serving Rothesay refilled his goblet more times than was usually wise.

He could not see Catriona, who sat again between Morag and Lady Ealga.

Occasionally, when Donald's voice or Alex's grew more intense, Ivor and Fin would glance at each other. But the third time it happened, Fin heard the Mackintosh mutter something that silenced them both.

Throughout the meal, a low rumble of conversation continued in the lower hall where servants, men-at-arms, and other guests sat at three long trestle tables.

At last, Rothesay rose, and perforce, everyone else rose as well. Nodding regally to the Mackintosh, Rothesay stepped past him and Shaw to speak to the ladies Ealga and Annis. His comments to them were brief, and when the lady Morag joined them, he turned away to speak with Catriona, offering her an arm as he did.

Fin imagined the lass turning on Davy as she had turned on *him* the day he'd met her, and slapping Davy silly. Sighing, he knew that she could not do such a thing without stirring everyone's wrath save his own.

The number of people between him and the far end of the dais blocked his view now of Catriona and Davy, so he went around the other end of the table, hoping to keep a close eye on them and wondering how to intervene if it grew necessary.

Rothesay's brittle mood was a clear harbinger of trouble, although Fin knew from experience that those not well acquainted with Rothesay would not realize that he was ape-drunk. Even if someone did, he was the acting King of Scots and thus ruler of Scotland. Moreover, he was a guest of both Shaw and the Mackintosh.

The two of them had stood between Rothesay and Catriona as everyone rose from the table, but both men had moved at once to talk with Donald and Alex.

Just when Fin got a clear view again of Rothesay and Catriona, as they stepped off the dais and joined the crowd in the lower hall, she shook her head and touched Rothesay's arm. He grinned, put his hands on her shoulders, and drew her close.

Chapter 12 _____

Rothesay was still grinning at his ribald jest, and although Catriona had told him he should not say such things to her, he clearly did not care what she thought.

He had come upon her so quickly, and when she had hesitated to take his arm, he had said he wanted only to walk briefly with her and not to be rude. No one else on the dais seemed to heed them, and she was sure that he could do nothing horrible in such a crowd of people, so she had obeyed him. He had put his free hand atop hers then and had urged her off the dais as he had told her his jest.

He'd frowned fiercely at her objection to his ribaldry, but the minute she touched his arm, hoping to show that she had not meant to offend him, he had grinned and put his hands on her shoulders. His intent now was clear, and she knew that no one nearby would dare to interfere with him.

Swiftly raising both of her own hands palm outward between them, she said, "Do not, my lord. You must not."

"Ah, but I must, lass. You are too enticing to resist." Stroking one velvet sleeve, he said, "I like this gown. Its softness invites a man's touch."

She had unexpectedly met her father after Shaw had left the meeting that morning, and had suffered a lecture on the behavior that he expected from her. Although he had readily agreed that she must not be rude to Rothesay, he had said simply that she should keep clear of him. To that end, she had managed to avoid Rothesay at the midday meal. But having worn her favorite gown to supper in hopes of impressing Fin, she had unfortunately lured Rothesay to her side instead.

Looking intently into her eyes, he said, "Be friendly, lass, unless you would dare to lay unfriendly hands on your sovereign."

"You are not King yet, sir."

"Ah, but as Governor, I wield the King's powers—all of them, including the power to issue and revoke charters to land. Your grandfather and father control much land hereabouts, I believe, but only at the royal whim. Sithee, my command is as law." He was still staring into her eyes, his grip strong on her shoulders and his desire for her radiating from every pore. "Come now, and walk with me."

"I must not, sir," she said, but she could scarcely get the words out and knew that she was trembling. She did not know if he spoke the truth, or if he would be able to take Clan Chattan's vast lands even with an army. However, whether he could or not, she knew that the men in her family would take a dim view of her conversing at all with him and a much dimmer view if she angered him. And she did not want to give Shaw, in particular, any further cause for disapproval.

That he did disapprove must have been plain to Rothesay after Shaw had twice sent her away when he'd seen them together. However, Rothesay just as plainly would dismiss any father's censure. But she could not dismiss Shaw's.

Rothesay had only smiled at her weak refusal.

She said more firmly, "Truly, my lord, I must not."

He continued to smile, his hands tightening on her shoulders. The thought flitted through her mind that even if she had had her dirk, she could not draw it on Rothesay. To do so would surely be committing treason.

When, slowly, hypnotically, he began to draw her closer, his purpose clear to anyone watching them, she knew that she had to stop him any way that she could.

His lips pursed expectantly, and she could smell the wine on his breath.

"God-a-mercy, sir, do you mean to kiss me here in front of everyone?"

"If you walk with me, we can be private," he murmured. His lips relaxed to allow the comment, but his gaze still burned into hers.

"Yon archway leads to the garderobe," she said with an edge to her voice.

"Aye, sure, but also upward to the ramparts and a fine view, I'm told. 'Tis your own choice. Obey me, or pay a pleasant and public forfeit."

Gritting her teeth and sending consequences to the devil, she pushed harder against his chest, letting more of her anger show as she said, "Now, see here, my lord, you are truly beginning to irk—"

Before she could finish or his lips could touch hers, a guttural clearing of a throat made her jump and snap her head around to see Fin quite close to them.

She was glad to see him, but the stern look on his face and her own embarrassment strengthened her irritation with Rothesay. She tried to wrench away, but Rothesay's hands tightened on her shoulders, and he held her so easily that anyone standing any distance away might easily fail to note her aversion.

"Let me go," she snapped, wondering if she dared stomp on his foot.

"In a moment, lass," he replied. He was looking at Fin but lazily, having neither jumped nor shown any other hint of the guilt that he ought to feel.

However, as he continued to gaze at the silent Fin, a frown clouded the royal countenance. "What the devil did you make that damned noise for?" he demanded.

"With respect, my lord," Fin said. "I would have a word with you."

Realizing that she was holding her breath, she let it out.

"Go away," Rothesay said, grinning but easing his grip on her shoulders. "You intrude, Fin, as you can plainly see."

"If I intrude, sir, 'tis better that I do so than that her ladyship's father or one of her brothers should more angrily protest the liberties you take with her."

"The devil fly away with you," Rothesay snapped. "You're a damnable nuisance, Fin. The lady is going to walk with me, and no father or brother would be such a dafty as to protest my attentions to her, whatever they may be. I find her beauty soothing to nerves overwrought by our discussions today. But you can say nowt about it in any event after so ruthlessly abandoning me earlier to my fate."

When Fin's lips tightened much as Ivor's did when that gentleman was about to explode, Catriona felt a thrill of anticipation at the base of her spine.

However, he said only, "If I abandoned you, my liege,

I did so at your command and that of the Mackintosh, as well you know."

"God's blood, man, such talk! Would you defy me then? Do you dare?"

Catriona was watching Fin, but at these words, the thrill of anticipation turned to a frisson of fear. She frowned at him.

If Fin noticed, he gave no hint of it. In fact, he displayed more temerity by looking with disapproval from one of Rothesay's hands to the other.

Again, she tried to step away from Rothesay. Again, he prevented it. She glanced up at his face, then at Fin's.

"Prithee, sir," she said to the latter. "There can be no good cause to—"

"Hush, lass," Fin said quietly but nonetheless firmly.

She swallowed a burst of anger but wished she could smack them both. It was as if two dogs circled a tasty bone.

Fin said, "By my troth, my lord, I do not want to fratch with you, only to preserve the benefits of your welcome here and the Mackintosh's goodwill toward your cause. We may forfeit that goodwill if he takes offense at such royal interest in his maiden granddaughter."

Rothesay looked long and searchingly at him, while Catriona fairly quaked with increasing unease. Then Rothesay's eyes began to twinkle.

Seeing it, she began to relax until he said, "By heaven, Fin, I see what it is. You've taken an interest in the lass yourself!"

~

Fin stared at Rothesay, stunned, while his imagination sought urgently for something sensible to say that would not be an outright lie.

Catriona was silent, but he had not missed her warning frown earlier. And he doubted that she would welcome a declaration from him even if he had the right to make one. However, if he said that he had *no* interest in her, he would be lying and Rothesay would try to walk off with her.

Just then Ivor appeared beside them as if a magician had conjured him there and said grimly, "Speak up, Fin. What *are* your intentions toward her? If you mean to offer for her, I'd have expected you to ask our father's leave to court her first."

"Aye, that is true," James said from Fin's other side. "I must say, I had no notion of this. Nor did my lady Morag ken aught of it, for she would have told me."

Fin, having looked from one to the other, now saw that Shaw had noted their gathering and was eyeing them sternly. Certain that he would be upon him next, he turned back to Rothesay, who returned his gaze with a mischievous one of his own.

"Sakes, Fin," he said. "Have you been keeping this attachment of yours a secret? Because, if you have, I'm thinking that the devil must be in it now."

Catriona, having kept silent throughout, suddenly sighed, looked right at Rothesay, and smiled ruefully, saying, "You are quite right about *that*, my lord. As you can plainly see, you have created an unfortunate situation by revealing our secret. But 'tis true, I'm afraid, that Sir Finlagh and I are in love."

Lowering her lashes next in a way that made Fin want to shake her until they fluttered off her to the ground, she added, "How could I have had enough strength to resist your so-flattering advances, sir, had I not fallen deeply in love with him?"

"How, indeed?" Rothesay said with a merry laugh. "But this is extraordinary! Here, Shaw," he added when Catriona's father strode up to them, "I have uncovered a secret for you. Your beautiful daughter and my man Sir Fin of the Battles here want to marry. I think it is a grand idea. Now, what do *you* say to it?"

Fin held his breath as Shaw looked from one person to another, letting his gaze settle at last on Catriona.

"I was just coming to suggest that it is time ye were in your chamber, lass," he said in his usual stern way. "We can talk more of this in the morning."

"With respect, my lord," she said, meeting that piercing gaze. "This concerns me as well as Sir Finlagh, because I am the one who told Rothesay. I think you will agree that it would be unfair of me to make Fin answer to you alone for that."

"Mayhap it would," Shaw agreed. "Nevertheless, he is going to talk with me alone. If ye do insist, ye may join us afterward to hear then what I will say to ye."

That was not what she had wanted, as Fin could plainly see from her look of frustration. But when Shaw nodded to Ivor and Ivor put a hand on her arm, she turned obediently if reluctantly away with him.

"Don't take her to the ladies' solar, Ivor, but to the wee room opposite the muniments chamber above it," Shaw said. "I will talk with her before she need tell your mam or grandame about this, so leave the gist to me. Ye're to go with them, James," he added. "Take your time, though. I'd liefer that nae one think aught of it or follow any of us upstairs. Do not speak to Morag, either, until I give ye leave."

"As you wish, sir," James said with a nod as he turned away.

Fin waited to hear his own orders while keeping an eye on Rothesay, who was still enjoying himself and clearly expected to hear what Shaw would say to Fin.

However, Shaw spoke to Rothesay first, saying, "One of your lads told my good-father that you can doubtless beat him at chess, my lord. He would welcome a match, if you would so honor him, and awaits you now in the inner chamber."

Rothesay grinned, saying, "I will, aye, and gladly, because I must tell you that I have been seeking a way to amuse myself tonight. But sithee, Shaw, I think that this secretive pair should marry at once. Forbye, it would amuse me more than a good game of chess and may lighten the mood betwixt my cousins and make them easier to bend to my will."

"As to that, my lord, we shall see."

"I could make this marriage a royal command," Rothesay said provocatively. "Mayhap I have not made it clear that the match has my blessing."

"An honor, to be sure," Shaw said in the same stern tone. "We can speak more of this if you wish, after I talk with Sir Finlagh and my daughter."

Seeing Rothesay's quick frown, Fin wanted to warn him to recall his need for Clan Chattan support. But Rothesay, glancing at him, clearly did remember, because his brow cleared, and he said, "I would like that, aye, Shaw."

"Good then," Shaw said. Turning to Fin, he added, "You come with me."

Hearing those words and Shaw's ominous tone, Fin's mind played him an unexpected trick with the sudden thought that had he known a month before that he would find himself alone in a room with the war leader of Clan Chattan, he would never have guessed that it would be for

such a purpose or that he would be hoping only to soothe
the man's rightful fury.

⁓

Appalled at what she had wrought and angry with herself
for putting Fin in such a fix, Catriona kept her emotions
in check until Ivor ushered her into the tiny room across
from the much larger one where the clan's important documents were stored. The larger chamber was also where
her father closeted himself when he had private business
to attend or a daughter to scold.

But when Ivor turned to shut the smaller room's door,
she said evenly to his back, "I don't want to talk to you
about any of this, or to James either. Not yet."

Ivor turned then to face her, and in place of the anger
she had expected to see, she saw compassion and a glint
of humor. "Do you not, Wildcat?" he asked. "I can well
understand that. But what devil possessed you to declare
such a thing?"

"I cannot tell you," she muttered.

"Cannot or will not?"

She did not know how to reply to that.

"I see," he said, "or mayhap I do not. But I suspect that
Fin will ask the same question, so you had better think of
an answer before he does. Have you any idea how much
trouble you have created for him?"

"I know," she said miserably. "I did not mean to do that.
When Rothesay urged me to walk with him, everyone
else had moved away, and even Father had said I could not
be rude to him. But when I said that Father disapproved
of my showing favor in such a way, Rothesay said I *was*
being rude. I think he must be ape-drunk."

"Very likely. He often does drink too much."

"I did think that I could take care of myself here in our own hall, but—"

"Nay, lassie, and never with Rothesay."

She drew a long breath and let it go, knowing that he was right. "How much did you hear of what we said?"

"Not much until Rothesay said what he did about Fin's taking an interest in you himself. Sithee, I was still on the dais talking to James when you left it, so—"

He broke off when the door opened and James entered as if the mention of his name had brought him. He stood there, looking at them, clearly deciding what to say.

Ivor said, "Shut the door, James. It won't do for Cat to see Father leading Fin into that room as he used to lead us when we were in for a raging or worse. I was just telling her what you and I saw and heard."

James gave Catriona a searching look as he reached back and shut the door. Then he said, "You should never have let Rothesay walk off with you like that, lass, but, by my troth, I do not know how you could have stopped him. The man believes that his position and the blood royal running through his veins grant him the right always to get his own way. We have all seen that."

Catriona looked from one man to the other and fixed her gaze on Ivor. "I expected you, especially, to be furious about what happened down there," she said. "Instead, you looked almost amused...and...and something else. Art worried, sir?"

Ivor looked at James, who shrugged. "Your emotions hardly count as the gist of the matter, I'd think," he said.

"Sithee, Cat," Ivor said, "by the time anyone but Fin noticed that you had left the dais with Rothesay, you were too far away and too much mixed in with our people in the lower hall for us to do aught save shout. We could only depend on Fin's ability to intervene diplomatically."

"He doubtless *would* have succeeded in diverting Rothesay," James said solemnly, "had you not interfered with him."

Catriona disagreed, since Rothesay had been in no mood for anyone to divert him, but she knew better than to say so.

However, Ivor said, "By the time you and I were near enough to hear what the three of them were saying, James, I warrant the matter had already gone too far."

"I did try to stop Rothesay," she said, hating the defensive note in her voice but unwilling for them to think that she had simply complied with his wishes. "He reminded me then of his great power as Governor. He…he made threats."

"Aye," James said, nodding. "The man does wield much power, lass, and often threatens to use it. But it did look at first as if you went willingly with him."

"You said yourself that you don't know how I might have stopped him, James. So how could *I* have known how? Just tell me what—"

"Enough, Cat," Ivor interjected, clearly impatient with James's need to explore details ponderously and at length or with her own reaction, or both. Ivor added, "Although Rothesay is but three-and-twenty, he does stand in the place of our King, so it is true that you cannot slap his face or order him to take his hands off you as you would with any other lad. Even so, many who saw you will believe that you found his attentions flattering and that you responded to them."

She nodded. "Morag said as much the first time I walked with him."

"Then we'll say no more about that," Ivor said. "We did soon see that you were unwilling and tried to get to you quickly but without stirring undue curiosity."

"Aye," James agreed, adding earnestly, "I did not mean to make ye think otherwise, Cat. Rothesay would be a difficult man for any lass to manage."

"I heard nothing clearly until Rothesay raised his voice to ask if Fin intended to defy him," Ivor said. "I saw you frown, and the next thing I heard was Rothesay declaring that Fin had an interest in you himself. And Fin did not deny that, Cat."

"Nay, he did not," she agreed, remembering. "He did not say anything, Ivor. That was when you demanded to know what his intentions were toward me."

"I did, lass, aye," he said. "Sithee, you or, more accurately, Rothesay had put Fin in an untenable position. He could not honestly say that he had no interest if he does. But I'll admit I just said the first thing that came into my head, hoping to give Fin more time to think. It was, however, not the wisest thing I might have said."

"That," James said, "is perfectly true. It may even be what put the notion into Catriona's head to say what *she* did."

Giving him a quelling look, Ivor went on, "When I said that Fin should have sought permission from Father, I expected Fin to reply that he *would* discuss any such intent with him. But before he could, you blurted your declaration of love and did it within earshot of God knows how many people, each of whom has doubtless told others. Sithee, lass, you tossed Fin into the devil's own fire with those words."

"But how?"

"Do you imagine that Fin is across the way now, declaring to our father that you are a liar, Catriona?"

"Mercy, sir, Fin makes such a thing of his honor that I *assumed* he would tell Father the truth. He must know that I spoke up when I did to *stop* Rothesay and get away from him without causing more of a disturbance than we had already caused."

"Whatever he tells Father, you've put Fin in a damnable position."

She had known when Shaw had forbidden her to be present while he and Fin talked that she had put Fin in an unfair position, but she had hoped that by declaring as much to her father, she had at least done something to help. Clearly, she had not.

"Sakes," she said, "I'll tell Father the whole truth, myself."

"Much good that will do either of you now," James said, shaking his head.

"I don't understand you, James. Prithee, say what you mean."

"He must not, Cat, for we've come to the gist of it," Ivor said gently. "In troth, Father would think that we had already said more than we should."

Looking from one to the other, she wondered what on earth she had done.

⁓

Following Shaw into a comfortable-looking chamber of a size that nearly matched the ladies' solar below them, Fin shut the door without waiting to be asked. The chamber's warmth was welcome, even soothing, because in the long

minutes that it had taken to cross the great hall and follow Shaw up the main stairway to the muniments room,
his thoughts had whirled like waterspouts on a windy
loch.

Inhaling deeply and letting it out, just as he would before
taking on an opponent in a tiltyard, he watched Shaw kneel
to stir embers to life on the hearth.

Then Shaw stood and looked at him for a long moment
before he said, "Ye should know, lad, afore we start this
conversation, that my good-father thinks ye'd make a
good husband for our Catriona. I'm not so sure I agree
with him. Not yet."

Everything that Fin had considered saying vanished
from his mind. With nothing else to say, he kept silent.

"Sithee, ye ken fine that he told us who ye be. Likewise,
Ivor told us about your part in the battle at Perth, including that he urged ye into the river so that someone from
your side would live to tell the tale. Have ye told it yet?"

"Only to Catriona, sir. I've not been home since then to
see the others of my clan." That fact alone had not seemed
distasteful to him when compared with his flight and his
father's bequest. But it did now when he admitted it to
Shaw.

"So although ye've not told your own folk, ye did tell
our Catriona, did ye?"

"I did, aye," Fin said. "She had befriended me—
mayhap even saved my life. I thought that she deserved to
know."

"And did ye tell her likewise that ye be brother to a
Cameron chieftain?"

"I did."

"And that ye were born at Tor Castle, a place over which

our two clans had long fought until the battle at Perth, and over which we still share much tension?"

Quietly, Fin said, "I did not tell her that."

"Doubtless the opportunity did not arise," Shaw said almost amiably.

"We did talk of Tor Castle," Fin admitted, feeling as if he were nearing a precipice...or a gallows. "She asked if I knew of it and said that the Mackintosh goes there every Christmas. I said only that I did know of Tor Castle and Loch Arkaig."

"I see." To Fin's surprise, Shaw's eyes twinkled. But he said only, "I expect there will come a time when ye'll wish ye'd been more forthcoming with the lass. But that is only one of the consequences that ye're going to face now."

"I could name several, certainly," Fin said, thinking not only about Catriona and the anger he had seen in her but also about Rothesay.

"Aye, well, I'm concerned with only one consequence at present," Shaw said. "Unless ye be meaning to give our Catriona the lie."

"I would not do that under any circumstance," Fin said. "However, I am sure she will clarify the matter as soon as she can. As easily as she speaks her mind, I'd not be surprised to hear that she has already declared that she spoke in haste."

"Now, lad, I'd remind ye that I put her in the charge of her brothers. So she's said nowt yet to anyone else. Nor will she. I'll not permit her to make a scandal of herself, nor ye to do it for her. Had I thought that ye had such a thing in mind," he added when Fin moved to reassure him, "I'd have seen to it that ye kept your mouth shut. As it is, I ken fine that I can trust ye to deal with the lass as ye should."

"As I should, sir?"

"Aye, sure, for ye'll have to wed her now, will ye not? Sithee, we've three powerful lairds here. And every one of them will expect to hear that ye'll marry."

Fin heard the words. But their impact on him, though strong, was much different than he might have expected. A hunger overcame him unlike any he had known. He wanted Catriona and suspected that he had never wanted anything more.

That he might win her...

His body stirred at the thought, and his mind hummed.

It was something of a shock, though, to discover that Shaw believed, exactly as *he* did, that the best punishment for any man was to let him suffer the consequences of his own actions.

Chapter 13 _____

Catriona paced while she waited with her brothers, annoyed at their refusal to tell her more but knowing it would do no good to press them. Neither Ivor nor James had made further comment. Both men sat silently, watching her pace.

When the door opened, she started violently and whirled to see Shaw filling the doorway, his expression grim.

"What have you done to him, sir?" she demanded.

Raising his eyebrows in clear objection to her tone, Shaw said, "Ye'll come into yon chamber with me now, Catriona."

She swallowed hard but said, "Prithee, sir, where is he?"

"I warned ye, lass, that I had things to say to ye. I would say them to ye now." He stood aside, gesturing implacably toward the chamber across the landing.

With much the same sense of doom that she had felt as a child ordered to that chamber, she collected herself only to feel shaken again when Ivor shot her a look of sympathy. Hoping that she could maintain her dignity through what lay ahead, she walked past her father, crossed the landing, and entered the larger chamber.

Fin stood by the hearth, looking solemn but otherwise at ease.

Her heart had been pounding, but seeing him apparently unaffected by whatever had occurred between him and her father steadied her.

She was about to speak when Shaw said, "Look at me, Catriona."

Closing her mouth, she turned to face him.

Instead of the scolding that she had expected, he said, "I have told Sir Finlagh that he may describe for you the discussion we have had as he chooses and the outcome that I expect from it, as well. I know I can trust him to make my position and that of your lord grandfather clear to ye, lass. I'll trust ye, too, to recall your own part in the matter as ye talk it over with him."

"Aye, sir, I will," she said.

Nodding, he went on, "When ye've finished here, ye'll retire to your chamber for the night. That will spare ye the need to talk with any of the other women. Likewise, ye're to spare Ailvie any details until tomorrow. I will be most displeased if she prattles to anyone about this. Do you understand me, Catriona?"

"I...I think so," she said, aware that she still understood little but hoping that Fin would explain what was happening. She had a strong feeling that if she demanded clarification from Shaw, she would get more than she wanted to hear and perhaps more than just words. He already looked most displeased with her.

She did not breathe easily until he had gone, shutting the door behind him and leaving her alone with Fin, who still stood quietly behind her at the hearth.

He had not said a word, so she turned slowly to face

him, vaguely aware when a glowing ember in the fireplace cracked and shot sparks into the air. Her gaze sought his, but when they met, her sense of increasing ease shifted to wariness.

He did not look any more pleased with her than her father had. His expression was not as intimidating as Shaw's had been, but neither did it give any hint of what Fin might say to her or what he was feeling.

"What did he say to you?" she asked with more force than she had intended.

He continued to hold her gaze, but his expression altered when she spoke, as if he were gauging her mood in much the same way that she was trying to judge his.

She felt herself begin to relax again. Something about Fin made it easy to be with him even when he was displeased. He might contradict her—sakes, contradiction was a habit with him—but he did not customarily dismiss what she said as James sometimes did, or tell her that she just ought to trust and obey him as Ivor far too often did. Fin talked to her as if she had wits of her own. In fact, if he became irked with her, it was usually because she was *not* using them.

At last, without moving toward her or suggesting that they sit but with his expression hardening as if he had resolved upon something, he said, "What you said out there to Rothesay . . . Was there even a grain of truth in it, Catriona?"

Remembering Ivor's declaration that she had thrown Fin into the devil's own fire with her words, she said ruefully, "I am sorry about that, sir. I'd meant to explain the whole thing to Father myself, although James said that it would do no good. But Father and Granddad can mend matters for you, I'm sure."

"What were you going to tell your father?"

"Why, that I had said what I did only to make Rothesay leave me be, of course. I thought you realized that."

"I did," he said.

Reassured, she went on, "Sithee, you had kept silent for so long by then that I did not know what to think. After Rothesay declared that you wanted me for yourself, I did *hope* that you would not proclaim to the ceiling beams that you wanted none of me. But, in troth, I could not be sure of that because of your so strong sense of honor. I certainly expected you to tell Father straight out that I had lied. But Ivor said that you would not."

"Ivor was right. Nor could I have reconciled it with my sense of honor to abandon an innocent maiden to Rothesay's clutches."

"I expect you mean that to call me a liar would be a sort of betrayal, but—"

"I do mean that," he said. "Recall that I know Rothesay's habits better than you do. But tell me something else. Why did you frown at me?"

"When?"

"Don't try me further tonight, Cat. My patience is spent."

"If you mean when you confronted him as you did—mercy, sir, you as much as challenged him! I could see that you were making him angry, and you had already annoyed him earlier, for he said that you had abandoned *him.*"

"To which *I* said . . . ?"

"That he had commanded you." She sighed, realizing that she had overstepped. "I expect the truth is that the two of you toe-to-toe like that frightened me witless, although you will say that I ought to have known you could manage him. Sakes, the plain truth is that I took umbrage when you told me to hush."

Fin replied mildly, "You were not helping, but I'm glad you realize that anyone who tells Rothesay that he is behaving badly treads on dangerous ground."

"Well, then—"

"Sithee, lass, your resistance to his advances merely spurred him on at first," he said. "But I could see that you were getting angry enough with him to behave in a way that he would not tolerate. You have yet to give me a clear answer, though, to the most important part of my question. Was there *any* truth in what you said to him about your feelings for me, or was that declaration just a lie?"

She hesitated, wondering what he hoped she would say and wondering, too, just how strongly she did care for him. A short while before, facing her father on his entrance to the room across the hall, Fin had been all that she could think about.

She had feared for him, feared what Shaw might have said to him, and feared that Fin might never forgive her for making him face her father in such a way.

The truth was that she loved being with Fin. He fascinated her, he made her think about things that she had rarely considered before, and he listened to her. He made her opinions seem worthy, even interesting.

His beautiful eyes let her see straight to his thoughts whenever he allowed it, and he had ways of looking at her that she could feel to her very soul.

But what did she know of him other than what he had revealed to her? And how fair would it be to let him think she cared enough to marry him but not enough to ride off with him and live among strangers...enemies...when he had to leave her?

"May I ask you a question, sir?"

"Aye, anything," he said.

"Anything? Sakes, but you say that so easily. Do you not fear that someone may ask you a question so personal that you have never had the courage to share its answer with *any*-one? Most people do have such personal secrets, after all."

There was, briefly, an arrested look in his eyes. But it vanished and he said, "I will answer any question that you ask me if I can, personal or otherwise."

She watched him carefully, determined to note his every move and catch his slightest expression, so that she could accurately judge his response. Then she said, "Have you told me everything about yourself that I should know?"

Fin considered her question and how he should answer it, nearly smiling at how quickly she'd fulfilled her father's prediction that she would call him to account.

Shaw had been right in saying that she would have to know about his family. Fin knew that would have to tell her more about himself, too, because sooner or later he would take her to Loch Arkaig and she would see that the original seat of the Mackintosh was also the original home of Fin Cameron.

Recalling Ivor's description of her as a wildcat, he suspected that fur and claws would likely fly when they did have that talk. So to have it now would be unwise. Only when he could be private with her without fear of interruption would he tell her *all* that she wanted to know.

He would not do so where Ivor or James might walk

in or where she could easily walk off, bolt her door, and refuse to talk to him.

At last, seeing clear signs of impatience in her expression, he said, "Cat, sheathe your claws. I cannot possibly have told you all that you may want to know about me. I can think of two or three things straight off that I can*not* tell you because they relate to people who would take a dim view of my sharing their confidences with you. I'll admit, too, that there are things that I have not told you as a friend that I would feel obliged to tell you under other circumstances."

"What circumstances? You cannot mean that you would tell an enemy."

He waited, knowing how quick she was, and she did not disappoint him.

"You mean if I do agree to…if we…that is if you were to…"

"Just answer my question," he said quietly when she faltered. "Did what you said to Rothesay reflect feelings that you do have for me, or did you lie to him?"

Visibly swallowing, she said, "I think I may regret saying this, but I…I believe that there may be some truth to what I said. Still—"

His heart leaped, startling him with the surge of emotion and more physical responses that coursed through him. "Art sure, lass?" he asked, hearing his voice crack on the words. "Recall before you answer me that you did apologize to me and tell me that you had said it only to make Rothesay leave you alone."

"Must you contradict even my half-formed thoughts, sir, and use my own words against me when you do?"

He took a step toward her, realized that he had done so

impulsively, and recollected himself to say, "I am not contradicting you. I just need to know what you feel now, to have some idea of how you will react to what must occur next. Sithee, there is one thing that I must be sure is clear to you before we leave this chamber."

Catriona stared at Fin as a flurry of thoughts danced through her mind, including the last thing that her father had said to her, that Fin would make clear what Shaw's position was, and that of the Mackintosh.

Abruptly, the truth dawned.

"God-a-mercy, they mean to *make* you marry me!"

"The Mackintosh and your father have discussed it," he said. "That is to say, they have discussed us and they have discussed Rothesay. Your grandfather has decreed, and Shaw agrees with him, that nowt shall happen to cause ructions between the house of Mackintosh and that of Stewart. So they do suggest—"

"They insist, more like! But I never meant—"

"Whatever you meant, you have wreaked havoc, lass. Try to imagine, if you will, what Rothesay's reaction will be if he learns that you lied to him to evade his attentions. He is young and gey proud, and such a tale would spread fast."

Wincing at the image he'd created in her mind, she said, "I do know that others were nearby. Ivor said that most of them would delight in telling the tale."

He nodded.

With a sigh, knowing that she could not defy them all and knowing, too, that she did not want to defy them if it meant never seeing Fin again, she said, "Very well.

They may give it out that we will marry. Then we'll see. But there is one thing that you should understand clearly about me before we do this, sir."

As she spoke, he had moved closer, much too close. He looked into her eyes. "What is it that I must understand?" he asked.

Striving to keep her emotions out of her voice, she said, "I do *not* like it when men assume that I cannot look after myself. Because I can, sir, and I do."

"Ah, lassie, come here," he said, pulling her into his arms. "I have seen that you can. You are intrepid. By my troth, though, that worries me more than any weakness you may have, because no woman is *always* capable of looking after herself—or any man, either, come to that."

"It is something, I expect, that you will admit *that*," she murmured, leaning into him and welcoming his embrace. As she did, she realized something else. "You have not said what *you* think of all this. You must be vexed with me and hate as much as I do that they are forcing you to do this. Also, if what I've done puts you in bad odor with Rothesay, whom you do serve..."

She sounded sincerely worried, so when she paused, Fin hugged her and said, "Davy will recover from his displeasure the first time he needs me, lass. And I am not vexed with you or even opposed to your father's plan for us, although it may complicate my life for a time. Especially with my family."

She nodded. "I expect it will. I doubt they will like our marrying."

"Whether they do or not, they seem to be honoring the truce," he said. "In any event, after we marry, they will want to meet you." He did not add that his brother Ewan would say that they ought to have met her long before then. What Ewan would say about Fin's marrying a Mackintosh, Fin did not want to imagine.

Catriona said quietly, "My feelings about leaving Loch an Eilein have not changed, sir. I have seen, with Morag, how hard it is to live amongst strangers even when their clans have never been enemies. We have nearly always been at odds with the Camerons. Also, if you have not seen your kinsmen for some time…"

"Not since the battle at Perth," he said.

"God-a-mercy, they must think that you died there!"

"I don't know what they think," Fin admitted. "I doubt that anyone but Ivor knew who I was when I left the field. So folks in Lochaber likely do believe that all thirty of the Camerons at Perth died there. But I like to think that my family will be glad to learn that I did not and will likewise welcome the woman who so recently kept another rogue from killing me. But if they are not glad about the first—"

"Why would they not be?"

He had not meant to raise that subject. But he said honestly, "The men of my family number amongst those who would think that leaving as I did was cowardly."

When she did not comment, he experienced a moment of uncertainty. "Look at me, Catriona." When she did, he said, "Art sure that you do not agree that it was? I would not blame you if you did. I know that we talked about—"

"Ivor believed that you should leave. That is enough for

me, Fin Cameron, just as it was for you. Sakes, no sensible person could believe that a man who outlasted his opponents and twenty-nine of his companions on such a day is a coward."

Her tone made it impossible to disbelieve her. He began to relax.

"There is another thing, though," she said. "Since you were able to intervene with Rothesay, I do think you might have stood up to my father as well. Marrying you is a far better fate than marrying Rory Comyn, but if you let them force you—"

"I think you know that at this point I have as little to say about it as you do," he said. "If you want me to tell them that *you* still oppose the match, I will. But you ken fine that they care more about protecting you than acceding to your wishes."

"Will you really tell them that I don't want them to *make* me marry you?"

"I will."

"They may listen to you," she said. "Go and do it then. I warrant Father must be waiting for you across the hall with Ivor and James."

Accordingly, Fin walked to the landing with her and watched until she had vanished around the first curve of the stairs. Then, rapping on the door across the way and hearing only silence, he opened it to an empty room.

"Beg pardon, sir."

Turning, he saw Tadhg on the stairs below him. "Aye, what is it?"

"The laird be in the inner chamber wi' the Mackintosh and them. He would see ye there now that her ladyship has gone up for the night. And, sir?"

"What else?"

"I say it be a fine notion that ye be going tae marry our lady Catriona."

"Sakes, does the whole castle know what goes on here tonight?"

"Nay, sir, but I were at hand when the laird told the Mackintosh it be all set."

"I'll go down at once, Tadhg. Prithee, go to my room and tell my squire that I shall be along shortly. He is to wait for me. But do not share this news with him."

Waiting only for the boy's assent, Fin went down to the hall.

When Aodán admitted him to the inner chamber, he saw not only Shaw and the Mackintosh but their ladies, Rothesay, and Alex Stewart as well. Donald had apparently retired for the night, and neither James nor Ivor was there, nor Morag.

Fin wished Ivor were there. Without him, he felt alone against many again.

Rothesay grinned at him, clearly still enjoying himself, and Alex also looked amused. Shaw looked as stern as usual, the Mackintosh quietly pleased.

Catching the lady Ealga's eye, Fin received a warm smile.

Lady Annis eyed him more measuringly.

"Is all well above?" Shaw asked him.

With Rothesay and Alex there, Fin said only, "Aye, sir," and hoped Shaw would know that he preferred to say no more than that in their presence.

Rothesay said, "How could it be otherwise? 'Tis grand to be so delightfully amused as we have been this evening. We must proceed at once with the wedding."

Catriona reached her landing to find Boreas lying at her door, his small gray shadow curled tightly atop him. The dog blinked at her, moving only its tail. The kitten raised its head and greeted her with a plaintive "mew."

Opening the door to let them in, she felt her mood lighten and realized that her last exchange with Fin had still weighed on her mind. She felt as if she had cast him into the briars again. But he did enjoy debating anything with her, so it had seemed reasonable that he might persuade Shaw and her grandfather that the wedding need not take place. Not yet. Perhaps later...someday.

She sighed. The fact was that she did want to marry him, very much.

Just thinking of his touch was enough to make her feel it again through every fiber of her body. When he held her, she felt as if she belonged in his arms.

She could recall no one since childhood who had comforted her so tenderly. Perversely, that thought made her wonder if her insistence that she could take care of herself had made him think her childish. He had called her "lassie" then, had he not?

Pondering that thought while Boreas and his kitten resettled themselves beside the bed, she realized that Ailvie ought to be there. But the washstand ewer was empty, so perhaps it was not as late as she had thought.

Moving to look out the window, she tried to decide if she would like being married. The thought of leaving home still chilled her to the bone. And Fin had not ever responded when she'd told him that she had not changed her mind about that.

Perhaps he understood her feelings and would live at Rothiemurchus. If so, when he had to follow Rothesay into battle or elsewhere, she could stay with her family instead of with enemy strangers whom he must barely know himself by now.

She was still pondering so when the latch clicked and the door opened.

Assuming that it must be Ailvie, she said without turning, "I wondered if I should have to send for you. Is it not growing late?"

The door shut, and the last voice she expected to hear then said, "Ailvie is not here because I sent my woman to tell her not to come until I send for her."

"Grandame!" Catriona exclaimed, turning. "What are you—? That is . . ."

"I have heard of some strange ways to announce a wedding, Catriona," Lady Annis said tartly. "But the usual custom is *not* for the bride to declare her intention so publicly, nor so directly to the heir to Scotland's throne. Do you not think that you might at least have told *some-one* before now that young Sir Finlagh attracted you? He *does* do so, I trust, since you must marry him tonight."

"Tonight! But he said—"

"Never mind what he may have said. Rothesay wants to see a wedding at once. And your grandfather means to provide him with one, because *he* decided some time ago that this Fin of the Battles is an excellent choice for you."

"D-did he?" Catriona could scarcely breathe, let alone respond sensibly.

"Aye, he did. Sithee, he knew from the moment he clapped eyes on him that the lad was a Cameron. And not just any Cameron, mind you, but the son of the great archer, Teàrlach MacGillony, which makes him perfectly suitable to marry you."

"It does?"

"Aye, sure, because coming from *that* branch of the family, he is just the sort of match, your grandfather says, to help him keep this truce in place betwixt the Camerons and Clan Chattan. *That* is of the utmost importance, he says."

"But, Grandame, I—"

"This decision is not about you, Catriona, so you can put that notion right out of your head. And if you mean to cause trouble by losing your temper or enacting some other drama, I strongly advise you to think again. Your father is not in a mood to be either amused or indulgent. In troth, you should be grateful that I persuaded him and your grandfather that I should be the one to relay their decision to you."

"Prithee, if you will just—"

"Hush," Lady Annis commanded, determined as usual to have the last word. "Rothesay means to have his way. So you will be sleeping tonight with the man."

Catriona's imagination promptly produced an image of Rothesay in her bed, but there was naught in that image to amuse her, and she knew that it was not what Lady Annis had meant. But she did not want to think about Fin in her bed either.

That image was much too disturbing, and if she was to retain any respect for herself, she could think about only one thing now.

As she strode to the door, Lady Annis exclaimed, "Where are you going?"

"To end this," Catriona declared. She could not recall ever defying her grandmother before. But she could not let them force Fin to marry her even if she was as angry with him now as she was with herself and everyone else.

⁓

After Rothesay's declaration that the wedding should proceed at once, Fin had tried to catch Shaw's eye, hoping to indicate that they needed to talk. But the conversation had immediately become general, with the women and Alex Stewart exclaiming and asking questions about how the wedding should proceed.

Lady Annis had exchanged a look with the Mackintosh and then left the chamber, declaring that she would inform Catriona of their decision.

"There can be no difficulty about a priest," Rothesay said in answer now to a question from Lady Ealga. "There are many ways around that, but we'll just roust out the real mendicant friar amongst Donald's lads and let him marry them."

Shaw, listening to them, seemed unaware of Fin's tension.

Alex still looked amused, as if he watched the antics of jesters.

Seizing on a pause that fell, Fin said, "With respect, my lords, I believe that such a hasty affair may not serve as well as one accomplished with more thought."

The Mackintosh said testily, "The lass blurted it out to all and sundry, Fin. So there is no reason to delay and every reason to proceed. I ken fine that this puts ye in an unfortunate position, lad—with your own folks not being here," he added with a glance at Rothesay. "In troth, though, ye've been spending so much time with the lass that it has stirred speculation, as such behavior always does. So unless ye expect now to give her the lie and look as if ye've been trifling with her—"

"You know I won't do that, sir. By my troth, I do want to marry her."

He meant that. No longer was he doing the honorable thing or one that he did not mind doing. Catriona had come to mean much more to him than that.

Even so, he had promised that he would speak for her.

"However," he added, looking from one man to the next, "I must tell you that . . . that even now her ladyship is having second thoughts. She—"

"Nae doots, she'll be nervous, what with Rothesay here, and all," the Mackintosh interjected. "But her grandame will see to her."

"Aye, lad," Shaw said. "'Tis better to do it at once before the rumors start."

"Then that be settled," Mackintosh said. "Sakes, but ye cannot wait about whilst she has bride clothes made and the like. Rothesay wants to get back to his own business as soon as he reaches agreement with Alex and Donald. Also, lad, if ye marry quick, ye'll have time to enjoy your lass afore ye have to leave with him."

As Fin opened his mouth to respond, the door flew open and the lass he was supposed to enjoy strode into the room, her golden eyes flashing.

She fixed her gaze on him at once. "I thought you were going to tell them, sir. Instead, we are *now* going to marry at once? Sakes, but I—"

Shaw said curtly, "Catriona, that will do!"

She turned to him next. "Will it, Father? God-a-mercy, you may order me to bed one moment and command me to marry the next, but you must not force F—"

Her words ended in a gasp and a cry when Shaw's hard slap silenced her.

"Not another word," he snapped. "To shame your lord grandfather and me by behaving so before such a company surpasses anything ye've done before! Ye'll do as we bid you, or by God, I will make you sorrier than you have ever—"

"No, sir," Fin cut in coldly. "You will not. Not unless you want me to call an end to my part in this marriage right now."

Chapter 14 ———————

Catriona had heard her father's threat, but distantly, because from the moment she put a hand to her fiery cheek, she had been gazing in shock at the others in the chamber. She realized with dismay that her anger had blinded her to the fact that Alex and Rothesay were there.

She had seen only Fin at first and had expressed herself as if they had been alone until Shaw's command had diverted her anger to him.

She did hear what Fin had said, though, and the ice in his voice sent shivers up her spine. Waiting for Shaw's response, she did not even breathe.

He'd flicked a glance at Fin and still glared at her, but he did not speak.

An ache filled her throat, and the silence lengthened until Fin said, "My lord Rothesay, I would take it kindly if you would allow her ladyship and me to be privy with her family ... for a short time, at least, sir."

Another silence fell, but it was brief, because Alex Stewart got up, saying, "Come along, Davy. We'll find someone to wake up that friar of Donald's."

Hearing Rothesay's chuckle, Catriona watched as he got to his feet, made her a slight bow, and left. Turning back to her father, she knew she ought to feel some relief with Rothesay and Alex gone. But, eyeing the still angry Shaw, she felt none.

When she heard her grandmother's voice in the background, bidding the two great lords goodnight, she felt worse. Lady Annis was only too likely to share her granddaughter's earlier defiance of *her* with the others.

However, everyone's attention shifted back to Fin when he said, "Pray, madam, be sure that that door is shut fast."

Catriona was astonished when her grandmother said quietly, "It is, sir."

"Good," Fin said. "By your leave now, Shaw MacGillivray, I would speak privily with your daughter. Before I do, though, I will make my position clear to you all. Davy Stewart has tried to make a farce out of this business simply to amuse himself. I will not allow that to continue."

"How d'ye propose to stop him, lad?" the Mackintosh asked curiously.

"You may leave that to me, sir. In return, I will endeavor to persuade the lady Catriona…again…that her best course is to accept this marriage, as I do. I will also insist, however, that we marry tomorrow instead of tonight. But," he added when Catriona stiffened, "I will not employ threats or allow anyone else to do so to achieve that course. I sincerely apologize for my curtness to you just now, sir," he said to Shaw. "But I will not accept a bride who must be beaten into marrying me. Nor do I think you want a good-son who would allow that. Would you, sir?"

"Nay, lad. In troth, I'm fast coming to hope that I'll have ye in his stead." Shaw put out his hand, and when Fin gripped it, Catriona relaxed at last.

The Mackintosh said, "If ye're sure about tomorrow, Fin, I'll tell Rothesay m'self. Ye can smooth over aught that ye need to smooth with him afterward."

"He has likely realized already that something has gone awry," Fin said.

"Aye, well, I'll draw on his vast knowledge of women, then," Mackintosh said with a twinkle. "I can say it be more seemly to wed by daylight and will thus make the lass happier. I've other things to suggest, too, and I'll want Shaw with me. Annis and Ealga will retire to the ladies' solar, so that ye two may bide here."

"Thank you, sir," Fin said. In a blink, Catriona was alone with him, but if she expected her trial to be over, she soon learned her error.

"I have something to say before we discuss any marriage," he said with the same chilly edge to his voice as when he had spoken to Shaw.

Swallowing hard, she said, "What is it?"

"Simply, that if I ever again hear you talk that way, to me or to anyone else in authority over you, I'll react much as your father did. I hope I would never slap you in the midst of such a company, but be sure that I would soon put you over my knee. So keep that in mind as we continue, for as much as I would dislike taking a bride whose father had to beat her into marrying me would I dislike marrying one who believed that I would *not* react as sternly to such rudeness."

"You do frequently stir my temper, though," she reminded him.

"And when I do, you may tell me so," he said, putting a warm hand to her sore cheek. His voice gentled as he said, "I'll expect you to tell me civilly, lass, although I will allow for temper, as I hope you will for me. Also, I'll have much more tolerance in private than if you hurl my faults at me before an audience."

"Particularly such an audience as I chose tonight," she said ruefully. "That was not well done of me. By my troth, though, I saw no one but you. I was furious to learn that after you'd said you would persuade them, they were going to force you to marry me at once. I...I don't remember ever being as angry with anyone as I was then with you, even though *they* were doing it. Why do you suppose that is?"

Instead of trying to answer the unanswerable question, Fin gently stroked her reddened cheek and said, "Art still angry with me now, little wildcat?"

"Nay," she murmured, and he was glad to see a tiny smile as she did. "I'm still unsure about all this, though. It happened so suddenly, and it seems so unfair to you, especially when it was my own unruly tongue that caused all the trouble."

"Davy caused it," Fin said. "He has complained of boredom, and when he is bored—or frustrated, as he also is—he makes mischief, with females or otherwise. In this case, it was both. But, see here, lass, you are wrong if you think they have forced me into a wedding. You heard how easily I can stop it, and I will do it if you are still reluctant to marry me. But if you are willing to risk it, I am more so."

"Do not try to cajole me, sir. You did not come here seeking a wife."

"Nay, but I did find someone who will suit me if she will just agree to it."

"I am not unwilling. I am terrified." To his surprise, tears welled into her eyes. "I don't want to live amidst strangers who have so long been our enemies."

"But you would live with me," he said.

"Only when you were at home. Men are forever going off—to battle, to St. Andrews, to all manner of places. And they always leave their womenfolk behind. I don't *want* to live as miserably in Lochaber as Morag lives here."

"I doubt that you would," he said. "You are too warm, too competent, and too wise to live so. You also dwell less on your feelings than your good-sister does. I believe that you will make fast friends easily, wherever we live."

"But I like solitude, too," she reminded him. "Would I be as free to roam the mountains in Lochaber as I usually am here?"

Knowing that any discussion of that subject would undo the progress he had made, he said mildly, "We can talk about that sort of thing anon. For now, I just want to know if you will marry me, Catriona. I hope that you will say aye."

"Aye, then, I will. But you don't fool me, Fin of the Battles. God-a-mercy, but we are going to battle mightily if you forbid me to do the things I most enjoy."

"All married people battle, sweetheart." Seeing her eyes widen at the endearment, he wanted to kiss her. But he needed to be sure they understood each other first. "Art truly willing, Cat—even if we must marry tomorrow?"

"Will you have to go away soon?"

"I mean to talk to Davy about that, to request leave so I can take you to meet my family. I promise you won't have to stay with them if I have to rejoin him soon, though.

I'll bring you back here before I do. I should have other options, too, but it will take time to sort them out."

"That is what you meant about this complicating your life, is it not?"

"It is, aye. Answer my question now. Art sure?"

"Do you think that anyone is ever sure about such things?"

"I know that I am."

"Are you?" She searched his eyes. "Then I am, too."

He kissed her then, and she responded at once, melting against him as she had before, her lips warm and soft beneath his. He kissed her many times, lightly and then more possessively. The thought that she would be his wife on the morrow stimulated every part of him and one in particular.

She felt his cock move, too, because her eyes widened again. When he thrust his tongue into her mouth, she moaned softly, and that moan was nearly his undoing. He wanted to sweep her up and carry her straight to her bed.

Reminding himself that Ailvie would be there, he went on kissing Catriona, stroking her slender body, achingly aware that it would soon be his to possess.

As he eased a hand gently over one soft breast, a double rap sounded on the door. The door opened on the sound, and the Mackintosh walked in.

Fin's wandering hand moved quickly back to her waist. She had stiffened and would have pulled away, but he held her where she was.

"Forgive the intrusion, lad," Mackintosh said. "I've talked with Rothesay and Alex, and I thought ye should hear what we have decided."

Again, Catriona stirred as if to step away, and this time,

Fin allowed it. As he did, he said pointedly, "I do want to hear what you would suggest, sir."

"Aye, well, 'tis more of a consensus, as ye might say. Sithee, Rothesay has agreed that a morning wedding will suit him. He also reminded me that Donald will be impatient to get on with our discussions. He's proving right difficult, is Donald. So I said we should dispense with everyone save the four of us until we sort out what exactly, if anything, Donald and Alex can agree to do for their cousin Davy."

"I'm guessing that Donald will agree to do nowt for him," Fin said.

"Mayhap that is so," Mackintosh said. "But whilst their so-called advisors make more trouble than not, as they have, we cannot know. Now, our James will stay for the wedding, but he wants to leave for Inverness afterward with Morag. They'll stay the night at Moigh, he said, and I thought that ye two might like to stay there, as well. Ye'd sleep in my chamber, for James has his own rooms above it."

Fin glanced at Catriona, but her grandfather did not allow for discussion.

"Ye'll have a few days to yourselves," he said, "whilst we sort an agreement out here. Then, when Rothesay is ready to depart, you can return. Sithee, Moigh sits just fifteen miles away, and the coming back takes less time than the going."

Fin said, "'Tis a generous offer, sir, that we will gladly accept. But I mean to talk to Rothesay about more generous leave. If he agrees, I'll take Catriona to meet my family before we return."

"Aye, well, ye'll decide that for yourself, I expect, or

Davy will. In the event, ye're always welcome here and at Moigh, so there be nae more to say about that. As for ye, lassie," he said, turning to Catriona. "What d'ye say to all this now?"

"I'm willing, sir," she said, flushing deeply. "I...I must apologize to you, though, for my behavior earlier. I let my temper overcome me, sir."

"Ye did, aye, but ye should be apologizing to your father as well, lass."

When she nibbled her lower lip, Fin felt a strong protective urge to say that that might wait. But he knew the Mackintosh was right, so he held his peace.

~

Catriona wondered if she knew what she was doing. Her grandfather was acting as he always did with her, gruff and stern but kindly withal. Still, he would do nothing to make her apology to Shaw easier. Nor, by the look of Fin, would he.

For that matter, she had known all along what she would have to do.

"I will do it straightaway," she said. "Did you and Rothesay decide exactly when this wedding is to take place, sir? Before we break our fast, or after?"

"Before," her grandfather said. "That way, ye and the lad here can have a wedding feast and Rothesay and the others can meet after your party has gone."

Fin said, "I've been wondering, sir, just what the situation is between Clan Chattan and Clan Cameron. I know our truce is still in effect, but I've heard—"

"Whatever ye've heard be nobbut mischief dreamed up by them who would keep us busy fighting each other, lad," the Mackintosh said firmly. "If the truce betwixt our two clans should fail, it will not be Clan Chattan that breaks it. Nor do I believe that any Cameron leader wants aught at present save peace."

"Thank you, sir. I had heard only whispers, but in such a case..."

"Aye, one's imagination can feed all manner of bad cess into one's mind. Let it rest, expect the best, and all will be well. I've a notion that a day or two at Moigh will ease your mind considerably. The place does have that effect."

A strange sensation stirred in Catriona as her thoughts drifted. She would sleep with Fin at Moigh. The thought stirred her imagination, serving up images of what that might be like. The image of him walking naked on the shore lingered longer than most, so when she realized that he was watching her, heat flamed in her cheeks. It spread quickly then through the rest of her as well.

"Is Shaw still in the hall?" Fin asked, bringing her instantly back to earth.

"Aye, he must be," Mackintosh said. "He said he would await my return."

"Then I suggest that we see him and then send this lass upstairs to her maidservant. They have much to do before they sleep to prepare for the morrow."

Catriona did not think it mattered how much she and Ailvie had to do. She would not sleep a wink.

Fin opened the door for her, and she saw Shaw standing just beyond it in the hall. He was clearly on the watch for them, because he came to meet her at once.

"Lassie," he said.

"I'm sorry I was so rude to you, sir," she said at the same time.

"Aye, me, too," he said, pulling her close. "Ye deserved a good smack, lass, but ye didna deserve to bear it in front of yon rascally Rothesay and Alex Stewart."

Glancing around to be sure that those gentlemen were not also still in the hall, Catriona said, "In troth, sir, had you not stopped me as you did, I fear that I might have said more than I should. Sithee, I was so angry that I was not thinking. I did not even see Rothesay or Alex Stewart *until* you silenced me. As it was, I am not sure but that Rothesay may have guessed I'd made the whole thing up. Do you truly believe it would not have been better just to admit it and apologize to him."

"I am, lass. This all amuses him now, which renders him harmless. But he is a powerful man and gey reckless. To learn that ye'd lied to him would soon lead him to imagine that others were laughing at him, which would lead next to a sense of deep offense. To offend the powerful is unwise at any time, lassie, and best to avoid."

"What did Granddad tell him?"

"Only that it never paid to rush a woman. He said he'd learned that lesson in his youth from your grandame, and he assured Rothesay that putting off the ceremony until morning would make ye gey happier and thus serve us all better."

Glancing at Fin, she saw him frown and waited for him to explain why. He said nothing, however, and she accepted his lead by bidding her father and grandfather goodnight. Then she let Fin escort her to her chamber.

"Ailvie will be in there," she said as they neared her door. "Grandame said that she would send her up, and I'm sure she must have done so by now."

"Come here then," he said, pulling her close and tilting her chin so that he could kiss her again.

She leaned into him as he did, savoring the warmth of his hard body against hers as well as his kisses. After a long and pleasant time, she said, "What made you frown so when Granddad told us what he had said to Rothesay?"

Without hesitation, he said, "Rothesay thinks only in terms of women making *him* happy, never in terms of considering any woman's wishes. He may still ask me some pointed questions about all this. You are not to worry, though. I have managed to work with and for him these past years without incurring much of his wrath. I was just thinking about what he might ask and how I might answer him."

"He can be gey charming," Catriona said with a rueful smile.

"Aye, and he does trade on that charm, too. But your Ailvie will hear us if we keep talking out here, sweetheart, and this is no place for such a conversation. So, kiss me again, and then it's bed for you."

She obeyed, although there was much more that she would have liked to discuss with him. When he reached to open the door, she said, "I am glad that James and Morag are going to see her family, for she has missed them. But I do wish that they were not traveling with us. I want to know more about you, Fin of the Battles, and such a journey without them would give us more time to talk."

"Aye, but we'll find time for talking," he said, lightly pinching her earlobe. Then, after one more kiss, he said, "Get thee in, sweetheart, and sleep."

"I do not think you can command me yet," she said. "I am not yet your wife."

"True. Now go."

She went.

Stirling Castle

The Duke of Albany was reviewing accounts with his steward when a minion announced Sir Martin Redmyre. Signing to the steward to leave and telling Redmyre to take a seat, he waited until the door had shut and said, "You have learned more."

"Aye, my lord duke. My man heard two days ago that the Mackintosh was apparently in daily expectation of visitors at Rothiemurchus Castle. It lies—"

"I don't care where it lies, Martin. Who are these visitors?"

"Comyn called them 'grand lairds,' sir. Three of them, his kinsman said."

"Three?"

"Aye, and Davy did meet with your nephew Alex Stewart in Perth, and with Shaw MacGillivray, who is now Laird of Rothiemurchus and good-son to the Mackintosh. No one seems to know the third one, but I'd guess it must be Donald."

"So would I if I could imagine how Donald could cross the entire western Highlands from the Isles to get to Clan Chattan country. But if Davy allies with Alex . . . I'll want to think about that. How long do they mean to be there?"

"I don't know, but my man promises that the Comyns have devised a plan to keep them where they are long enough for us to get there. However, if you are thinking of sending someone at once to catch them conspiring together, whoever you send may meet with difficulty. There are, as you must know, only two possible routes for a force of any size."

"I know the one through Glen Garry. Is there another at this time of year?"

"Aye, sure, or so Comyn said. The other is through the Cairngorms to the east. Its snowy passes must be hazardous, but he swears that the route is feasible by now."

"I've no intention of risking myself on such a route. This country needs me. But you will take my men and your own that way. If Glen Garry is the easier route, I'll send the Earl of Douglas that way. He can gather his Border army quickly, and he has much the same reason as your own to interfere with any plan of Davy's. After all, the Douglas's sister is Davy's unhappy wife. Also, Redmyre..."

"Aye," the other man said, raising his eyebrows.

"If your men there can hold them for you, you know what will serve me best."

"I do, my lord. I do, indeed."

Satisfied, but not one to count a deed done until it was, Albany dismissed him.

Fin would have liked to go straight to his own bed, for although it was still relatively early, he had had his fill of emotion for the day. However, he knew that he would be wise to ask Rothesay straightaway for leave to take Catriona to Moigh and, if Davy would spare him longer, straight on to Tor Castle.

Finding the hall empty of everyone except those trying to sleep there, he went to Rothesay's chamber.

The gillie who always slept on a pallet before the door was awake. Scrambling to his feet, the lad said, "My lord duke did say ye'd come, sir."

"I want to see him if he is still awake," Fin said.

"Aye, he said ye might wish it. But he said tae tell ye he'd be fast asleep by now." Glancing toward the door when sounds came from within that included a feminine giggle, the lad said stoutly, "He'll talk wi' ye on the morrow, sir. Afore the wedding, he did say. Be there going tae *be* a wedding, Sir Fin?"

"Aye," Fin said, wondering if the Mackintosh or Shaw knew that Rothesay had a woman in his bed. He hoped that she was as willing as she sounded and a maidservant rather than a noblewoman or a Mackintosh tenant's wife.

On that thought, an image of the redoubtable Lady Annis rose in his mind, so he was chuckling when he added, "If you see him when he wakens, tell him that I do hope to speak with him privately before the ceremony. You may fetch me from my chamber as soon as he finds it convenient."

Returning to his room, he woke the dozing Ian and informed him of the wedding and the journey to follow while Ian aided his preparations for bed. Having little to pack, he soon sent Ian to bed in the hall as usual, and put out his candle.

Lying in bed, he wondered if Catriona was asleep yet and how different things might have been—or if they would have ended up the same—had he insisted on continuing to Moigh the day they had met. If the arrow had killed him, he would never have met her. But what if the arrow had just missed him and he had returned to Rothiemurchus in a normal way after learning that the Mackintosh was there?

Would the Mackintosh ever have trusted him alone with her then? Or was it the fact that they had been alone in the woods that had made the man trust him?

As he tried to imagine how the order of things might have progressed, the images faded and dreams of Catriona in his arms replaced them.

When he awoke with the dawn, he was sweating, erect, and annoyed that a most satisfactory dream had ended moments too soon with the entrance into his chamber of gray, early-morning light.

The night before, the thought of marrying her had produced delightful, sensual anticipation. Now it produced a clearer, much more urgent desire for her.

Rising hastily, he dressed himself without waiting for Ian and waited impatiently for Rothesay's lad to fetch him.

"Take off your shift for me, lass," Fin said, smiling in much the same hungry way that Rory Comyn had always smiled at her. But Fin's smile did not discomfit her...at least, not in the same way that Comyn's had.

Feelings roared through her body much as the river Spey roared in full spate through Strathspey after a mighty rainstorm or when the high snows were melting fast and racing into it from every rill, rivulet, and burn.

She gazed up at Fin from under her lashes, wondering what he would do if she refused to obey his command. A husband, after all, had every right to command his wife, but if he thought that he was going to order her every breath and step from his wedding day forward, he was in for a fine surprise.

Faith, but she was flirting with him, with her own husband, whilst he stood naked before her, his eagerness plain... and she with only a thin shift to protect her.

"Take it off, Catriona," he said, moving toward her. She felt his warm hand on her bare upper arm and heard a low, rumbling moan in his throat...

Catriona awoke with annoyance to discover that the low rumbling sound in her dream, as well as the warmth against her upper arm, was merely Boreas's kitten curled up against her, purring loudly.

As she lay wondering if her interesting dream might otherwise have included what else would happen when she lay naked beside Fin, a memory flitted through her mind. Her grandmother had been talking to Ealga about Morag.

"James should be more masterful with that lass," Lady Annis had said tartly. "Faith, but he should give her a good hiding to cure her low spirits."

Catriona's mother had protested that James was rather more prone to lecture a woman than to behave masterfully. But Lady Annis had said, "Pish tush, he must learn to take a firmer hand if he would stop her complaints. All women prefer men who will stand up for themselves to those who will not."

Catriona had a strong feeling that she would never complain of Fin's failure to stand up for himself. She was not as sure as her grandmother seemed to be that she would prefer that he always be masterful.

Ailvie's entrance put an end to her fantasies, so she got up to prepare for what promised to be a long day. When she descended to the great hall a half-hour later, she found everyone else gathered near the huge fireplace, waiting for her.

Swallowing, hoping she was not making a mistake that would end in misery as Morag's had, she obeyed her father's gesture and went to stand beside him.

As she did, she heard Rothesay say in a voice that carried to every corner of the hall, "But of course you cannot ride off with the lass before you consummate your marriage, Fin. Bless us, man, it will not be a *real* marriage until you do."

Conscious of a strong desire to throttle Rothesay, and not for the first time, Fin said, "We are eager to consummate our union, sir. But I'd liefer reach Moigh at a good hour than linger here. James and his lady ride with us and are eager to be off."

"Don't be daft, man. Your bride is his sister, and his lady will do as he bids."

Fin knew he had erred in mentioning Morag's wishes. But he'd seen Catriona come in and knew she had overheard Davy's comments. Even in the dim morning light, he saw her cheeks darken but could not tell if she was vexed or just embarrassed.

Hearing James clear his throat behind him, Fin hoped that his soon-to-be good-brother would support leaving as soon as possible.

James said, "Your company would be gey welcome, Fin. But I did promise Morag that we'll take no more time than necessary here or at Moigh. Sithee, my lady would prefer to spend the night with our kinsmen at Daviot, five miles nearer to Inverness. That would shorten our journey tomorrow and likewise leave Castle Moigh to you and Cat for your wedding night."

Looking again at Catriona, who stood by Shaw and

gazed into the fire, Fin said, "I will talk with her, James. You and I can easily find time to discuss this more before you must leave."

James nodded, but Rothesay said, "You are a fool, Fin, if you think these Mackintoshes will let you leave with their lass still a maiden. They'll not risk your returning her in a like state and demanding annulment due to lack of consummation. Mayhap they should watch it, just to be sure," he added with a mocking grin.

That grin made Fin nearly certain Davy had guessed that Catriona had either exaggerated their relationship or lied about it. That he was still enjoying himself was likely due to the evident intent to conceal the fact.

Fin glanced then at Mackintosh and got a curt nod, indicating that Rothesay was right about one thing. The family—the head of it, at least—would insist that he and Catriona consummate their marriage before departing.

Mackintosh came forward then to say lightly, "It takes little time, lad. The first coupling is a shock to any young bride, but if ye've a good appetite for her, it need take just a minute or two. James can wait that long. I'm thinking, too, that ye'll have more energy for it if ye eat first, and will thereby enjoy yourself the more."

Rothesay's grin widened, making Fin wish fervently that one could horsewhip the young Governor of the Realm without hanging for it.

James, still behind him, said quietly, "A private word with you, Fin?"

Nodding, Fin moved away with him, and James added softly, "My lass says she wants time alone with me. She says such time has been sadly lacking in our marriage. It may seem a small thing—"

"Nay," Fin told him. "Catriona and I have things to discuss, too. But we can all travel to Moigh together and still give ourselves distance enough to talk with our wives. Then, too, you will be alone with Morag from Moigh to Castle Daviot."

James agreed, and they saw Morag approaching, so Fin moved to join Shaw and Catriona by the fire. Donald and Alex entered together shortly afterward, followed by their retainers and Donald's mendicant friar.

Catriona turned to Fin when he neared the hearth, and as her gaze met his, a slight smile touched her lips, lingered there, and grew warmer.

Feeling himself stir in response, Fin smiled, too.

Chapter 15 _____

Catriona's first thought as she watched Donald and Alex enter with their attendants was that the friar looked too shabby to be performing a wedding.

She wore a gown of soft tawny velvet, and Fin looked particularly fine in a green velvet doublet and darker green hose that she had not seen him wear before. All the talk of their consummation and the thought of coupling with him had stirred her curiosity again. When he looked at her, she felt suddenly shy.

She had no time to think after that, because the friar said to Fin, "We'll begin at once if ye please, sir. The ceremony be short, and the Mackintosh said that nae one wants to sit through a nuptial mass. We'll eat when we're done here, he said."

Rothesay, having moved near enough to overhear him, chuckled and said in his usual, carrying voice, "Everyone, gather round. Our priest would begin, and I smell roasting beef, so do not dawdle."

Catriona saw Fin's lips press together, but Rothesay's behavior no longer disturbed her. Her gaze rested on Fin, and her thoughts lingered there, as well.

His lips relaxed, and a twinkle lit his eyes.

Without thinking, she reached out a hand to him.

"Nay, not yet, m'lady," the friar said. "Ye'll be letting me say the words over ye first. Now, Sir Finlagh, d'ye take this woman to be your wife ... ?"

Catriona listened and enjoyed the sound of Fin's voice as he plighted his troth to her in all manner of ways, "for this time forward, till death us depart."

The friar said then, "Ha' ye a ring for your lady, sir?"

Catriona, watching Fin, saw consternation in his expression. But before he could speak, aid came to him unexpectedly.

"Aye, he does," the Mackintosh said, stepping forward. "I have the ring right here, lad." As he handed something to Fin, Mackintosh looked at Catriona and said, "'Twas me mother's ring, lassie. I promised her that I would keep it for my favorite granddaughter, and so I have if ye'll accept it from us now."

Her eyes awash with sudden tears, Catriona caught hold of his arm and stood on tiptoe to kiss his wrinkled cheek. "I do accept it, sir, and proudly. I thank you, too, for I will think of you both, as well as of my husband, whenever I look at it."

Slipping it onto her finger, and at the friar's prompting, Fin said, "With this ring I thee wed, and with its gold and silver I thee endow. With my body I thee worship, and with all my worldly cattle I thee honor."

Obediently repeating vows similar to his first ones, Catriona also promised to be "meek and obedient in bed and at board," as she plighted her troth to Fin.

And that was apparently that, because the friar turned to face the audience and said, "My lords, my ladies, and all here watching, I pray you, take heed now of this married couple, Sir Finlagh and Lady..." Pausing, he looked ruefully at Fin. "Bless me, sir, I did forget to ask ye what her ladyship's proper styling be."

"Lady Finlagh will do for now," Fin said.

"...Sir Finlagh and Lady Finlagh," the priest repeated.

"Have ye whisky nearby, Mackintosh?" Davy Stewart demanded. "I've a thirst on me now that nowt save whisky will slake."

"I do have some, aye, as any good Highlander does," Mackintosh replied. "Fetch the jug from my chamber, James, and send one of the lads to fetch more. Everyone should drink to this wedding, especially Fin and Catriona."

Catriona wrinkled her nose at the thought of drinking the fiery stuff. But when she did, Fin leaned close and murmured, "You'll drink with me, lass. It will warm you for what is to come after we have broken our fast."

"I'd liefer drink it after I eat something," she whispered back. "I don't mind whisky with honey when I've an ague on me. But, other times, nay."

"Then we'll drink our toast from one goblet," he said. "You need only touch your lips to the whisky to avoid bad luck in our marriage. But if you will heed some good advice, you'll take some claret with your food. You did hear that your grandfather expects us to consummate our union afterward, did you not? And that James and Morag will be waiting for us to get on with it?"

"Aye, sure," she said. Feeling suddenly shy, she looked away, adding, "I ken what we'll do then, because my grandame told me. She said it will be pleasurable."

Lady Annis had said more than that, for she had been as blunt about sex as she was about most things. But that had been nearly two years ago. And Catriona remembered the physical description and promise of pleasure, but little else.

Fin put two fingers under her chin, making her look at him. Smiling warmly, he said, "We'll see that it does become pleasurable, lass. I mean us to practice as often as possible. For now, though, I'll just treat myself to one wee kiss."

With that, right there in front of everyone who cared to watch, he put his free arm around her and slowly, tantalizingly, bent nearer until his warm lips touched hers. Then, as if they were alone instead of in the midst of a large company, he drew her close enough to feel his length against hers and shifted the hand at her chin to the small of her back, pressing her closer.

His lips ravished hers, and his body stirred against her own. When the tip of his tongue sought entrance to her mouth, she resisted briefly and then submitted to its penetration. Closing her eyes, she moaned when his tongue began to joust with hers. The sensations he stirred stimulated others, a whole host of others.

He ended the kiss at last but did not release her. And her eyes stayed shut, because her mind had filled with images of what lay ahead of them.

When applause broke out, and cheers, her eyes flew open. Dazed, she felt as if some strange spell that had overcome her had ended abruptly with the noise.

"You're blushing, sweetheart, but you need not," Fin said. "A man has a right to kiss his bride after the ceremony."

She smiled then. "I didn't mind at all."

As they turned toward the high table, the Mackintosh approached them and said, "Ye'll take time to meet with me in the inner chamber after we break our fast, lad, and ye'll bring your lass with ye."

"Granddad, you cannot mean for us to consummate our marriage in there!"

"Nay, lass, although I'll admit that I did think it would be a grand honor to let ye. But your grandame called me a dafty and said ye'd prefer your own bed to any other. Ailvie and the women be preparing it for the two of ye now."

Relieved beyond measure, because she could not imagine consummating her marriage in the bed that her parents shared and that her grandparents had slept in for a month, Catriona went contentedly with her husband to the high table.

Rothesay awaited them there. "The Mackintosh said that you should take the central chairs, Fin. So I'll sit beside you. Having given my blessing to this marriage, it is right and proper that I do. I do have a question, though."

"Aye, sir?"

"Why Lady Finlagh? Why not Lady Cameron?"

⁓

Wondering what mischief Rothesay was up to now, Fin said, "So you know my clan, do you, sir? I thought that you must." Noting a flash of disappointment on the prince's expressive face, he felt a twinge of unease.

"Aye, sure," Rothesay said. "I've known all about you from the start. Bishop Traill told me that you had cause to keep your identity to yourself. And knowing how fractious our Highland clans can be, I decided that that cause was likely a matter of self-preservation. Is that how it was?"

"'Tis close enough," Fin said.

"I see. But the great feud *was* between your confederation and Clan Chattan," Rothesay said. "So, I did wonder if the Mackintosh knew. But your lady showed no surprise just now when I asked, and one does assume that if she knows, he does."

"Aye, sure, he does," Fin said.

"Then, I repeat, why 'Lady Finlagh'?"

"Because I am a younger son, of course," Fin said with a shrug. "'Tis how folks will style her at home, where my brother's wife is Lady Cameron."

"Aye, sure, 'tis the usual way. That reminds me, though, of *why* I wondered if the Mackintosh knew about you. It was not just that Camerons and Mackintoshes were foes in that battle at Perth. It was also that you belong to the same Camerons who began that feud, over who owns Tor Castle and the Loch Arkaig estates."

For the second time in less than an hour, Fin indulged in murderous thoughts about Rothesay. And one look at Catriona told him that she had indeed recalled his equivocal reply when she'd asked him about Tor Castle the day after they had met.

Catriona had heard Rothesay's comments plainly. But it took a moment to realize that the heat she felt rising in her was no longer sensual but emotional.

By the time she recognized her feeling of betrayal for what it was, she likewise realized that she could not vent her reaction to it then and there. But when she shot Fin an oblique, speaking glance, she saw that he was already facing her and had been expecting such a look, if not more.

"Lass," he said quietly. "I should have told you. We'll talk about it later."

Nodding, she dared not speak lest she say exactly what she was thinking.

She was still thinking about what he had said about Tor Castle that day, when she heard Lady Annis, just to her left, say, "That friar of Donald's did better than one hoped of such a ragged creature. Ye be well and truly wedded now, dearling. And your granddad thinks ye've done gey well for yourself withal."

"Does he, Grandame?" Grateful for an excuse to look anywhere other than at her husband, Catriona added, "I expect Granddad also told you that we mean to stay at Castle Moigh for the next few days."

"Aye, sure. When he sent the messenger to warn them of your coming, I made sure that all will be in readiness for you. I expect James told you that he and Morag will ride on to Daviot, so ye'll have the place nearly all to yourselves."

"I overheard him telling Fin," Catriona admitted.

"Your Fin is a fine man," Lady Annis said. "Mind, though, that ye do not let him see that temper of yours until ye've taken measure of his. I have seen signs in the man much like those that ought to have warned me to tread warier than I did with your grandsire at the outset of our marriage. We lived here, then, of course."

"What happened?"

Lady Annis smiled reminiscently. "He scolded me for doing what I thought had been a natural thing for me to do. So I pitched a basinful of cold water at him."

"You didn't!" When she nodded, Catriona said, "What had you done?"

Her ladyship shrugged. "I climbed a tree to get a wider view of the loch."

"Well, I think that does sound perfectly natural. Why did it anger him?"

"Perhaps I ought to have explained that I was wearing only my shift at the time. We had been…um…getting better acquainted, as one might say."

A gurgle of laughter rose in Catriona's throat. "Where *were* you?"

"On the west shore yonder, near the landing. By my troth, though, he lectured me in the coble, all the way back to the castle, and all the way upstairs to our chamber. So, when I'd heard enough, I pitched the water at him…*all* over him."

Catriona grinned. "And then?"

"That is all I am going to tell ye, Mistress Impertinence. Ye ken your granddad fine, so doubtless ye can use that fertile imagination of yours for the rest. But I am telling ye—I, who know men—that I see similar signs in your Sir Finlagh. His eyes narrow in the same way, and his jaw tightens so much that wee muscles jump in his cheeks. If ye would be happy, tread softly when ye see those signs."

Catriona smiled and nodded but decided that in the next hour or so, it would be Fin, rather than she, who ought to be watching for signs of temper.

Tadhg interrupted them by extending a platter of thinly sliced beef to Catriona. She nearly reminded him that he should serve her grandmother first before she remembered that, as the bride, *she* was the ranking lady of the day.

Applying herself to her breakfast, she hoped that Fin would talk to her and not just try to assuage her displeasure so she would couple with him. She soon realized, with some indignation, that he was not paying her any heed.

A brief glance, however, provided an explanation for his neglect.

Rothesay, on his other side, was holding forth about something. After his recent behavior, she suspected that he was trying to make more mischief.

Someone, she decided, should have thoroughly acquainted Davy Stewart with a good stiff leather tawse during his childhood, to teach him better manners.

No sooner had she nodded to a gillie that he could clear her place than her grandfather stood and raised a goblet. "We'll be drinking to the bride and groom now, if ye please. They'll want to be getting on with the grandest duty of marriage."

Delighted laughter greeted his announcement. Goblets were filled and raised and the toasting soon over—too soon to suit Catriona. Worse, she had drunk some wine with each toast and could tell that she had had more than she should.

"Come now, into the inner chamber with ye," the Mackintosh said, putting one hand on Fin's shoulder and the other on Catriona's. "Ye can take the service stair up to your bedchamber from there, so ye'll have nae need to pass this way again. Our lads be already taking your things across the loch and loading the ponies. So everyone can go straight outside to see ye off after ye've dressed."

As Catriona followed him into the inner chamber, she could feel Fin's presence beside her as if he were touching her. Still irritated, she wondered what he was thinking and decided that he'd better be kicking himself for not being more forthcoming about his close connection to Tor Castle.

Wondering what the Mackintosh wanted with them, Fin followed Catriona, enjoying the enticing sway of her hips as she passed her grandfather into the chamber but trying to measure, too, just how upset she was.

Inside, Mackintosh shut the door and crossed to his table, from which he took a foolscap document. An ink-pot and a sharpened quill lay nearby.

Turning to Fin, he said, "I'll not take long with this, lad, for I ken fine that ye're impatient to claim your bride. Also, we both know that James and Morag be champing at their bits to be off the island and away."

"James promised to wait, sir," Fin said.

"Aye, sure. Now this be the charter for Raitt Castle. I have signed it over to ye for your lifetime as a wedding gift. I'd be fain to see it go next to your heir, but I ken fine that ye'll never change your name to Mackintosh, nor should ye. Not after nearly giving your life for Clan Cameron."

"You are right, sir," Fin said.

"Mayhap, though, if ye'll choose to live much of each year at Raitt and one of your sons would agree to take the name, Shaw can arrange for it to pass to him. Sithee, he agrees to the notion. If aught happens to ye afore ye have a son, Raitt will revert to Catriona unless she remarries to an outlander. Agreed?"

Fin did not hesitate. "You do me great honor, my lord. I will agree, aye."

"Good, then. Sign right there at the bottom," the Mackintosh said, dipping the quill and handing it to him. "Nae one has lived there for a time, but 'tis a sturdy place and can soon be made comfortable for a family."

Fin signed, received yet another goblet of whisky, and drank with his new kinsman to their agreement. Catriona stood nearby, and other than hugging her grandfather and thanking him, she remained silent.

"The door's yonder, lad," Mackintosh said. "Ye've nae reason now to tarry."

Putting a hand to Catriona's elbow, Fin urged her toward the door and ahead of him up the narrow stairway. He was thankful that they would have privacy.

Many weddings, as he knew, ended in a raucous bedding ceremony that was highly entertaining for the company but rarely so for the couple. He was sure that, under the circumstances, having to endure such a ceremony would *not* be helpful.

When they were safely in her bedchamber, she turned to face him. "Do you still think we must bed at once, sir, after what Rothesay said below?"

"I do, aye," he said. "We have a duty to consummate our marriage, and you are as aware as I am that James and Morag are waiting for us. We can fratch later."

"But I don't understand why you never told me."

Taking a step toward her, looking right into her eyes as he did, he said, "I should have told you, but we can discuss the matter as we travel, lass. We will not discuss it now. Not with everyone waiting downstairs to bid us farewell."

She stepped back.

Annoyance stirred, but he knew that she had cause to feel as she did. However, such discussions took time, and he did not believe that the people waiting below in the hall and in the yard would be patient. He glanced at the door to the main stairway. "Does that door have a bolt?"

"Nay," she said. "I have never needed one."

"Aye, well, beddings often become public affairs, lass. The reason your grandfather sent us up the service stair was to give us privacy. But if we do not go down soon, they will come up. I don't think you will like that."

Her face paled. "Then perhaps you should go down and tell them..."

"Tell them what?" he asked when she paused uncertainly.

When she did not answer, he took another step, saying gently, "We are the same two people we were earlier. The only difference is that now we are married. We can still talk to each other, and we will. Now, come here to me, sweetheart."

She turned away.

"Catriona..." His patience was ebbing.

⁓

Catriona recognized the warning tone. Turning, she saw that his lips had formed a straight line hard enough to make a tiny muscle twitch in one cheek. Recalling Lady Annis's warning, she felt an odd little thrill dance up her spine.

"We have made vows to each other, Catriona," he said evenly. "I will keep mine, and I expect you to keep yours."

"What will you do if I don't? Ravish me or beat me?" But her heart was pounding, and the way he looked at her now made her want to touch him.

"You know that I would not hurt you or force you," he said, clearly keeping his temper in check.

The tension in the room had increased tenfold, much of it within her own body. Her anger had ebbed with that tension, too, as if she could not contain two strong emotions at once.

He was determined, and that determination stirred indescribable feelings inside her. From her tingling skin to the core of her body, every nerve had come alive. When he took yet another step toward her, they vibrated as if someone had plucked a harp with strings attached to every part of her.

He reached for her.

She licked her lips, eyeing him warily but without fear. Anticipation of what he might do warred with her own desire to touch him, to let him know how she felt deep inside. Then he touched her cheek, the palm of his hand warm against it but making it ache a little, too, reminding her of her father's fury the night before and how Fin had responded to it.

"We can deal better than this, lass," he said, his voice low-pitched and husky. "I promise you, we will discuss whatever you like for as long as you like whilst we travel. James said that Morag seeks privacy with him, too, so they will leave us to ourselves. Now, unless you want me to have to tell them that we have failed to consummate our marriage..." He paused.

She certainly did not want that. "Would you really tell them?" she asked, although she knew what he would say.

"I will not lie to them," he said. "Nor, I think, would you. Forbye, they will examine the sheets."

Experiencing a sense of relief just to know that she had judged him aright, she felt the warmer sensations increase.

The hand on her cheek shifted to her left shoulder, and when she did not object, both of his hands moved to her laces. When one of them chanced to brush across the tip of a breast, the feeling it caused made her gasp.

Lingering warmth from the wine she had drunk enhanced the feeling. She felt as if it spread its heat all through her.

He opened her bodice, stroking the tawny velvet as he did. The cool air in the room made her tremble as he untied her shift ribbons and bared her breasts.

"Ah, lassie," he murmured, "how beautiful you are. I wish we could take our time, so that I might show you how pleasant this can be. But I fear..."

"...that someone will come, I know," she said. "I do know something of what must be done, because Grandame did tell me. But *can* it be done so swiftly?"

The question alone was answer enough for Fin's willing body, which leaped mightily at the vision she produced in his mind. But he did not want to hurt or frighten her, so he said, "It can be done, sweetheart. But I'd liefer have your dress off first, for you will be more comfortable so."

She reached for her gold-linked girdle, unclasping it and setting it atop a kist. He helped her slip off her velvet tunic, its matching skirt, and her red flannel underskirt. Standing before him in only her shift, its top still agape to reveal her firm, rosy-tipped breasts, she was even more magnificent than he had imagined.

Stripping off her shift and casting it aside, he picked her up and carried her naked to the bed, which the women had turned down to reveal the pristine sheet. Laying her down, he took off his shoes, hose, and netherstocks. His cock was ready for her, and he saw her eyes widen when she saw it, but she did not protest.

"You did not say if your grandame warned you that the first time may be painful for you," he said. "But I'll do all I can to make it easier, especially since we have a long ride ahead of us. We need only couple, though, no more, so—"

"Aye, sure, I know that," she said as if she wondered why he would say something so obvious.

"Ah, but there *is* more to this than you may be thinking after we've finished. So you should know before we start that to do what I mean to do will deny me much pleasure. That denial will weigh heavily on me until I can ease its weight, which," he added, grinning now, "I mean to do before we rest tonight."

Catriona could scarcely breathe as she watched him. He had taken off only his hose and netherstocks. But it was enough to tell her that Lady Annis must be mad to think that a man built as he was could ever couple with a woman as small as Catriona.

He glanced again at the door to the main stairway.

"In troth, sir, I doubt that anyone will enter without rapping first," she said.

"Likely, you're right," he said. "We'll just snatch blankets over us if they do."

On those words, he got into bed, stretched out beside her, and raised himself on an elbow to lean over and kiss her. His breath smelled pleasantly of whisky, and the velvet doublet he still wore caressed her bare breasts, stirring new sensations wherever it touched her. "Breathe deeply, and try to relax," he murmured against her mouth as he stroked her belly. "I'll be as gentle and as quick as I can be."

With that, his stroking hand moved toward the juncture of her legs. When she stiffened, he shifted his hand to her thigh, stroking it gently but moving slowly, inexorably back toward his objective until his fingers brushed lightly over the curls there. When he slid a finger inside her, she started.

"Easy, sweetheart," he murmured, kissing her again. "I think your body is more prepared to receive me than your mind is. Don't think, just feel."

Chapter 16 _____

I'm feeling so much that I *can't* think," Catriona muttered. Then Fin touched something that made her earlier feelings seem tame by comparison. Fire shot through her. His lips claimed hers again, holding them captive as his fingers teased her more.

His tongue invaded her mouth, and she responded at once with her own.

She barely realized that she was moving against two fingers now, trying to increase the pleasurable sensations they elicited within. Then he withdrew them and moved to replace them with a larger part of himself.

Straddling her now, bearing his weight on his legs and his hands, he looked into her eyes as he pressed himself gently inside her. Catriona tried to relax, moaning in soft protest to a dull ache. He paused, eased out again, and repeated the movements. Now resting on his knees and forearms, he no longer kept her mouth occupied with his lips and tongue, but the sensations below, both mesmerizing and somewhat worrisome, kept her mind well occupied.

Moving one hand to cup her left breast, he used his thumb to tease the nipple, diverting her attention just as he pressed himself fully inside her.

Gasping at the increasing pain, she felt her body respond nonetheless to his. She had closed her eyes, but she opened them to see his face contorting as if he were the one in pain. His body gave a sudden start, and his grimace became more profound as he drew in a long deep breath and let it out again. Just as she wondered what would come next, his face relaxed and he eased himself out of her.

"That should satisfy anyone bumptious enough to inquire into the matter," he said gruffly as he shifted to lie beside her. "Was it so painful, lassie?"

"It ached some, but now it feels only hot and a bit prickly," she said.

"A good word," he said with a chuckle. "We'll get you cleaned up then, or do you want me to shout for Ailvie? I do need to change my clothes for the journey."

"Prithee, don't call her until I can tidy myself, but you must do as you like."

"I don't like it at all," he said with a wry smile. "I'd rather stay right where I am. And I should warn you that all I'm going to be thinking about until we're safely in bed together at Castle Moigh is that I have unfinished business with you."

She nearly told him that she would be thinking much the same thing. Then, she remembered that she was still annoyed with him. Somehow, that little detail had flown right out of her head the moment he had touched her.

Since she still wanted to make her feelings clear, she thought it might be wiser not to admit the effect that his touch had on her, so she said lightly, "You may not be safe as soon as you think, sir. We still have matters to discuss, you and I."

"Aye, sure, lass. In turn, I'd remind you that a husband

has greater rights in such discussion than a guest or a friend does. You have given your temper free rein several times since we met. I prefer that my wife remain civil in her manner to me."

"Do you, sir?"

He gave her a direct look. "I do, aye."

"Then do not give me cause to lose my temper, and all will be well."

Holding her gaze, he said, "We'll see just how well it is, won't we?"

Fin grinned at her as he got out of bed and was glad to receive a wry smile in return. He did not want to debate anymore until they were on the road.

Shortly afterward, wearing suitable attire for riding, they joined James, Morag, their attendants, guests, and family members at the boat landing, where the travelers piled into one of the larger boats. Fin was thankful for all the company, the activity, and his mantle, because his body still expressed its disapproval of his decision to remove himself from the velvety warmth of Catriona's sheath.

All the feelings that she had engendered remained wide awake in him, albeit not as strong as at the time of his withdrawal. Then it had elicited a surge of instinctive, primitive yearning to conquer her. His cock still twitched in awareness of her nearness, but at least it no longer ached.

That his decision had been the right one, he knew. Just watching her on the landing with the family, seeing how naturally she smiled when she spoke with the others and how gracefully she got into the boat assured him that their brief coupling had not hurt her enough to cause her distress as they traveled.

If God was kind, He would reward them both by nightfall. If He was in a more fractious mood, He would resurrect the earlier, more irritable lass.

Fin would do his best to prevent the latter choice.

They reached the opposite landing to find Toby and Ian waiting with a string of Highland garrons, the small, sure-footed horses that could travel nearly anywhere in mountainous terrain without missing a step. Four of them were sumpter ponies.

The others bore minimal leather saddles similar to those that Borderers used. Like the men, the women rode astride, their skirts made full enough for discretion.

Having said their farewells on the island, they mounted quickly.

Fin had not ridden a garron in years and recalled Rothesay's description of riding such a horse. His feet seemed awkwardly close to the ground, but garrons were strong and could carry weights greater than his with ease.

After setting out on the trail that he and Catriona had followed to the loch's outflow, they rode only a short way before they saw a half-dozen men striding toward them. All carried swords and dirks.

Toby Muir said, "Master, that be the gallous young slink that lost his sword tae ye the day we met ye and her ladyship just yonder."

"Rory Comyn," Catriona said at the same time. "What is *he* doing here?"

"I can guess," James said. "We heard that he and other Comyns have been casting threats about and saying that he'd have you for his wife before the month is out. We ignored them, suspecting that Granddad had other plans." He looked at Fin.

"Well, he means to make a nuisance of himself now," Catriona said.

"Wait and see, lass," Fin said. "We are too many for them to stir mischief."

"Sakes, sir, all six of them are armed. And although our party is larger, our gillies carry just dirks. You, James, and Ian are the only well-armed men with us."

"I'm here, too, m'lady," Toby said indignantly. "And yon other lad, as well," he added, gesturing to James's equerry.

"So you are," Catriona said. But Fin could see that she still believed that if the six Comyn men attacked, the Comyns would win.

He did not think that they would attack. Glancing back, he saw that the boatmen were still within call. Also, the six men approaching looked purposeful rather than dangerous.

Knowing that the garron would be of no use to him, he told Catriona to stay on hers and swung his leg over to dismount. He saw James and Ian do the same. But he did not notice until Catriona strode ahead of them that she had also dismounted.

He opened his mouth to call her to order just as she said, "Good morrow, Rory Comyn. 'Twas thoughtful of you and these others to come and bid me well."

Fin shut his mouth when, except for their redheaded leader, the other Comyns halted. Rory took a few more steps toward Catriona, but after a glance at Fin and another at James, he stopped before he got too close to her.

"What be this, then?" he demanded. "Why should I wish ye well, lass?"

"Because I am now a married woman, sir," she said with a smile. "As I ken fine that you had some thought of taking me to wife, I think it was kind of you to come all this way to help us celebrate the day."

"I heard nowt o' this," he muttered, frowning at Fin. Then he looked more measuringly at James, Ian, and the others behind them.

Taking his cue from Catriona, Fin moved to extend a hand to Comyn, saying, "I can understand your vexation. I'd be wroth if you had been before me, too."

"Aye, well, I *were* before ye, and I'll be after ye, come to that," Comyn growled, ignoring Fin's outstretched hand. Looking at Catriona, he said, "So, ye be celebrating the day. D'ye mean to say the event has only just taken place, then?"

"Hours ago," she said, nodding. "And a fine day it is for a wedding, too."

"There will be a reckoning for such betrayal, lass. The Mackintosh—aye, and your da, too—knew I wanted to speak more wi' them. Yet they put me off. I came here today to make that plain to them and demand that we continue our talks."

"There were no true nego—" Catriona broke off when Fin put a hand to her arm. She glanced at him, clearly eager to challenge Comyn's words.

Aware that the man had talked himself into a temper that would seethe into fury before long, Fin said, "Gently, my lady. One can see that he believed that your kinsmen were still considering his suit. Forbye, when we met him before, you told me that they were. Sakes, any man would be irked by such treatment."

"Aye, anyone would," Comyn agreed. "But dinna think

to cozen me into friendship wi' such words, because I'll see ye dead first."

"Mayhap you will, Comyn," Fin replied calmly. "But not today. The guards yonder at the castle will have noted your presence. They will likewise be eager to discuss your unwelcome presence further if you do not leave now."

"Aye? Well, I dinna fear them, nor the Mackintosh, nor Shaw, nor any grander laird wi' them wha' thinks he wields power over any Comyn. Not one o' them does, and so they should all ken fine. We'll meet again, Fin o' the Battles. Make nae mistake about that!"

Fin's hand was still on Catriona's arm, and he felt her stiffen. Believing that she was about to add her mite to the conversation, he squeezed her arm in warning.

Glowering at them both, Rory Comyn turned and strode away, signing to his men to follow him.

James and the others remounted, but instead of following them, Catriona turned to Fin and said testily, "Why did you not let me speak?"

"I did let you speak, as long as you were encouraging civil conversation," Fin said quietly. "But when I saw that he was getting angry and that you were about to make him angrier... If you will recall, lass, I *told* you to stay on your horse."

She grimaced but said nothing, turning abruptly toward her garron.

He followed, caught her at the waist, and put her on the horse himself.

～

Fin's action caught Catriona by surprise. When he put her on her garron with enough force to make her teeth snap together, she drew breath to tell him what she thought of such behavior.

His expression made her think again.

"We'll talk soon," he promised. "First we'll let that lot get well away from us whilst I have a word with James."

"What about?"

"Aye, what?" James asked curiously.

"Comyn knows about your exalted guests," Fin said.

"I don't see how he could," James said, frowning. "Rothesay rode into the Highlands as one of Alex's men, and Donald came to us as a mendicant friar. Nae one can have recognized either one of them."

"One would hope not. Yet Comyn suggested that Rothiemurchus houses 'grander lairds,' wielding more power than the Mackintosh or your father."

James's frown deepened. Turning to his man, he said, "Ride back and tell the boatmen what just happened here. Tell them to report it to the Mackintosh and Shaw. Tell them, too, that we think that Rory Comyn kens more than he should."

As they watched the man hurry back, Catriona said gently to Fin, "'Twas my speaking to Rory that earned us that information, was it not?"

"It was, aye," he admitted.

"It is good then that I did annoy him a trifle."

"The man was angry from the moment he saw us," he said flatly. "I'd wager that when he departed, he'd have hurled much the same words at us."

"But he had come to negotiate with my father, so he was *not* really angry until I told him that you and I had married."

"You made the matter personal, Catriona, a matter

betwixt you and him, Mackintosh and Comyn. A woman telling any man who wants her that he can never have her utters fighting words, words that *beget* trouble."

He had given her something to think about, but his calm voice did not fool her. She decided that she would keep her thoughts to herself for a time.

When James's man returned, they continued on their way, watching the now distant Comyn party until all six of them vanished over the ridge north of the loch.

Their own party followed the barely discernible track that she and Fin had followed the day they had met, when she had led him to Rothiemurchus. At the top of the ridge, they headed northwest and downhill to the river Spey. Fording the river, they splashed out onto a wider, more traveled path that followed the river for some fifty miles to its outlet into the Moray Firth near the cathedral town of Elgin.

Fin had not tried yet to open a discussion with her, so as they rode, she mentally practiced what she would say to him. But their party remained tightly grouped, and she had no more desire than he did for James or Morag to hear what she said. So she bided her time.

When she saw Fin look back across the river and then at James, she realized that they had been waiting until the Spey lay between them and the Comyns. At that time of year, the next ford lay ten miles to the north. Moreover, they would soon be in the heart of Mackintosh country and less likely to meet any Comyn.

Armed Comyns would certainly draw notice, and word of their presence would quickly spread until Mackintoshes confronted them in great number.

Fin said, "Do you know the turning we want, lass?"

"Aye, sure, I do," she said.

"Then you and I will ride on, so we can talk of anything you like."

His matter-of-fact words had an odd effect on her. Although she had been waiting for such an opportunity, now that he was granting it to her...

"What now?" he asked, raising his eyebrows.

"I was ready and willing to tell you just what I think," she replied. "But I did not think you would be so willing to hear it. In troth, sir, your invitation has acted like a damper on the heat of my anger. And I am not sure that I like that any better than other things you have said or done of late."

"Is that all?" he asked with a twinkle in his eye.

That look had another effect, a deeper one. But she fought it, determined to hold her own and have her say. "Faith, do you laugh at me?"

"I am not such a fool," he assured her. "Now, shall we discuss what Rothesay said to anger you just before we left the hall, or have you another topic that you would prefer to offer first?"

She sighed. "By my troth, sir, I think what angers me most is almost the same thing in every instance."

"And that is...?"

"You used to listen to my opinions and seem to respect them. But now you either ignore what I say to you or you dismiss it as unimportant. But if I do the same to you, you get as irritated as Ivor does."

"You will have to explain to me how that applies to what Rothesay said about my having been born at Tor Castle."

"God-a-mercy, you ken fine that you misled me when I asked you if you knew the place," she said.

With a wry and rueful look, he said, "I did not tell you the whole truth, but we had met just the day before."

"Then what about when I asked you yestereve, before I agreed to marry you, if you had told me everything about yourself that I should know? *Then*, you made it sound as if the only things you had *not* told me were things that you had not thought of or secrets that belonged to other people. *That* was not true, sir."

"I should have told you then, aye," he admitted. "I do see that now. At the time, I was acting on your father's orders to persuade you to our marriage. The truth is that I wanted to persuade you for my own sake, sweetheart. But I feared that if I admitted that I was born at the very place over which our clans had fought for decades, you would be as irked as you are now. And our fratching over it would have done nowt to change your father's mind or that of the Mackintosh."

His explanation took the wind out of her sails. But she soon rallied, saying, "That is all very well, sir. But when you told me that you had only *heard* of Tor Castle, that was deception, plain and simple. How can you expect me to believe what you tell me when you do such things?" Tears welled unexpectedly into her eyes and she stared straight ahead, hoping that he would not notice them.

He reached over and caught hold of her hand. "Look at me, lass."

She ignored him. She would not let him see that her own words had stirred such foolish emotion in her. When he squeezed her hand, a tear spilled over. But it fell from her left eye, and he was on her right, so he could not see it.

"Sweetheart," he said, "I wish I could promise never to do such a thing again, but I cannot. Sithee, I serve a man who behaves impulsively and holds his secrets close. That means that I often have to keep my activities secret, too. I have spent years keeping personal secrets as well. Sakes, I thought that even Rothesay knew nowt of them. I was wrong about that, as we have seen, but even he knows nowt of one dilemma that I failed to resolve before I met you."

"You did resolve it then?"

"I did, aye, and I am sure that I chose the right way."

"Will you tell me what the resolution was, and why it was such a dilemma?"

"A fortnight ago I'd have said that I could never speak of it to anyone," he said solemnly. "I am still not persuaded that telling you would be the right thing to do. But that is not because I don't trust you, so I make you this promise. I will never forbid you to ask me about it, and mayhap the day will come when I can tell you."

The tear dried on her cheek as she considered his promise.

At last, still watching the road, she said, "I must be able to trust you. But how can I when I'd often wonder if you were parsing your words or just lying to me?"

"Will you agree to let a matter drop if I tell you that I cannot discuss it?"

She glanced at him, saw him looking intently at her, and could not look away. Something in his expression challenged her to think before she replied.

At last, licking dry lips, she said, "If I say that I agree, will you promise never to say those words just because you don't *want* to answer me?"

"I will promise that without hesitation."

His voice sounded hoarse, and his gaze was more

intense than ever. The way he was looking at her sent new sensations surging through her, touching her in the very places that had reacted earlier when he had stroked her breasts.

She muttered, "Will you promise never to mislead me again?"

"With respect, Catriona, I did not really mislead you about Tor Castle. You asked me if I knew of it, and I said that I did and that I knew its exact location. We were on the loch trail then, and we met Comyn, which ended our conversation."

"But by not being forthright…"

"That *was* just after we'd met. Recall that I still did not know how the people of Rothiemurchus felt about members of the Cameron confederation. I had good reason to tread cautiously."

"We do have a truce," she reminded him.

"Aye, but truces are not set in stone, lass. Men break them all the time."

"Men break many things," she said. "How will I know I can trust your word?"

"Because I will trust yours if you say that I should. Should I?"

⁓

Fin saw color fire her cheeks and knew that he had touched a nerve. He decided to press the advantage. "We need to be able to trust each other, lass. I know that it angered you when we met Comyn today and I told you to stay on your horse."

"And I irked you when I dismounted and said what I did to him."

"Aye, but I quickly saw that you could manage him, so I let matters be. Then you began to contradict him about his so-called negotiations, and I could see that you were going to make him even angrier than he had been."

"By my troth, sir, had I not been thinking as much about how you would react to my defiance as I was about what I should say to him—"

"Don't you see, sweetheart? That is just the sort of thing we need to learn about each other. Until we do, I would ask that you obey me when I make it clear that I expect obedience, if only because I have more experience of the world than you do. In return," he added before she could argue, "I will do my best to give you the same respect when we speak of things about which you know more than I do."

"What if I don't obey you?" she asked, regarding him now from under her lashes. "Sithee, sometimes I just act because it seems right to act."

"Then I fear you must accept whatever consequences I impose. I am your husband now, Catriona. So, law and tradition accord me certain rights and likewise certain duties. The greatest of those is the duty to protect you from others. And from your own folly," he added bluntly.

When she licked her lips, his body stirred in response, making him wish James and Morag to perdition. What he wanted to do was snatch his defiant, beautiful wife off her garron, carry her into the nearby woods for privacy, and master her so thoroughly that she would know forevermore that she was his woman.

⁓

Catriona could not mistake the heated desire in Fin's eyes, and since her own body had reminded her any number of times that they had consummated their union too hastily, his desire and even his threat stirred other, much stronger feelings.

Preferring not to think about those consequences he had mentioned, because she knew he would never approve her habit of taking her own road whenever she could, she was glad to see the turning they wanted ahead. As they ascended the steep, wooded trail into the mountains, she remembered his penchant for waterfalls.

Shouting to James, she suggested that they stop at the one they knew and eat the midday meal they had brought with them. That plan being heartily approved by everyone, they ate so near the tall, spectacular torrent that they felt its mist on their faces. Watching Fin, she saw him relax, grinning, and knew she had chosen well.

When they had finished, everyone remounted and they returned to the trail.

James and Morag seemed happier, too. When James suggested that they all ride together, neither Catriona nor Fin objected.

They reached Loch Moigh well before sundown, and the guards on the castle ramparts were watching for them, because a boat with two oarsmen set out at once. The castle occupied a sizeable island, and the loch was larger than Loch an Eilein.

When the boat neared the landing, James shook Fin's hand and said, "We'll be off now straightaway, because we want to reach Daviot by suppertime. But I do wish you the best of luck in taming our wildcat, and all happiness for you both."

Catriona hugged her brother and Morag, then stepped into the boat when it arrived at the landing. Fin followed her, leaving Ailvie, Ian, and Toby to supervise the unloading of the sumpter ponies and tend to the garrons.

"'Tis a beautiful place, is it not?" Catriona said as the boat left the landing.

"Aye, but frankly, lass, I'm thinking about my wife and our bed," he said.

Grinning, and aware of heat swiftly rising within her, she saw a man in a tunic and a blue-green plaid emerge from the castle and stride toward the landing, evidently to meet them. Feeling Fin stiffen beside her, she said, "Do you know him?"

"I do, aye. That is my brother, Ewan MacGillony Cameron."

Chapter 17 _____

Still stunned, Fin stared at Ewan in disbelief.

"Why is he here?" Catriona asked.

"I don't know," Fin said. "But I discern the fine hand of your grandsire in this. He knew I'd not seen my family since Perth and that I want to present you to them. But, for Ewan to be here now, he must have sent for him a sennight ago, long before knowing we would marry. I just hope Ewan did not bring the whole family."

"God-a-mercy!"

Seeing her face pale, he said, "Don't fret, sweetheart. If he did and they expect to upset *my* plans whilst we're here, they will soon learn their error."

She looked uncertain, and he hoped he was right. Ewan could be fierce, and despite the friendly wave, Fin had no idea how his brother would receive him.

When they reached the landing, he stepped out of the boat and extended a hand to Catriona as he said, "This is a fine surprise, Ewan, and a welcome one. How many of our kinsmen did you bring in your tail?"

"Nae kinsmen, just a half-dozen of my own lads," Ewan said, grasping Fin's hand warmly. "Ye've brought even fewer men with ye, I see."

"My liege lord was reluctant to extend my leave beyond a few days, although I did mean to go on to Loch Arkaig to ask your forgiveness. Now, though..."

When he paused, Ewan said heartily, "I'm glad to see ye hale and well, lad. Sithee, we all thought ye must be dead. So ye could have knocked me down with a broom straw when I got the Mackintosh's message that, if I were willing to accept his hospitality, I might meet ye here. D'ye mean to present this bonnie lady to me?"

"If the wily old man told you nowt of her, then I have a surprise to match yours," Fin said as Catriona curtsied. "She is the lady Catriona Mackintosh, my wife. And if you are wroth with me for marrying without your consent, Ewan, you may roar at me later. For now, we are both tired from our journey and—"

"Be damned to your weariness, lad! How long have ye been married?"

Fin relaxed then, recognizing Ewan's hearty mood as a friendly one. "Since sunrise," he admitted with a rueful smile.

"Sunrise! Bless us, why did ye no invite your own family to the wedding?"

"That tale will take some time to tell," Fin said. "And I'd liefer tell it over a good supper, because we ate only bread with some beef and cheese at midday. But what I want now is for us to settle in, tidy ourselves, and eat. After that, I'll thank you to remember that this is my wedding night."

"Aye, sure, I'll remember. But ye'll tell me your tale straightaway. I've nae doot that your lady will want a bath after her long ride. But unless ye've forgotten how to swim since ye left home, ye'll make do with a dip in the loch. If

I'm wroth with ye, Fin, 'tis not for marrying. But ye do deserve my anger, do ye not?"

Fin could not deny that, and Ewan's tone had changed enough to tell him that he'd better tread lightly for a time and remember that Ewan was not just his brother but also a chieftain of their clan with rights of punishment. Accordingly, Fin said, "A swim is just what I'd like if you will let me see my lady wife settled first."

"Aye, sure," Ewan said, smiling at Catriona. "Did I understand him to say that ye be a Mackintosh, my lady?"

"You did, sir, aye. My grandfather is the Mackintosh."

"Himself, eh? Well, 'tis grand to make your acquaintance. I wish ye happy in your marriage and bid ye welcome to our family."

With a smile, she thanked him and turned to Fin. "We are to use the inner chamber, sir. Shall we go in?"

Glancing back across the loch to see Ian and Toby helping Ailvie into another boat that was doubtless already carrying their baggage, he agreed.

"Don't be long, Fin," Ewan said. "I ken a good place for swimming a few steps from this landing. I'll await ye here."

Agreeing, Fin escorted Catriona inside, where she introduced him to her grandfather's steward and issued orders for a bath. She also asked that he delay serving supper until they had had time to get settled.

That done, she took Fin to the inner chamber. The bed there, he saw with approval, was much larger than Catriona's was.

"Is your brother angry with you?" she asked when he had shut the door.

"He is glad to see me," Fin said, looking around and

noting the cheerful fire that leaped in the fireplace and the basket of extra wood. "But he does have cause to be wroth with me for not telling him where I've been and what I have been doing."

"Will you tell him everything? Even the bits you have not yet told me?"

"I will answer his questions honestly," he said. "As to what more I'll say, I must first see how our talk progresses. For now, though, I ken fine that you and Ailvie can see to stowing what we brought with us and to your bath as well. But one day soon, I'd like to assist you with that latter task myself."

"We'll just have to see about that, too, won't we?" she said, dimpling.

"Don't tempt me, lass. I must talk with Ewan, but I will try not to fratch with him. Our supper will be more pleasant so, as will its aftermath."

Hearing footsteps approach the door and pause there, he kissed her quickly and turned away as Ailvie entered, carrying a sumpter basket.

Informing Ailvie that the steward was ordering water and a tub, Catriona watched Fin walk away across the great hall and wished that she might be a fly on a nearby rock to hear his conversation with his brother.

Not to have told his family that he had survived the great clan battle at Perth must, she feared, be a choice that such a brother would not easily forgive.

She did not have to strain her mind to imagine how she would feel had Ivor or James done such a thing. She would want to see the offender smarting, at least.

Fin and Ewan seemed more alike than her brothers did. Ewan looked seven or eight years older than Fin and a stone or so heavier. Both had powerful bodies, dark hair with auburn highlights in the sun, and gray eyes. But Fin's eyes were lighter, his body lither, and his movements more graceful.

She had detected signs of a temperament similar to his in Ewan, however.

"Your grandame did say that I should root through her things to find aught that ye'd need," Ailvie said as she shut the door, recalling Catriona's attention.

The maidservant bustled about then, finding places for the sumpter baskets and seeking French soap and towels for Catriona's bath.

"I want to wash my hair," she said. "We can brush it dry here by the fire."

"Ye'll be glad to put up your feet after this long day," Ailvie said. "I'm still wondering about them Comyns, though. Did ye no think they submitted too quick?"

"Quick or not, they had to submit," Catriona said, dismissing her own earlier concerns. "Our boatmen were nearby, and the men on our wall could see us."

"Even so, I dinna trust any Comyn. And Rory ha' been talking these six months past o' taking ye to wife. I ha' never heard o' him walking away from nowt."

Although she recognized truth in Ailvie's words, Catriona had little concern. Against Fin of the Battles, Rory Comyn must always lose.

⁓

Eyeing his brother's posture as Ewan looked out over the loch with his back to him, Fin recognized familiar signs that Ewan had been suppressing his stronger emotions for Catriona's sake. With that in mind, before he got too near, he shouted, "Where is this swimming place of yours?"

Ewan turned, nodded silently, and led the way along the shore to an inlet boasting a smooth granite slab that sloped into the water.

"Shall we swim first or talk?" Fin asked, still trying to gauge Ewan's mood.

"We can do both if you like. I found another such inlet some hundred yards north of here, round yonder point. Nae one will be there, whilst someone from the castle might disturb us here."

"Just promise that you won't try to drown me on the way," Fin said.

Ewan looked at him, eyebrows raised, then smiled. "Nay, laddie. I won't pretend that I'd not like to give ye a fierce drubbing, but I'll hear ye out first."

Fin nodded, relieved, and bent to untie his boots. When they had shed their clothing, Ewan led the way into the water, saying, "I'd wager this rock be gey slippery by midsummer. But for now it does give a man's foot good traction."

He dove in and Fin followed. They soon found the inlet, sun drenched and warm, and sprawled on the granite to dry.

Ewan remained silent. So, although Fin would have preferred to bask in the warmth, he gathered his thoughts and said, "What did you hear about the battle?"

"Only that we'd lost and that all of our men died on the field or afterward of their wounds," Ewan replied, raising his arms to fold them beneath his head. Staring up at the azure sky, he added, "Plainly, though, you did not die."

"I was the only Cameron who did not," Fin said quietly. Without waiting for the obvious question, he turned on his side to watch Ewan as he added, "The fighting had well nigh stopped. But there were four men still hale on their side when I...I dove into the river Tay and let it carry me toward the sea."

"Sakes, I ken fine that ye swim well, but that firth widens quick beyond Perth and grows gey rough, too," Ewan said, scowling. "Ye might have drowned!"

"I swam to the Fife shore and made my way to St. Andrews."

"Where, nae doots, that old scoundrel Traill hid ye."

"He did not hide me, nor did he offer much solace," Fin said. "In his opinion, I had merely chosen the most practical course under the circumstances."

"But not the honorable one? Is that what the man did say?"

"Not in those words, but I felt that way myself," Fin said. "Sakes, there were eleven Clan Chattan men still alive, the others sorely hurt. But nevertheless..."

Ewan frowned but looked thoughtful rather than angry. "Ye've never done a cowardly thing in your life, Fin, unless ye've altered mightily since ye left home."

"I did think that I must have changed and that others would say so, aye."

Ewan started to speak but did not. He was silent long enough then to remind Fin that Ewan himself had been one of those "others."

At last Ewan said, "Ye've made me think, lad. I had nae authority then and small understanding of such, or of men, come to that. Likely, I would have thought such a thing, and others surely would have. Ye might not have been safe."

"I didn't think about safety," Fin said. "But there were other reasons, too."

"D'ye chance to ken what happened to our father?"

"He fought near me, Ewan. I was with him when he died."

"Bless ye, lad, that must have eased his way. Did he say aught to ye?"

Tension swept through Fin, but it carried no urge with it to equivocate. "He told me that I must swear to take vengeance on Clan Chattan, that he was bequeathing that charge to me as a sacred duty."

Ewan said curtly, "Did ye not, all thirty o' ye, swear at the outset that yon trial by combat would settle the matter betwixt our clans and result in our truce forbye?"

"We did swear so, aye," Fin said, feeling his tension begin to ebb.

"And did not that vow lead to our current agreement?"

"It somehow kept you living at Tor Castle as well, aye. I have never heard how, exactly, that did come about after Clan Chattan won the battle."

"It did because yon Mackintosh is a canny man, is how. 'Tis no for nowt that he has led Clan Chattan nigh onto forty years. Sithee, with all from our side dead at Perth, some at home suspected treachery. He kent fine that if he ordered us off our Lochaber lands, that truce would no have lasted a heartbeat longer. So, he proposed that if we'd honor the ancient agreement and begin to pay the yearly rent again, we could continue to lease our lands from Clan Mackintosh and be peaceable."

"Did the Camerons really have such an earlier agreement, then?"

"Aye, sure, but don't ask me when or why we stopped

paying. 'Twas before I was born. The old man kent fine the amount and said it would stay as it were till matters sorted themselves out elsewise. We're content, and so are they, I think."

"I did hear that you are now Constable of Tor Castle."

"I am, aye. I collect the rents and act as host when the Mackintosh comes each Christmas to stay, as he still does. And when he dies, I'll see that he's buried in the graveyard there. But how the devil did ye come to marry his granddaughter? I'm thinking 'twas yet another canny move on *his* part, to see that we all keep the truce."

"He said that if anyone did aught to break it, it would not be Clan Chattan."

"We'll see about that, I expect. He won't live forever and nor will I—or our clan's captain, come to that. So tell me about this marriage of yours."

Fin explained what had happened, and although he thought that Ewan laughed at inappropriate times, the tale clearly entertained him. However, when Fin had brought him up to date, Ewan was silent again for a time.

Then he said, "This about the Comyns...D'ye ken aught more about it?"

"Only that they are weak and resentful," Fin said. "The Mackintosh and Shaw have had occasional trouble with them for some time. Why do you ask?"

"Sithee, I keep lads out and about with their eyes open and their ears aprick, because our truce is central to the general peace. Of late, the name Comyn comes up whenever anyone talks of trouble anywhere east of Tor Castle. Some do say that the Comyns seek to aid the Duke of Albany by making trouble for the Lord of the North, mayhap by stirring the coals of our old feud into something fiercer."

"It is no secret that Albany wants his own son to replace Alex Stewart."

"But d'ye ken aught more of what they all be up to? Sithee, I'm thinking that troubles for Alex may encourage Donald of the Isles to attack us here in the west."

"I do know more, aye," Fin admitted. "But as I told you, I serve Rothesay, so I cannot tell you all I know without breaking confidence with him. I will tell you that Donald takes more interest than he should in extending his power to the western Highlands. He wants more now than just his wife's inherited lands."

"I do ken that, aye," Ewan said. "What more of Alex?"

"His interest is solely in Lochindorb and retaining the Lordship of the North."

"Keeping it away from Albany, ye mean."

"Aye, but I believe that he will also defend it against Donald." A breeze stirred then, bringing a chill off the loch, so Fin sat up. Meeting his brother's gaze, he said, "Are we good, Ewan, or do you still want to try giving me a drubbing?"

"Och, laddie, the past is gone, and I'm no one to be telling ye what ye should or should not have done whilst I were safe at home. I'm just thankful that your notion of vengeance against the Mackintosh was to marry his granddaughter."

"Did I mention that her father is the Clan Chattan war leader?"

Ewan chuckled. "Ye left that out, but I'll warrant ye don't mean to murder either one, and I'll thank ye for that, too. Peace is always preferable to war, but it will last only until it does not. So 'tis good to know ye've nae intention of breaking it. But I'll expect to see more of ye now, mind. Ye'll come to Tor Castle to stay with us, the pair of ye, after ye've sorted out whatever ye be into now with Rothesay and them."

"The Mackintosh granted me a charter for life occupancy of Castle Raitt as a wedding gift," Fin said. "My lass loves her home, and Raitt lies but two miles from it, so I expect I may find myself a Highlander again before I know it."

"Ye're a Highlander born, lad. Ye cannot be aught else."

Fin drew a long breath and let it out, feeling a sense of ease that he had not known since long before he had flung himself into the Tay. He had not told Ewan everything, because he had not mentioned Ivor's part, but his brother now knew more than anyone other than Bishop Traill did about what had happened at Perth.

⁓

Catriona paced Castle Moigh's great hall, wondering how much longer Fin and Ewan would be. Her hair was dry, she was freshly gowned, and she was hungry.

She had gone out to the rock where she assumed that Ewan had meant for them to swim and had found their clothing there. Seeing no other sign of them, she had returned to the castle but only because it was the courteous thing to do.

Ewan might be one of those rare men who preferred not to parade naked where women, particularly his new good-sister, might see him. And she was in no hurry to see any man naked but Fin.

That she looked eagerly ahead to that made her wonder if all newly married women felt the same way. She remained uncertain about the future, because she was sure that she and Fin would frequently argue about all and sundry, as they had. But she hoped that he would also continue to elicit the strong responses she had felt with him that morning just as frequently if not more so.

Consequently, she paced, and when the two men finally strode into the hall, she greeted them with, "At last! Faith, but I was beginning to fear that you had both drowned and I would have to go without my supper!"

"You may have to go without your supper in any event if that is how you greet a guest of this house, madam wife," Fin said before he caught her by the shoulders and kissed her thoroughly.

Pushing him away as soon as he would let her, she swept Ewan a curtsy. Rising, she said, "If you are as daft as your brother, sir, and believed that I meant aught but teasing, I do humbly apologize and swear that I will mend my ways."

Laughing heartily, Ewan said, "I think you are just what he needs to keep him out of trouble, my lady. If ever I can aid you in that task, however, you need only ask. Sithee, he has earned a drubbing, so he still treads on thin ice with me."

"Even so, I trust that all is well between you now, sir," she said.

"It is, aye," he replied, smiling at Fin.

Fin said, "As I do not see Ian here, I shall require your help to don a clean tunic for dinner, lass. You may come with me and see what *you* have earned."

"I, too, want a fresh tunic," Ewan said. "I doubt that ye'll need my aid in managing him just now, Lady Catriona, but if ye do—"

"Nay, sir, I will not," Catriona said. Despite her confident words, though, she did wonder if her saucy greeting might have irritated her husband.

As they turned toward the inner chamber, he put an arm around her shoulders, but he did not speak. She hoped he was just giving her back some of her own for teasing them, but she could not be sure. Looking up, she saw that he had pressed his lips together, which was an ominous sign.

Aware of her unease, Fin was enjoying himself a little, believing that it served his wildcat right to wonder if she had overstepped the bounds of what he would tolerate. Heaven knew, she had a bad habit of speaking impulsively and would be wiser to take more thought before she did offend someone.

Nodding at the young gillie who hurried to open the door of the inner chamber for them, he urged Catriona inside but did not release her when the door shut quietly behind them. Instead, he turned her to face him.

Looking sternly at her, he said, "Do you know what you deserve for teasing your husband and his guest so?"

"Aye, sir, more kissing."

Having no desire to argue about that, he kissed her again but did not stop there. Scant seconds later, he had opened her bodice and was gazing hungrily at her enticing, rosy-tipped breasts as he stroked them.

Scooping her into his arms, he carried her to the bed and, stripping her of her clothing, began to discover just how fast her body would respond to his touch. He wanted her hot for him. At the same time, he did want to teach her a small lesson.

"Lie still now, lass, and close your eyes," he said, casting aside his mantle and boots. "I want you to think only about what you feel."

Retaining his tunic, he climbed onto the bed and straddled her, catching her wrists and pressing them to the bed before bending to kiss her again.

She opened her eyes wide and gazed into his but responded eagerly to his kisses. Capturing her mouth, he eased his body lower, still pinning her wrists and bearing his weight on his elbows and legs. Knowing that his tunic was rough enough to tease her nipples, he moved so that it brushed against them.

She tried to free her hands and then tried to pull her mouth away from his, clearly wanting to speak.

Briefly freeing her lips, he murmured, "Hush now. Just let be."

"But I want to hold you, too, and touch you."

"Nay, sweetheart, not yet. For now, you will be as meek and obedient in bed as you vowed this morning to be. That is to say," he added, "you will do as I say now if you want to have a try later at being meek and obedient at my board."

"I'd remind you, sir, that 'tis my granddad's board and not yours at all."

"Ah, but here at Moigh I am *his* guest. And you ken fine that a guest in any man's house may command his own pleasure."

"Aye, and so you may until I shout for the servants."

"Do you think that any one of them will disobey me if I countermand an order you give?" he asked gently.

Seeing the answer in her grimace, he murmured, "Just so, sweetheart. Now, do as I bid you. I promise, you will not be sorry . . . well, not in the end, at all events," he added conscientiously.

~

Catriona stared up at him, wondering what he meant by those last, ill-omened words. But she could not deny the feelings he stirred in her.

Her body had come alive and clamored for his attention.

He inched lower to kiss her breasts, and as he did, his body and his tunic set new nerves aflame wherever either one touched her. "You smell good," he said, as he laved a nipple with the tip of his tongue. Both of her breasts swelled in response.

Gasping at the sensations that raced from that nipple to other parts of her body, she stammered, "'Tis Grandame's French s-soap. Ailvie f-found it."

"I like its scent. You must ask Lady Annis where she purchased it." Attending still to her nipples, and without releasing her hands, he shifted his knees lower.

Knowing that she could not escape him unless he allowed it stirred new feelings in her, stronger than before. She felt helpless, as if she were his captive. But as long as he went on as he was, she had no wish to be free. He slipped one knee and then the other between her legs, easing them far apart.

Laying a trail of warm breath and kisses along her belly as his head moved lower, he nipped her skin between his lips and even now and again, gently, with his teeth. So focused was she on what he might do next that she failed to notice that he was shifting her hands lower, too, until they were nearer her waist than her head.

"What are you doing?" she demanded when his breath tickled the curls at the juncture of her legs.

"Shhh," he said, and she trembled when his breath sent a rush of heat through her most private parts.

Her hands were even with her hips now, and still he held them. The things he was doing affected her senses so that she wanted to cry out and tell him to stop. But the torment was too pleasurable, and the last thing she wanted was for Ewan to pound on the door and demand to know what was going on, or even break it down.

It was a near thing, though, when Fin touched her with his tongue, and nearer still when his tongue invaded her most secret places, caressing the spot that had sent her soaring that morning. His tongue's touch was softer, more engaging, and far more stimulating. Her body heaved, encouraging him of its own accord to do as he pleased. The sensations increased, sending her higher and higher until he stopped.

"Oh, prithee, don't stop," she breathed. "That feels wonderful, and it was beginning to seem as if something even more were about to happen. 'Twas the strangest, most wonderful sensation that I have yet felt, and gey promising, withal."

"But recall that I had a long swim, sweetheart, so I'm hungry for food now, and *you* said you wanted your supper," he added with a teasing smile. "We can continue this later if you like. As your grandfather said only this morning, we'll enjoy it more if we have sustenance first."

She nearly shrieked, "What! But why did you begin if—?"

"Now, lass, we must rejoin Ewan," he interjected. "He must fear by now that we've forgotten all about him."

"But, surely, if he has waited this long, he will wait a few minutes longer."

"Mayhap he would, but I don't want just a few minutes more with you. I want to take my time and enjoy every minute."

"God-a-mercy, when you let me up, Fin Cameron, you had better take care!"

"There is no need for me to let you up at all," he said, grinning now. "I might command you to stay here and wait for me instead, just as you are."

Glowering, she said, "Very well, sir. But do *not* think I will forget this."

"Sweetheart, I mean to make certain of that—right after supper."

Still smiling, albeit with more difficulty than she knew, Fin released her and picked up his mantle. He was achingly aware that at least one body part meant to let him know that in punishing her, he was likewise punishing himself considerably.

After he arranged his mantle, he helped her dress, noting with delight that every time his fingers brushed her skin, she reacted. As he urged her back into the hall, he swore to himself that if Ewan had dawdled, the man would go hungry.

But Ewan was on the dais, examining the baskets and platters of food already on the table. Looking at Fin, he shook his head. "Ye took your time, lad."

"Not nearly enough of it," Fin said, grinning again and more easily. "I mean to desert you again right after supper, so you must entertain yourself this evening."

Chuckling, Ewan said, "Since it *is* your wedding night, I expect I'll manage. But do not think that ye'll keep to yon bed all morning. I want to hear about all of your adventures these past four years, and I warrant that will take some time."

"You may have me until midday if you like, because I mean for my lady to be so tired that she will sleep the whole morning away."

Glancing at Catriona, he saw that her cheeks were as red as fire. Her eyes flashed, though, and her rosy lips formed a straight line, indicating that she ached to tell him what she thought of his tactics. They seemed to be working, though.

Catching her gaze, holding it, and noting that her breath caught audibly when he did, he knew that her heat had not ebbed in the slightest.

When she did not speak, he devoted his conversation to Ewan until they had finished the meal, the entire time as aware of her presence beside him as he knew she was of his. Only once or twice did he move a hand to touch her warm thigh, or let his leg brush against her. Her reaction each time encouraged him to believe that even if she had harbored the slightest lingering fear that she might again suffer the painful ache she had described that morning, she was *not* thinking about that now.

Catriona had begun the meal with a strong urge to kill Fin for exciting her senses to such a point and then stopping too soon. But so aware was she of every move he made and every time he inadvertently touched her that long before the meal ended, it was Ewan she wanted to murder for having such a healthy appetite.

At first, Fin offered him more and more food, as if he were still teasing her. But she had noticed in the past quarter-hour that he had not only stopped offering but was barely replying civilly to his brother's comments.

At last, Ewan pushed his trencher away. But when the gillie picked it up, the fiendish man ordered another jug of wine. Catriona gritted her teeth, then sighed aloud when Fin got up, saying, "If you will excuse us, we'll bid you goodnight."

"Aye, I thought ye might," Ewan said, grinning at him.

Catriona could have sworn that she heard Fin growl, but her thoughts swiftly flew ahead to what would happen in the bedchamber. She had no time to think long though, because when he'd shut the door, he wasted no time disrobing her.

Fire spread through her everywhere he touched her, but when she reached to put her arms around him, he stopped her as he had earlier. Then he scooped her up and carried her to the neatly turned-down bed, laying her naked upon it.

When she reached to pull up the covers, he said, "Nay, sweetheart, leave them. 'Tis warm enough in here, and I want to think of you lying as you are whilst I stir up the fire and light more cressets. Then I want to look at you."

Chapter 18 _____

Fin attended quickly to the fire and the cressets, but the image of Catriona as he had left her stirred him to even more haste in doffing his clothing. It occurred to him as he did that a tunic and mantle were much more convenient in such situations than a man's doublet, shirt, braies, nether hose, and shoes or boots.

"The two of you said naught to me or to each other about your talk," she murmured as she watched him fling off his tunic. "What did Ewan say to you?"

"Not enough, since he clearly thought that I still needed some of my own sauce served to me at supper," he said as he moved to join her in the bed. "But we are not going to talk about Ewan. Where were we before we stopped?"

"*We* did not stop," she muttered, only to gasp when he recalled what he had been doing and reached to see if she was still as ready as she had been then.

She was nearly so, and he noted how eagerly she welcomed his touch.

Knowing that his control was limited due to his earlier tactics, he forced himself to disregard a nearly overwhelming urge to take her hard and swiftly.

She was already moaning at his slightest touch and

arcing against him. So he gently kneed her legs apart and positioned himself. Easing himself into her silken sheath, he waited to see if she might reveal any sign of lingering discomfort.

Instead, she rose to meet him as if to aid and encourage him.

Instinct took over, and the result for him came swiftly. Aware that she had neared her own climax, he stroked her until she, too, gained release.

Afterward, lying beside him with the coverlet over them, his arm around her, and her head resting in the hollow of his shoulder, she sighed and said, "Grandame said that it could be pleasurable. And you promised earlier that I would not forget it. But I had no idea what either of you meant."

He chuckled. "Do you think that you might like this aspect of our marriage?"

"I do, aye, although it did last but a short time. And *you* said—"

"Sakes, lass, we've only just begun," he said, still smiling.

They lay quietly for a time before he pushed the coverlet away with his free hand and began to caress her again. The cressets still cast a golden glow over the room; so rising onto an elbow, he delighted in watching her reactions for a time while his hands sought to memorize the wondrous planes and curves of her body.

Moving purposefully, he made slow, sensuous love to her until she squirmed with pleasure beneath him, gasping his name, and begging him for release.

Midway through the night, he took her again. And then, in the gray dawn light, she reached for him. Afterward, as they lay beside each other, sated, he knew that God had spoken at last and all was well.

As he had promised, he spent the morning with Ewan, while Catriona slept. But she was up before midday to rejoin them and beg to hear their reminiscences of their years together at Tor Castle. She listened raptly, too, as Fin recounted more of his adventures with Rothesay and others.

They retired early again that night and spent Thursday in much the same way. Shortly after midday on Friday, Tadhg arrived, big with news.

"Himself said ye're tae return at once, Sir Fin," he said as he ran across the hall to the dais, where they were sitting down to their midday meal.

"Why such hurry?" Fin asked him. "We'd return tomorrow in any event."

"Them bloody Comyns, sir. They killed three o' our men ashore, and Himself did hear that a large force o' Albany's be gathering this side o' Perth and mayhap a Douglas army near Glen Garry. He thinks they be meaning tae join wi' them Comyns to try and take Lochindorb Castle and mayhap even Rothiemurchus, too, if the Comyns did tell them that three great lairds all be there."

"What has he done with our noble guests then?" Fin asked.

"Donald o' the Isles did leave yestermorn afore word o' the army at Perth did reach Himself. But the Duke o' Rothesay do be there still."

"And the Lord of the North?"

"Him, too, aye. He and your da were talking o' sending for more men when I left, but Himself did say that the Laird o' the North should no leave the island until they kent that he'd be safe. He said they should send Sir Ivor tae fetch men from Lochindorb, 'cause the laird's men do ken Sir Ivor fine and trust him well."

"If Sir Ivor left when you did, he should be at Lochindorb, for 'tis nigh the same distance that you've come," Fin said. "I have few men here, though."

"Himself said tae leave the Moigh men here, and that Ewan Cameron should choose what he'll do. But he said also that wi' ructions threatening, mayhap Ewan Cameron should be away to warn Lochaber that uproar in Strathspey may hearten Donald o' the Isles to attack them in the west. Who might this Ewan Cameron be?"

"This gentleman here," Fin said, gesturing. "He is my brother and a chieftain of Clan Cameron of Lochaber. You've done well, laddie."

"Aye, sure, but I did wonder about Ewan Cameron, 'cause Himself did say that if he be still here, ye should tell him the lot and then let him choose how."

"I'll do that, but you go and get yourself some food now," Fin said.

"Don't leave the dais yet, Tadhg," Catriona said, gesturing to a gillie. "You may sit here at the high table and tell me the news from Rothiemurchus whilst we wait for them to bring your food. You deserve a treat if you ran all *that* way."

"Hoots, m'lady, I didna run but from yon boat landing up to this hall, 'cause Aodán let me ride a garron. He said it would be safer and more like tae get me here." But he took the seat she indicated, grinning, clearly delighted to sit at the high table.

Fin left them chatting and bore Ewan outside to tell him all that he had not yet revealed to him about Rothesay's presence in the Highlands.

When he had finished, Ewan said, "I must get back then.

With Alex and Shaw at Rothiemurchus, ye'll have men aplenty without me or mine, and Mackintosh is right. I must let men in the Great Glen and west of it know what is happening. Donald uses the same network of informants as his late father did, and he is sure to see Albany's invasion of the Highlands as an occasion to make mischief himself."

"Donald and Albany are competitors for power, not allies," Fin said.

"But Donald will seize any opportunity that offers gain to him," Ewan said.

~

Catriona was still talking with Tadhg when Fin and Ewan returned. Greeting them, she said to Fin, "I must tell Ailvie and Ian to pack our things at once." But when she began to rise, she saw that he was shaking his head.

"You'll stay here, lass. You will be much safer so."

"Don't be daft, sir. Of course, I shall go with you. I must."

His expression altered to a sternness that shot a thrill up her spine. But after a glance at Tadhg he said, "You'll do as I bid, Catriona. I am not leaving you with strangers. You know your grandfather's people as well as you know your own."

"Ye canna leave her," Tadhg said earnestly. "Himself did say he'll put lights on the ramparts for ye tae see when ye top the ridge. A host o' them if all be well, three if there be Comyns about, and nobbut one should ye no come down at all."

"I can remember all that without her ladyship, however," Fin said.

"Mayhap ye will," Tadhg replied with a near cheeky grin. "But Himself did say that ye'd be less likely tae be doing aught tae make her a widow if she be with ye. So they'll no put any boat in the water nor open the gate till she makes her owl's cry like she used tae do tae waken yon echo. But ye'd best bestir yourselves," he added, glancing from one to the other. "There do be black rain clouds rolling in."

Catriona nearly offered a smile to match Tadhg's but thought better of it when Fin frowned at her. Soberly, she said, "Truly, sir, I won't slow you down."

Still frowning, Fin said, "The Mackintosh leaves me no choice but to take you, lass, so tell Ian to see to our things. Tadhg, you find the kitchen and tell them to put up food for us. Come, Ewan," he added. "We'll collect your gear and your lads. Then I'll go across in the boat with you to speak to Toby."

Catriona waited until they had left the dais before quietly sending the gillie who had served Tadhg to fetch Ian Lennox and Ailvie.

When she told them to pack and explained why she and Fin were leaving, Ailvie said, "What about us then, mistress?"

Ian said, "Sir Finlagh will take Toby and me, lass. So I expect that he'll take you as well, unless you want to stay warm and dry here instead."

"I *want* to stay, sure enough," Ailvie said with a grimace. "But me place be wi' the mistress, come wha' may, so I'll go."

Ian nodded, and the two packed the sumpter baskets. By the time Fin returned, all was ready for their departure.

⁓

To Fin's relief, and somewhat to his surprise, the journey proceeded without incident, although darkness had fallen an hour before they forded the Spey.

There was no moon and only a sprinkling of stars, but he was sure that Rory Comyn would not expect them yet if he expected them at all. Just as Fin knew how long it should take Ivor to reach Lochindorb, gather Alex's forces, and return, Comyn would know that, too, and would expect it to take at least until late the next day for any reinforcement to reach Rothiemurchus.

As they rode side-by-side through the woods in near pitch darkness to the top of the last ridge, Fin realized that Catriona was thinking along similar lines when she said quietly, "Do you think Rory knew we were going to Moigh when we met him?"

"I don't know," Fin murmured, as aware as she clearly was of how easily sound traveled at night. "But we'll assume that the Comyns know we're here."

"Rory's lads are not keeping a close watch *here* tonight, though," she said. "There are many lights below on the castle."

"Or the Comyns have somehow lulled the castle into a false sense of security," he replied. "They could up to mischief, and no one from the castle has caught them at it. We should proceed as if that were the case. Recall that they have killed three of your watchers. I'll wager that Shaw has put more lads out, doubtless two by two, to look after each other. But the long perimeter of the loch makes it impossible to secure entirely, especially on a moonless night like this."

"At least, those clouds have yet to produce rain," she said. "We have seen patches of starlight ever since it got dark."

They had used torches at first, but Fin had ordered them doused as soon as they had safely forded the Spey. Nevertheless, instinct warned him that the Comyns had likely kept track of them both going and on their return.

Warning the others to keep a close watch as they guided their horses down the hill, Fin kept his right hand poised to draw his sword at a moment's notice.

All remained quiet when they reached the shore. The host of lights on the castle ramparts should have reassured him, he knew. But they did not.

"Waken the echo, sweetheart," he murmured.

With a low chuckle that stirred him to think briefly of more pleasant things, she hooted softly. When the echo failed to respond, she hooted again with more energy, and the sound echoed back to them. As it faded, another hoot sounded.

"That's Aodán, not the echo," she murmured. "Watch for the boat to come."

The rowers made little noise and collected them swiftly. Fin told Toby, Ian, and Tadhg to remove the sumpter baskets and turn the garrons loose.

"Aye, sir," Tadhg said. "They'll find grass and feed on their ownsome."

They made the trip back without a hint of trouble, and Aodán assured them that all had been quiet. "The laird do be away, gathering men to head for Glen Garry whilst Sir Ivor and the Lord of the North's forces keep to the east," he said. "But the laird left enough lads here to stand regular watches. We'll be changing the guard in an hour or so, and we'll ken more when our lads report aught they may have seen."

"The Mackintosh is in charge then, is he?" Fin murmured.

"Aye, sir," Aodán replied. "He said to tell ye, though, if ye did make it back here tonight, that although Sir Ivor and Shaw should be able to keep the trouble well east and south o' us for a time, all here will obey ye as they would

Himself. And we will, sir. See you, he and the ladies be already thinking o' their beds."

By the time Fin, Catriona, and their attendants entered the great hall, it was plain that the ladies and the Mackintosh were ready to retire.

Fin talked briefly with Mackintosh, who assured him that their guards would give warning of any trouble in good time. Then, wondering if his usually reliable instinct for danger had simply misled him, Fin took his lady wife to her bed, lingered there most pleasantly with her, and slept until Aodán woke him.

"Them devilish Comyns ha' captured our lads ashore," he breathed in Fin's ear. "Worse than that, sir, they've kept our last boat and mean to drown us all as we sleep, because they've dammed up the loch at the outflowing burn!"

When a wet paw stroked Catriona's cheek, she awoke to find Boreas's small shadow shivering on her pillow and Fin no longer lying beside her.

Rising and donning a robe, she gathered up the shivering kitten and, noting that its paws and belly were wet, cuddled it as she went to the window and opened the shutter. Instead of the rain she expected to see, she saw stars amid the clouds.

She could see only three lights on the ramparts, so the watchers had sighted Comyns, and Aodán had left a signal. She hoped it meant nothing worse than that.

Leaving the shutter open when she turned back, she could see that Boreas was not in the room and the door stood ajar. Through the crack, about the width of the kitten, dim golden light from a cresset on the landing peeked in.

Drying the kitten as well as she could and leaving it in her still-warm place on the bed, she grabbed her shift from the floor where Fin had flung it and took her old kirtle off its hook. Dressing hastily, she belted her dirk around her hips under her skirt, snatched a warm shawl from the same hook, and hurried downstairs.

Peeking into the great hall from the landing to be sure Fin was not there, she went on down to the scullery and the postern door. There, she set aside the bar, opened the door, and moved quickly to scan the yard. The lights above revealed that it was empty, and she saw only two men on the ramparts, both looking outward.

She hurried to the gate and found it a couple of inches open.

Wondering how far Fin might have gone, she eased the gate open more to let herself out and then pulled it nearly shut again.

When she saw no torch and heard naught to indicate where Fin might be, it dawned on her that he might just have gone to the garderobe. But Boreas would not have followed him there, and the kitten had got wet somewhere. Instinct and logic told her that the open gate meant all three had gone outside the wall.

As she turned toward the landing, she heard footsteps approaching. Although she hoped it was Fin, she stepped silently into the shadows until she could be sure.

Instead, she recognized Aodán's shape against the watery flatness behind him as he strode to the gate, eased through the opening, and shut it with a click.

She realized then that if Fin was *not* outside the wall, she would have some uncomfortable explaining to do. A shiver shot up her spine, and she amended that thought. He

would be furious and would say she ought to have spoken
to Aodán and gone back inside with him. She could still
rap on the gate, but she told herself that she did not dare
make such noise. Besides, she was curious.

The woods were black. No moon shone yet, and clouds had
moved in to hide the stars. Had it not been for the faint
gleam of water to guide them through the thickly growing
trees, he and Aodán would have blundered into things.

After Aodán had wakened him, he had dressed and
come outside with him to see how far the water had risen,
bringing Boreas along to keep the dog from waking Catriona. When the kitten darted through the doorway and
down the stairs, he had left the door ajar so that it would
not scratch to get back in.

The two men had not talked until they began sloshing
through water. Even then, the woods gave them cover, so
Fin doubted that anyone saw them.

The night was still, though, quieter than usual.

"Ye can usually hear the roar o' the water running out
on such a still night," Aodán had said then. "How fast will
it rise, sir?"

"Depends on the weather," Fin said, looking up to see
that clouds hid most of the stars. "No one here will drown
for some time, though." He hoped that no one at all would
drown. But the plain fact was that the steep bowl formed by
the hills, plus its single outflowing burn, and many tributaries, meant that the water would rise to whatever height the
Comyns had built the dam. And Aodán had said it was high.

Also, they had no boat. When the men being relieved
ashore had not returned in it, Aodán had worried enough

to swim over and look for them. Avoiding the landing area, he had scouted the west shoreline to see what he could see before swimming back to wake Fin. The Comyns had struck and struck hard.

But Fin meant to have the last word.

"Sir? There be summat I should ha' told ye afore," Aodán muttered.

"What?"

"The lad, Tadhg. He were wakeful, sir, and I let him go wi' the boat."

"We'll find them all," Fin said. "When you go in, wake what men you have in the castle and secure it. I'm going to swim across and see what I can see."

"Do I wake the grand lairds, too?"

Knowing that Rothesay and Alex would each then insist on taking charge, Fin said, "Let them sleep. If you need anyone, wake the Mackintosh first."

"Aye, well, wi' the gate closed, the place should be impregnable to all but the rising water. But I do wish we had a boat. If they've destroyed it..."

Not wanting to think about that, Fin had sent Aodán back and devised his own plan. His night vision was excellent, and he knew that when he was in the water he would see enough to know where he was. In any light, one could tell the difference between water and land, but finding a place from which to swim was less certain.

Not only was the water higher, but he had always swum the longer way to the loch's east shore. So he did not know the west shoreline well enough to be sure of the best route to reach it from the island. He would have to feel his way in without splashing about, and the water, he knew, would be icy cold.

His intent was to see exactly what the Comyns had done and to judge how hard it might be to undo it. He and Aodán had collected a few things that he could carry with him and that might or might not be of help.

A cold nose touched his hand, and he saw that Boreas had not returned with Aodán. Patting the dog's head, he murmured, "You'll have to stay here, lad."

He would swim quietly, and most of the enemy would be asleep. But they would have guards at the dam and with the prisoners. Doubtless, they had others to watch the castle and loch, too, as well as they could in the increasing blackness.

Even so, all of their watchers would get sleepy.

"I thought you must be out here."

Catriona's quiet voice preceded her as she came up behind him. She was all but invisible when he turned, and he had not heard her approach. The truth was that even now, he could feel her presence more easily than he could discern her shape.

"What the devil are *you* doing out here?" he demanded, realizing that Boreas might have tried to warn him that she was coming.

"The kitten woke me. It was all wet. Why is the water so high?"

"The Comyns have dammed the outflow. They also captured both sets of guards at the change of watch, and they kept the only remaining boat, too."

"Then you will need help," she murmured. "Whatever you mean to do, you should have someone with you. And since you did not keep Aodán..."

She left the sentence hanging in the air.

"I am going alone because one person can keep silent

more easily than two," he said. "Moreover, much of this trouble springs from my having come here."

"Piffle," she said. "Rory Comyn was making mischief long before you came. Granddad did try to make peace with the Comyns. But peace requires that both sides want it, and although many Comyns may agree that they do, Rory is not one of them. But this is foolish talk," she added. "What else have they done?"

He told her all that Aodán had discovered. "And Tadhg was with the lads."

Exclaiming her shock about the Comyns' perfidy, she added, "God-a-mercy, at first I thought it had just rained hard whilst we slept! Do they want to drown us all?"

"They may hope," he said. "But to do that, the water will have to rise high enough to submerge most of the castle. Their dam cannot be so high, be—"

"Not yet," she said grimly. "But we must get rid of it before the water rises higher. How can we do it without a host of men or even a boat?"

"Until I see the dam, I won't know whether anyone can dismantle it without getting himself killed," he admitted. "Once I know just what we face, we—"

"You have no intention of trying to dismantle it alone, do you?"

He did not reply.

After waiting impatiently for an answer that did not come, Catriona said tersely, "Just how do you think you *could* dismantle such a dam by yourself?"

"Lass, go back inside before I lose my patience with you."

"What will you do then, sir? You can scarcely shout at me or beat me without making enough noise to spoil any chance that we have tonight."

"I'll have plenty of time to attend to you later, however."

"Well, if you have failed to learn that I do not respond well to arbitrary orders, you should have paid more heed. Did Aodán describe this dam to you?"

Fin sighed audibly. "He said it looks as if they used two rows of posts with planks stacked on their sides between them to hold back the water whilst they piled logs, branches, and dirt behind them, like a beaver dam behind a board wall."

"Then I suspect you mean somehow to bore holes in those planks, because you cannot safely remove them *and* all that debris alone. But if you don't bore large enough holes in them, or *enough* holes, you'll just make water-spouts to spit through to the other side. And if you bore too many *large* holes, the force of water pouring through will destroy the dam before you can get away, and the torrent that results will carry you all the way down to the Spey. So, how *do* you intend to proceed?"

"Lower your voice, sweetheart. Recall how easily it echoes here."

Obediently, she murmured, "But I am right, am I not? You did listen to me."

"I did, aye."

When he did not go on, she knew that despite the endearment, he was still vexed with her. He wanted her to go inside, and he did not want more argument.

"Don't tell me again to go back to bed," she said. "I mean to stay here or go with you, and I *won't* promise not to follow you. I swim as well as you do."

"Do you, lass? Mayhap that is true, but you have not pitted your skills against mine yet, so I doubt that it is. You are not as strong as I am."

She could not deny that, but the knowledge did not dissuade her. "I don't need to be as strong as you are," she said. "I can take the raft."

Fin had forgotten about the raft but considered and dismissed it. "Too noisy," he said. "Trying to paddle that raft from here to the dam would be tiresome as well. It is small, aye, but with you standing on it, they might see it from shore."

"Sakes, it is too dark out there to see anything. I can barely see your shape right in front of me. I could hear you breathing as I approached, and I knew that Boreas was out here, too," she added hastily, not wanting him to think that she would have spoken to just anyone she had met out there.

"Cat, think," he said. "Even on the darkest night, can you not see the water well enough from your window to tell that it is not the shore?"

"I can, aye," she admitted. "But any watcher seeing the raft would more likely think that it had just floated away from here when the water rose."

"You stand whilst you paddle the thing, do you not?"

"Aye, sure, but if I keep low, I can easily follow you. Sithee, I ken fine how to paddle without making noise. I have often—"

"Often what?" he demanded sternly.

Clearly unabashed, she chuckled low in her throat. "Stop trying to come the ogre over me, sir. I'm just thinking that you are more likely to get back safely if we do take the raft. We can swim beside it if you think that would serve us better."

"*We* are not going."

"Ay-de-mi, but you *will* take the raft. If you mean to put holes in that dam, you will need it just to keep you afloat if the dam breaks before you expect it to."

"As you said yourself, lass, if it goes, I'll go with it, raft or no raft," he said grimly. "And so will anyone else who is nearby on the loch. The current there will be fierce until the loch returns to its natural level."

"Then it will be as well if we … that is, if *you* … are out of the water long before then," she said. "To avoid disaster, you must mean to plug your holes somehow. Or do you simply mean to bore holes *until* the dam breaks?"

"I do have rags to plug them and a large ball of twine," he said, realizing that she thought such plugs would keep the dam strong enough to hold but unwilling to increase her fears by explaining that each hole he drilled would weaken that plank regardless of any plugs, that they would just keep outflowing water from interfering with him as he worked his way down to the most vulnerable planks. He would tie the plugs together so that he could pull them free quickly in a hope of *relieving* the water pressure if any plank began ominously bowing or cracking as he worked.

That small relief would, he hoped, give him time to get out of the water.

"A ball of twine is not enough," she said. "We … *you* need a rope, a long rope."

"I mean only to set the plugs in place tonight if such a plan proves feasible," he said. "At the pace the water is rising, it won't reach the great hall until tomorrow afternoon or evening. Tomorrow night, Aodán and I can return if that becomes—"

"Listen," she murmured.

He heard it then, too, the sibilant whisper of raindrops in the canopy above.

"All the better," he said, reaching for her and pulling her close. "The rain will help conceal me, sweetheart. I must go, but I will be back as fast as I can. Now, kiss me, cease your fratching, and get back inside that castle and to bed."

She leaned into him, putting her arms around him and holding him close. Then she tilted her face up and kissed him, pressing her tongue to his lips.

Parting them, he savored the taste of her, aware that he might never taste her again if anything went wrong. Plunging his tongue into the softness of her mouth, he moaned softly, wishing that he could carry her back to bed and stay there.

Reluctantly, he released her.

"How will you go?" she asked.

"I had thought of swimming straight down the loch from here," he said. "But now that the rain has come, I think I can safely swim to the shore instead and walk at least partway and possibly as far as the turning if I can keep near the water."

"That path will still be above water, I think. But won't they be using it?"

"If any Comyn is wandering about at this hour in the rain, I will attend to him," Fin said. "He won't be expecting anyone, and I will. Don't fret."

"Nay, then, I won't, I promise."

"I want you to promise me something else."

"Aye, aye, I ken fine what *that* is. Now go, so you can come back to me."

He gave her a hug and stripped off his mantle, keeping only the thin tunic he had donned to come outside, and he kept that only to cushion his sword as he swam. After weeks of hardening, his bare feet were tough.

Handing her his mantle to hold while he fastened the belt that held his dirk in its sheath, he tied the cloth sack that contained his rags, twine, and auger to it. The sack would hamper his swimming more than the sword but was a necessary burden. He had a shorter distance to swim, so it would not hamper him much.

Confident that Catriona and Boreas would return to the safety of the castle, he walked with her to the place where she said it would be easiest to get in, kissed her once more, waded in, and silently pushed off.

Rain pelted the water around him, but even angling north as he did, the swim was short, his sense of direction reliable, and he soon decided on his destination.

Chapter 19 ——————————

Catriona watched Fin swim away, relieved to see that he *could* swim with the heavy sword strapped to his back. But she soon lost sight of him in the rain.

Satisfied that even a Comyn dependable enough to keep watch in the middle of a rainy night would not see him if she could not, and certain that Fin would win against any single opponent, she turned from the shore but not toward the castle.

Instead, she went back through the woods and sloshed to the raft tied on end to its tree. Setting Fin's mantle atop a shrub with thick foliage above it, she began to unwind the long rope binding raft to tree.

Boreas pressed his nose into her hand.

"Good lad," she said. "But you'll stay here." Coiling the rope, she tipped the raft over, its cumbrous weight defeating her so that it made a great splash when it landed. She was sure that the noisier rain hid the sound, and as she had hoped, the water was deep enough there for it to float. She would take the rope with her.

Tying the raft to a sapling, she went back for her paddle. As long as the rain continued, she would paddle standing, as she and Ivor had done as children. There would be no current as there had been then to aid her tonight, though.

As that thought crossed her mind, another followed. There *would* be a current after she and Fin destroyed the dam, so getting back to the island might be hard. She wondered how long it would take the loch to return to its normal level.

Fin clearly had not thought about that. Of course, if he meant just to bore his holes, plug them with his rags, and then connect all the rags with his twine—

Another, horrifying thought struck. What if his intent all along had been to sacrifice himself to save them all as penance for killing Clan Chattan men at Perth?

A raindrop slid beneath her kirtle and down her back, jerking her from the dreadful image and restoring her common sense. Fin would not sacrifice himself on purpose. But if his plan was going to work, it had to work that night. Even the daft Comyns would examine their dam by daylight to be sure that all was well. If they saw twine or rags, any chance of removing them later would be lost.

Aware that if she fell in, she would swim better without her kirtle, she nearly took it off to leave it behind. But it occurred to her that the current created by the water pouring out of the loch would likely prevent any return before morning. If so, she would have to face her grandfather and others wearing a soaked shift with her dirk strapped round her hips, and escorted by an equally underdressed Fin.

On that thought, she went back and collected his mantle and decided to keep her kirtle on rather than chance losing it in the dark if she did fall off the raft.

Wet clothes would be better than facing *anyone* in only a thin, damp shift.

~

Fin reached shore without seeing any sign of human movement there. Although he knew that a sensible watcher would conceal himself, he also knew that at two hours or more past midnight, all men were less alert.

However, the Comyns would have set at least two men to keep an eye on the narrows between the island and the shore. A short time later, he was satisfied that they had posted *only* two and that neither need concern him any longer.

Aodán had said that the prisoners were on the hillside above the landing, but Fin could not be sure they were still there or how many guards they had.

His primary objective was the dam.

Moving as fast as the darkness and his night vision allowed and keeping to the grassy verge where possible, he soon realized that the rain had eased although it remained steady. It was also warm. If it continued so overnight or grew heavier again, the rate at which the water rose would increase significantly, because it would melt most of the remaining snow above them on the surrounding hillsides.

The Comyns, without interference and given the time, could raise the height of their dam as high as necessary. The granite cleft into which the outflowing burn passed was narrow with steep sides tall enough so that if their dam held, it could easily force the water of the loch high enough to cover much of the castle.

Fin was glad that he had not promised Catriona that

he would do nothing dangerous by himself. He had to do what he could do to avert catastrophe.

He reflected then on the promises that she had made him. At the time they had eased his concern for her, but something about them nagged him now.

A sound diverted his thoughts. Realizing that it was a once-trickling rill ahead, now full of fresh rainwater and snowmelt, rushing downhill to the loch, he focused his mind on other sounds of the night. If he allowed his thoughts to wander again, he risked walking right into trouble.

When he reached the curve where the track forked over and around the hill near the outflowing burn, and slowed his pace, he heard a soft thud as of wood against wood a short distance to his right, on the loch.

Drawing his dirk, he stepped off the path and eased downhill through waist-high shrubs until it felt soggy underfoot. Then he crouched in the bushes to wait.

∼

Freezing in place, mentally cursing her clumsiness in letting the raft bump the shaft of her paddle as, kneeling, she had reached with it to feel for the shore, Catriona knew that she had reached the inner curve just before the shoreline curved outward and around to meet the burn that the Comyns had blocked with their dam. She had often swum near that shoreline and knew it well. Wary now, she remained watchful.

The slope there was steep, as were most of the slopes around the loch, but she managed to float the raft near enough to grasp shrubbery and pull herself toward the granite shelf from which she often swam. The raft made a whispery noise as she eased closer, and she realized that it was scraping over other shrubbery underwater.

Kneeling as she was, she would have to sit to get safely off the raft. She did not want to step barefoot into a bush or fall into the water as she secured it. But she was in a good place. A deer trail led up from the shelf to the path around the loch.

The rain gently continued and dripped from her lashes, making her blink and wipe water from her eyes. She reached for another branch...

"Don't make a sound," Fin muttered from the darkness, startling her nearly into a shriek. Only by what she deemed superhuman effort did she stifle the sound in her throat. Jerking her hand back served only to make the raft tilt dangerously, but a warm, strong hand gripped her quickly outflung wrist, steadying her.

"Can you get off now?" he asked. His voice sounded quiet and calm, as if he were only inquiring about the weather or the state of her health.

James would have begun scolding at once. And Ivor would have revealed the side of him that set the earth trembling from his wrath. But Fin...

She wished she could see more than his shape, because although she knew he must be angry, she could hear nothing in his voice to tell her *how* angry he was.

"Careful," he said as she used her free hand to shift her skirts out of her way and gingerly swung her bare feet off the raft to seek purchase on the granite.

"I brought your mantle," she murmured. "And the rope from the raft."

"You brought company, too," he murmured as he dragged the raft ashore.

Glancing over her shoulder, she saw the vee-shaped wake in the loch before it registered that she had neglected to tell Boreas to stay behind.

Fin watched the dog's silent approach, reminding himself that wolf dogs were naturally quiet animals. Even so, he wanted to shake Catriona, or worse.

Instead, he said, "I'm glad Boreas came with you, because I must leave you here—" Hearing her indrawn breath, he broke off long enough to put a firm finger to her lips, silencing her, before he added, "Just listen, Cat. Don't speak."

She nodded, which he thought was wise of her. Boreas, emerging from the water a short distance away, shook himself and waited where he was.

"I'm going to leave you both here, and you *will* stay," Fin said, "because I must see what lies ahead. I don't want the distraction of wondering if you will keep silent or if one of you will somehow warn them of our approach."

When she nodded again, he took his finger away.

"How long?" she whispered. The whisper indicated naught of her emotions. Nor did he want to know what they were.

"It will seem long to you, staying here," he said. "I'll make my way up that hill to see what I can from the top. I must know how many guards they've set near their dam and how high it is. I'll leave my tools with you."

"I can be patient if you will be careful. I just hope you can find us again."

"I'll find you," he said. "But do not be congratulating yourself, lass, because I am displeased with you. Your coming here makes my task more dangerous than it would be without you. Moreover, you promised—"

"I promised only not to *worry* about you," she reminded him. "If you recall—"

"I do, and I recall, too, that afterward, when I said I wanted a second promise from you, you cut me off and said, 'Aye, aye,' did you not, as if you—?"

"I did, but I—"

"You did, and you *know* I took it to mean that you understood the promise I sought and had agreed to it. Nay, do not try to defend yourself," he added, hearing her draw breath to do so. "You ken fine that you are in the wrong, Cat. But if you want to pretend that you *don't* know it, I'll make it quite clear to you later."

Catriona squirmed, feeling none of her usual eagerness to debate with him. His tone made his feelings as clear as they would be if she could see his expression. Indeed, she could easily imagine it, and she had come to know him well enough to be certain that she did not want to test his tolerance now by reminding him that she had also said earlier that she would *not* promise not to follow him.

"We'll wait for you," she said. "I should tell you, though, that even if you punish me sorely for this, sir, I'm glad I came. If aught should happen to you—"

"I know, lass, and I wish I could promise you that nowt will happen, but I cannot. Your grandfather thinks nowt of the Comyns, but they did succeed in this venture, and they may even have men surrounding the loch now, watching and waiting until Rory Comyn summons them."

"You don't believe that."

"I don't. But in my experience, it is better to assume that the other fellow knows more than I do and is as smart, or smarter, and as skilled with a sword."

"God-a-mercy, even Ivor says that no one can best you with a sword. I worried about you swimming here with it, but I'm glad that you did."

"I have my dirk, too," he said. "Now, take these things we brought, and Boreas, and go uphill till you find a place where you can see the path but not be seen from it." He paused. "I must know that I can depend on you this time to obey me."

"I will, sir." Following him up to the path, she clicked her tongue to Boreas.

When she could discern the dog's moving shape, she gestured widely toward the hillside and felt more confident when she saw Boreas cross the path and begin to range back and forth. Fin said no more to her and soon vanished into the darkness.

By the time she had settled where she could still make out the path, she decided that he must have reached the hilltop and would return before she knew it.

The rain eased more. The minutes crawled by.

Taking his time, Fin wended his way to the top of the hill, careful not to disturb any Comyn who might be nearby. Telling himself that he needed to live at least long enough to deal properly with his erring wife, he knew that his true intent was to live long enough to make love to her until they wore each other out.

Despite that pleasant fantasy, his battle-honed senses remained alert. The rain eased to gentle mist. When he reached the crest and found a vantage point, he soon discerned movement beyond the dam, near the silent bed of the dammed-up burn.

A male voice drifted to his ears. "Be they all asleep below?"

Another said, "All save two watchers, aye, and all be nigh the burn. D'ye think this thing will hold? Because they'll get a right dousing down there if it fails."

"Aye, sure, it will hold. We've piled wood and rocks high to hold the planks in place against the rising water. It be rising quick now, too. If this rain picks up again, it may get high enough to drown the lot o' them by morning and mayhap Shaw's men, too. I just hope our lads a-watching them do keep themselves safe."

"I'm surprised Rory didna want them all kept below with the others."

"He didna want to hear them Mackintoshes bemoaning their lot all night, he said. Come what may, I mean to find me a place to sit well above this great pile."

"Me, too, aye. But we'd best keep one o' us to each side like Rory did say."

Satisfied with what he'd heard, Fin shifted to a better position, drew his dirk, and waited for the one who would guard that side of the dam to come up to him.

The result was almost too easy, because the man came carelessly, paying heed to naught but where he put his noisy feet.

Clapping an arm around him from behind, Fin put his dirk to the man's throat. "One squeak and ye're spent," he muttered, affecting the local accent. "How many watchers d'ye keep round yon loch?"

"Two at their landing, and three others, if ye dinna count us two here."

"Who guards your prisoners?"

"Them other three I told ye about. All the others returned to our encampment below. Nae one else be out yonder, for nae one can see nowt tonight!"

"How many sleep below?"

"Nigh a score to send out and about at dawn. That be all o' them, I swear!"

"Is that counting Albany's army or that of the Douglas?" Fin asked dulcetly.

His captive stiffened but kept silent.

"Ah, now, ye're a fine honest chappie," Fin said. "A feather in your chief's bonnet, ye be. I'll just go and see if your friend yonder be as fine and honest, shall I? Nay, now, cease your wriggling. I'll no disturb ye more, I trow."

Catriona was sure that something horrid had happened to Fin. She had heard nothing since he had left her with Boreas, and the dog lay dozing beside her.

She kept her dirk in hand, just in case, and had wrapped herself in Fin's mantle. Although she was grateful for its warmth, its dampness permeated to her skin, making her think longingly of the hall fire at Rothiemurchus.

The dog raised its head, and a moment later, silently, a shadow loomed over them. "God-a-mercy, I hope that's you," she muttered, gripping her dirk tighter.

"It is, aye," Fin said. "I've come to fetch that sack and your rope."

"How many guards are there?"

"None who will disturb us," he said. "Now, come, for I want to get this done. Albany's army will come round the Cairngorms and Douglas from the south through Glen

Garry. They could be here tomorrow if Ivor, Shaw, and their men cannot stop them. Albany expects the Comyns to capture Rothesay and Alex Stewart for him, and as many Clan Chattan prisoners as they can. I won't let that happen."

Indignantly, she said, "Neither will my father or Ivor. And even if they should somehow fail, do you think Rothesay and the Lord of the North are such cowards that they would leave those of us here to face Albany and Douglas alone?"

"Nay, but if Albany captures them, it will put everyone here in danger, because he will declare us all part of their conspiracy. I agree that Shaw's men and Ivor's from Lochindorb will likely stop Albany's armies or the terrain and bad weather will, because neither leader has experience in the Highlands. But if Albany is determined enough to get his hands on Rothesay and Alex, he may just do it."

"In this weather, we cannot use our signal fires to bring more aid," she said.

"Nay, but if we can avoid armed confrontation, we'll sort things out. However, we must defeat the Comyns here. Then, if Albany does win through, he'll have to deal with your grandfather. The Mackintosh can handle him if anyone can."

"He has cowed fiercer men than the Duke of Albany," she said. "And my father and Ivor *will* succeed. But what about Rothesay and Alex? Neither one will like being out of the action and neither is easily persuadable."

"I hope that Alex will persuade Davy to go with him," he said. "But I cannot think about that. First, I must see if I can perform a feat of magic with this dam."

"What can I do? And, prithee, do not tell me that I can do naught."

"You and Boreas are coming with me to keep watch whilst I bore my holes and plug them," he said. "Three watchers guard the prisoners on the hill above your landing, but the two watching the dam expected no relief for anyone before dawn."

"How do you know all that?"

"I asked them."

"You *asked* them?"

"Aye, sure, how else was I to get such information?"

"But you said they won't trouble us. If there are *two*, won't they rouse—?"

"Nay, they will not. Now, are you coming?"

Realization of what he must have done struck hard, and remembering his first words to her about the guards, she knew that she ought to have taken his meaning then. She did not speak, not knowing what to say.

He kept silent, too, so she knew that he was waiting for her to ask him if he had killed them. Instead, she stood, shook out her skirts, and said, "I am wearing your mantle, sir. Do you want it, to warm you as we go?"

"Nay, it must be damp, too, and my tunic will suffice as long as I keep moving. I see no sense in warming up just to go back into that water."

~

They went quickly back to the dam, with Boreas loping silently ahead of them, ranging back and forth as he always did.

"Don't let him get too far ahead," Fin warned Catriona.

"He won't," she said. "When he comes to the fork, he'll wait for us. And, as you've seen, he'll also stop if he senses anyone approaching."

Going around the hill instead of over it as Fin had before, they reached the front of the dam without incident. The water had climbed several feet above normal.

He thought that he could stand up to bore many of his holes but knew that he would have to bore others with his head underwater just to get the angle of the auger right. The planks near the bottom were the most important ones, because no matter how high the dam was, it would all go when its underpinning went. Even so, he could not be sure that his plan amounted to more than wishful madness.

As he stripped off his sword and tunic, he handed her the latter and said, "I'll be in the water for some time, so tuck this under the mantle to warm it against your body. But go back to the top of the hill now, and keep hidden in the bushes."

He moved nearer the water and was putting his sword down close to where he would be working when she said quietly, "How are your feet?"

"They'll do. They've toughened since I came to Rothiemurchus."

The truth was that they hurt, but the pain was bearable.

He could feel her watching as he picked up the sack and waded down the granite slope toward the center of the dam. The water there was up to his armpits.

"How are you going to manage that sack *and* the auger?" she muttered.

Without taking his attention from what lay before him,

he replied in the same tone, "I'll hold it in my teeth, lass. Now, go. You must keep watch."

Hearing only a brief rattle of pebbles in response, he felt relief sweep through him. She would be safer atop the hill, with Boreas.

Catriona moved far enough away to be sure that she had faded into the darkness as Fin had when he had left her earlier on the hillside. She stayed until she thought she had given him enough time to push her out of his mind. Then, quietly commanding Boreas to stay on guard, she made her way back toward Fin.

If he was like most men she knew, once he began boring his holes, he would concentrate completely on them. But he would need help. It felt as if more than an hour must have passed since they'd left the island, but she could not be sure. It had seemed at least twice that long when she had waited for him before.

She knew it had not been anything like so long. But with Comyns still lurking in the area and Albany and Douglas on their way, every minute counted.

The rain had stopped, and looking up, she saw a few scattered stars.

Boreas would warn her if anyone came, and she would be able to warn Fin more quickly if she was near the water than if she stayed obediently atop the hill.

But she had known better than to suggest that to Fin.

She could hear him moving, then the sound of water sloshing as he set the auger to a plank and began to bore, turning the handle swiftly enough to splash. The sound seemed loud, but she doubted that it would alert anyone unless that person was nearby. And, thanks to Boreas, she knew that no one was.

⁓

Fin's work went smoothly despite devilish conditions.

The rough-hewn planks sat tightly between two rows of distantly spaced support posts, just as Aodán had described them. The water of the loch crept higher as he stood there, but he had to bore near the center of the planks to have any hope that his two vertical, closely spaced lines of holes would cause them to break.

The higher the water rose, the more weight it would exert on the lower planks. He knew that once they cracked and water started flowing with speed, its force would carry away the planks and all that the Comyns had piled behind them.

Boring steadily, plugging each hole as he went, he wound twine around the rag plugs, cutting lengths long enough to connect them all. Crouching lower as it became necessary, working with his head underwater now most of the time, he worked his way down from the waterline, finding it harder to keep his balance as he bent and harder to press the auger efficiently into the wood.

Before he had finished boring the third plank from the bottom, he realized that the second one was too far under for him to crouch without floating. Surfacing, trying to think and thinking only how cold he was, he muttered a frustrated curse.

The water stirred, and he felt a warm hand on his shoulder. Reaching for her, he discovered that she was naked.

"What's wrong?" she murmured. "Can I help?"

"You are supposed to be watching for Comyns," he muttered back.

"Boreas is doing that. I will hear him growl if he hears or smells anyone coming, but we need to finish this and get back."

"I still have to bore holes in the two bottom planks," he told her. "Sithee, the lower boards bear more of the water's weight than the upper ones do, and so the dam will most likely break from the bottom up. But when I bend so low, my body wants to float. Do you think you can hold me down?"

"I'll stand on you, if necessary," she said. "I can balance myself against the dam. You need only touch my foot when you need to come up for air."

⁓

Although Catriona had expected Fin to refuse her help, he said, "If you stand on the slope, you can step onto my back when I bend over. Then I can brace myself as I work. And I'll warn you, aye, before I straighten up."

He finished quickly after that, although standing on him as he worked proved to be more difficult than she had expected. She nearly fell in more than once, and just before he touched her foot, she heard an odd moaning sound and felt the planks against which she was steadying herself shudder. She shuddered, too, but relaxed when nothing further happened.

She got off him and moved to where she could stand, and he straightened but only to scoop her up and carry her out of the water to where they had left the rope.

She saw Boreas rise from the shrubbery above them, alert to their approach.

When Fin set her on her feet, she reached for the rope, but he said, "Never mind that now, lass. We should get round to the other side of the hill because the dam may break with enough force to fling plank pieces and other debris about."

"But we must pull out the plugs first."

"Nay," he said. "The two lower planks had begun to bow outward, and I heard creaking, so I stopped. It's too dangerous now to go back in."

"I did hear an odd moan," she said, feeling for her kirtle. "But I don't hear anything now. How long will it be before it breaks?"

"I don't know," he admitted. "But unless you want to go naked, hurry."

Keeping an ear cocked for other ominous sounds as she dealt with her wet kirtle, she could see enough of his shape to know that he had already put on his tunic, belt, and dirk. Before slinging on his sword, he helped her with her lacing.

As he did, he said, "The pressure at the bottom will grow as the water rises, and I do think that it must be about to go. But I dared not wait to bore the last plank, especially you standing atop me, lass, so I don't even know for sure that this will work. I'm tempted to stay just to be sure that it does."

"Do you mean that if it doesn't, you would go back in and bore more holes?" she demanded, feeling an icy chill of fear at the thought of the dam breaking with him still standing in the torrent's path.

He was silent for much too long.

"Don't be daft!" she snapped, forgetting to keep her voice low. "Sakes, sir, we still have to do what we can to save Tadhg and the other prisoners."

He put a finger to her lips. "Shhh," he said. "We're not out of this yet."

"But you can't stay here. I won't *let* you!"

"Won't you?" His voice was soft, even gentle.

She put a hand to his cheek and her face close to his. "Nay, Fin Cameron, I won't. This is one battle that you will *not* fight alone, sir. Rothiemurchus is my family's home. If you must stay, then Boreas and I will stay, too."

"Nay, we'll go," he said. "Rain or no rain, that dam will break before the water gets high enough to drown anyone."

He hugged her then, the strong warmth of his body warming hers.

"You're shivering," he said. "But we'll walk fast, and you'll wear my mantle until you feel warmer. The thing smells of wet wool, but you won't mind that."

"You'll freeze," she muttered as he wrapped the damp mantle around her.

"Nay, then, I did not freeze in the river Tay at the ice end of a September. I'll not freeze here when it's nearly summertime."

"It is barely the first of July, sir, and still snowy above, come to that."

"Strap your dirk on over your skirt, sweetheart, not under it. We'll let Boreas lead the way," he added, grasping her hand warmly when she had signed to the dog.

"I keep expecting to hear the dam go," she said as they hurried along the path.

"The trick will be for us to get back to the castle when it *does* go."

"The current on the surface may be too strong then,

aye," she said. "But we do still have one boat unless the Comyns destroyed it, too. If we *can* get back, our men will be able to row Rothesay and Alex ashore so they can leave."

"I've been thinking about that," he said. "If they follow the Spey, they will likely run into Douglas's forces, coming here. Good routes from here are few."

"Mercy, sir, you contradict yourself as well as me," she said.

He chuckled, and the sound warmed her more. "I don't contradict you," he said. "I just raise fresh points to discuss." Before she could counter that daft statement, he added, "I suspect that Alex will know how to get them both away safely."

"He will. Not that they need go at all. The men of Clan Chattan and the North *will* prevail. We must tell Granddad what you heard those two guards say, though."

"Not we, sweetheart. *I* will tell him."

She did not argue, knowing that she would willingly escape that discussion. In her absence, Fin would not make a point of telling the Mackintosh or Shaw that she had been with him. However, if she were there, facing them with him...

She sighed. The likelihood was that the Mackintosh, her father, and Ivor would somehow learn all there was to know and would have much to say to her. But Fin was her husband. They would leave any punishment to him. And although he had been vexed with her, he no longer seemed to be.

"Keep Boreas close," he said. "I don't want him running into an errant Comyn."

"You said there were only the three left, all guarding the prisoners."

"I don't trust any Comyn to be where I expect him to be, not tonight."

Just then, Rory Comyn stepped onto the path ahead, his sword in hand.

Chapter 20.

Fin knew that he was tired, because until he'd recognized Rory Comyn, he had scarcely noticed the moon beginning to peek over hills to the east. Stepping swiftly in front of Catriona and pulling his sword from its sling, he said brusquely, "Get well away from us, lass, and keep Boreas with you. Do not let him interfere."

She did not respond, but he heard her moving off the path. And he knew enough about the dog to be sure that it would stay near her.

Eyeing Comyn, he said, "I expected you to be sound asleep."

"I'm none so daft as that," Comyn retorted. "I should be asking what mischief ye've been up to, should I no? I didna ken that ye'd returned."

"Then you must have been elsewhere when we did," Fin said. Testing the ground beneath his bare feet, he noted grimly that they would have scant room to maneuver. "We made no secret of it."

He heard the dog growl low in its throat and hoped that Cat could control it. He did not want to see Boreas spitted on the other man's sword. Nor did he want the dog to interfere with him. But the growling ceased, and Comyn leaped forward.

Parrying his first sweeping stroke, Fin focused on the next one, preferring to let Comyn tire himself while giving Catriona time to get well away.

⁓

Catriona watched the two men long enough to be sure that Fin was in no immediate danger. Unless she was much mistaken, though, he was letting Rory Comyn lead the swordfight, choosing only to defend himself.

She had watched her brothers practice their swordsmanship often and easily recognized James's chief defense against Ivor.

But she had understood Boreas's growl if Fin had not. That Rory would be walking alone had seemed odd to her at once. Hoping that whoever was in the woods where they dipped near the trail ahead was more interested in the swordsmen than in her, she eased her way up the hillside, taking care to keep her wet skirt from catching on every branch of shrubbery she passed.

As the moon rose, its light increased. It would not be full but the sort the Scots called an aval moon, because it was the shape of a pregnant woman's belly. She was grateful for the light but hoped that Boreas's silence meant that no one lay in wait ahead of her and not that he was still obeying her earlier command for quiet.

Confident that he would keep her from walking into danger, she moved with more speed. In the woods, enough moonlight pierced the canopy to let her find her way, but knowing that an ally of Comyn's stood somewhere ahead, she took care to make no avoidable noise.

Passing a deadfall, she saw a stout branch that might serve as a club, picked it up, and then touched the hilt of her dirk to be sure that she could find it quickly if she needed it. Holding the club firmly, she listened to the clanging swords on the trail as she moved on, reassured by the even rhythm of their clashing.

Then she saw him, a lone shadowy figure standing by a tree with his back to her, watching the fight. Amazed that he seemed unaware of her presence, she saw the reason when he held a bow out near his right hip and nocked an arrow to its string. The shape of bow and arrow against the moonlit water made his intent unmistakable.

Signing to Boreas to stay behind her, she moved as swiftly as she dared.

When the archer straightened away from the tree, raised the bow, and drew the bowstring to his cheek, Catriona gripped the club tightly in both hands and struck his head as hard as she could.

He dropped at her feet with no more sound than a dull thud and a hushing of leaves. The moment that she'd struck, a voice deep in her mind had murmured that he might be one of theirs. A surge of relief engulfed her to see that he was not.

He was dead or unconscious, the bow and arrow lying half under him. Signing to Boreas to guard the villain, she turned to watch the swordsmen.

Fin looked tired, as he ought to be, she thought. She remembered his so recently tender feet and was sure that after being in the water so long, they must have been as numb as hers were. Hers were leather tough, though. His still were not.

On the other hand, the cold did not seem to bother him, and Ivor was the same. Ivor had only to see sunlight to bare his torso and bask in it.

Fin looked as if he were handling Rory as deftly as he had before. Then he stumbled, and Rory drove his sword at him. As Catriona gasped, Fin deflected the murderous blade and recovered his balance, but she had seen enough.

Looking warily at her victim and seeing that he was as still as a man could be, and that Boreas was watching him closely, she pulled the bow out from under him and yanked the arrow from beneath his elbow. Then, moving prudently away, she watched the two swordsmen on the trail.

Neither man's movements were as agile as they had been before, but although she hoped that Fin would soon pick up the pace and go on the offensive, he did not. He stumbled again, and Comyn leaped forward.

Again, Fin deflected the blow and recovered.

Catriona nocked the arrow to the bowstring and prepared to draw. She was no highly skilled archer, but Ivor had taught her, just as he had taught her to use her dirk. Taking her stance, she drew the bowstring back far enough to make sure that she could. Assured that, although it was not an easy pull, it was possible, she took aim at a point in the shrubbery some yards to the left of the two swordsmen, waited until they danced farther apart on the path, and let fly.

To her shock, just as she did, Comyn leaped to the hillside above Fin, turned to attack again, and the arrow struck right between them.

Both men started at the sight of it, but Fin recovered faster. With an upswing of his sword and a flick of his wrist, he sent Comyn's sword spinning up and over his own head and back toward the loch, where it made a large and satisfactory splash.

Comyn roared toward the woods, "Ye daft bastard! Ye nearly killed *me*!"

That was all he said, though, before Fin's fist connected with his chin and he collapsed much the same way that the man lying a few feet from Catriona had.

Tadhg's quiet voice from behind startled her nearly out of her skin: "Sakes, m'lady," he said, "ye missed the villain. He'd ha' looked better wi' your arrow through his lugs!"

~

Fin crouched low, waiting for the hidden archer to reveal himself. When four brawny figures stepped into the moonlight from the forest shadows, he felt the same sense of fatalism he had felt at Perth upon realizing that he was alone against four more Clan Chattan men. Rory Comyn still lay where he had fallen.

As Fin set himself he saw that the others did not. Then Tadhg and Catriona walked out of the woods behind them, and Boreas loped toward him.

Catriona ran ahead of the others, and Fin caught her in his arms. "Don't tell me that you freed our men whilst I played out here with Comyn, lass."

"Nay, *I* did that," Tadhg said, dancing up behind her. "A score o' them Comyns was a-waiting for the nine o' us new lads when we come over in the boat, Sir Fin. But when they sprang out o' the woods, they went for all our big lads without heeding me. So in the tirrivee, I went tae ground and hid in the bushes."

"Good thing for us that he did," one of the other men said.

"Tadhg was very brave," Cat said. "He'll make a fine knight one day."

"Aye, I will," Tadhg said. "That 'un there that ye clouted took another 'un and they went looking tae see had they got all o' our watchers. So, I waited long, sithee, till I thought they were no coming back and them guards was all a-sleeping. Then I crept about and untied a couple o' our men. But that 'un and his man came back then, so we had tae lay low. Then them two said they'd best be getting back to the dam. Next we knew, swords was a-clanging. Their guards looked to see what were happening, so our lads what I'd freed took care o' them. Then we freed the others."

"You said there were two men, Tadhg, but I've seen only Rory Comyn," Fin said. "He challenged me alone, but he had a bowman hidden in the woods, because Comyn shouted at him. Sakes, but you must have seen the chap, lads," he added. "He shot at me just before you came out of those woods."

"Nay, then, she didna shoot at *ye*!" Tadhg said indignantly. "She—"

Fin had already felt Catriona stiffen. Holding her away from him, he snapped in amazement, "*You* shot that arrow?"

～

Catriona heard astonishment in his voice but wished that the moonlight were not behind him so that she might see his expression. His hands gripped her tight.

The other men and Tadhg had fallen silent. No one moved.

"I meant only to startle Rory, sir, because I could see that you were tired and that your feet hurt," she said. "I aimed well to the uphill side of you both, but he jumped that way just as I let fly, so my arrow struck between you."

"Where did you find the weapon?" he asked.

Although his voice was quiet, its tone increased her tension.

She tried to think how best to answer the question.

"Tadhg," Fin said. "Did you see where the weapon came from?"

"Nay, but it must ha' come from the chappie laid out by her feet," the boy said. "A couple o' our lads be a-trying to wake him up now. I tellt her that she'd ha' done better to put that arrow straight through that Comyn's thick head, but then ye clouted him, so that be fine. Be he dead, Sir Fin?"

"I hope not, because I want to make a present of him to the Mackintosh. But first, madam wife," he added, "I want to know how you got that bow."

Knowing that he could see her face better than she could see his, and well aware of their audience, Catriona did not want to discuss the matter there. "We should be getting back," she said.

"In a few minutes," he said, the warning note now clear in his voice.

"Aye, very well then. But you won't like it, because when I saw that man, I—" She stopped when her sharp ears caught a strange sound through the night.

Fin heard it, too, and looked toward the north end of the loch.

The water looked calm, gleaming silver in the moonlight, but she heard a scraping, creaking sound. Then came a chaotic mixture of louder sounds, followed by quieter ones. Moments later, she heard men shouting in the distance, a second explosion of sound, and the roar of rushing water.

"Look," Fin said. "The surface of the loch is moving."

"The dam broke!" she exclaimed, and turned to him, grinning. "We did it!"

He put an arm around her and held her close again. "Aye," he said, "we did."

"And not before time neither," Tadhg said. "Look at them clouds. I'd say they be a-gathering up tae rain again afore morning, and I'm still that wet from before."

Fin's mood had lightened with the collapse of the dam, but Catriona knew he had not forgotten the bow and arrow. She was sure that he had deduced most of the truth, because he would not imagine that she had just stumbled across them.

But she wondered if he was grateful for what she had done. Men could be unpredictable in such matters.

⁓

"We'll not be taking Rory Comyn back with us, sir," a man who had knelt by Comyn told Fin. "His head's bad split. Likely he cracked it on the rock here when he fell, although ye might ha' split it yourself when ye clouted him."

"Saved Himself the trouble o' hanging him," another man said. "And I'm guessing the old gentleman will be glad to hear it. Will we be going across now, sir?"

Despite the black gloom of lowering clouds above, moonlight still gleamed between them, and Fin recognized an oarsman among the erstwhile prisoners. "What do you think about that current?" he asked him. "And do we have a boat?"

"Aye, sure, sir," the man said. "The boat be at the landing, because the villains thought they'd want it. And we'd be rowing wi' the current, which be easy as breathing. Rowing back will be another matter until the water rests easy again."

"I don't want us all to go," Fin said. "The eight who came to take the guard until dawn will stay, and any who got some sleep. Treat Comyn's body and the two you'll find near the landing with respect, for we'll give them back to their kin. Other Comyns will be awake if the torrent didn't get them, and there were a score of them, so keep your eyes open. The rest will come with us if we can all fit."

The oarsman chuckled. "Sakes, if Lady Cat could row ye and that Boreas in the coble, I'm thinking we can row the three of ye in our boat with ourselves."

"And me?" Tadhg said hastily.

"And you," Fin said, clapping him on the shoulder.

As they turned toward the landing, Fin became aware again of rushing water to the north and decided that the burn was likely making a fine waterfall now.

They made the return trip to the castle as easily as the oarsmen had foreseen. The boat was crowded, but Fin knew that the added weight helped its rowers keep it on course. The current was strongest in the narrows, where the oarsmen used it to their own advantage to make the landing. Thanks to the lingering moonlight and watchers on the ramparts, Aodán and another man-at-arms were there to aid them and help pull the boat from the water.

Noting how quiet Catriona had become, Fin put an arm around her shoulders as they went with the others to the gateway. "Cold, sweetheart?"

"A little," she admitted, "but not as cold as I probably should be."

"I'm not going to murder you, Cat," he murmured close to her ear.

"But you *were* vexed with me."

"A little, aye," he agreed. "But not as vexed as I might have been."

Smiling, she leaned into him. "Must you talk to Grand-dad straightaway?"

"Aye, and to anyone else who might be awake. We won't wake Rothesay or Alex, because with a boat here, we can easily get them away early if we must. But you will go straight upstairs and get into bed even if the others are waiting for us."

"One of them may order me to stay," she said.

"I won't allow it," he said.

⁓

Catriona believed him, although she was not sure that Fin could countermand an order from Rothesay or Alex, or her grandfather.

However, her grandfather was the only one in the hall when they entered, and although he gave her a look that seemed to be half-relief and half-annoyance, he spoke only to Fin. So when Fin nodded toward the stairway, she silently handed him his mantle, which she had kept wrapped around herself.

"It will help you maintain your dignity, sir, because your tunic is still damp," she said. "The mantle will keep you warmer, too."

"I'll warm soon enough. And if I don't, you can see to it when I get to bed."

Her body responded instantly to those words, and she hurried upstairs to find Ailvie asleep on a pallet by her bed. The maidservant awoke and jumped up, exclaiming at her mistress's appearance.

"What are you doing in here?" Catriona asked. "It's the middle of the night."

"Aye, sure, and what d'ye think I thought when Aodán woke me to say that yon kitten were a-mewing so loud that he went up to slip it into your room only to find the door ajar and ye naewhere to be found?"

"Oh, Ailvie," Catriona said, understanding her grandfather's expression now. "I'm sorry if my absence frightened you, but I was with Sir Finlagh, and now I am back."

"Ye are, aye, so I willna ask why ye be damp from tip to toe and nae doots shivering yourself nigh to fits. I'll just get ye out of them clothes and into that bed."

She soon left, and Catriona lay naked in bed with a purring kitten to warm her. Boreas had not followed her upstairs, doubtless preferring the hall fire's warmth.

Although, listening to the soothing sound of gentle rain outside, she expected to fall quickly asleep, she soon found herself trying instead to imagine what was happening downstairs and what Fin might say to her when he did come to bed.

By the time he did, she was dozing, but the click of the latch brought her wide awake. When she recognized his figure against the cresset's glow from the landing, she said, "What did Granddad say?"

"Since you're awake, I'll light a candle or two," he said. Taking one from a nearby small table, he lit it from the cresset and then used it to light two more. When he had finished, he stripped off his mantle and tunic, tossed them aside, and got into bed beside her. The kitten fled.

"You feel warm," she murmured, as he gathered her close. "But I don't know why you lit candles only to come to bed."

"Do you not?" He moved a hand to cup her left breast, brushing its nipple with his thumb.

"What did Granddad say?" she asked him again, trying to ignore the sensations he was stirring in her long enough to get an answer to her question.

"Not to worry," he said.

"Fin, if making me wait to know is another of your ways of punishing—"

"It isn't, sweetheart. I just want to make love to my wife."

"And so you may, but what about—?"

"I told you, he said not to worry—not about Albany or Douglas. He said the weather and our men waiting in good number to meet them will drive them back."

"The rivers *will* be roaring high," she said, nodding. "Not just from the rain but also because the rain is warm and will melt what's left of the snow. There must be few fords safe enough to use anywhere hereabouts, or in Glen Garry."

"So he says, aye, but we'll hear all about it tomorrow."

"Did you tell Granddad that I was with you at the dam?"

"I did, aye. He asked for the details, Cat, so I told him everything."

She sighed. "He'll have much to say to me, and so will my father and Ivor."

"I don't think so, my love."

"You don't?" The new endearment warmed her.

"He may expect me to have things to say, or even things that I ought to do, but I am your husband now, so he won't interfere. Neither, I think, will your father." He chuckled then. "I won't speak for Ivor."

"Ah, but you can protect me from him. Even he says that you are much better with a sword than he is."

"I am, but you did not think so tonight, did you?"

She swallowed hard, and an ache filled her throat. When he did not continue, she knew he was waiting for her to speak, to explain about the bow and tell him why she had shot the arrow.

"It was not what you thought," she said.

"How do you know what I thought?"

"You just told me," she said. "I was terrified for you, because I could see that your feet were sore. And that horrid man was about to shoot you from the woods."

"Aye, but I'm curious about that. How is it that he failed?"

Opting for the truth, she said, "He was concentrating on what he was to do, so I crept up and hit him with a stout branch I'd found near a deadfall."

"And then?" His voice had an odd, tight sound to it, so she decided that she would do better not to look at him until she had told him everything.

"I saw you stumble twice."

"Comyn also stumbled, several times. That path is rocky. You know that."

"Aye, but I never *saw* him stumble, and the bow was right there. I thought I could startle him if I shot an arrow near him. I never meant for it to go between you. I might...God-a-mercy, I might have shot you!"

At first, she thought he was trembling, even shivering. But then she realized that he was shaking more, and she looked at him. "You're laughing!"

"I…I am," he agreed, nearly chortling. "The thought of you just walking up and clouting that villain…"

Fin thought she looked ready to murder him, so he kissed her and said, "You most likely saved my life again, sweetheart, and I know that you would not have shot me. If you'd shot anyone, it would have been Comyn for being daft enough to jump in front of your arrow."

"Are you suggesting that for me to hit anything it would have to jump in front of me?" she demanded.

"I am not. Recall that you told me you can shoot. I deduced from that that Ivor had taught you, and although I doubt that you are as fine a shot as he is, I would trust you not to hit me in error. Call it instinctive trust, if you like. I don't think I'd be daft enough to think such a thing just because I love you."

"Do you?"

"Can you doubt it? Would I have trusted a lass I don't love or who does not love me to stand on me whilst I was underwater boring holes in that devilish dam?"

"You can trust your instincts, sir," she said, putting a soft hand to his cheek. "I do love you, and I have seen that your instincts are sound."

"I should have trusted them myself long before now," he said soberly. "I came to realize that whilst I was boring those holes."

"Mercy, how?"

"Since I did not think it helpful to ponder what might happen if the water's weight alone should bring down that dam, or to fret about the icy water, I turned my thoughts to other things. Mayhap it will help if I explain that I once told Ian I believe in teaching men to learn by their own mistakes, because I think that teaches them to make better decisions. Then you asked me if a man's training was not the very thing that develops the instincts he trusts in battle...and in life, come to that. You also reminded me that an honorable man cannot kill to protect his honor. In short, lass, I came to see that one can make a decision by *not* making it. I did that."

"Your dilemma," she said. "That is what you were thinking then? Does that mean that you are ready now to tell me about it?"

"I thought you must soon have deduced that the friend whose dilemma I told you about was myself. I can remember Ivor telling tales like that before he learned that he could tell me anything."

"You're right," she said. "Who was the kinsman you found dying?"

"My father."

"Oh, Fin." She moved closer and put her arms around him. "And who...?" She stiffened but soon relaxed. "Your father was the war leader," she said. "So he would have wanted vengeance against my father, at least. And you came here—"

"I came because Rothesay sent me. I did not know that Shaw was your father until you told me so, and I accepted your hospitality here because I had to see the Mackintosh. But, sweetheart, what I'm trying to tell you is that I had already made my choice between those two oaths. I just hadn't known it. Cat, it is four and a half years since the battle at Perth. Had I believed that killing your father was right—"

"You'd have done it long since, aye. I do see that. So,

I agree that you made the decision without realizing it, simply by not choosing. That was instinct, was it not? It would have been better, though, I think, if you had recognized long ago the plain fact that one should always choose life be over death."

"Aye, perhaps, but I'm a warrior, sweetheart, and a good one. The likelihood is that I will kill again, and you know it."

"I do, but I don't want to talk about war or killing now. I want you to hold me. And in troth, sir, if you want to take me, you'd best do it soon, because much as I love you, I am so tired that I can scarcely keep my eyes open."

"You don't know how glad I am to hear that," he murmured, kissing her. "I'm going to put out those candles."

"There is something I should tell you, too," she said. "Sithee, for those four and a half years, I thought all Camerons were sons of the devil. Then I met you and came to think of you as a good friend. So, later, your being a Cameron didn't seem so dreadful. But I assumed that your family would feel about Mackintoshes the way I'd felt about Camerons. Then I met Ewan, and he was just your brother and I your wife. I doubt that I thought of him as a wicked Cameron even when you told me who he was. I like him, and I want to see Tor Castle with you."

"I think we'll still spend most of our time at Castle Raitt," he said. "But we'll see Ewan often, too. And we'll all spend Christmas together at Tor Castle."

Cat watched him put the candles out and felt him climb back into bed but knew nothing more until the kitten demanded release the next morning. Even then, she barely noticed Fin getting up to let it out and was asleep before he returned.

When he woke her, midday sunlight was streaming through the open window and he was already dressed.

"It is nearly time to eat," he said. "And Ivor is back."

"Already?"

"Aye, and grievously annoyed."

She raised her eyebrows. "Why? If he is back, then Albany must have turned back at the Cairngorms. So whatever nuisance he intended to create—"

"Need no longer concern us for now," he said. "But although the army that tried to get through there did fly a royal banner, it was Sir Martin Redmyre, one of Albany's captains, who led it. There was no sign of Albany, or so Ivor heard from watchers who met him and told him that the weather in the high pass had defeated them. He would have been back sooner if the rain had not come down so hard, but they took shelter and made camp. So he is annoyed that he missed all that happened here, as well. And your father sent a messenger."

"Then he must have routed Douglas's men in Glen Garry."

"Aye, and likewise without a battle," Fin said. "He sent two lads ahead to meet Douglas, pretending to be Comyns. They told him that Rothesay and Alex had fled and assured him that the wicked weather would prevent the other army from making it through the high passes. They also mentioned that your father's army was waiting at the top of the glen. Douglas turned back at once."

"But Rothesay still has no alliance," she said.

"Alex will do what he can, but Donald will do nowt," Fin said, stripping off his tunic. "Shaw's messenger brought more bad news, too. Douglas told his men that the Queen is ailing. They say it is not grave, but Rothesay is upset."

"So would anyone be," she said. "She is his mother, after all."

"She is more than that, lass. She is his strongest ally. Annabella Drummond has powerful allies of her own. But without her to stir them to his defense, they may not be so eager to support him. If Davy loses her…"

"He will have even fewer friends than he has now," she said. "Why are you taking off all your clothes if we are about to dine, sir?"

"Because we can have food anytime, my love, and I believe we began something last night that we were both too exhausted to finish. Move over, so I can teach you more ways to please me."

After that, their activities took on a sense of urgency. As soon as he lay beside her, she felt his cock throbbing eagerly against her, seeking her nest. Her own body responded at once, but Fin eased lower, stroking her, teasing her with his caresses, and kissing her, lingering to savor her breasts while one hand sought to see if she was ready for him.

She could tell that she was, but he took time to trail kisses down her body, teasing it more until she was pleading for release. At last, grabbing a handful of his hair, chuckling, she twisted up and tried to get out from under him. But he caught her and pressed her to her back, leaning over her as he had at Moigh, grinning.

"Would you conquer me, lass?"

"I thought I might try," she said, twinkling at him.

"Sakes, I'll show you how myself."

She had already learned ways to excite him, but he

showed her a few more, and she responded eagerly to his instruction. He also taught her new ways that he could excite her, especially with his agile tongue.

At last, though, he took her swiftly and hard, demanding more and more of her until their passion sent them soaring at last to ecstasy.

Lying in her husband's arms afterward, sated, Cat purred.

Dear Reader,

I hope you enjoyed *Highland Master*. The story evolved from a Mackintosh legend about the Comyns damming a loch. The incident, never dated, may have taken place at Castle Moigh or the island castle at Loch an Eilein, known as Rothiemurchus (as was most of that part of Strathspey then and as much of it is to this day). I chose to set the book at Rothiemurchus, because the basin in which Loch an Eilein sits seemed a more plausible location for such an effective dam than Loch Moy would be.

Wolves were common in Scotland and northern England in medieval times, and there are many tales of their extinction. The last wolf in northeast Scotland died at Kirkmichael, Banffshire, in 1644. Sir Ewen Cameron of Lochiel at Killiecrankie killed the last one in Perthshire in 1680. And a MacQueen, stalker to the laird of Mackintosh, killed the last wolf of all in 1743 *(Dictionary of Scottish History)*.

The Clan Battle of Perth, September 1396, is much studied, but controversy still exists over which two clans were involved. Nearly all historians agree that the victor was Clan Chattan, but many have suggested clans other than Clan Cameron as their opponent. The only one that makes logical sense to me is Cameron.

Clan Cameron was not only another powerful confederation but one with whom Clan Chattan, specifically the Mackintoshes, had been feuding forever over land that both clans claimed. That a continuing feud between two confederations, with many tribes in each, might make enough trouble in the Highlands that the King would bestir himself to intervene makes sense.

Also, a truce did exist between the two of them for a

number of years, which began shortly after the clan battle. The legal issue was not resolved until the sixteenth century, however, when the courts decided in the Mackintoshes' favor. One sticking point with regard to the Camerons' being the second clan was that they continued to reside at Loch Arkaig in Lochaber, which was the land in question. Logically, the Mackintosh ought to have been able to kick them out.

I consulted my chief expert, however, and we agreed that my solution to that question in *Highland Master* is the most likely, given the circumstances.

Albany's armies and those of his allies frequently attempted to pursue Highlanders into the Highlands but rarely with much success.

Readers often ask where I get information about wedding ceremonies. The words for the one in this book come from a missal used during the reign of Richard II in England (1377–99). The Scottish and English churches at the time both derived their rites from the Roman ones, so the ceremonies would have been the same.

After serving as Captain of Clan Chattan for nearly forty years, Lachlan mac William Mackintosh died at a ripe old age in 1407, leaving, by his wife Agnes, daughter of Hugh Fraser of Lovat, one son, Ferquhard, who succeeded him, and a daughter, whose name probably was not Ealga and who married Chisholm of Strathglass, not Shaw Mackintosh. He married "a daughter of Robert mac Alasdair vic Aona," and therefore his daughter here, Catriona, is entirely fictional, as is Fin.

My sources for **Highland Master** include *The Confederation of Clan Chattan, Its Kith and Kin* by Charles Fraser-Mackintosh of Drummond, Glasgow, 1898; *The*

House and Clan of Mackintosh and of the Clan Chattan by Alexander Mackintosh Shaw, Moy Hall, n.d., and, of course, the always impressive Donald MacRae.

I must also thank my webmaster, David Durein, for sharing his expert knowledge and personal experience in both creating and removing a similarly placed but well intended dam, and the always efficient Julie Ruhle, who keeps me sane by dealing with the trivia whenever she can.

As always, I thank my wonderful agents, Lucy Childs and Aaron Priest, my terrific editor, Frances Jalet-Miller, Senior Editor Selina McLemore, Production Manager Anna Maria Piluso, copyeditor extraordinaire Sean Devlin, Art Director Diane Luger, Cover Artist Claire Brown, Editorial Director Amy Pierpont, Vice President and Editor in Chief Beth de Guzman, and everyone else at Hachette Book Group's Grand Central Publishing/Forever who contributed to this book.

If you enjoyed *Highland Master*, please look for *Highland Hero*, the story of Sir Ivor Mackintosh, an impertinent lass who ignores Sir Ivor's infamous temper (and happens to be the King's ward), and a seven-year-old prince with a habit of commanding all in his orbit. It should be at your favorite bookstore in October 2011.

In the meantime, *Suas Alba!*

Sincerely,

Amanda Scott

www.amandascottauthor.com

Don't miss the second
book in Amanda Scott's
tantalizing Scottish
Knights Series!

Please turn this page
for a preview of

Highland Hero

Available in mass market

in October 2011.

Chapter 1 _____

Her bare skin was as smooth as the silky gown she had worn before he'd helped her take it off. His fingertips glided over her, stroking a bare arm, a bare shoulder, its soft hollow, and then the softer rise of a full breast heaving with desire for him.

Cupping its softness, he brushed a thumb across its tip, enjoying her passionate moans and arcing body as he did and feeling the nipple harden.

Part of him had hardened, too. His whole body urged him to conquer the lush beauty in his bed, but although he was an impatient man, he was also one who liked to take his time with women. Experience—rather a good deal of it—had taught him that coupling was better for both when he took things slowly.

Neither of them spoke, because he rarely enjoyed conversation at such times. Preferring to relish the sensations, he favored partners who did not chatter at him.

Stimulating them both with his kisses, he shifted an arm across her to position himself for taking her. As she spread her legs to accommodate him, she caressed his body with her hands, fingers, and tongue, sparking responses from every nerve.

Her motions and moans fed his urges, making it harder for him to resist simply taking her, dominating her, teaching her who was the master in that bed.

The bed shifted slightly on the thought, and he had a fleeting semiawareness that he was dreaming—fleeting because he ruthlessly shoved the half-formed thought away lest, if true, he might awaken too soon.

Somehow in that moment, in the odd way that dreams have of changing things about, the beauty had got to one side of him and he could no longer see her in the darkness. Ever willing, he shifted to accommodate the new arrangement.

Finding the warm, softly silken skin of her shoulder, he reached for her breasts again, rising onto his elbow and leaning over her as he did. He felt her body stiffen, and when his seeking hand found one soft breast, it seemed smaller than before, albeit just as well formed and just as soft. Sakes, but the woman herself seemed smaller. Most oddly, though, he touched real silk there instead of bare skin.

Undaunted, he ignored her increasing rigidity and slid his hand down to move the annoying silk out of his way and gain access to his primary objective.

As he did, her body heaved under him, a gasping cry sounded near his right ear, and in a flurry of movement, she slid from his grasp. Flying out of the bed, she managed on her way to deal him a stunning blow across his face. Then he saw only flashes of movement and light, and before he could collect wit enough to know that he was awake and had been toying with an unknown but very enticing female in *his* bed, a sound near the door told him that she was rummaging through the kist there.

Leaping from the bed, he shot toward her, but the door crashed back just as he reached for her, clouting his outstretched fingers and hand hard as it did.

The glow of torchlight in the corridor revealed long, lush, dark-red hair; a drab robe hastily flung over a pink shift that barely concealed long, lovely legs; curving hips, and a tantalizingly small waist as she ran. His aching hand and stinging cheek provided excellent cause for retaliation, but he no sooner started to give chase than he recalled his own state of naked readiness and swiftly collected his wits.

Chasing a nubile beauty by dead of night in a state such as his own just then might find favor in some masculine establishments that he had visited. But his grace the King's royal castle of Turnberry was definitely *not* one of them.

The young woman dashing up the corridor did not dare to look behind her, lest her pursuer know and recognize her. But as she gripped the handle of the nursery door, she could not resist glancing back and felt a surge of relief to see that the dimly lit corridor behind her was empty.

She had been sure that he would pursue her. But what a coil if he had and worse had he chanced to recognize her or seen her clearly enough to know her later.

Shoving the nursery door open, she whisked herself inside. Then, relieved, she quietly shut the door, eased the latch hook into place, and bolted the door, giving thanks to God as she did that Hetty had not already done so.

Glancing over her shoulder, she noted in the light of the single cresset still burning in the chamber, and the dimmer glow of embers from the well-banked fire, that Hetty was fast asleep on a pallet near the hearth. In the far corner of the room, the drawn curtains of a cupboard bed warned her to wake Hetty quietly.

Moving swiftly to the pallet, listening all the while for sounds from the corridor that might herald a search by the man who had been sleeping in Hetty's bed, she gently shook the plump, middle-aged mistress of the royal nursery.

"Hetty, wake up," she murmured. "Oh, don't screech, but do wake up!"

The woman's eyes flew open, and she sat bolt upright. "My lady!" she exclaimed. Softening her voice, she added, "What are ye doing in here?"

Seventeen-year-old Lady Marsaili Drummond Cargill grimaced. "I could not sleep, Hetty. I went to your room and climbed into your bed as I have bef—"

"Och! Ye did nae such thing! Not tonight of all—! What time is it then?"

"I don't know, after midnight I think. Oh, Hetty—"

"Good sakes, but his grace's man did say—"

"Someone was *in* your bed, Hetty. A man!"

"Is that no what I was just trying to tell ye? His grace's gentleman—"

"It cannot have been his grace's man," Marsaili said. "His grace's man—"

"Whisst now, will ye whisst? I'm trying to tell ye, if ye'll just listen to me. Sakes, but I thought ye'd learned to curb such foolish, impulsive—"

"Hetty, he was naked!"

Henrietta Childs, Mistress of the Royal Nursery, grabbed Marsaili firmly by the shoulders, gave her a shake, and looked into her eyes. "Now, Lady Marsi, have done! Ye'll tell me right now, was the man awake?"

"Not at first."

"At first!" Hetty's voice went up on the words, and with a swift look at the curtained bed in the corner, she lowered it to a whisper to add, "What did he do?"

"He rolled over and…and, before I realized that it wasn't you—"

"Ay-de-mi, did he touch ye?"

Remembering, and instantly feeling the strong, hitherto unfamiliar but most pleasurable sensations that his touch had first stirred in her, Marsi swallowed. But Hetty looked fierce, and Hetty had known her from her cradle and was reminding her of that with every word and look, so Marsi said, "He did, aye. But he did not see me, Hetty. I jumped out of the bed, snatched up my robe, and fled here to you."

"Snatched up your robe, did ye? What more have ye got on under it?"

"My shift. But, Hetty, who is he?"

"I dinna ken his name, and I'm no to tell anyone about him."

"Hetty, it's me. Who would I tell? I haven't a friend in this whole castle except you, and haven't had since Aunt Annabella died. What's more, they say that the Duke of Albany is on his way to Turnberry right now. He may arrive tomorrow, and if not tomorrow, then on Tuesday. His grace warned me that the duke is most impatient to arrange my marriage and has no intention of waiting the year that I *must* wait, in order to mourn Aunt Annabella's death properly."

"My lady, I ken fine that the Duke of Albany comes to Turnberry. See you, that is why that man is in my bed now."

"He is *Albany's* man?"

"Nay, he is not." Hetty looked upward, as if seeking guidance from above. Then, drawing breath and letting it out, she said, "I'll tell ye, then, but only so that ye do not go about trying to find out for yourself, as I ken fine ye'll do if I do not tell ye. But ye must no breathe a word to anyone else of what I say. Swear it now."

"You know that I will tell no one," Marsi said. "I keep secrets even better than I ferret them out, Hetty, and well do you know that."

"I do, aye, or I'd no say aught of this to ye. Our wee laddie's life may depend on it, though, so see that ye keep your word. See you, his grace did send for that man to take Jamie away from here to greater safety."

"Away? But when do they go, and where will he take him?"

"Mayhap as soon as tomorrow, for I was to pack for him," Hetty said. "His grace's man did not tell me where we will go, nor were I so brazen as to ask him."

"Aye, sure, his grace must mean for them to leave tomorrow if Albany is on the way. Dearest Annabella feared mightily that Albany would take Jamie in charge if he could but think how to manage it. But must you go with them, Hetty?"

"So his grace's man did say," Hetty said with a sigh. "I cannot say that I want to, for I ken fine that ye'll miss me sorely, my lady. But if Albany does come, he will take ye both, and I'd have naught to say to anything that *he* might do."

"Faith, but I did hope that he would just lecture me and say that I must obey him even though I am the King's ward, not his," Marsi muttered. "But I warrant you are right, that he will take us both in charge. As set as he is on marrying me to one of his toadies, if he takes Jamie, he'd be unlikely to leave me with his grace."

"He might, though," Hetty said. "His grace has stood against him before."

Marsaili gave an unladylike snort. "Mayhap he has, once or twice. But you ken fine that his grace cannot hold out long against him if Albany gets him alone and says he must not. What can I do, Hetty? Albany terrifies me."

"Aye, he terrifies most folks who have a grain of sense."

"Come with us, Marsi," piped up a third voice. "Wherever we go, it would have to be a happier place than Turnberry will be whilst my uncle bides here."

Both women turned toward the curtained bed, where the tousled auburn head of seven-year-old James Stewart, Earl of Carrick, peeped between the blue curtains.

"Jamie, were you listening?" Marsi demanded. "Naughty laddie!"

"I couldna sleep," the dark-eyed lad who stood second in line for the Scottish throne said soberly, sounding, as he always did, much older than his years.

Hetty got up and reached for her yellow robe, which lay across a nearby stool. Putting it on, she said, "I'll warm ye some milk, sir. It'll settle ye again."

"I don't want milk. Must I command ye tae go with us, Marsi?"

"Oh, Jamie, I wish you could. But your royal ways

don't fool me, laddie. You fear your uncle Albany almost as much as I do."

"Aye, sure, but he canna find either of us if we are not here," James pointed out. "When he leaves Turnberry, we can come back and be comfortable again with my royal sire. Do come, Marsi. Ye make me laugh, and Hetty does not."

Marsaili hesitated, thinking furiously.

Hetty gave her a stern look. "My lady, ye must not. For once in your life, I pray ye—me, Hetty, who kens ye best—heed the dire consequences of such an act."

But Marsi rarely heeded consequences. Before her doting parents had died and left her a ward of her aunt, the Queen of Scots, most consequences had been pleasant ones. And when they were not, they were nearly always soon over.

However, now that Annabella was dead and could no longer protect her, the consequences of remaining to face Albany would likely be worse than anything she had ever known.

"I could pose as your assistant, Hetty, and help you look after Jamie."

"And *I* could help ye look after Marsi, Hetty," James said.

Henrietta looked dourly at Marsi. "Good lack, what was I thinking to tell ye that ye must *not*?" she muttered. "A body would think that after knowing ye for all of your seventeen years I'd ken better nor to challenge ye so."

"Is anyone else to go?" Marsi asked. "Any of Jamie's gentlemen?"

"Nay, for the King's grace kens fine that some of them

be in Albany's pay, and nae one save Albany kens which ones. We'll leave before they arise, I expect."

"Then there is naught to stop me," Marsi said. "I must get some of my clothing, but then I'll come back here."

"Ye've nowt that be suitable for a maidservant to wear, my lady! Nor would ye fool anyone for long in such a menial guise, for ye were no born to it."

But now that she had made up her mind, Marsi dismissed such objections without hesitation. "I can easily talk as a common maidservant would, Hetty, as you know gey well, having often scolded me for doing so. I shall say that I served Annabella and that she gave me some of her cast-off clothing. She did give it away, after all. Then I can say that since you and I hail from the same part of Scotland, when my position ended with her grace's death, I offered to help you."

"I can say that I know her well, too, Hetty, for I do," Jamie said.

"Faith, but I can also say that I just want to go home," Marsi said. "After all, wherever we go from here, we are likely to go north or east. If worse comes to worst, I can tell whoever escorts us to take me to my uncle Malcolm at Stobhall in Perth. He wants me to marry his second son, and I can tell you, Hetty, if the choice is between a toady of Albany's and my dullard cousin Jack, I'd *prefer* Jack."

Two hours earlier

Striding across the flagstone floor of the royal audience hall at Turnberry, the tall, broad-shouldered young knight filled the room with crackling energy even as he dropped to a knee before its sole, elderly occupant and bowed his head.

"You sent for me, sire?"

"If you are the knight that other men call Hawk, I did, aye," the King of Scots murmured, his raspy voice barely above a whisper. "I have sore need of you, lad."

"I am Hawk," Sir Ivor Mackintosh said, fighting to conceal his dismay at how much the King had aged since the only other time he had seen him, three years before. "How may I serve, your grace? Your messenger said it was gey urgent."

"'Tis my Jamie," muttered Robert III of Scotland, a king who had never sought or enjoyed his exalted position.

Ivor said gently, "Jamie, my liege, your younger son?"

A log shifted in the nearby fireplace, and sparks leaped before the King nodded and said, "Annabella... m-my Queen..." Pausing when his voice cracked, he added with tears welling in his pale blue eyes, "Annabella feared mightily for Jamie. Sithee, she had great fear of my brother, Albany. I canna believe he would harm a child, but 'tis better, I trow, to see the laddie safe than to weep for him if Annabella should prove to be right."

"But what, exactly, are you asking of me, sire?"

"Albany sent a message a fortnight ago to say that he has business here that can nae longer wait upon the pleasure of those most concerned in it. He will be here tomorrow or Tuesday and he wants to take Jamie into his own custody. The Bishop of St. Andrews once told me that *he* can keep our laddie safe at St. Andrews Castle. You also ken Bishop Traill, he said, and St. Andrews as well."

"I do, your grace. Had you a particular plan in mind?"

With a feeble gesture, the King said, "I want to ken nowt of any plans, for I am incapable of lying to my brother. Just get Jamie to St. Andrews."

"I can be away in the morning if James can be ready by then," Ivor said.

"You need only give the nursery mistress your orders when you arise," the King said. "Henrietta already knows that Jamie may be traveling tomorrow."

"Then, by your leave, sire, I will sleep, too," Ivor said. "If you can tell me—"

"Aye, sure. My own man will show you to a room near the royal nursery."

Bowing, Ivor bade the King goodnight and retired to bed only to awaken betimes when the lass in his dreams became real. However, afterward, thanks to years of knightly training and preparing for battle, he soon slept again and awoke only when the dawn's gray light crept into the room.

His bruised hand reminded him of the lass, but he dressed nonetheless hastily. Then, deducing which door was that of the royal nursery, he rapped on it lightly.

Marsi opened the door, took one nervous look at the tall, well-formed, stern-looking man who stood at the threshold and quickly swept him a deep curtsy. Then, speaking over her shoulder as she rose again, she said, "Mistress Henrietta, methinks 'tis the gentleman ye're expecting, though he do be earlier than ye said he'd come."

"Do not chatter, lass, but come and assist his lordship to dress whilst I talk with the gentleman," Hetty said sternly. "I am Henrietta Childs, Mistress of the Royal Nursery,

sir," she added, and Marsi moved to obey her, glancing
back as she did.

Without awaiting further invitation, the man stepped
into the room and shut the door. "I believe you understand, mistress," he said, "that we must be away as soon
as possible and without any ado. His grace's man awaits
us near the sea gate."

"The sea gate!" Marsi's exclamation was out before
she knew she would speak. Trying to conceal her dismay,
she glanced at Jamie and saw that his eyes were wide with
delight. Turning next to their visitor, she said, "But where
do we go?"

The man looked at Hetty, who said sharply to Marsi,
"Hold your tongue, lass. Ye ken fine that ye've nae call
to put yourself forward so. I did say that I would have
need of ye, but if ye cannot behave, we will leave ye right
here."

Quickly bowing her head, Marsi strove to look contrite,
but James said in a tone just as stern as Hetty's, "Marsi
must come with us, for I want her. And if we are to go on
a ship, I will *need* her, Hetty. Ye ken fine that boats always
make ye sick."

Eyeing their visitor again, Marsi saw that he was
looking sterner than ever, but before Jamie had stopped
speaking, the man's gaze shifted to her. Feeling herself
tense, she took a deep breath, but his expression had
already turned thoughtful, and he said only that Hetty
should hurry her charges along so they could all get
going.

The man had forgotten all about *her*, Marsi decided, so
he could have no suspicion that she was the girl who had
fled from his bed the night before.

To be sure, she had put on a plain moss-green kirtle and a simple white apron. And, fearing that he might recognize her hair, she had covered it completely with a frilly white cap. Even so, and although she was relieved that he did not seem to recognize her, she felt an odd sense of disappointment, as if he *should* have.

THE DISH

Where authors give you the inside scoop!

From the desk of Jane Graves

Dear Reader,

Have you ever visited one website, seen an interesting link to another website, and clicked it? Probably. But have you ever done that about fifty times and ended up in a place you never intended to? As a writer, I'm already on a "what if" journey inside my own head, so web hopping is just one more flight of fancy that's *so* easy to get caught up in.

For instance, while researching a scene for BLACK TIES AND LULLABIES that takes place in a childbirth class, I saw a link for "hypnosis during birth." Of course I had to click that, right? From there I ended up on a site where people post their birth stories. And then . . .

Don't ask me how, but a dozen clicks later, my web-hopping adventure led me to a site about celebrities and baby names. This immediately had me wondering: *What* were these people thinking? Check out the names these famous people have given their children that virtually guarantee they'll be tormented for the rest of their lives:

Apple	Actress Gwyneth Paltrow
Diva Muffin	Singer Frank Zappa
Moxie Crimefighter	Entertainer Penn Jillette
Petal Blossom Rainbow	Chef Jamie Oliver
Zowie	Singer David Bowie
Pilot Inspektor	Actor Jason Lee
Sage Moonblood	Actor Sylvester Stallone
Fifi Trixibell	Singer Bob Geldof
Reignbeau	Actor Ving Rhames
Jermajesty	Singer Jermaine Jackson

No, a trip around the Internet does *not* get my books written, but sometimes it's worth the laugh. Of course, the hero and heroine of BLACK TIES AND LULLABIES would *never* give their child a name like one of these . . .

I hope you enjoy BLACK TIES AND LULLABIES. And look for my next book, HEARTSTRINGS AND DIAMOND RINGS, coming August 2011.

Happy reading!

Jane Graves

www.janegraves.com

From the desk of Cynthia Eden

Dear Reader,

I love strong heroes. When I write my romantic suspense novels, I try to create heroes who can save the day while barely breaking a sweat. Men who aren't afraid to face danger. Men who are comfortable taking out the bad guys—even while these heroes successfully romance their heroines. Oh, yes, I'm all about an alpha male.

And when it comes to my heroines, well, my response is the same. *Give me a strong heroine.* I don't want to write about a heroine who needs rescuing 24/7. I want a woman who is strong enough to defend herself (and her man, if need be).

When I began writing DEADLY HEAT, I knew that my heroine would have to be a strong match for FBI Special Agent Kenton Lake. Since Kenton appeared in my previous "Deadly" book, DEADLY FEAR, I already knew just how powerful and capable he was. Kenton hunts serial killers for a living, so weakness isn't exactly a concept he understands.

I didn't want Kenton to dominate his heroine, so I made sure that I created a very strong lady for him . . . and firefighter Lora Spade was born. Lora is a woman who fights fire each day. She's not afraid of the flames, but she is afraid of the way that Kenton makes her feel.

Physically and mentally, my characters are strong.

But emotionally? When it comes to emotions, both Kenton and Lora are in for a big shock.

After all . . . love doesn't always make a person weak. Sometimes, it just makes you stronger.

Since Kenton and Lora are about to track an arsonist who enjoys trapping his victims in the flames, they sure will need all the strength they can get!

Thanks for checking out my Dish. If you'd like to learn more about my books, please visit my website at www.cynthiaeden.com.

Happy reading!

Cynthia Eden

♥ ♥ ♥ ♥ ♥ ♥ ♥ ♥ ♥ ♥ ♥ ♥ ♥ ♥ ♥

From the desk of Cara Elliott

Dear Reader,

Yes, yes, your eyes do not deceive you. Just when the brouhaha in Bath had calmed down a touch, a new scandal popped up. The Circle of Sin is spinning into action again. Alas, trouble seems to follow our intrepid heroines, when all they really want is a life of quiet scholarly study. . . . Actually, I take that back. They do realize that there is more to life than books (a handsome rogue . . . but we'll get to that later).

As you probably suspect, this time it's Kate, the feisty free spirit of the "Sinners," who has landed in hot water. She's spent most of her life gallivanting the world with her American sea captain father—some high sticklers may call him a pirate—so it's really no surprise that her life in London, where she's come to live with her imperious grandfather, the Duke of Cluyne, is not sailing along very smoothly.

But honestly, it's really not *all* her fault. That rascally rake, the Conte of Como—Marco, to his more intimate friends—is the one making waves. He's an unexpected guest at her grandfather's staid country house party, and when one thing leads to another . . . all hell breaks loose.

Trouble takes Kate and Marco from London to Vienna, where the various rulers of Europe are gathering to discuss politics now that Napoleon has been exiled to Elba. Now, now, don't roll your eyes. It so happens that Vienna was *the* ultimate party town at the time. Anybody who was anybody wanted to be there, to rub shoulders (and other unmentionable body parts) with the kings, princes, emperors, and other high-profile celebrities.

The Emperor of Austria hosted many of the dignitaries at his magnificent castle, and his poor aides spent countless hours trying to figure out the room assignments, taking into account who was sleeping with whom, so that late-night tiptoeing through the corridors wouldn't result in any embarrassing trip-ups.

Glittering balls, sumptuous banquets, fanciful medieval jousts, spectacular fireworks—the daily list of extravagant entertainments was mind-boggling. Party girls Princess Bagration and the Duchess of Sagan vied with each other to see who could attract the most influential men to their soirees. As for other pleasures, well, let's just say they all were intent on having a good time. In fact, the Tsar of Russia—a notorious skirt-chaser—had to have a whole new wardrobe sent from St. Petersburg because he gained so much weight partying every night!

But why, you might ask, is Kate plunging into the midst of such frivolous festivities? And how is a rake like Marco going to help her get out of hot water? Well, you'll just have to read TO TEMPT A RAKE to find out!

Cara Elliott

www.caraelliott.com

From the desk of Amanda Scott

Dear Reader,

Most books grow from the seeds of isolated ideas. One reads about an unusual historical incident, or finds an odd phrase that triggers a string of thoughts, or overhears a comment on a bus or plane that stirs an idea for a situation or a character.

I was seeking such seeds as I began to plot HIGHLAND MASTER. I'd started with a vague notion of Romeo and Juliet, simply because I always want to create a basic conflict between the hero and heroine. But I did not want the simple "Capulets think Montagues are dreadful and vice versa." When I found myself wondering what would happen if a Montague were dropped into a nest of Capulets with a mission to accomplish, the gray cells began churning. That is the moment when a writer begins asking herself, "What if?"

What if my Scottish Romeo had sworn to kill Juliet's father? In medieval Scotland, blood oaths and blood feuds were common. What if someone in authority over that Scottish Romeo, knowing nothing about his oath or the feud, sends him on a vital diplomatic mission to the Scottish Capulets?

Then, since one also seeks to raise the stakes, what if Romeo has somehow managed to swear a second oath in direct conflict with his oath to kill Juliet's father? What if he cannot keep either oath without breaking the other?

What if he meets his Juliet and falls for her without realizing that her father is the man he has sworn to kill?

Research soon drew me to the great Clan Battle of Perth in 1396, which was to all intents and purposes a trial by combat between Clan Chattan and Clan Cameron, the two largest, most powerful Highland clan confederations. Thirty "champions" from each clan fought on the North Inch of Perth before the King of Scots and his court. When I read that only one (unknown) Cameron had survived, and did so by flinging himself into the river Tay, which swept him into the Firth of Tay and most likely on into the North Sea, I knew that I had found my hero.

In my story, Scotland's finest swordsman, Sir Finlagh "Fin" Cameron, the last man of his clan standing against eleven men of Clan Cameron, escapes from the great clan battle, manages to avoid being swept out to sea and—calling himself simply "Fin of the Battles"—joins the service of Davy Stewart, the bedeviled heir to the Scottish throne. Seeking to ally himself with the Lord of the North and the Lord of the Isles against his scheming uncle, the Duke of Albany, Davy sends Fin of the Battles back into the Highlands to arrange for a secret meeting with the great lords, hosted by the powerful Captain of Clan Chattan, known to all and sundry as "the Mackintosh."

Entering Clan Chattan territory, Fin is felled by a mysterious arrow and rescued by the lady Catriona Mackintosh, granddaughter of Clan Chattan's captain and, yes, also daughter of the clan's war leader, Shaw Mackintosh, the very man whom Fin swore to his dying father on the battlefield that he would kill.

I hope you enjoy HIGHLAND MASTER. In the meantime, *Suas Alba!*

Sincerely,

Amanda Scott

www.amandascottauthor.com

Find out more about Forever Romance!

Visit us at
www.hachettebookgroup.com/publishing_forever.aspx

Find us on Facebook
http://www.facebook.com/ForeverRomance

Follow us on Twitter
http://twitter.com/ForeverRomance

NEW AND UPCOMING TITLES

Each month we feature our new titles
and reader favorites.

CONTESTS AND GIVEAWAYS

We give away galleys, autographed copies,
and all kinds of exclusive items.

AUTHOR INFO

You'll find bios, articles, and links to personal
websites for all your favorite authors—and
so much more.

THE BUZZ

Sign up for our monthly romance newsletter,
and be the first to read all about it.